I0537281

Collateral Damages, Kept Secrets

Julian M. Stephens

Copyright © 2018 Julian M. Stephens

All rights reserved. No part of this
book may be reproduced or
transmitted in any form or by any
means, electronic or mechanical,
including photocopying, recording,
or any information storage and
retrieval system, without
permission in writing from the
publisher. This is a work of fiction.
Names, characters, businesses,
places, events, locales, and
incidents are the author's
imagination or fictitious products.
Any resemblance to actual persons,
living or dead, or actual events is
purely coincidental.

Secret Kept 2 Teens Publishing—Wylie, TX

ISBN: 978-0-692-19725-7

Collateral Damages, Kept Secrets | Julian M. Stephens

Available formats: eBook

Hardcover distribution

Paperback distribution

Dedication

Collateral Damages, Kept Secrets
are dedicated to the family I hold
dearest and nearest to my heart.
My memoir and life story are good,
bad, happy, sad, and genuine. My
mother, Mrs. Ludella Stephens,
never allowed me to become
comfortable with small successes in
life but encouraged me always to
stay humble. To a wonderful wife,
God blessed me to share my life
journey on earth. And to members
of the first home team, my
daughters Jana, Kareesha, and
Madelynn. And to the most fun-
loving individuals to call you Paw
Paw, Undrea, Leaondria, Taurus,
Devin, Jayla, Kamani, Londyn,
Ken'Zel Julian great-
granddaughters Za'Coriya, Akari,
and A'Mora.

A man who endures trials is blessed because when he passes the
test, he will receive the crown of life that God has promised to those
who love him. **James 1:12 HCSB**

CHAPTER ONE

COLLATERAL and DAMAGES

There are many events in my life experience, and some of them haunt us because we are bothered by the outcome or unanswered questions. Collateral Damages, Kept Secrets has many storylines about a young man (Collateral) and a young lady (Damages). The main characters in Collateral Damages and Kept Secrets are Jeremiah Micah Ford, the collateral, and Annie Mae Sims, as damage.

Collateral Damages, Kept Secrets, reveals the defacing or marring of something beautiful. The damage usually is costly and can take a long time to repair. The one thing we treasured was our heart, and if broken, there is a domino effect that sinks the soul, kills morale, and loses faith.

I am Jeremiah Micah Ford, the sixth of eight children. The Ford children knew what things we should not touch to break it. By always being careful not to touch or damage an item, we were prewarned not to handle it, or we would feel the wrath of our parents. If something is forbidden was accidentally broken, the culprit would usually try to hide it, fix it, or cover it up. We always sought ways to mitigate the level of our parents' pain inflicted upon our rear ends. Although we knew who the responsible party was, we tried keeping it a secret. We knew our parents would find out who the culprits were because we were children and our parents and they knew us very well. Which meant our parents were not as gray matter challenged as us and could figure things out. The question is, why didn't we just come forth and own up to the mistake instead of trying to hide it? The book Collateral Damages, Kept Secrets, tells the story of two individuals who developed a love for one another so strongly. Their story stems from two young people who fell in love for the first time. But just as their first whirlwind love rocketed to outer space, it succumbed to a crashed landing and shattered it into many pieces. The reason for writing this book is that neither of them accepted fault. They each kept secrets of things that shamed them into silence by hiding tragedies and calamities that haunted the two before of them, during, and long after the final curtains were lowered.

I AM Collateral

I am Jeremiah Micah Ford, and I grew up wishing my parents would appraise me as valuable collateral. Being aware of this is separate from the love of a mother and father. Had my parents passed on, such knowledge would have prepared me for the world that I would soon face and learn how to explain or express my valuableness because of the lack of understanding of why my black skin was valuable collateral. I should not allow anyone to play with it as it was expendable. I did not hear people say little dark skin boys like me as adorable. Such praise was generally heaped upon the light, yellow-toned boys. Like all kids, I wanted to be accepted, and in my make-believe world, I considered myself valuable. The appraisers assessed me as damaged based on my exterior because they were too shallow to know to judge the content inside me. I am sure I may have contributed to their lack of understanding whenever they verbally challenged me by jostling back and forth, trying to outwit the other. And I could feel the anger on their voice and see the disdain on their faces when you knew they lost the debates. I took great care always to keep a stoic look on my face. Keeping my facial expressions under control always made it difficult to read me.

I thought about changing my name to distance myself from my family as I was not entirely convinced I belonged. I was hoping for a newer and lesser complex Jeremiah when I reached the end of the road. My attempt to runaway only introduced me to the Jeremiah that would make me stand and fight to find my niche in this world. Thanks to my family, who kept me tied to the values taught and grounded. I had the choice of being a dreamer or darer. I could live as a loner and be satisfied or try and conceal myself in a crowd much like a chameleon. I am a deep thinker who tries to be both empathetic and sympathetic. I associate myself with no group because none will have me because of my opinions. In other words, I try to stay within my lane and stand on my own beliefs. I hid behind the curtain to conceal my shame.

My battle started early in life as I was wounded early and often, although I pretended nothing people said about me or did to me hurt. I wore my feelings on my sleeves, and I was bruised much easier than I let on to my perpetrators. Imagine trying to figure out how to fight every day at the age of five or six and defend a blessing from God. Having dark skin wasn't my choice. I can genuinely say that I do not know of a time or recall a single moment in my life when I wished my skin was lighter so that I could be accepted. I never found myself angry with God or my parents for the dark skin that enveloped my body. But as I would learn along my life journey, it has been the most valuable thing I have ever owned. Because of my dark skin, I try to lull people into believing that I am inferior because that is what I think they see me as, and by the time they realize I am equal, it is too late because I am too far ahead of their leader. Before gaining wisdom to create my pathway, I relied on my mind and anger to protect my collateral. It seemed logical because most people would always focus on the visual. I was aiding them to sell short the blessing from God. I still try and convince myself that I am shy and not afraid of being out front or the center of attention. I reflect on my past life in my senior years, and I still have difficulty admitting or speaking of my accomplishments.

I have given more blessings and credits of achievements to others to remind hidden. And I recently discovered it wasn't me being shy as a kid growing up, but ashamed of how I was poor and made fun of because of how we lived and our house. Before I go too far and make some disparaging comments about my family, my parents did the best they could to raise a family of seven children in the fifties, sixties, and seventies. We were reared to be respectful, kind, loving, and appreciative. I tried to instill these characteristics in my children, and I see our daughters impressing them upon our grandchildren. We were never taught or told to feel or think of ourselves as inferior. I lived in a home where my mother would take in other relatives and their children for long periods. In reflecting on how I grew up, neither the house I lived in that caused me to feel ashamed nor the fights were about my skin, something I could not do a damn thing about and didn't want to because God had blessed me with this ebony skin for a reason. It was not the home I grew up in but more about the skin I had to live within. Still, after taking this deep dive back into my past, I how having dark skin was not my problem but those who made it their problem. But it had become my fortress and served as a place of protection. I could keep hidden the bruises, both physical and mental. It helped to repel ignorant beliefs and assumptions of irrelevant people's comments about how black my skin was. I now realize how I have used my dark skin as a battering ram to break through barriers. And to open doors, raise windows, and pave roads for myself and others because I was more motivated by the words no and cannot; instead, my mantra was, I will show you what a black self-driven black boy from East Texas can do. I had become so engulfed in fear of failure and proving by naysayers to be right I ignored my shamefulness; it frightened me to smile.

The Genesis of Jeremiah and Annie

The story of Jeremiah Micah Ford and Annie Mae Sims was an example of innocent young love. And how their love changed the outlook on life for them, causing one to ascend and the other to descend. Jeremiah's demeanor did not show emotions, and he was more stoic. And Annie was animated and in your face. Angry or flustered, Jeremiah would smile, and silence becomes silent as if he was ignoring his surrounding by turning a deaf ear to the noise I felt unworthy to be heard by my ears. My shame was so deep that I almost missed the opportunity to have a first girlfriend. I delayed asking her for the chance to become her boyfriend, and would she be my girlfriend? When I asked Annie to be my girlfriend, and she accepted, she never mentioned my dark skin. And as our relationship grew, she spoke only about how I made her feel special, and she always wanted to be a special girl to someone. It was much later when I realized the stigma of having dark skin had gone away. I can pinpoint my fear left me, and it was when I decided to pursue and dedicate myself to bestow happiness in the life of Annie Sims. My pursuit of her had forced me only to allow loving her to occupy my time and thoughts. The courage I had mustered up helped me to ignore past rejections by venturing outside of my dark skin comfort zone for the first time. It was like I was finally free from a closet nailed shut and has lost hope of ever seeing the freedom to love. It must have been the heat within my soul. In Annie, I found a love and companion of a beautiful, funny, and talkative girl. The thing I feared the most and had caused me to hesitate when it came to pursuing the opposite sex. And the first confirmation that my dark skin was a valuable commodity and have learned inside of this black skin that God blessed me to display daily is because others dig the pit for you to jump in doesn't mean you have to climb in and dwell in it.

Did Jeremiah Make Dark Skin a Problem

What I thought would be a deterrence, I learned how to accept I had dark skin and live inside and outside my soul. I learned how to navigate and function in society as a civil and intelligent individual and avoid being dubbed an angry Black man. By the grace of God, I crossed paths with many decent people. I learned to feel as good about my outside as I do about my inside. Today, if anyone has a problem with my skin color, it is their problem and not mine to deal with or broaden their narrow-mindedness. My real value is wrapped up in my collateral which is my dark skin. I will face many trials and encounters before the final chapter of Collateral Damages; Kept Secrets. But it will be my God-given collateral for which I will draw much strength many times. The safest place to talk about some of my life's challenges was to write them in a book. Some of those challenges I believe are worthy of being shared. And perhaps one day another Jeremiah who may find himself locked in the kind of closet that almost paralyzes me with fear, they will have a paved road to find the type of freedom and enjoyment as I. I do not anticipate my family reading Collateral Damages, Kept Secrets because reading is not where they want to hear about my life.

Before Annie, I wrote about my hurts, pains, and disappointments in notebooks and then destroyed the documents. I can see the problem, rationalize, and move past the pain by etching the words in my mind. I don't write this book to be a best-seller, nor promote it. It is medicinal and allows me to tell all by putting behind the hurts and disappointments I suffered because I wore the skin color I was blessed with by God. Based on where God has taken me in life,

I would choose the black paint job as my favorite color in the next ten lives.

I am finally brave enough to tell my story with some input from Annie Sims, my first girlfriend. Annie and I disagree with how our relationship ended; neither wants to blame destroying a once successful courtship. We agreed to try and collaborate on writing Collateral Damages, Kept Secrets. For full disclosure, I am happily and faithfully married to my wife Ruth of more than twenty-five years. So, there will be no rekindling of an old romance of Annie and Jeremiah. However, breaking up with each other was not the problem that had caused us so much consternation between us. It was the secrets that we kept hidden from one another. I saw Annie for the first time in 1994 after many years. I was disappointed with the person I saw standing before me because the girls I knew as Annie Mae Sims were very bitter people filled with hate and writhing in self-pity and feeling that someone owed her something. I could not bring myself even to want to shake her hand because I instantly felt the presence of evil and disdain for her. After all, she had not taken proper care of the girl I had stuck in my memory of her. To collaborate with Annie in writing this book, I feel I have a lot to lose and a vested interest in keeping my marriage happy and healthy.

Annie, I think, is planning on having me as the guest of honor at her pity party. I will not jeopardize my marriage to elevate her value and create collateral damage in my life. Not since we were together as lovers have, she showed that she could be trusted with my heart, mind, and indeed, not with my soul. Our perspectives on life are polar opposite. She sees her life as a glass half empty. I am a half-glass full kind of person, in filling the forty-year void when we first vowed to love one another for a lifetime. We did not make it to a decade, let alone a lifetime. We found ourselves on opposite ends of the spectrum before we even started; This time around, I will try and offer to help pull her out of the ditch; she seemed to want to wallow in a sad situation if she chose to stand on her own two legs. But I won't carry her imaginary woes or allow her to drag me down to her level of bitterness. Neither will I let me feel one iota of pity that would give her any reason to think we will try and go back to where we split. The story of Humpty Dumpty best describes our relationship today. I learned to be content with my life but remained curious to discover why Annie did some strange things. The peculiar behavior of Annie convinced me to flee her as fast as I had fallen in love with her. I had plans to fulfill my dreams by going places and doing things in my life before settling down and getting married. And actions also convinced me to go on with my life, minus her. Only time will show whether or not I made the right choice to move on when I did. For some strange reason, I always felt indebted to Annie and always wanted to be available should she ever need me. I could not utter the words today I needed to express yesterday that had caused me to suffer the pain of the secret I held inside me for so long. As we began writing this book, I noticed a lot of hostility between us. The mere thought that we are attempting to collaborate on finding out what happened to our magical love story was worth sharing. There is and will be nothing nefarious happening during this time. My wife's confidence and trust in me to pursue this mystery in my past because she knows our marriage will never be in jeopardy. Any attempts to rekindle their old and dead relationship will be nipped in the bud immediately. I love my wife Ruth; we have known each other since the third grade, which is longer than I have known than Annie and I were a couple. We have more than twenty-five years invested in a beautiful marriage that I have enjoyed immensely. There is nothing that Annie could offer me to derail my marriage to Ruth.

Another challenge in collaborating on this book with Annie is to find out why the relationship with so much promise went wrong. Although Annie was my first true love, Ruth was the first girl I liked three weeks before dumping me. Annie stated the voices inside of her head tormented her. Her comment had piqued my interest because I wanted to know. Hmm!! There were times when Annie displayed odd behavior, like marriages without at least telling me that she wanted to move on or refusing to press charges against individuals who violated her body. And I hope during the writing of this book, I can return the favor by helping Annie find the strength to escape the clutches of the unwanted guests who torments her.

After this venture of writing Collateral Damages, Kept Secrets is finished, I do not even want us to be friends, perhaps friendly and cordial because of Annie's hostility toward me. I believe it is misplaced. But I feel that I must reassure her one more time that we are seeking to find one answer, and that is to answer the question of WHY our split was never explained. Maybe we will see the cause and agree on the explanation. I think it bears repeating that I owe Annie a great deal of gratitude. She was instrumental in freeing me from my secret closet and giving me the courage to flee my nemesis by finding the strength to fight back and face their attacks. If Annie had rejected sixteen-year-old Jeremiah, I believe that my life could have been much different today. Annie Sims was my first lover, and I will repeat how grateful I am to her for rescuing me many times. What is the reason for our disdain for one another today? Is it something I hope we will also learn why? I feel she ruined a good thing and gave me the impression I ran out on her. I point to our demise began when she transferred schools. Since gaining my freedom, this was the first time I would have to face my nemesis alone. But I was not as horrified to the point that I would return to the closet Annie had opened the door to free me. I felt alone, empty, and numb by not knowing when Annie and I would see each other again. But this time, instead of fear, I was filled with anger, a rage that seemed to go looking for someone to take out my pain and frustrations on, by not knowing when Annie would be in each other's arms and kissing by pressing our lips together for a long passionate kiss. Reflecting, I realized Annie had served the purpose God had intended by helping me to gain the confidence and courage to discover how to utilize more fully the talents I had been blessed with to the fullest. I was now on my own but not content, and I felt a sense of restlessness and anxiousness to challenge my foes and not back down. I had become the aggressor. Although Annie was far away, I kept her in my heart. But I could not be sure that she still loved me. I spent most of my nights lying awake wanting her, and she was nowhere close to soothe the pain deep inside of my heart. When I sit and talk with male friends, they all seem to remember that first love, and I guess you can never forget the person who stole your heart for the first time. Because you still recall those special moments, you remember, and you are over that love, but you learn to move on without them to someone new, and perhaps the next one is your life partner. After splitting, Annie and I met many times, but we never talked about rekindling our relationship. We just assumed that we were back together. This kind of misunderstanding left me feeling free to go and come as I please. These kinds of efforts were more destined to fail than survive. When I say that I will always love Annie Mae Sims, it is not the kind of love we shared when we were kids and finding love for the first time. I appreciate someone who gave me a chance by trusting my heart. The Annie I am facing today makes me APPRECIATE and love my wife more. I made the mistake of marrying the wrong woman, but now I have gotten my business straight. I will not betray her trust her in me.

It isn't easy to know where and how to start telling the love story of Julian and Annie. We have a consensus on when our relationship started to erode. When Annie transferred schools, she put me in a position where I needed to test myself. I wasn't excited to find out if I would ever love again or be loved again, but I understood that I would have to seek the magic Annie and I once had together to move on with my life. I shudder to think what my state of mind would be today if I had not fought after being freed of the closet Annie found me in. Would I, too, be entertaining unwelcomed guests inside of my head today. I had witnessed and experienced the beauty that life had to offer and that there were both good and evil in people. Before Annie, I had established some goals and had dreams of my future. I did not know how to overcome my shyness and fears, and I never thought falling in love would cure me. I probably would have given up on all my goals and accepted the fate plotted by naysayers. Her coming into my life was a blessing because I had the opportunity to experience interacting with other people who were not so mean and vindictive. Finding the goodness in one person caused me to expand my horizon because it mushroomed and dwindled all of my apprehensions. And I was no longer afraid like the many moments in my life. I discovered someone deserving of all my respect and someone wanting to give me all their love in the same person. All it took was for someone to say they loved me. When I think of all the nights, we talked on the phone and the amount of time we spent together at school. I never shared with Annie my complexion fear, and she never told me of the molestation and incest she was encountering. I feel sorry that she didn't feel like loving me was an open door for her to exit her secret closet and flee to freedom. Today, she describes me as selfish and an S.O.B. because I am nothing like the sixteen-year-old boy who fell in love long ago. At age sixteen, when we met, I was broken and looking down. I also lacked the necessary wisdom I enjoy today in my sixties to discern danger and pain. She had spoken of an uncle that let her sit on his lap to drive his four-speed Roadrunner. It never came to my mind that it was odd for a fifteen-year-old girl to sit on the lap of a grown man. I think back, and I remember the excitement I experienced when Annie used to sit on my lap. I failed the pastor of my church growing up, and he would always stress kindness and helping others by saying, *"when you help someone else up a steep hill. You get closer to the top yourself."* He failed to explain how you help someone heading in the opposite direction. I guess the test was to see if I cared enough to look beneath the surface by turning around and coming down from my ascending ladder to help someone else to turn their life around. The voice I heard inside of my head said, keep walking. I went to Church as a kid and stayed awake! So, I listened to that voice and kept pushing toward a higher mark in life because I knew what misery loves company meant. Since I did not care for pain of any kind, I do not think suffering together would have held us. There are miserable people in this world, some by choice. Those are the ones that will go out of their way to make you feel bad because they are sorry human beings and cannot stand seeing someone else happy. It was evident that Annie became unhappy and was filled with bitterness. Instead of getting in the line to succeed, she chose to remain in the pity and complaint line. Today, her chief complaint is that everyone wronged her that ever touched her life and, most of all, me, Jeremiah Ford, with my shit-eating grin on my face. I am the only one alive that she holds responsible for hurting her and letting her down. She expects to unload all of her anger on me. Jeremiah, I would describe myself as a dark chocolate brother, introvert, passionate, extremely shy, do not like to be the center of attention, and love seeing others happy and excel in life. You would think that someone who grew up as one of eight children and the sixth as an introvert does not make sense. And being a member of such a group would mean you are not afraid to come out and fight. But I never liked conflict and always wanted to get along with everyone. But once the light switch was in the on position, I became a no-nonsense kind of person. I felt safe building a wall around me to keep away other Blacks with a hang-up about my dark skin. The more I succeeded in life, the higher the fence became and a reminder I can never feel safe or free from the ignorant; it does not protect me entirely from the idiots who try to be insulting when I return fire. Imagine everyone born into the world giving their input to God on how to assemble their body and choosing the preferred paint job. If it was permitted, I must have missed that day of work since I could not pick my skin color like an automobile. There has never been a day in my life when I questioned God's chosen skin color for me. At first, I had difficulty confronting people with hang-ups about my dark tint job even though I had no dents or dings, just dimples. I remember hearing a pastor saying *God doesn't make any junk*. I was born with this skin color, a part of the package God believed best fitted me. And God makes no mistakes either. Since we agreed to collaborate on writing Collateral Damages, Kept Secrets, I wonder is it worth drudging up our forty-five-year history. The secret closet that trapped me inside was minute in Annie's opinion and perhaps even others. But because of her help, the belief that if I kept quiet, I hoped that no one would see me become a non-issue where my skin complexion was concerned. Over the years, I have often wondered how odd it is I join an organization and sit in a crowd mining my own business, and somehow, I will get drawn into the mix. I always get asked for my input or invited to become the leader when I want only to be an observer. I had come a long way from when I accepted my dark skin as taboo and not worthwhile. The hateful and hurting words I used to hear no longer stings or make me feel ashamed. Neither did the insults from individuals who tried to put me in my place because of my dark skin. I feel good because they now know that I will return whatever insults delivered posted paid for shallow individuals. That is from the old playbook and no longer makes me feel ashamed. It only awakens the giant slay killer in me. More than sixty years later, I remember the first time I felt hatred toward another human being; I was about six years old. I dub them the Malign Twins; it involved two teenage girls. The cliché that sticks and stones may break my bones, but none of your words will hurt me. That is not always a true statement. I was victimized by words that hurt as painful as a rock or stick. They threw stones in my direction unprovoked as weapons to destroy me. I had to develop a retaliation mechanism to deter them from coming after me. I would make sure they also felt some pain from the massive chips I carried on both of my shoulders. I dubbed the two evil girls as the Malign Twins. After all, they deliberately sought to hurt a six-year little boy. They were the first to tell me that I was dark and unattractive to look at when my mother and father took me to enroll in school to start the first grade. I was already uncomfortable around other people, especially if their skin was lighter than mine. I allowed myself to be intimidated by people, not because they were more intelligent than me. But because I thought their light skin automatically made them wiser and superior. Although those were my thoughts and beliefs, they did not keep me from rebelling against such notions. It was finally my turn to get kicked out of the house and start school. I was excited and dreamed of what it would be like to attend school with my older siblings. I remember riding with my parents to enroll me in school. And even though I was six and my brother was four, they left us in the car while they went inside to register me. Like most six-year-old kids, I was curious about the surroundings. And could hear the voices of other children playing, which piqued my curiosity. I was bothering no one, and I suppose no one would bother my brother and me, as my parent thought. I imagined what school would be like when I started in my small world. And up came two teenage girls. I will refer to them as the Malign Twins. They saw me looking out the window of my parent's car; I smiled at them, thinking they were friends and not foes. They turned the smile on my face upside down very quickly. By hurling insults at me by calling me a little black tar baby, monkey, and anything ugly, they could think of in my direction. As a six-year-old, it seemed like the insults went on forever. I shrunk below the window, hiding in the backseat of the car, so the Malign Twins could no longer see me. I could still hear their voices continuing to spew out mean and hateful comments about me. Although I could no longer see them, they knew I listened to their every word and did not stop throwing their insults at me. Suddenly the belittling stopped, and there was silence. The barrage of insults and laughter ended. In my mind, they were waiting for me to rear my head again from the back seat of my parent's car so that they could continue to belittle me. Even today, I have panic attacks thinking about the Malign twins. I remember hurting inside, as this encounter made me sad and was hurtful. I could not allow my parents to see tears flowing from my eyes and flowing down my cheeks. Inside, I was crying, shaking, and shamed by everything said about me. I had never experienced this kind of hurt in my young life before meeting these two girls. I believe this incident was when I entered this secret closet of pain by hiding my emotions in my mind's closet and watching others like the Malign twins. The sudden silence by the two girls was because my parents returned to the car. I remember my mother looking at me as if she knew something had occurred while they were away and asking me why I hid behind the seat. Were you afraid? No, I replied. Feeling that if I told her what the girls had said about me would require my repeating their hurtful words. I never wanted to hear a repeat of those nasty words spoken by the Malign twins, not even out of my very own mouth. If I had cried aloud, my mother would have told me that I needed to be a big boy because big boys shouldn't cry for no reason even though I did have an explanation but was too hurt and ashamed to tell my parents what had happened. I was too shocked to explain my hurt feelings; I had no physical bruises to show where the pain was; this was inside me where not even I could rub or soothe the pain away. My father would have just told me to shut up, or he would give me something to cry about if I did not stop crying. I slammed the closet door and tried to deal with my dark skin being a problem to some people. I had never allowed myself to think about my black skin as bad but instead just knew how I was always uncomfortable around other people, especially if their skin was lighter than mine. I allowed myself to be intimidated by people, not because I was afraid of what they could do but what they might say about me referring to dark skin. But because I thought their light skin automatically made them superior. Although those were my thoughts and beliefs, they did not keep me from rebelling against people who presented such views. The Malign twins' evil and vile words had caused me to shut myself inside the closet of my mind, trying to hide but not disappear. Later in life, if I had not met Annie, I probably would have remained shut up and silent in the closet of my mind, consumed by fear, too afraid to turn the knob to exit, and afraid someone may attempt to enter. Because of those terrible Malign twins gone was the excitement of attending school and getting on the bus with my sisters and brother. I no longer wanted to go to school with my older siblings, feeling that there were many more children like the two bullies I had encountered. If I were going to overcome this stigma thrust upon me, I would need to find a way to combat it by developing a formidable weapon to fight back against my enemies by making my sticks and stones. Yes, words hurt the same as sticks and stones because people use words to batter your inside, affecting the mind. Perhaps this kind of assault is not a crime for bruising someone's mind with hurtful words. It is a sin and shameful. It hurts when you have your heart set on love, peace, and having a great day, and someone ruins it by saying words to damage you. I will not tell anyone that words do not hurt because I believe that they can cut to the very core of your soul, and sometimes the scars last longer. And no thanks to the Malign Twins, I was personally affected negatively early in my life. But I also discovered that words could not stop me from reaching my destiny. I was forced to see myself as different, and I didn't want my voice to repeat the words I heard that created this fear that had frozen me. I will never wish anyone to feel the pain and hurt I experienced when encountering the Malign twins. I must revisit some painful places and find refuge to protect my feelings from writing this book. Out of fear, I tried to flee the criticism and opinions of those who sought to speak negatively. I thought I had escaped their clutch only to discover they were just lying dormant. When I fear failing, I think of Albert Einstein's quote; *a person who never made a mistake never tried anything new.* The further I get into writing this book, it reminds me of the shy little boy bullied into a closet of shame and shyness. I think the book is appropriately titled "Collateral Damages, Kept Secrets" because two individuals get to rid themselves of demons of their past. I considered my skin color as collateral. The value I placed on myself was worth more than my verbal and physical abusers. I had earned the kids' in my class and the school's trust because I didn't tell secrets or violate their confidentiality by revealing secrets shared with me by other people. I find myself in a dilemma that, in the past, I would have never given a second thought to share secrets. Today, I tell of my own secret story and the person who helped me overcome my shyness. I felt filled with information that someday I could help another little black boy, but I also needed to empty my soul for self-preservation and cleansing. I hope it will help others face the challenges in their lives that may have held them back from realizing their full potential. Because *we cannot solve our problems with the same thing we used when we created them.* Albert Einstein

CHAPTER TWO

MY COLLATERAL

The Skin Color That God Chose for Me

I learned that my skin color was collateral given me by God and a blessing, not a problem for me anymore, only for ignorant people who considered themselves intelligent. I became driven and determined to overcome the various obstacles in life; I did not know how to face nor tackle them in my teen years and early adulthood. I stopped listening to the angry voices that once occupied a space in my head by refocusing my energy. I could not show godliness with revenge against stupidity with like actions, but instead, I used words of encouragement spoken into my life by people who spoke positively. The two places my skin color should have never been an issue were in my home and the Black community. Even today, I still get stupid comments and insulting remarks on my skin color from people in my ethnic group.

They Chose The Color Green

It has been an adventure and a blessing. I realize how much I appreciate God for His many blessings and good he has allowed into my life. I did not choose the dark ebony skin I have lived in and sported for my entire life. I get a hearty laugh and yet a small amount of pity for those He did not make green, but they still chose that color to hate me. My heart jumps with small leaps of joy when they reveal who they are and their elected color. They decided to gree (envy) God's skin color, a gift specific to me. And they are not satisfied with the paint job he put on them. Because of their lighter skin, they are advance two rungs up the latter of success and life, while I have to start from the ground up trying to avoid kicks in the face or stepping on fingers.

Black Don't Crack, But Jealous Shows Lack

I see those individuals as having an identity crisis and one-on-one confrontations with themselves. I recently had a fellow deacon at my Church who felt it was alright to belittle me by making a rude comment about my dark skin. Have you ever been suckered punched by stupidity?

That is when someone says or does something stupid that you thought highly of them, only to learn their opinion of you is low. They say things so dumb that you refuse to dignify the ignorance coming out of their mouth with a response. When I need to school an idiotic comment, I give them some salient advice by telling them that green looks ugly on them and perhaps you should try something in black. The jet just went flying right over his head, and he is still trying to make sense of what I was telling him. Jealous is green envy. After getting called black Tar Baby, Sambo, monkey, and poked fun because of my dark complexion as a kid. I realized that I could never overcome someone else's hang-ups until they learn to love themselves. I grew up dealing with people who thought that light/bright skin was more acceptable and automatically passed to loftier status or clubs. But not so if blessed to have been born with dark skin and tightly curled hair, you were considered taboo. **MY CONFIDENCE LEVEL INCREASED** when I

learned to accept my dark skin as a blessing and not a curse. I
eventually learned how to deal with other human beings' different
treatment and resentment and one of God's creations. I learned
how to deal with small-minded individuals whose skin might have
been a shade lighter until a not-so-shy girl helped to bring me out of
the shadows of my fears. I never let on to any girl I might have liked
that had light skin. Their parents forbade some and would not allow
them to date me because of my dark skin. It kept me strong-minded
by constantly seeking to prove that people like Mrs. Louser and
others were wrong, and I was as good as if not better than the bright
and fair-skinned students in my class. After my divorce from Sarah
and before Ruth and I were married. I occasionally returned home.
The off-limit girl's mothers urge me to visit or drop by and see their
daughters. That I should give them a call; they would be glad to
hear from me. Many young ladies whose parents didn't want them
to date me because I was too dark later tried to hook me up with
their bright-skinned daughters. They were good enough for me
after failed marriages or having children with multiple men. My
mother always taught me to be kind to everyone, even my enemy
and those that dissed me, by keeping my head up. The daughters
they once believed were too good for me to date; I consider myself
too good to want to date them now. I would not give them a second
look now and cast what they viewed me in the past onto the junk
heap. I think it was dumb on the parents who insisted their
daughters not date a boy with dark skin with nothing to base it on.
I could sense the parents' phoniness that did not want me dating
their daughters, especially the mothers. And I will not write what
came across my mind about them, but it was not flattering. I
wonder why they assumed that I want to see their daughters after
they have been dragged through hell and back by some fair-haired
light, skin beau? I am a gentleman and never want to make women
feel put down or undesirable, so I pass on their newfound interest

in me. If I accidentally bump into one of them, I lie by telling them how good they look and leave it at that, no matter how they may try and compliment me. After years of rejection and being made to feel that my dark skin was a contagious disease, I no longer felt the desire to talk to my daughters years ago. I was not allowed to date. If I showed interest in a girl whose skin was bright, I was put in my place according to their once dyslogistic way of thinking because I was sub-human and not proper for their daughter. From those experiences, I promised myself I would not spend an inordinate amount of time revisiting potential relationships, missed love connections, and seeking revenge on girls who could not make their own choices as to who they should date. Many of the young ladies I wanted to date married their parents wanted them to. My complexion is still as dark today as the day I was born. And I learned I could be picky by rejecting handed-down girls forbidden by their parents to have relationships with me because of my skin color. I also knew the difference between my character and the desired boys that met the girl's parents' approval. Each of those guys indulged in alcohol, drugs, cigarette smoking, and womanizing. I appreciated the people who persuaded me not to give up as a young man. And the adults gave me nicknames such as Reverend and Deacon because of how I carried myself and was active in the Church. One would think that good character and manners would garner some favoritism. I was a good student in school; I made the honor roll, served in the student government, and t highly of my teachers and principals. I believed myself to be a loyal friend and trustworthy. People have shared some of their most intimate secrets with me. But when it came to dating girls, it was a no-go and no starter. I remember one girl telling me she wanted to date me, but her mother said boys with dark skin were evil, mean, and brutal. I find that amusing today when I think back to how this beautiful, very bright mind and skin girl married a boy whose skin complexion was what her mother felt was best for her daughter. I knew of his character before they dated and long before they married. He was the kind of guy who believed in thumbing his women's heads like watermelons. And they were married, he kept her busy in the maternity ward with four back-to-back babies. That must have been his occupation because he would not hold a job. Neither of my two wives ever had to worry about working and being a provider for them. The young lad whose mother thought she was too good for me, I wonder if she ever had any second thoughts.

CHAPTER THREE

ONCE YOUNG, DUMB, and DARING

And Two Fat Lips

Despite being a shy little boy, I did not mind taking a dare when I was a ten-year-old, especially if it questioned my bravery. The starting point of your life should never assume it will be your destination. You should never relinquish your mind to mindless people like the Malign twins and their mother, Mrs. Louser. You cannot give credence to meaningless comments with no facts to support what they say. You allow yourself to promote and peddle their short-sighted and misinformation of ignorant individuals. And most of all, you should consider their words as hollows like an empty wagon and the noise that comes from empty heads. It was unfortunate that I encountered the Malign twins and their mother, Mrs. Louser. I had to find the strength to harness the penned-up anger inside me.

Daring and a Hot Head

Having older brothers and sisters, I was competitive and relentless. When told I could not do something, my ability came into question. When I was ten years old, I learned that I was allergic to wasps and bees. One weekend my grandmother had all the grandchildren at her home. One of my teenage girl cousins, Coleen, discovered this giant wasp nest hanging on the side of my grandmother's house. She dared me to take one of my grandmother's fishing poles and knock the nest down. Well, you haven't said anything but a word. I reached and grabbed one of Grandma's fishing poles and gave that wasp nest a hard whack, and for my effort, I received a kiss on my lips from some angry wasps. My lips blew up like two balloons. I managed to get two fat lips without having a punch thrown my way. When my mother saw it, she went into a rage, asking all kinds of questions, of which I could not answer clearly. So, off to the doctor, we go.

At the hospital, Dr. Garrett asked what had happened? My mother tried to tell him, but he insisted that I explain how I came about getting stung by a wasp and wanted me to tell him all about the two large soup coolers I was now sporting. So, here is how I explained it to him, blubber, blubber, wobble blubber. Dr. Garrett said I see that

will happen with a grin on his face from time to time. I was given a
shot in the buttock and sent home with my two big soup coolers.
One girl told my sister that I was cuter with bigger lips than regular
ones. I guess I will be ugly again for a few days until after the
swelling is gone. When the swelling had subsided, I told my
mother that Coleen had given me the fishing pole and dared me to
knock the wasp nest down. She was none too happy about that, nor
was my grandmother because she always called me her boy, and I
just loved that lady. I wanted to move out with my family and live
with Grandma Minnie. I would convince my mother to let me
spend the day with her, and it would be just the two of us. As I
grew older and taller, I became meaner and more quick-tempered. I
could not define or describe what was inside me until later in life. I
know that there was a tremendous amount of anger to defend
myself, coupled with anxiousness to prove myself worthy. It was a
kind of rage that forced me to focus on overcoming stereotypes. I
never initiated any maliciousness toward anyone but felt compelled
to return to serve. One of my best friends had a severe speech
impediment, no one could understand him, and I could not see him
initially. But I discovered that if I slowed down and listened as he
spoke, it became clear what he was saying to me, and I could
understand him. I became one of his interpreters, especially when
other kids or teachers would make fun of his speech. I would tell
them what he was saying word-for-word. I realized that the Malign
twins and Mrs. Louser offered me a dare. I accepted their challenges
by pushing myself to set goals in life so that I could cram as much
good inside of me as possible in the dash after birth and before
death. I wanted to be a decent

person, someone doing as much good as I could while living. The
propensity to feel I must make up a lost portion of my life when I
allowed others to force me to lock myself inside my closet of fear
and shame because of their ignorant disdain for the brother with the

dark skin. Life comes with trials and tribulations, and we do not know when or how to get tested. God's hand always guided me when I did not know who he was, he knew me and my destiny, and I cannot give credit to the anger or anxiousness. But the confidence of a child, with the faith of a mustard seed, believing I could move the mountain of fear if I were brave enough to run from the closet when the door opened. Hope is what you rely on when you are trying to overcome it. And not allow anyone to deter or dare you two reach outside their limitations for you when God gives you unlimited possibilities. Traveling the narrow trail is a good thing because eventually, you will find yourself on a broader road.

CHAPTER FOUR

It Started

"Because of My Dark Skin"

Before writing Collateral Damages, Kept Secrets, I never told anyone of the terrible encounter I had with the Malign twins and all of the nasty names they called me. It is only now that I have ever allowed myself to think the words of the Malign twins. I did not know how to fight back when someone called me ugly names. I to hide and try not to let negative comments written or spoken affect me in the future.

I also lived up to the reputation of having a short temper from my brothers and sisters. It was a stark difference from the little brother with dimples when he smiled. The dimples were seldom seen because I rarely smiled. I was an ugly little black ape. At six years old, I knew that it was no compliment when someone called you a black tar baby.

CAUTIOUS

My first school day finally arrived, and I started the first grade. I did not want to go to school and tried to stay at home with my mother, younger brother, and sister. I was afraid that I would encounter the Malign twins, and they would start on me again. This time I would not have the back seat of my parent's car to hide behind. I guess you can say the first horror movie I saw starred me. It was scary and hurting. The Malign twins must have practiced their lines because they were effective and landed solidly in my mind. But strangely enough, some of those words I had heard also fell the lips of my father, whom I adored and admired the most. That is another reason I did not tell my parents what the girls had said. If my idol thought it was alright to say, it must be true. The Malign twin's opinion of me had crushed me, and perhaps they were validating my father's description of me.

I Had the Best Teacher

I was surprised, after starting school, how I enjoyed attending school. I had a fantastic first-grade teacher who spoke softly and was kind to me; her name was Mrs. Miller, a lady with light skin.

And like all first-grade boys, I developed a crush on Mrs. Miller; I studied hard to learn and enjoyed pleasing her by always giving my best effort. On one occasion, when the school had a parent-teacher night, she told my parents that I was a smart little boy, well-behaved, and a fast learner. As lovely and kind as she was, I kept waiting for her to say something about my dark skin. I remained a shy little six years old boy, looking for the bad guy to dress me down again. But I stayed on high alert and afraid because I did not understand how to deal with hatred. I did not know how to respond or answer why I had dark skin. And it appeared as though that seemed to have been the only flaw everyone would point to when referring to me. All of my girl classmates in the first grade were like Mrs. Miller seemed to like me. And of course, there was this one high yellow boy named Anthony. It is funny because all the girls preferred to play with me and despised Anthony. They just flat-out rejected him. None of the girls seemed to be hung up about my dark skin, only Anthony. I was the one that kept it at the forefront of my mind because I knew how hurtful it was to be called nasty names. I supposed it helped strengthen the wall and used it as a guard, not allowing anyone to get too close by putting up a fence to guard my feelings.

Their Words Were Lasting

Their words would far outlast physical bruises and scrapes I occasionally would get placed upon my body because they were etched in my mind. If they attempted to draw blood, they succeeded. For some reason, I needed to identify the semi-trucks license plate that ran over me, driven by the Malign twins. I still remember the names of both of those two girls even today. I would have to say that those two won the prize fight and were declared the victors of the first round. Yep! It was a beat-down of the dark skin kid. I had a fear of feeling that kind of pain again until I was sixteen. So, I always stayed on high alert, expecting a tar baby or monkey comments to come my way at any time. If things did not go the way another kid wanted, I would pay for it with insults about my skin color. But except for Anthony, it never happened. I finished the first and second grades with Anthony, the rejected and sore loser who tried to get his punches. By now, I had also developed quite a temper. I would look to retaliate with physical blows to the noggin or anywhere else when they were kids my age and size. You could see Anthony's bruises but only scratches on my arms from our confrontations.

After passing the first to the second grade, I enjoyed my first year of school because I had a great teacher in Mrs. Miller. I did not know that she would also be my second-grade teacher, twice as lovely, having Mrs. Miller as my second-grade teacher. The second grade went much like my first grade, smooth without incident. Even old yellow Anthony straightened up and was walking right. At least nothing like the berating I received from the Malign twins before starting school. The Malign twins' belittling started me on the road to believe that I was nothing and should expect this kind of treatment from everyone. And the action of some other individuals almost convinced me that they were correct about me.

I Am Still be Afraid

After completing the first and second grades, I gained a little confidence. I thought I would probably never get bullied again by those terrible Malign twins, anyone as insensitive. They shook me up, and now it was time to start the third grade with a new teacher. It would be my first time without Mrs. Miller as my teacher as my security blanket. There were issues initially for a couple of days; for one thing, I did not want to leave Mrs. Miller and go on to the third grade. I would have been entirely comfortable being a lifer in the second grade. So, I did not report the first two days to Mrs. Louser's third-grade class. Instead, I would camp out at Mrs. Miller's second-grade class. After Mrs. Miller would finish calling the class roll, and asked if she missed anyone's name? Yep!

Mrs. Miller did not call my name, and I am sitting right in the front row for the first two days. She would kindly march me down the hall to my third-grade classroom taught by Mrs. Louser. The second day she advised me She would spank me if she had to bring me to the correct class again. That love affair was over, which resolved the matter without any aches and pains applied to my behind. From then on, I reported to my third class without further incidents without Mrs. Miller escorting me to my correct classroom. But Mrs. Miller continued to watch over me years later and into my high school years. Once in high school, I remembered the first Christmas Annie and a couple.

We took a walk to the back of the school. And I was leaning on a large oak tree. I pulled Annie close to me to kiss her on the lips. Me being slightly taller than Annie, who had to look up when we kissed. She whispers to me; someone is watching us from the window as she points up toward a window. I looked up, and it was Mrs. Miller, my first crush. Had I come this far from being this shy little dark skin boy to be brave enough to kiss a girl out in the open? One of those flashback moments to a happier time was growing up, and so was my courage increasing. There were other times when Mrs. Miller would see me at Church away from school in the community and ask me how I was doing and whether I was behaving? There is so much more to tell and talk about Mrs. Louser and my third-grade experience that became another low point and deflating. When I think about it, the third grade became the most controversial and most motivational in my entire school experience for both elementary and high school. I was always determined to be one of the best students in my class. It was essential for me to prove that Mrs. Miller was correct when she bragged on my parents that I was intelligent and capable of learning quickly. In the third grade, I met my present wife, Ruth Allen, for the first time, and she became my girlfriend for about two or three weeks before she dumped me for no reason. Ruth had an aunt in our class that was a few months younger, a busybody, and a bit of a dictator. If you knew my wife Ruth, you would understand because she is loyal and sweetheart.

I Hated the Third Grade

Other than Ruth agreeing to be my girlfriend in the third grade for a couple of weeks before dumping me. The most eventful thing that happened had to deal with Mrs. Louser, our third-grade teacher (she could have been the Malign twins' mother). Mrs. Louser was convinced that I had cheated and knew precisely why I could not get good grades on tests. She accused me of cheating on a spelling test. To prove her theory, she summoned me to the front of the classroom and told me to stand and face my third-grade classmates. I walk up and stand in front of the class, happy, thinking she would praise me as Mrs. Miller did well on all my tests. Instead, it was to present me as the class cheater. She says, class, I want to introduce you to a cheater and how one looks in a growling voice. There went my happy feeling and a smile on my face. I denied her claim that I was not a cheater. But she disagreed with my plea of not being a cheater and liar.

Mrs. Louser railed even more challengingly by declaring that I was a cheater and she had proof. She eventually would share her evidence with the class and how she knew I could not get hundreds in her classroom. She was sure I was a cheater because *you are too black to get good grades*. I was a crushed nine-year-old boy. My opinion and view took another step back into the muck and mire created by the Malign Twins. I could not tell anyone about the inferiority complex I had about my dark skin. I didn't trust anyone with this piece of knowledge, yet it was hurting me deep down inside my gut and piercing my heart. I did not tell my parents what the mean Malign twins had said about me and how they made me feel. I needed to decide if I would reveal to my parents what Mrs. Louser said to me before the entire third-grade class or accept her horrible comments to be pushed back into my closet. I was seen as a piece of junk and not valuable collateral. After all, if my skin color was supposed to define me and who I am to become. I must make myself into a silhouette with no features, feelings, or future. I needed to avoid mirrors that possibly could reflect a human being. Who was right, Mrs. Miller or Mrs. Louser? One spoke of me as value with no reference to my skin color, and the other determined I was dumb because of my dark skin color. Mrs. Louser's comment told my classmates and me that I was stupid because of my skin color. All I wanted was to please and impress Mrs. Louser with my ability and show excitement about learning. She chose to throw my spirit down to the floor and stomp all over it.

I did not realize how much the Malign twins were right because my father, Mrs. Louser, and now my classmates must think the same way about me. These three seemed destined to pummel me by their devastating blows that were discouraging me. And I think they enjoyed and rallied as they drove home their point to plant as many hurtful words and deeds into my mind often as possible. Their voices became relentless and manifested themselves in my life day and night. Today in my sixties, I have difficulty sleeping because their voices became louder and echoed over and over inside my head. I thank God every day of my life. Somehow, I learned to use Mrs. Louser, my father, and the Malign twins for motivation by carrying this large-sized chip on my shoulder. A chunk is so massive that the weight would constantly remind me of the damage they inflicted on me. Before meeting Annie, I had a passion for writing poetry, where I found peace and solace by just writing about love. And as evil as some people, I do not recall ever writing a single poem I ever wrote that was hateful. I would often write asking why so much bitterness was inside those two girls. And why was I the recipient of their vicious tongue lashing of a little boy who did not have a defense for their vocabulary and did not find them humorous? I would love the opportunity to give the Malign sisters a lesson in kindness. I would admonish them with a huge grin that says, and you failed to destroy me to show them this same face. And let them know how they almost crushed me but instead only became the plinth that I used to drive me and get up off the mat each time knocked down or deterred. They were not alone, and it was not long before I discovered other ways to get attacked because of my skin color when I entered the third grade.

A Great Smile

"Stolen by the Malign Twins"

Before entering the first grade, the two nemeses I encountered must have been too dumb to graduate from high school. It seemed like they stayed in school forever, as I would occasionally see them walking on the school grounds. Ironically, I can only recall two times where I lost my desire to smile, and this happened to be one of those times. Incidentally, the twins were friends with my oldest sister Mattie. And one day, when I was with Mattie, I came face-to-face with those two imps. They tried to dote me by pretending to like me and telling my sister Mattie how adorable I was with cute dimples. They were opposite what they had said about me when they were spewing nastiness my way and crushing my little six-year-old spirit. I believe they are reasons I never let my guards down around people, even today. As an adult, I always wait for that individual to show up when I meet new or visit acquaintances to point out my dark skin. I wonder if people are dumb or unaware of what they say because I know I have dark skin. Hell, I have lived inside this skin every day of my life since birth. And those who try to sly will subtly, saying something like my cousin or friend is your complexion or so-in-so is much lighter, so I know you are not that person. I don't even dignify such ridiculous comments spoken by uncouth individuals. I give them my go-to one of the dyslogistic looks for morons. If you cannot describe a relative or friend without bringing up another individual's skin color? How stupid are you? I think to myself. I am always suspicious of friendly people and wait and look for their motives. I guardedly watch to see if their words match their actions. Before Annie, I would not smile or show my teeth because of the negative comments about my dark skin, not because they were stained, crooked, or were gapped. It was a long time before I felt comfortable smiling; yes, those two wrecking ball girls, I named the Malign twins, also took my pleasure to smile away from me. I was embarrassed by this occurrence, and this is the first time I have ever shared this story with anyone. Those Malign twins, along with Mrs. Louser, made me feel like it was a curse to have dark skin. The harsh words and comments get thrown my way when I was a young boy still resonated with me. People sometimes make me feel uncomfortable, especially those with light complexions, as some remarks, although directed at someone else. I recently visited with some of my in-laws, and one of the ladies equated black skin to being out in the sun too long. I am so sick and tired of explaining to the dumb-ass people that sitting outside in the sun doesn't cause you to have an ebony skin tone. I usually remove myself from such environments and go outside or walk or ride to relieve my anger. I recently visited the Veterans Medical Center, where I worked for five years. I never like visiting my former employment places or the people I once worked with because they are still working. A visit would be a distraction keeping them from doing their work. I decided to call one of my former co-workers because I am her daughters' pseudo guard parent. While sitting outside visiting with her, another former co-worker walked out to take a smoke break and came over to join in our little reunion. The second lady my age, a long story short, asked what I had been doing since retirement and if I enjoyed it? I told her yes and was trying to finish writing a book. I am excited for me as she is with anyone who works to do something positive with their lives. She asked what the book would be in my book. I shared the book title that I had settled on and the storyline. Primarily it is about people with hang-ups on skin color and the rape of my first girlfriend. These things sometimes affect others mentally, sometimes causing them to withdraw and suffer inside, hiding behind their pain. My friend Frances, a tall, attractive African American lady, never married and had no children. I shared with her my book about some of my life's highs and lows and how I was teased as a kid because of my dark complexion. And there are times today when people still try to insult me by pointing to the fact that I was born with dark skin. My friend Frances began to wipe the tears from her eyes. I wonder why she is crying. Was it for me, or perhaps she knows of the pain I describe from personal experience? Frances states I will be sixty-six soon, and I remember being called horrible names because I was dark and skinny. Frances explained that she could never maintain a meaningful and long-term relationship throughout her life. Because the guys always found my dark complexion to be a problem as if there was something that I could change. I have always been a tall and thin person; perhaps if it were a matter of weight, I could consider adding a pound or two. Jeremiah, those voices haunt me still and remain in the back of my mind. I am okay and in a peaceful place, so much so that I can talk about the experience. Since she was a child, Frances has suffered in silence because she was mistreated or talked to because her skin was darker than other family members. If you were to meet her and hear her speak, you would not know that she was in pain from childhood bullying and ridicule because of her dark skin. If someone saw or met her for the first time, they would be impressed to find that she has a bright personality that shines through her words and enthusiasm about life. But like me, Mable long to be a human with the same emotions and cares as every human being. It is sad for two reasons: the missed opportunity of this dark skin woman to be an ebony queen to a king worthy of someone like her. And second, it tells me that far too many men may have crossed paths with either passed her by or looked over because they failed to look beneath the sand for a pearl that God placed along their route. Perhaps a child or children missed being born to a dark skin mother that would have loved them even if they too had dark skin. Mable's story mirrors mine because I also hid inside me by relegating myself to living inside a closet. It was the epitome of collateral damage caused by some dumb individuals. We both were chased from the public view by the hurtful comments made by family and friends, finding comfort in talking within ourselves and never entirely giving upon us. I pray for my friend Frances and hope she will join me by shattering this myth that dark skin is taboo someday when she will not allow the past to cause her to cry or feel saddened. To some, it is an obsession to try and destroy individuals with dark skin instead of enjoying another of God's beautiful creatures. It is a sad commentary that in 2018 we still have to keep our guards up because of past painful and hurtful comments. The ignorance of people who use color as a barometer determines a person's character rather than the content and depth chart that flows deep in all directions (depth, profundity, understanding, perceptiveness, wisdom, acuity) inside the individuals' God chose to wear his prettiest color. I no longer use my skin as a curtain of protection but allow others to see what I am inside. Today I see myself as a secure individual with a great personality, three daughters, eight grandchildren, and one great-grandchild that loves me. I am aware that falling in love for the first time in 1969 helped me shed that negative image of myself and stop calling it shyness, but it forced me to cope with ignorant people. I am an introvert by nature, but not because of my skin; it is just my personality. I am most comfortable and at peace if I have paper and pen in hand. As an adult, I still take to heart the hurtful things people say to me, the same as when I was a kid. I sometimes hear some of the same things, but I stay prepared for whatever may come out of their mouths. I no longer enable the stigma imposed on me by ignorant, uninformed individuals to force me to hide my face or mute my voice hoping to avoid the ridicule. I find myself happy that I do not have to deal with people a lot because I am never sure who the newest version of the malign twins will be. The one word that best described me today would be happy. Ironically, I have known Annie's closet secret for more than forty-five years. Still, I have never shared my closet secret with her before writing this book.

And despite her reading about it, she has yet to address it or say whether it had any bearing on our past relationship. As my sisters and brothers described me as quick-tempered, I remain ready. I always keep a fungible jar of oral ribald on the shelf for dispensing with plenty of refills. That usually cures a case of stupidity fast. Despite what most might say, we all want acceptance as a person inside and outside. I used to hang out with the children with whom other kids poked fun by making unkind jokes about them. I wanted to help them fight back and not accept the abuse. Since they did not resist or fight back, I felt it was my place to do something by not allowing them to get bullied. I did not endear myself to the bullies, but they learned to respect me because I refused to back down or be driven by pinheads. I wanted to be invisible and not heard. Still, something inside of my conscience would compel me to stand up and speak out by always fighting back and retreating to my closet. When I am with other dark skin individuals, they share their stories of humiliation and shame. And how they were treated only because of their skin color. For the most part, they appear to be intelligent, educated, thoughtful and reserved chiefly to themselves. I have a handsome, smart, kind, loving, and genuine grandson that happens to have inherited my hue, and I am now once again an ally to a dark skin brother. It seems never to stop, and I can never let up out of fear someone will say the stupidest crap. Just let me get away from these people.

CHAPTER FIVE

DIRTY HANDS

"A Dusted Behind"

To finish up this incident, after disputing Mrs. Louser that I was not a cheater. I was not with clean hands on my way back to my desk. I was so angry, hurt, and ashamed, patting my behind at her as I walked back to my desk. That used to be a way of telling someone to kiss your butt. And she got the last word by whipping me behind and didn't kiss my butt as I had offered her. But I must explain why a child of hers would be so disrespectful. I could not explain to my mother why I had made such a gross gesture to suggest my teacher kiss my behind. My mother was a parent who believed children were always to respect adults. I was found guilty of showing disrespect toward an adult. She rendered this decision even if the teacher was wrong for what she said, and I was worse. So, I got a twofer; that is two butt whippings for you thick-minded individuals. My mother instructed me to move to another seat in the classroom, not accuse me of cheating again. I followed my mother's advice, moving off by myself. I continued to receive hundreds and A's in Mrs. Louser's class, and she never apologized. And neither did she ever acknowledge that I was still getting hundreds on her spelling tests and in her class. After this incident, I returned to my shell before starting the first grade. I learned to cope and blend in without bringing more attention to myself.

I remained in my shell until I was in high school. I would stay locked in this closet of fear guarding my emotions against evil people like Mrs. Louser and the Malign twins. And from the third grade until I was a Junior in high school, Mrs. Louser won the battle because she had silenced me just like the Malign twins. I hid in the corner of my mind with the pain and hurt of a teacher and educator. As she explained to my classmates, Mrs. Louser's reasoning for accusing me of cheating was because of my dark skin. She assumed my skin color was a learning impediment. Mrs. Louser might as well have hung a handicap placard around my neck because, according to her, my black skin equated to a permanent learning disability. Therefore, rendering me unable to learn or to be taught. When I graduated from the third and fourth grades, I entered with no expectations about my next teacher. Honestly, I did not even remember going through the fourth grade. After the third-grade experience, I became so withdrawn that I remember the teacher's name, but that is about everything I remember. As harsh as Mrs. Louser's words were toward me in the third grade, they did not forever take me out of the game. I became detached and wanted to live inside the closet of my mind. I found comfort in hiding away from the fear of being told that I was too black again. Mrs. Louser accurately described my skin as black, and her declaration was as if an old fart like her first encounter with someone born with black skin color. After all, she was black, and only it describes the heart that I supposed beats in her chest. But she was wrong to equate someone having black skin with their intelligence. My black skin was not a determining factor in my intellect to learn or if I could love someone.

I am the only class member with a four-year college degree from the third grade. So, here is to Mrs. Louser.

You Missed Your Mark

To Mrs. Louser

If you thought I would fail because you ridiculed me for my skin color.

You missed your mark.

Mrs. Louser, you thought you could destroy me by spewing mean and hurtful words.

You missed your mark

If you planned to destroy me by weakening my confidence;

You missed your mark.

If you thought calling me names and beating me would deter me.

You missed your mark.

If hating a little nine-year-old boy made you big and him small.

You missed your mark.

None of your thoughts, intentions, plans and hateful ploys worked against God's vision for my life.

You missed your mark.

CHAPTER SIX

ATTEMPTS TO DAMAGE MY COLLATERAL

"Jeremiah Micah Ford"

Step back, Jack, your hands are too black! Whites were not the only ones who perpetrated the disdain for dark skin. Other Blacks hurl insults as many if not more distasteful insults at those with skin color like ebony and Irish mocha and farther from vanilla. I thought this meant I was supposed to step aside and allow the light, bright, and darn near white group to go before me. I was willing to concede to their ignorance and lack of pigmentation knowledge. But when I think about it today, I tried my best to avoid confrontations or draw attention to myself. I attributed my shyness as an excuse to deflect attention from having dark skin.

By allowing myself to believe black was inferior and the light was superior. I was the first someone to fail myself long before anyone else by accepting the low-value others had placed on my exterior. When Annie came into my life, I saw value inside me much more significant than those who could only see the physical me. I knew in my interior was a heart filled with love and mind. She would benefit because I was willing to pour all of my kindness and loving compassion if she accepted me. I would reveal the type of love expressed only through service, romance, and caring of someone I would be happy to please. I knew I've always had qualities but was too afraid to express them but never had anyone to bestow or share them freely. Once we were into each other, we realized that the group's mission was to separate and destroy us. Although, outsiders did not share their sentiments because they knew how much our love meant to one another. I supposed they desired to have company in the valley of misery. I have Annie to thank for my new or changed attitude. Because of her, I became an unwilling participant in letting anyone wreck my chance at happiness with someone I hope to love a lifetime.

This experience resurrected a spirit of insubordination in my life. I stopped allowing others to define who I was or could be in life. No longer would I let anyone affect my life or write their narratives and beliefs inappropriate or demeaning. I found someone to love me. I first saw Annie Sims and purposed in my heart to someday have her as my lover. I recognized I was deserving of someone to love and love me. This determination became a worthy reason to stop allowing myself to be minimized and see what I had to give as below value collateral based upon my skin color. So many unexplained things and events have occurred in my life. I only give God credit, who I believe predestined and ordered my steps in life, and only he has the final say and no one else. I fell in love with the self for the first time when I learned to stop hating and listening to other people's opinions and whether their comments were good or evil. I didn't have a Columbus moment in my discovery of who was Jeremiah Micah Ford. I was there, and I discovered that I could deny or hide my ebony complexion in the skin I was born to cover my exterior. I devised a way of protecting the Black man that I am. There was nothing to fear about me unless you were disrespectful or dismissed me as though I was inferior to them or less knowledgeable. My dark skin color was damaged and not collateral like my fair-skinned classmates and friends.

Before I experienced discrimination by other races, I experienced it within my race of people. Because of my skin color, even people within the Black race thought it was good to separate me from the kids with light skin.

Inspired to Write

In Collateral Damages, Kept Secrets, I found real love when I fell in love for the first time. After this life-changing experience, I never allowed skin color to define me or force me to hide in a closet again. At the same time, I had to cope with the artificial stigma surrounding my skin color and her abuses and abusers. In Collateral Damages, Kept Secrets, Annie and I finally revealed all of the secrets we had kept from one another. We were fortunate that we found each other and remained together as long as we did. As much as I wanted and wished Annie and our relationship could have ended as a true love story. I do not believe Annie, and I was together for a lifetime. Because we found each other stuck in ditches and in need of tow trucks to come and hitch their hearts to pull us out of the mess or pathetic lives we lived at that particular time. We both had allowed evil and ignorant people to cause us to hide instead of building a defense to combat the bullying and ridiculing. As for me, it must have confused those whose skin was much brighter than mine when they heard my name associated with intelligence. These attributes contradicted their impression of what an intelligent individual personified. If God has something for you in life, I learned my choice to attempt to settle for bashfulness was a good line of defense but not a sustainable one for life. I wanted desperately to change others' minds and spent nights lying awake to thinking of ways.

It was difficult, if not impossible, for me to get up enough nerves to talk to her while hiding in a closet of fear. Listening to other people's opinions almost caused me to miss the opportunity to share my love with someone starving for what I had in my heart to give freely. I had a few scars and memories to warrant such hesitation and the reluctance not to expose myself to the fear of rejection. I decided that I was a worthy suitor for her love and affection. And suppose I never venture outside of my safe zone, not pursue Annie. In that case, the negative naysayer's opinions win, and I will be the forever loser. But the stars were aligned, and she could not say no to a handsome big bright, eyes nine-year-old boy with a note requesting her to be my escort for homecoming. Enters the girl who would steal my heart and chase away my greatest fear. Annie was the perfect girl for me, and I could have missed out on having Annie Sims, my first girlfriend. I never shared my fear of being rejected by her because of my dark skin. I was too afraid and shy to share this with her when we dated. Why did I fear getting rejected by her because of my dark skin? I am sure if I share this bit of information with her when we meet and talk about old times? All that mattered was I muster together enough nerves to approach her, and this is the beginning of our story.

I always thought it was genius of me to use my nine-year-old little cousin, but standing on my own two feet, I found a way to ask her to be my homecoming escort. And it was a genius idea. But had I remained sitting on my brain (butt), it would have remained numb and deprived me of the use of my ability to function adequately. I asked myself what I enjoyed doing most to relax and cope with stressful situations? Answer. I get great pleasure in writing poems and letters to imaginary girlfriends. I met a young lady named Annie Marie Sims, who unknowingly hid in a closet and kept secrets about her life. Annie was an excellent reason for me to eventually leave my closet of shyness and venture out into the harsh world, no backing down this time. So many unresolved issues still force me to remain cautious and play close to the vest when dealing with people even today. I never want to let my guards down or show signs of sympathy for Annie because she will treat such gestures as a potential opening. And I am for sure that it is over between us. I tried to empathize with her because of her abuse. I could not come to her rescue when she told me she had been raped and was pregnant. I forced myself to intervene because I felt I needed to help her, I suppose as she had once helped me.

CHAPTER SEVEN

MY FATHER LINGERS

I have often asked one question from relatives and others who knew my father and have never received a satisfying answer. Why does my father hate me? To include my mother and the answer was always the same. Your father did not hate you. What makes you think that he hated you? My father sang the loudest in the negative choir, along with the Malign twins and Mrs. Louser ridiculing me. His words always seemed sharper, louder, and more hurtful because they came from my idol and the man I loved most and wanted to be like in life. I believe I loved Mrs. Miller because she was more like my mother away from home, protective, and someone's approval I cherished. Suppose Mrs. Miller had continued belittling me like the Malign twins I encountered before enrolling in school, reinforced by my father. In that case, I think that it would have been over for me. I could not fight against my father and was too afraid to challenge Mrs. Louser and the Malign twins. I am eternally grateful to God for his protection.

I learned to write by dreaming pleasant thoughts each day. I now know that it was God's way of protecting me. Psalms 30:5 For his anger lasts only a moment, but his favor lasts a lifetime; weeping may stay for the night but rejoicing comes in the morning. Learning how to read and write became a godsend. I wrote poems and letters about the beauty I saw in other people. I wanted to show kindness to those whose lives I may touch. Having this desire or gift to help others strengthened me to stand and fight instead of running and fleeing from those who would try and bully me. Those experiences helped shape and motivate me to fight back when dealing with such dumbness.

And when things become weighty and not a clear path, I recess into space to hide myself to escape. There are days I find myself sitting alone and weeping from thinking about some of the harsh things that were said to and about me because of my skin color. The one constant of my hurts is my life ups and downs have always been God. I thank my first Sunday school teacher for introducing me to Jesus, and the clarity she gave of him caused excitement in me at age nine that has never left me. Before Jesus Christ came into my life, I knew what my dreams were, what I would be when I grew up or what trails I would have to travel to reach my destination. I remember thinking that I had no assurance that I would have friends to encourage me along the way. But when I dreamed, I was always far away from East Texas and in a sunny place.

I allowed fear to paralyze me and keep me from facing my foes, who were trying to block my path. Their weapon was their tongue to try to destroy me. I used people's ignorance against them to overcome their plots. I am sure my skin will be a dark shadow, but my body will radiate bright with hope and compassion inside. The darker some tried to paint my destiny, the more hopeful I would shine because others saw a bright future for me. I will focus on the knowledge that matters the most from grey matter. Someday I will look back on my life and recall my most considerable pain came not from fighting or spankings but because of my dark skin. I am not responsible for the skin color that God blessed me to have on earth. The people who sought to destroy me and keep me too bashful to speak because they knew their words were painful and affected me because of how I always responded. It made them feel good about themselves. When I stood up for myself and those who would be so foolish to think that someone's skin color was the best judge of their character, they did not know what I would become or where the trials were on the trail life would lead me. No one can write a resume with experience without first getting an education and gaining work experience. I was a little black boy written off just because someone with a poisonous eraser sought to try and deny me my future. They intended never to allow my ability to go from potential to kinetic. I refuse to let anyone make me a victim of collateral damage at the hands of individuals that were too lazy to look inside of my soul. If they had to look inside, they would have discovered my dark skin was no more complicated than any other skin color. Evil does not necessarily correlate with color but wrong intent within the heart. It is only difficult for the simple-minded who refuse to come inside. I attributed my timidness because of all the times I was teased by kids. I found myself off to myself and daydreaming about the future. I always dreamed of living a long way from East Texas, driving with my wife and kids. And to have my father, whom I adored, to support the insults hurled at me by other kids and some adults made, we want to be invisible.

I was the happiest and most excited when I had a pen and paper in my hand. I loved to write love letters, poems, short stories, and even a couple of skits for my Church. I needed to get over myself because people would put me down because of my dark skin. It seems like double that number thought I was talented and could make something out of myself if I put forth the effort. My History teacher, one day, called into his class to lecture me about my choice of friends and the difference in our future potentials. I did not understand what my History teacher Mr. Spillman meant when he talked and gave me that bit of unsolicited advice. He instructed me to look at the two boys hanging around. And he called each by their names and said those two boys are not going anywhere in life, and if you continue to hang with them, they will drag you down. We believe that you can make something of yourself, but you need to watch who you pick as friends. Taking Mr. Spellman's advice, I started to withdraw from the two boys. And today, I found his warning to be spot on and served me well throughout my life.

It appears others could see potential in me, although my father refused to recognize or believe in me. Nonetheless, that question, why my father hated me; he took to his grave, never revealing the answer, and I assume in his heart. It does not matter what other people told me that my father always spoke highly of me; he never said to me. I have heard my father say he loved me and wanted the best for me. He never said I am proud of how you grew up to be a respectful young man. I really would have relished that moment and hearing those words come out of my father's mouth and the chance to have a moment with a loving father and an admiring son. Instead, the only good thing that I can attribute to my father as positives in my life was he taught me how to drive. Also, I learned to do everything opposite him by doing the right thing and being a good father to my children.

I always wanted to know why my father hated me, he is deceased, and I am grown and should have moved on by now. Unlike me and Annie, my father and I will never sit down and discuss our differences. It will, likely, remain an unknown secret unless he left this secret in some locked box. Like Mrs. Louser and the Malign twins, my father also served as one of the motivators in my life. After being told a few times by my dad that I would amount too much. I focused on my education by staying as one of the top students in my class.

After Annie transferred to another school, I didn't engage or get involved with another girl. I decided to concentrate more on my future, and the day of high school graduation seemed to be fast approaching. I envisioned getting the hell out of James Ford's house as fast as possible and never looking back. My mother never liked expressing my desire to flee this popsicle stand. I had already earned enough credits to graduate from high school early, but my father insisted that I stay in school. Early in life, I had aspirations to become a lawyer someday and help other people. I wanted help to be kind to other people, especially those I felt were being given an unfair shake in life. My father was not down with his sons being white-collar professionals ambitions. He was an excellent mechanic by trade and wanted my brother Joseph and me to follow in his footsteps. When my dad learned I was not interested in being a mechanic, we became adversaries when I showed no interest in becoming a mechanic.

In 1974 when I decided to join the military, I had to take a battery of tests. One of the tests involved motor mechanics. When the recruiter went over the test with me, he pointed out how well I had done on the entry exam but noticed I did not like mechanics and the outdoors. The Recruiter Sergeant Sikes asked me what it would take to join the Army? My reply was indoors when it is hot and indoors when it is cold. So, I think that battery of tests I took a few years later confirmed my lack of interest in becoming a mechanic. And I did not see anything wrong with the profession, but it just wasn't my cup of tea.

Anyways I wanted to spend as little time in his presence as possible after high school. He was a darn good mechanic, and everyone wanted him to work on their vehicles. But becoming a mechanic just was not my passion and did not sit well with my father. I could do the work, but I just was not interested in it. I enjoyed using my brain more than my brawn. Who in the heck wants to be cursed at and called stupid in front of strangers just because you do not know what a three-quarter inch wrench is since you have never been taught or shown?

A Lasting Whipping

Dad was a great referee that settled disputes. My younger brother Joseph and I shared the same bed until our older brother moved out. My younger brother Joseph had a habit of rolling up in the blankets, leaving me out in the cold. Every night I had to wrestle him for a portion of the quilts. I had had enough, so I decided to allow him to remain rolled up in the blanket. I was able to thump his head, and he couldn't fight back because I tied his arms down from being rolled in the bed covering. And I was helping him to understand why rolling up in the blanket wasn't a good idea.

All he could do was cry out for our mother to come and help him. Someone did come to his rescue. Whoever came into our room did not turn on the light. They just started grunting and swinging their weapon of choice. I think I got the worse of that deal because Joseph was well insulated, and I was not as quick as the whipping started. It stopped. After that individual exited the room, I could hear our father's voice mumbling. I better not have to come back in here.

That was the last fight between my brother and me. Dad had settled the blanket issue forever. I guess this night, and he proved to be an excellent referee, as he took the fight out of me and my brother Joseph.

Challenged by My Father

In the ninth grade, I took typing in school, and my mother purchased me a portable typewriter. My father's response, you better hope that you get a damn good job pecking on that typewriter, or your damn ass will starve. I was a decent typist. When one of the pickiest teachers asked our typing teacher, Mrs. Anderson, an excellent typist, she recommended that I type a document.

Driving My Daddy

The feud between my father and I started back when I was about eleven years old. Like many that I had a part in, I was supposed to participate in a school program and needed a light blue shirt. James being my father, I asked if he would purchase me a blue shirt. If my mother could not get it for me, I did not need it, nor did I get it. I will not burden you with all the curse words and black ass, so-in-so my father called me. When he finished dressing me up and down and calling me everything but his son, I was happy to depart from his presence. But I made myself a promise that I never broke. I would never ask my daddy for another thing.

It was a rare Saturday evening when our entire family was home. My father was in a good mood (likely alcohol-induced) suggested that he teach me how to drive soon. I replied, I already know how to drive a car. My father was someone that enjoyed seeing eggs on my face. So, he would embarrass me in front of my mother, brother, and sisters on this day. Come on, show me, handing me the keys to the car. When you mess up, I will slap you upside your head. I started the car, looked behind me, put it in reverse, and back down the driveway, into the drive, and we proceeded down the street for about a mile from our home. He instructed me to turn the car around and head back home. After steering the car around, he says stop. He opened the passenger door, exited the vehicle, took it back to the house, and parked it. I successfully returned the car to where we had started, and the rest is history.

My Dad was a Cad

The one outlet that my father or anyone else could not take from me was that I enjoyed writing. It was my place to escape to go wherever I desired. The physical beatings with fan belts, extension cords, and having to lay on the ground with his foot on my neck while he beat us for something he made up in his mind. It mostly happened whenever something did not go right between him and one of his girlfriends. I was a teenager, and I recalled my father threatening to shoot me because he thought I had snitched on him for screwing around with one of my mother's lady friends. I told my mother about a situation between my friends who lived in the same neighborhood as my mother's friends and me. He had seen my father earlier that evening; I guess old pop was trying to get a little nookie on the side this day. Anyway, he asked dad to tell me to come by and pick him up for a basketball game that I would attend that night. Dear old Dad did not give me the message from my friend, and consequently, my friend missed the ride to the game. I meant it when I stated that I would never ask my father for anything else ever. So, the following day, my friend gets on the school bus and lights into me for not picking him up for last night's game. Dumb me. I tried to explain that I did not know I would pick him up for the game. And he did not believe me because I told your father to ask you to come by and pick me up. It upset me because we were such good buddies, and I was dumb and clueless. So, I shared how upset my friend was with my mother.

Today, I hate math because I came close to losing my life because I was not smart enough to solve a simple problem by adding one plus one to get two. However, my mother was much better at figuring the math. My mother had put one and one together. She determined that my father was sniffing her friend, which explained why he didn't deliver my friend's message. That would have given his whereabouts away before coming home. My mother confronted my father with unknowingly provided facts by their dumb son (me). He assumed I was informing him and threatened to blow my brains out. I wonder how much of a mind he thought I had; I could not figure out that one plus one equals two. He mentioned a few times getting his gun and shooting me. However, I was both innocent and dumb to what my parent's argument was about, which gave me more reasons to be quiet and standoffish, and even more of an introvert. I would look for motives, and there were none to be found.

Even though I wanted to avoid my father, I still tried to do things that would hopefully be proud of me as his son. I was a good friend with two white players on our football team that was brothers, and after some of our games, their father would come to our house to drink with my father. They sat in his car in our driveway. He would ask my father to wake me up because he wanted to give me something; it was always money. Mr. Edwards would tell my father, James, that is a good son you have; my two boys talk about him all the time, my father's response would always be, *he ain't s--t. No, James, listen to me, you got a good son here.* And I never heard my father say anything different, not one encouraging word. Nobody was going to make him think that I was worth anything.

You start to believe what people say about you as true when your father seems to find more pleasure in talking about using words laced with profanity.

When we had visitors come to our house, he would find a way to be insulting and say hurtful things; he appeared to have gotten great pleasure at doing so. The physical beatings with everything from fan belts of automobiles, extension cords, iron cords, sticks, sometimes forced to lie face down in the dirt with his foot on our neck, did not take away our desires in life. As stupid as it sounds, the beatings went on longer when you would not cry. I know that my body was numb, especially when it came to my father, and I could not shed tears. I had become numb to the beatings. He called a bull for some reason; I guess he was complimenting me for not crying. However, if I had light skin, the red did anger me.

Someone To Believed In Me

And I do not think he appreciated or believed my teachers when they told him that I excellent students, a smart boy, would say. A lady named Mrs. Davis all but adopted me as her son and would get me and take me to places to speak, sing, and to get the exposure of interacting with other kids and adults. I represented my Church as a delegate when I was thirteen years old until I left home for college at eighteen. I remember telling Mrs. Davis I wanted to stop being a leader and less involved in so many activities because I would like some kids to start grumbling. Other children complained that I was doing everything, and they felt overlooked. In a very stern tone from a very gentle lady, do not you ever let me hear you speak the words quit or stop again. And do not ever think about not using your God-given talent just because others do not have your ability or are too lazy to apply their skills.

Great Advice, Mind Your Own Business

Mrs. Davis's words of advice supported one of my high school teachers' advice she had given me about focusing on my own business. I was beside myself that another student received an A on her report card. The girl was a distraction in class, did not do her homework, flunked multiple tests, and the teacher still gave her an A for his class. That is the same grade that I have earned. Seeing me walking down the hall with a look of concern, she called me over to inquire about the look on my face. I explained to her what was causing me this distress. She asked me two questions. (1) Where is her A, and if she knows the material? No, I replied. (2) Where is your A, and can you do the work? Yes, I replied. Jeremiah, when she leaves this school, her A will remain here, yours, you will be able to take with you the rest of your life. I suggest that you focus on your learning and leave coasting through school to the likes of that girl. Mind your own business and focus on yourself, she concluded. I never forgot that conversation and that salient advice telling me I had enough on my plate to worry and concern myself.

Mr. Sage Visit

When it came time to graduate from high school, different recruiters came to our school to try and recruit students to their institutions. One such recruiter from a school in Arkansas, Mr. Sage, wanted me to attend this school. But there was one small problem; I needed to pay a thirty-five-dollar application fee. I told him, Mr. Sage, I do not have thirty-five dollars. Oh! Do not worry; I will ask your parents about it; I will come by and talk to your father. I begged this man not to approach my parents, especially my father, for any money on my behalf. But true to his word, he came to our house and approached my father. He said Mr. Ford, your son Jeremiah, is a very bright young man with excellent scores on his school's aptitude test. We would like to have a young man like him attend our school in Arkansas. All he needs is for you to invest in him by paying the thirty-five dollars application fee. Suppose Jeremiah is going to your school in Arkansas. In that case, Jay will go by paying his way because I will not waste thirty-five dollars on him. My father calmly and succinctly informed Mr. Sage that his recommendation for Jeremiah was to finish school and get a job to help support the family.

I knew I wanted to be exactly like my father until I was eleven. I am not too fond of it when someone says I looked and walked like my father, which puffed me up because he was my hero. But from eleven on, if anyone made those statements, I felt insulted because I wanted nothing about me to resemble my father. I asked my mother if I could change my name. Later, when I joined the military, I changed my middle name to five generations. I no longer wanted to be recognized as the son of James M. Ford. This hostile father and son relationship was wearing on my mother. She would talk to me, telling me that your father is your father, and you should love and respect him. The only good thing he ever did for me was that he taught me how to be the right provider for my family. Everything he did or did not do, I would do the opposite, and that was how I knew that I was heading in the right direction. Ironically, two weeks later, after the visit from Mr. Sage, I was summoned to the principal's office and informed that I had earned a full academic college scholarship. I thank my mother for always sticking by me, but on this day, I told her that when I leave home, I will not be coming back ever again. I could see tears welling up in her eyes as she asked me if I meant that and that I would not go back to visit her either? Maybe to see you, Mama, but I do not care if I never see daddy again. I have an awful lot to love for my mother, and I favored her over my father. My mother is responsible for five of her seven children graduating from high school. My mother did not graduate from high school. She also was a peacekeeper and wanted me to love my father. In 1989 I wrote my father a letter asking him why he did not love me as his son, and I would like to meet with him to discuss his hatred for me. I mailed the letter to his last known address. After a few weeks, I received the letter back because it was undeliverable. While in San Antonio attending a course, my ex-wife (Sarah) called me, and before she could tell me her reason for calling, I said my father had died, hadn't he? She wondered what I how knew. I said I just felt it and could hear something in her voice. We never reconciled our differences, and I never learned why he had such disdain and hatred for me.

More than one individual wrote that I would miss talking to you in my high school yearbook *because everything I ever shared with you I never heard again.* Today, I still have that same mentality, and some burdens are difficult to bear. Still, I remain hush and a safe deposit of information. It even caused me to wonder how easy to talk about anything and anyone. But found it difficult to share with others about my fears and hurt. I kept hidden from everyone as if I had no troubles of my own. I really would have liked to have learned the secret to my father's hatred for me. Was I his son? Did he think perhaps that I was not his child despite our resemblance? I know today that their plights helped me deal with my own because some of the things they shared with me kept me safe in my closet.

When I went off to college, I could land a job on campus, and I did not need a lot of money to send my mother half of my earnings each month. I remember coming home for spring break, and my father was acting a fool, brandishing his pistol, walking back and forth across the floor in front of me. Finally, he shared why he was pissed. Jeremiah, you send your mother money, but do not send me a dime blah! Blah! Blah, this, and that. It could have been a night of death, anticipating my father would push me into a fight with him.

I had placed a knife beside me in the chair I was sitting. As my daddy walked toward me, and I did not move but watched with an icy stare, I was going to defend myself if he continued to approach me. I would stab my father as many times as it would take to end his life. He stopped suddenly, standing in the middle of the floor, said I better get out of here before someone is hurt, and walked out on my mother and two children still in high school after being married for twenty-eight years. He left and never returned. Hoping that we would become destitute, but instead, we began to flourish in life, and things got better for us. He was the dead weight, always holding us back. His little evil beanie brain figured that we could and would survive without him always dragging us down and through the mud. Still, his sorry ass was not working, except to use his pecker and drive women around in a car that my mother had purchased.

I Never Heard Him Say It

Family members on my father's side say he bragged about his son and that he thought the world of me. I sure would have loved hearing that from him for myself. One of my older cousins shared that I had accomplished some of the things in life that my dad wanted to achieve. He felt that he had given up his dreams when the children started to come almost every year. That is a cop-out because all he had to do was stop being horny with happy pants. I do not buy it that the children he chose to make were at fault for his failures. That still does not explain why he hated me, or at least he made me feel unloved. Was this his way of pushing me? I do not think either because I have always been self-driven by aspiring to do something with my life. Then why didn't my mother hate me too? Why did I have only one teacher ignorant enough to emphatically state my dark skin was why I could not learn? Why didn't he believe others when they commented on me favorably? Why was his voice one of the ones in the chorus belittling me because my skin was dark?

I Wonder If

In a conversation I had with my mother recently, she asked, " What would your father say or think of his children today? I wonder whether he would be surprised or proud of how well you all turned out. My response to her questions was he still would not find it in his heart to encourage us or say that he was proud of us. Again, she was asking for something good to come from a man who never told his kids I love you or you did a good job. Perhaps time would have softened his heart and changed his mind about the children of his loin because through Christ Jesus, anyone can have a change of heart. I only wished my father's heart would have changed and been a part of the wind beneath my sail by helping his children soar. All of my parent's children left home with their blessing or well wishes. I remember it because we became of age and tired of the depression from having no plan for our lives. Throughout the community, we were all well-mannered and reared by our parents. That was mostly out of fear and hoping that the man we called "My Daddy" would notice our effort to please him enough that he would heap some of the praise he always found for other people's children upon his own. I know that when I left home, it was to keep a vow and a promise I made to myself. And a secret I shared with only my mother. Mama, when I leave home, I am never coming back. I will try to stay in touch with you and tell you where I am and how I am doing, but I don't plan to return to this place again. I was hoping it would hurt my father if he never saw or heard from his oldest son again after he left home. But I never thought how this drastic move might hurt someone I loved, like my mother, for one. I observed my three older sisters and older brother leave without promising to come home or occasionally calling. They went off and started new families of their own and created their happiness.

We all learned to care for and love our children and spouses was a miracle because we had no example or pattern. Perhaps we all had the same dream of what we hoped to have as a family, and each in our way realized our fantasies. We all tried to honor our mother, who preached and encouraged us to stay faithful to God and men and women of our word. Where one parent put us down and never lifted us, the other encouraged us and forced us to see good in ourselves and not worry about what others said or thought about us. I believe we got our strong work ethics from our mother—she would go to sick and could barely raise her head up.

CHAPTER EIGHT

OUR MOTHER IS OUR SHERO

My mother is an extraordinary woman. If I can recall, no one on earth has always wanted to please more than my mother, and I never disappoint her. For some reason, both she and my father seemed harder on me than my other siblings; I was not given breaks or allowed to make excuses for my mistakes. When I was eight years old, and my parents were about to leave the house to go somewhere, I do not recall where or for what. But I do remember them putting me in charge. I thought it was a joke, just as my older siblings felt they were also joking until my dad used some profane words and said, I mean, he is in charge until we return. To this day, I can still see that dumb look on my face, wondering what made them decide to put me in order of three older sisters and a brother. Also, I had a younger brother and sister. And speaking of my younger brother, it seems I was always looking out for him and getting burned for doing so.

One day we disobeyed our mother, and mom was not having it and vowed to whip us. Joseph had this habit of walking around without a shirt during the summer. Mom was not threatening this time; she was coming for flesh and blood. I did not want my brother to get a whipping without a shirt. I took the shirt off my back. I handed it to him to put on while he received his punishment, thinking that if mom whipped him first, she would be too winded when she got to me, and he would return my shirt to me. When it was my turn, my brother refused to give my shirt back. He ran off with my shirt, and I had to take my whipping shirtless. And my mother thought it was funny, as she lit me up like a Christmas tree, next time you will keep your shirt, won't you? I guess this is what people mean by keeping your shirt on. And he looked up to me. We would often get left at home alone while my parents visited, took my sister, and left us at home alone. He was easy to frighten when we walked together down dark roads, and I would tell him that I would always take care of him. When I left for the military, we hardly ever saw each other. He was either in prison or out in the drug scene, always something he should not be involved in at all. When my brother was ill from cancer in 2014, my sister Linda told me that she had gone to see him and did not recognize him except for his voice. She would take him to his next scheduled doctor's appointment, which happens on my birthday; I volunteered to take him and took the day off from work. She warned me of our brother's unrecognizable appearance. I drove to the location where Joseph was living. As I approached him, I could see what my sister Linda had told me. My brother appeared to be in terrible condition as I hugged him. I could only feel this skeleton body, and I could not imagine seeing the person before to be my brother. He would not see me crying. I told him to wait inside; I needed to return to my car and call my job about a private matter. After fifteen minutes, I compose myself and off to his doctor's appointment. We proceeded.

Our personalities were opposites; he was called "Cat," the life of the party. And I was given the nickname Deacon. My brother promised to take care of him and not run off and leave him. Two years later, Robert's bout with cancer ended on January 29, 2016; he passed with me standing by his bedside just as we walked hand and hand down the country road where we grew up. Here I am again, standing at the bedside watching another one of my siblings pass away. A few years earlier, it was my oldest sister Mattie whose hand I was holding as she drew her last breath. Of eight children, only two remain alive today, my youngest sister Linda and me. We grew up in a house that always appeared to be too crowded. And now, I live in an empty world where there is too much space as all, but one of my siblings still lives. Some days, you must prioritize your pain and hurt. I miss them.

For a mother to see six of her eight children go on before her, she must be a strong woman. I sometimes think about how she made a home for us despite my father's best efforts to hold us down. I learned how to be responsible, be a person of your word, and punctual from watching my mother. She taught me more things than she will ever know because I did not need all her advice at once, but I have often relied on it throughout my life.

I take pride in giving my word and fulfilling my promises by taking responsibilities seriously. Another good thing from Mrs. Louser's (Malign) class was when she gave us the assignment to determine our parent's birth dates. When I asked my parents about their birthdates, I did not forget them. Ever since I was nine years old, I always saved my pennies, nickels, and dimes to purchase my mother a gift when I was ten years old. I remember the first gift that I purchased my mother for a birthday gift: a jewelry box. This birthday, she was sick, and she could barely open her eyes in bed. I went into my parent's bedroom to give her the gift I had purchased, which seemed to perk her up. I could see the tears flowing from her eyes as she struggled to open the wrinkled paper I had wrapped her gift. I thought the tears were because she was in pain from being sick. Later that night, my dad came home, not sober, and my mother mentioned to him that he knew that she was not feeling well and asked why he did not come directly back after work. How do you know that I did not need to go to the doctor? He showed no real concerns and was being a total butt. Then I heard her say to my father that today was my birthday. The only person who remembered my birthday was Jeremiah. My father's response was, yeah! At ten years old, I vowed that I would never forget to give my mother a gift for each of her birthdays for now own. A promise that I have kept faithfully.

My Mother Saved My Right hand

Before remembering to honor my mother on her birthday, I remember when I was five years old. I was hardheaded once and disobeyed her after instructing my younger brother and me not to play with some glass jars that she had stored outside our house. Her instructions were clear and directed at my brother and me. But we needed just two to do something, and I do not remember what was so crucial that I disobeyed her. I sneaked and grabbed a couple of jars and ran with them in my arms, and I accidentally tripped fell, severing a tendon in my right wrist (dominant hand). I looked down at my wrist and could see nothing but white. The blood was starting to spew out like a Texas oil well, and picking myself up and ambling back calmly to the front door of our house.

Me - Mama

Mama -Yes.

Me- I cut my hand.

Mama- Okay! I will be there in a minute, which was the longest minute ever.

Me -Calmly called her again, mama.

Mama- I could hear her coming, sorting of fussing, Oh! What did you do? Sit down there on the porch.

Me -I cut my hand.

Finally, she walked to the door and saw me standing there, holding my wrist and bleeding profusely.

Mama- Like any mother, she became unglued and screamed out, baby, what did you do?

Me- I fell on the jar, and it cut me when I fell.

I could feel her picking out glass pieces from my wrist before wrapping them with a large rag. We did not have a telephone.

Mama – Went next door to our neighbor's home and asked if she would stay with my younger brother and sister while she went to get my father. He worked about five miles from where we lived. I think she ran all the way, probably where I got my running ability. Finally, she and my father arrived to take me to a clinic in Carthage, Texas. For many years, I walked around with a limp wrist, and the best that they could do was tie the tendon I severe together. I remember the two doctors' names were Dr. Garrett and White. The only way the doctor could repair the damage to my wrist was to tie the tendon together, and God only knows how many stitches it took to sew up the wound. The doctors informed my parents that I would never use my right hand again.

When I extend the fingers on my right hand, you can see a funky-looking scar and indentation. My mother has never had any medical training and a high school diploma. Both she and my father heard those gloomy doctors' outlook for their son's right hand, but she chose not to listen to that noise. My Mom purchased me a rubber ball and made me squeeze it every day multiple times a day. I felt like I was in a hospital room because she kept waking me up throughout the night to change bandages and keep me comfortable for a long time. My mother thought the rubber ball was my best friend every time she would see me without it. She would ask where that ball was? I was incredibly young but sensitive and could sense when things were incorrect. I saw the sad look on my mother's face, and it did not sit well with me. One night I was feeling a little down around bedtime. I told my mother that I would be with God if I were not here in the morning when I woke up, and I would tell him that I loved him. That night she must have awakened me a hundred times; Jeremiah, are you okay? Because my mother refused to let me speak, the doctor's prognosis proves untrue. I have full use today of my right hand; it is more robust than my left. I did not become handicapped, and I went on to play sports, serve twenty years in the military, and hopefully will someday write a book to tell this story. When I got older, I gave my life over to Christ; I look at the miracle on the inside of my right wrist and marvel at what God did through my mother.

My mother thought that I did not remember all that had happened to me and was doubtful until I described my great-grandmother to her. My mother said you were only three years old when your great-grandmother died. I said, but I remember she would fuss by saying that all that boy does is cry (me) when my high tone, Cousin Bruce, did all the crying. I described her as a short woman with long hair and bright skin. Whenever things did not go Bruce's way, he would run to her, and she would swing the situation in his favor. When I started the first grade and started learning my alphabet, my mother would have me show her how I would use that hand to write with my crippled hand. I would hold the pencil so tight in my right hand and could almost snap it into two pieces. The weaker side that was supposed to be weaker became the stronger one.

Whipping the Repairman's Butt

The year before I started the first grade, the oven on our stove played out and needed repairing. So, this fat greasy white guy that my father knew came to the house to fix it. When he completed the work, my mother asked him how much was it? His reply was, I do not want any damn money. You know what I want. He proceeded to try and rape her. Our neighbor, Mrs. Lewis, saw his pickup truck parked in front of our house and recalled that he had tried to rape her once. Thank God she decided to come over to warn my mother about him. When she got there, they were in a battle, he had ripped off my mother's blouse, and she was not giving in to him. Mrs. Lewis joined my mother as they teamed up and commenced whipping behind; now, the hunter is getting hunted. My mother and Mrs. Lewis darn near stripped him naked. Instead of getting nookie, he got his butt kicked by two angry Black women. They put him on the run, raggedy and eager to get out of our house to get in his station wagon, leaving all his tools. When my father came home later that evening, my mother told him what had happened. Dad was not a happy camper. Taking his rifle off the wall, he went looking for this guy, a Black man in the 1950's looking to put a bullet in a White man who was unheard of back then. I do not know if my father ever found him or not, but he did get a set of tools.

My mother always stayed busy doing something, and I would find myself sitting and talking to her about many things. I learned how to cook, wash clothes, comb hair, and treat my wife from my mother. In 1991 all these things except for how to love my wife came into play. I became a single parent responsible for rearing two beautiful daughters. Thanks again to my mother, I learned the above-mentioned skills that kept me from relying on other women to do them for me. I could concentrate solely on putting our lives back together. When my older sisters had babies while I was still in high school, my mother made my brother babysit me. We had to go the whole nine yards, which included wiping baby's behinds, combing hair, and teaching us how to cook and clean house. She said when you get married someday, your wife is sick or in the hospital having your baby. You can help while she is getting back on her feet; you all can take care of the baby and house. Thank you, mother, for that came in handy. But then, I always cared and looked out for my girls from when they were born. My wife and I did not plan or schedule to take turns getting up during the night; I just got up and took care of my little princesses without a rotating schedule.

A Compassionate and Caring Mom

One of my father's nieces came to live with us, along with her husband and their seven children. How did we do it, you ask? We did it out of love and our parents' expectations to be kind to visitors, especially family. One of the daughters and I learned how to tie a necktie using the encyclopedia. And my favorite little cousin was Duke; he delivered the note to Annie, my first girlfriend. So, Duke was pivotal in that transaction. And he was my favorite little cousin. I saw him more like a little brother than my younger brother. Duke and I would hang together.

We all got along with each other, which was not an option. So, we all grew up in a home full of love and a close-knit family. Some people who called themselves friends of my parents were frauds. I thought it was strange that people would speak favorably about my parents to their faces and how they admired them—the things people would say behind their backs by making fun of my family. And looked down on because we were a poor family, especially about how my parents gave birth to us close together. As you can imagine, back in the 1940s and 50s, the invention of cable television had not come onto the scene. The TV was not a part of today's family's quality of life. So apparently, my parent's favorite past-time was playing doctor and nurse. I suppose having children was their form of entertainment. I was the sixth of my parent's eight children as we lost a sister when she was eighteen months old with pneumonia. I was always somewhere in earshot to hear some of the comments made about us. Therefore, I am easily embarrassed and shy away from people even when they speak well. It was a cowardly façade saying one thing but meaning something opposite. And some were so bold to think that the tailored made insults lobbed my way. I was too ignorant to know that their comments were backhanded and meant to be insulting. The character I had allowed myself to fall prey to is nothing like my personality today or even before graduating high school. And for a moment, I let myself get snagged by the STUPIDITY hook cast by sick and shallow idiots I encountered.

I learned that you should never allow anyone to define you by writing their narrative to describe you early. And secondly, I learned never to let anyone minimize me when trying to determine my value. And last, most importantly, remember that your beginnings are not the decider of what or who you will become in life. It is God who predestines us and not humanity. I learned less about myself when listening to other opinions of me. It seemed as though the more negatively some spoke of me or viewed my skin as a problem they would not want for themselves, I understood that they could not handle the blessing God had bestowed upon them that they saw as a curse. I have come to grips that I will never outlive being a Black man in dark skin. I try my hardest to be respectful, polite, and caring toward my fellow man. But I will not allow anyone to think that my skin color determines the depth of my soul, the width of how far I can stretch my gray matter. I never shared with my mother the mean things said to me by the Malign twins. I did not allow their words to deter me from facing and climbing to higher heights up the ladder of success. Mrs. Louser and the Malign Twins were too shallow to hold me back because my focus and aim in life required that I continue to grow to reach my fullest potential in life. Just so that they know the height for which God's talents and ability are unlimited and not yet in sight.

The time was nearing when I must stop dreaming and come into the real world. I needed to stop shopping by finally buying. I had rehearsed all of the lines and scenes when finally I would have the courage to introduce myself to a girl by asking her to allow me to love her unconditionally. It was time for each letter I wrote, and the poem I composed would mean something for that special girl because I would give her my heart and soul for a lifetime.

CHAPTER NINE

SOMEONE TO WRITE I LOVE YOU

Before Annie came into my life, I found enjoyment writing love letters and poems to make a belief girlfriends as a way for me to relieve my feelings to an imaginary somebody. I used those moments of loneliness to write letters to see my words outside my head and in print. I longed for the day when I could share my love and companionship with someone. I wonder if the opportunity will ever come when my feelings bring pleasure to a deserving girl. And I would only focus on loving and writing I love you to one girl. One day, I hope to trust one particular young lady to enter the boundaries I had put up to protect my heart for the first time. Because of me, our Junior Walker, and the All-Stars forty-five record *What Does It Take to Win Your Love* was scratched and skipped in my home. I would play this record over and over and over. I was free to say I love you and ask questions in my letters because I only imagined myself asking that question to a girl. A true story when I reached the fifth grade, I had a small business. I wrote letters for other boys in my class and some sixth graders. I even had one girl who likes poetry and paid me to write her a poem for her little pinhead boyfriend. Writing letters and poems for other boys helped subsidize my brokenness (lack of funds). And if the boys wanted to impress the girls, I would add some poetry for an additional fee, of course. Despite being one of seven children, it might seem challenging to believe that I had difficulty being bashful. Writing the letters gave me relief and was an outlet to try and communicate with other kids. And I lay awake most nights staring out the window at the stars and listening to strange sounds. But yes, I was the shyest kid in the family and still hold that title of being the most bashful individual you will ever meet. During my first year of high school, our English teacher Mrs. Brock issued an assignment for her ninth-grade class to write a poem about the moon using aglow. So, I am the kid who enjoyed writing poems and was the only one in the class to complete the assignment. The title of my poetry was Moonlight Aglow. Mrs. Brock enjoyed the poem so much that she called me out of each of my classes to read my poem before her sophomore, junior, and senior classes. It also included me standing before my oldest sister in class; before allowing me to leave, she chastised the seniors and praised me for having such a talent at such a young age. But you all are about to graduate and cannot write a single sentence. I received boos, and my sister said the boys in her class called me a show-off.

I was born in the fifties and growing up in the sixties when the skin was a real problem before James Brown made the hit record, *I am Black, and I am Proud*. I was black and afraid because I had not yet overcome being called Sambo or having other derogatory names hurled my way by other Blacks. Today, some will still try to be insulting by pointing out my dark complexion, showing their stupidity by thinking they can affect me as an adult. I see their puny machination with that impolitic crap for what it is, but as an adult in 2017. Like Jeremiah, the adult, I responded by telling the village morons that green (jealousy) is an ugly color on you. And perhaps you should stop wearing them. But I must continue rocking this black for the rest of my life. Mrs. Louser and the Malign twins helped dispel the myths and my father. He also offered his opinions about my complexion.

CHAPTER TEN

DISCOVERING LOVE

I only allowed myself to dream of actually having a girlfriend for a long time. I was a sixteen-year-old young man, and my curiosity was starting to pressure me to step outside of my shyness and be bold in my pursuit. I must find the path and road to finding a lover for my heart. The course for me would be one I have only dreamed of and never traveled and more difficult for me. I eventually saw myself standing beside a paved road, wondering should I cross it or choose which direction I should go. Whichever I decide to take, I must be prepared to follow it to the end and never look back or turn back by doubting my decision. It was not a narrow-paved road; this was Broadway, yes baby, showtime. I was to star in my first significant transaction (love), and I was about to start my real-life movie in October 1969. It premiered one October night when Annie whispered into the right ear of Jeremiah. Jeremiah, I want to be your girl. The leading lady was a girl that intrigued me so much that I could not get her out of my mind. The girl's name was Annie Marie Sims; she had big beautiful brown eyes and a giant smile. After much deliberation and chicken-ness by me. I found a way to make her notice me and become my girlfriend. It was our first time to experience the excitement and joy of love for both of us. I had finally found someone to love, and having them love me back was like opening the door at a surprise party. Like any love, first-time love comes with no instructions or how to behave or what to expect, and it is more than just when a boy and a girl meet. Then, what else is it?

I must take you back two months when I first noticed her and started dreaming of becoming my girlfriend someday. After our first one-on-one conversation, and was convinced this was the girl for me. I was with a desirous kind of feeling, wanting to have more than an occasional and casual conversation with her. My thoughts became more frequent of her each day, to eventually, they became hourly. I continued to imagine what it would be like to have her as my girlfriend. The more I thought about her, and the more intense the thoughts were racing through my mind. I was free to dream more intently and not bridle my mind, but what was different about my dreams now? There are names and faces to go with the person in my imagination. I love you. The reason that I was reluctant to tell her how I felt about her as I still had a severe hangover from the punches delivered by Mrs. Louser and the Malign twins. I stayed in my lane out of fear of being rejected. It reminded me that I was perhaps because I was a dark skin individual, not deserving of someone like Annie's to love. The ridicule that I received at various points in my life. It was not like the insults were not always in the back of my mind. The blows that landed were precise punches to my gut. The kind you lose your breath is not an episode you will likely forget or want to repeat too many times, frightening. Yes, I was afraid and was willing to use every excuse for why I should not approach Annie by making her aware of my feelings for her. But I also realized that I had been relegated to the Maligns if I ever escaped from the restricted small closet space. I must find the courage and a cause worthy enough for me to venture outside those walls and walk through the closet door. I habit assessing situations too long before executing plans that I have designed, and thought would work.

Annie sat at my desk during the last school period every day because my homeroom became a study hall for her class. And since I practiced football, I left my belongings in a drawer underneath my desk in the final two periods. My school did not have student lockers to store your books and other belongings. So, after football practice, I needed to pick up my things from beneath my desk. She had her coat and textbooks all over, making it difficult to retrieve my stuff without asking her to make some adjustments. There were times when she was a little too comfortable because she would have her stuff sprawl all over the place. So, I would tease her by saying something insulting but playful. She was quick-witted and always responded rapidly when I kidded her. I felt comfortable teasing her and less shy but was nearly frightened to death to tell her how I felt about her. I had been reminded so many times about my dark complexion. I seemed to succumb to skin tone issues and believed that I could not deserve anyone to love. A great fear prevented me from approaching her; I must find the strength by getting over all the past insults and turning off the voices that repeatedly play in my mind. Although I had matured in some ways, I did not lack self-confidence in my ability, but I did in my appearance. I must overcome this if I am interested in girls and ever hope to have a girlfriend. I wanted her as my girlfriend and someone to love and love, but this fear of approaching Annie prevented me from just rushing past the fear of getting rejected. So, I chose to prolong the disappointment that would bring our daily interactions most likely to an abrupt end when I expressed how special she was. I assumed that she was more cordial than falling for me like I was for her. What drew me to Annie was I saw her as a beautiful girl with brown eyes, a contagious smile, and a captivating laugh. It took me almost two months to get up the nerves to approach her. Finally came a day of reckoning, the now or never moment that forced me to make my move sooner than I had planned. On Monday, the week of homecoming, the football team decided to have our girlfriends escort us onto the football field before and after the homecoming game. They were assuming we all had girlfriends for the Friday night game. I had gone the entire week trying to figure out how I would get Annie Sims to be my escort for homecoming without getting my feelings hurt?

The fear and belief that I am not deserving of anyone because of dark skin were starting to resonate with me even more. Finally, I figured out how to ask Annie and still landed in a soft spot after rejecting me. So, the plan was, I would not ask her myself but instead write her a note and have my little nine-year-old cousin Duke deliver the message during our pep rally. I took the corner of a sheet of paper and wrote, Annie, will you be my escort for tonight's homecoming game? The giant chicken that I was, I found a spot to hide so that I could see her reaction just in case I needed to rescue my brave little cousin. From where I was hiding, I could not tell if her response were yes or no because she did not nod or shake her head to give me any indication as to whether she answered yes or no. I could see her saying something to Duke and caught him by the arm, and proceeded to walk to where I was hiding. No, hello, hi, or anything, she just asked why didn't you ask me yourself to be your escort to the football game tonight? I responded by saying that I was afraid you would say no or get angry with me for asking you. It was to my amazement that Annie said yes. My knees buckled under me because I was nervous about getting her response even after rehearsals. I had played over in my head for two months. I struggled by giving her the time to meet and the location. I do not remember a single word or line said after she agreed to escort me on and off the football field that night. And the plan was for us to meet at the gym at 6:30, and she would accompany me onto the football field. Annie was a no-show, and I thought to myself just as I figured she was playing me for a joke because she was not present when it was time to be escorted onto the football field. I was disappointed but not as hurt as I would have been had Annie put me down in front of my little cousin Duke that afternoon.

Before the first quarter was over, someone tapped me on one of my shoulders as I stood on the sideline. I turned, and it was Annie's little brother. Annie said to tell you that she was late but will be here to walk you off the field after the game. I was once again happy, and my mind was racing for thoughts and words to say to her when we would later walk back to the gym after the game. Still, I do not recall anything I said to her, but I remember what she said to me as we walked off the field. She stopped me in my tracks and faced me so that she could look into my eyes and said Jeremiah, I want to be your girl, but I am not the kind of girl you think that I am. I cannot do what you are expecting me to do. I was shocked by the comments and needed to regain my composure, but I assured her that I would not try anything. The thought of me even asking for a kiss on the cheek was not in tonight's plan. So, the mere suggestion of sex indeed was not part of my plans to get through this night. Later I thought to myself if she only knew how long and difficult it took for me to get up enough nerves to ask her to be my escort and want to ask her to be my girlfriend. She would have realized that she was safe. Her little brother and sister were accompanying us on our walk off the football field. One little sister did have a problem with my complexion and stated how dark I was, but this could not knock me off cloud nine.

All I Needed Was a Chance

Finding Annie and accepting me into her life was an excellent cure for my shyness. Still, when we met years later, I have failed to tell that I was too shy about approaching her, but I felt too dark to expect her to want to be my girlfriend. But when Annie said that she wanted to be my girlfriend, it exceeded all of my expectations. She gave far more than I had asked for when I only wanted a date for homecoming. Instead, she was my first girlfriend, and she was the key that opened the closet door of fear and let a shy, dark, skin boy come out to experience the joy of love and to shine a light where I only saw darkness. I thank God for her love because it helped give me the courage and strength I needed to move past my fear. God had given me a heart filled with love and real emotions to share with someone outside my body and mind. Annie became that special someone to give my heart to and the opportunity to use talent, to reveal my passion by writing it and no longer being squelched. For the first time in my life, I was free to transfer the words in my mind onto paper, giving them the freedom to enjoy the light of another human. Finally, I was out of my closet of fear and shame. I enjoyed the view of darkness filled with the hurtful memories of past comments hanging in my closet of fear that caused so much collateral damage due to fear. Annie was about to receive a lot of love, care, and passion that I had stored up inside of me. I never dreamed I would ever get the chance to share my love with a woman as beautiful as her. I had hoped someday to bestow upon someone special. After the night was over, I was lying in bed awake because the night's excitement kept me from falling asleep. I just kept replaying our walk off the football field over and over in my mind. I could not sleep thinking of all the beautiful things I wanted to say to her the next time we would meet on Monday. Yes, like my birthday, I remember the day I started to erase the years of black tape reels from my mind filled with years of insults and negative comments. The long winning streak was over for the evil ones who intended to destroy me. I replayed this night so many times over in my mind, so much so that I sometimes, even in my advanced age, still get that same warm feeling that I felt on that night. But I soon get over it, something like gas! I have replayed those moments repeatedly in my head like the favorite scenes in a movie. I was now in control of the remote and could stop, rewind, and replay our relationship; it erased the years of negatives with positive, loving thoughts. I will always be grateful to her for being a girl. I first experienced the joy of what I believed was true love. Annie afforded me the pleasure of mutual feelings with another human. The dark closet is a place to hide and suppress imposed hurt inflicted by my perpetrators. I was in this closet space because I was bullied and shamed into submission, allowing others to render me feel hopeless, worthless is, ashamed, and devalued.

CHAPTER ELEVEN

I CAN'T WAIT TO LEAVE THIS SCENE

And here is why

It was finally graduation night. As sad it was that after this night, the classmates that I had spent most of my life with, we would never be together in one setting ever again. I am thinking back to the third grade when my teacher told me I was too black to learn.

My father cursed Mr. Sage because he asked him to pay thirty-five dollars for me to attend school. Absent on this special night was Annie Sims, the girl that saved me from shutting down and closing myself inside a closet. The teachers spoke well of me and encouraged me to keep going. Someone wrote in my yearbook *if the elevator to the top is crowded, take the stairs.* It was not easy, and so the stairs just seemed natural. During the proceedings, they called the names of the scholarship recipients. As I write this piece, I still get goosebumps from that night because I felt I had finally accomplished something to make both of my parents proud. Hearing my mother say how proud she was of me meant the world. I genuinely believe that God has blessed me throughout my entire life. By some, I was to be a failure in life, but God blessed me to go on and have two careers and be able to retire from both. It provided me with a means to free my mind from negativism by surrounding me with people who saw me as a glass half full. He gave me a passion for writing as a place to escape. Since high school, I have met some wonderful people and was exposed to many beautiful experiences.

Writing a book titled Collateral Damages, Kept Secrets allows me to share many stories about my life.

I thank God for my mother, for always being in my corner. Even when I decided to join the military, she was against it but understood when I used her words. Many of our conversations were about becoming a man and taking care of my wife and kids. The day I left for the military, she tried to talk me out of it. I reminded her that she always told me to be a man, stand on my own two feet, and do not be afraid to chase my dreams. I also reminded her that she raised me to be an independent man. I did not want to remain in East, Texas, working Monday to Friday, and have nothing to show for my efforts. Before I reached the point where I could take standing still and work on jobs that only paid minimum wage, I needed to leave. I had dealt with some difficult things already in my life that I never told my mother. I could not bring myself to say to her how the Malign Twins humiliated me when I was six years old. But I overcame Mrs. Louser's attempt to destroy me. I loved the girl, raped her uncle, and had a baby that was not mine. The real reason I transferred back home was to continue my college education to be near Annie.

And going off to college was another lesson in life about the world outside of East Texas. And college life started to mature me; it seemed to have been an extension of high school with newer and more problems. It was much faster, as college was more like the Beverly Hills Billie's truck trying to race a Ferrari.

The once-promising and loving relationship deteriorated after transferring to high school in the middle of the school year. And how her moving had affected me in a way I could not explain. It left me feeling empty, and I needed to prove I was not afraid to venture outside the protective fortress we built for each other's protection. The sudden departure was also right because we did not get a chance to say goodbye or do anything stupid like agreeing to try and have a baby. And yet, it was the making of a baby that ruined our chances of a future. It also involved me losing my first love. But eventually, I realized that leaving home to attend college helped me refocus while recovering from the absence of Annie's love. Also, going away from home took me further from my dad bullying me. And possibly a third one, which was the poor communication between Annie and me. I had already survived the twelve years of the secondary school experience. I overcame the third grade's pain and now celebrating the twelfth grade from a valley to a hilltop. I learned my nemesis and how to deal with them. Because of Annie, I could come out of my shell and no longer be shy. She was the distraction to buffer me and give me a soft and comfortable spot to land. This part of my life resolved, and I need to focus on was how to continue my journey alone.

CHAPTER TWELVE

COLLATERAL DAMAGES EXPOSED

Secrets Revealed

The collateral damage of two former lovers as teenagers is revealed as they try and tell their secrets hidden from one another. For the first time, we found the courage to talk about our love for each other and how it helped mass the painful secrets kept shut away in recesses of our minds and hearts. And how the pain and disappointment still haunt us many years later. We are both angry and upset with the other for not being allowed to say goodbye, or our love has come to an end. Annie accuses me, Jeremiah, of hiding, which I vehemently deny. I hold Annie at fault because she never responded to my letters after transferring schools. So we both found reasons to blame the other for our eventual demise as a couple. About forty years ago, the version of Jeremiah and Annie was too young and not savvy enough to take the appropriate actions to deal with the tragedies in each of their lives. Although the lack of understanding alone did not cause collateral damage, pride and shame played a huge role.

Currently, I plan to forgive Annie on full display because of our relationship with life experiences. The events had humbled me and taught me the importance of forgiveness. And perhaps I could convey to Annie that I was willing and ready to forgive her. And by asking for her forgiveness. Perhaps my forgiveness of Annie could provide her the freedom she needed to move past the pain and hurt she suffered and not accuse Jeremiah of going into hiding.

Annie desires to hold onto the memories from the pain and injury inflicted on her to build walls of lies and excuses best served her but did nothing to repair the damages. Unlike me, she continued to use the pain and hurts as motivation to escape and rebuild positive life for himself. There is no doubt that our love at the beginning for one another was genuine and magical. Still, the intense love for each other also faced obstacles and untold tragedies, making it challenging to overcome them together. Instead, they proceeded to succeed in destroying any possibility of their love beyond repair. Our actions eventually brought destruction to each other lives. The mountaintop we once stood atop madly in love became the valley of sorrows and disappointments. Our anger imploded the big house of love these two individuals' built. Annie's critical question is, could they rebuild it by joining together as friends and forgiving each other and the perpetrators who caused their pains. I will repeatedly state I was not interested in reviving or rekindling their teenage love affair. Because being happily married makes it doomed and a none starter. I am only curious why I could find a way to escape but couldn't reach Annie and pull her out?

I could sense Annie wanting her handheld and be walked step-by-step back into the past. And hoping Jeremiah would change his mind about never pursuing or restarting a defunct relationship. In that case, was it not for the festered hatred they seemed to develop, their love could have welded back together again during the years they were both free. And Jeremiah is convinced that what is needed is not rekindling a dead love affair but forgiveness to be potent.

Annie complains of many things that went wrong in her life, and it was not just one incident causing her to have a permanent mental scar. The unwanted attention and involvement played a big part in destroying each of their first-time true lovers' love. And the rift created a permanent parting of ways for two longtime young lovers. When Annie transferred to another high school, the distance grew wider because of no communication. We were never close again due to a lack of trust. And the secrets and unforgiveness of those who wrongly harmed each of them destroyed their loving relationship permanently. Who is actually to blame for the collapse of our teenage love affair? We are meeting many years later to discuss what happened and why.

Accept Having Black Skin

I also learned how to prepare myself mentally when people approached me, which helped me understand how different aspects of my life were the cause for their envy. I prefer to say green instead of saying envy. I delight in other people's successes and dread seeing anyone fail. But this is not always the case when the wind blows my way. I could sense but not understand why green (envy) individuals could not be happy for me. All that is well for me in my life. God blessed me with the wife I am married to, a home that we live in, cars we drive, the jobs and opportunities my wife and I are blessed to have worked. I realize their green was because they were the ones who doubted me and my ability and secretly spoke negatively behind my back. Many doubters suspected two people could live in harmony and love and respect each other as my wife, Ruth, and I care for each other. You would think they would seek to find our secret instead of hating our success. It would be a one-second class, God. Yes, God did it all for us, and we take no credit other than we obeyed and tried to remain faithful to him. I take a lot of the blame for the length of time it took for us to hook up because of the scenic route I traveled to get here. I wrote a book because I knew people would never read my opinions. After all, they never valued my feelings. It does not bother me as much as it may have in the past because I understand. After all, some people need daily gossip. They are only doing what green people do — hating and naysaying.

When Love is The Problem

Many side stories and events are told in Collateral Damages, Kept Secrets, involving Jeremiah Micah Ford falling in love with Annie Marie Sims. Together Jeremiah and Annie loved each other as much as any teenage couple would like. Still, their passion for one another could not pry the deep secrets they kept hidden from one another. A dramatic and crucial part of Collateral Damages, Kept Secrets, involves Annie Marie Sims's hardships as a young girl. The stories will reveal how their high school courtship unraveled and how they weaved together a life for themselves.

Annie was the first someone Jeremiah trusted with his heart. He allowed himself to venture outside of his area of protection. He would tell someone I love you, and I hope their response would express the same sentiment.

CHAPTER THIRTEEN
AND WHO WAS ANNIE MAE SIMS

Told by Annie Sims

I was born Annie Marie Sims in Houston, Texas, and the oldest of six children to a mother that did not want me and was not ready for motherhood. We never bonded as mother and child with my other siblings. I grew up convinced that my mother never loved me like my other siblings. And I learned the emotion of hate long before discovering the joy of love. All I knew was that I was her daughter because she gave birth to me. I never felt the warmth and loving care of having her as my mother, and it was not until I fell in love for the first time that I discovered what I believed to be true love. Before I learned to trust people, I knew not to love anyone. There were times when I wished that my mother could be there to comfort me and help me fight the evil uncle and male cousins that were molesting me from the time I was a little girl. The people who were supposed to protect me also had complete control over it and did not save me. I did not know how to tell or explain what was happening to my grandmother. I was molested because I did not know what it was called when grown-ass men sought pleasure in touching me in my private parts. Each time I would ask my grandmother to allow me to go and live with my mother and other siblings. She would say ain't happen because you are bought and paid for, and I will never let you leave.

What Was the Price Paid for Me?

I think back to try and understand my mother's reason for not taking me with her when she decided it was time for her to move out of my grandmother's home and why she could not take me. She tried explaining it was because my grandmother refused to let her take me. When I was about six years old, I asked my grandmother to allow me to go and live with my mother and other sisters and brother, but she scoffed at me, saying I bought you and paid for you. And you will never be allowed to leave and go live with your mother. How was I purchased and paid for by my grandmother? What did that mean? I never stopped asking to go live with my mother, and her response was always the same. I told you that you are not going anywhere. I bought them and paid for them. I wonder if my mother owed my grandmother a debt that she had failed to repay.

Was it the hospital bill that grandmother paid, and my mother could not repay her? Was I supposed to be held as collateral until she could repay the debt? I was collaterally damaged before going on the market, and who wants damaged goods? I often wondered if Jeremiah would want me if he knew male family members were molesting me? It left me with many questions, and I grew up feeling abandoned unloved. Damaged products were cast aside because of what was happening to me at the hands of grown-ass men. Ironically, my mother gave birth to another child a year after birth. She kept and raised that child and all my other siblings she gave birth.

There are days I wished I had the same fate as the child that Jeremiah and I once made but was refused to give birth. I was misled by one woman who said she owned me and another who abandoned me, telling me it was best for me. I grew up resenting my mother because she never fought to take me with her. Loretta, my mother, never stood up to any of my abusers. I told her about the things the male relatives in our family were doing to me. She responded like it was just some minor scrape on my knee from a fall. She expected me to go on about and play with the other children as if nothing were happening. Things done to me were more than boo-boos or minor scratches. I had enough darn sense to realize this at an early age. My mother never showed me that she cared as much about me as my siblings. She appeared even less interested in knowing that I was getting molested. I thought my sisters and brothers were all spoiled brats. My other siblings thought they were too good to live in the country for just one night. They would cry until my mother would come back to pick them up and take them home. Goodbye, damn it, and I hope you never come this way again, was how I felt about them and their behavior. I blame many people for the voices trapped inside my head and the unrelenting mind that never shuts off from terrible acts perpetrated against me. So, if people think I am angry or bitter when I speak of my mother and siblings, there is resentment. It is not a façade or joke; it is for real. My siblings lived a more privileged life growing up with my mother because they had her protect them.

In contrast, I had no one to depend on to protect me except Jeremiah, and I was afraid to tell him I needed protection. Today, I live a double life and find happiness in neither one. It seems like everything associated with joy in my life comes back to my time with Jeremiah. At least once, I did get to know true love once in my lifetime. I have had three husbands, and neither one was what I would consider a true love because they all hurt me emotionally and physically. Still, maybe out of necessity, I found myself settling for whatever happiness presented itself to me each time. And since I am damaged collateral, what else could I expect other than to be abused?

A Wish That Became A Nightmare

As quickly as I found true love in October 1969, I lost it in December 1970. Because my mother finally got the courage to come and take me with her, moving me away from Littlefield, Texas. Like a thief in the night, gone were the holding hands, kissing, hugging, receiving letters almost every day, and the nightly phone calls. It was fast like that; I lost the joy of being with Jeremiah every day, having a happy heart and a peaceful mind. I do not recall all three of these since I was with Jeremiah on the same day.

Early in my life and before Jeremiah came into my life, I was headed for the wrong side of life's ledger. I was so rebellious and downright hateful as a young kid that I refused to learn to read and write until I was ten years old. I was not a good student from the first grade to the third grade. I did not see the need or benefit of getting an education, and I certainly did not want to bother the teachers and other kids. If I had to give a one-word description of myself during this time, it would be "MEAN" I was downright mean toward everyone. I found more pleasure in being alone and off by myself.

A Late Bloomer

I would describe myself as reclusive during this time and did not want to be bothered. I did not learn to read until the third grade because school was not necessary, in my opinion. I resented every teacher that I had from first through third grade. I was mad as hell because I felt that my mother did not want me and had abandoned me. I was so low and forced to accept hand-me-down clothes. I was so desperate to have some of the things my siblings had. I started stealing money from my grandmother's purse. And would give the money to one of my teachers or a neighbor lady who lived across the street to buy me some new clothes. My rebellion ended, and I decided to learn to read and write. By learning to read and write, I discovered that the money I was stealing was a monthly health and welfare check my grandmother was receiving for me.

When I was about twelve years old, I ran away from my grandmother's home over a pair of gray socks that she refused to allow me to wear; they just hung on the back of a door. So, I decided to wear them anyway and put on the socks. I tore a hole in them because they were too small. I knew this would cause big problems between my grandmother and me, so my next adventure in life was to run away from home. Before they found me and brought me back to my grandmother's house, I reached the next town—no further comments or commentary on how that ended for me.

I did go on and graduate from high school and earned my college degree; otherwise, I would not have been able to read the love letters written to me by my first love, Jeremiah.

It was not just the men in my family who molested me and made me feel like trash. I recall when my grandmother would strip me of my clothing and scrub me in my private area because she thought I had had sex with Jeremiah. But she never once asked me about the semen on my gowns or pajamas, a gift from my male relatives who were molesting me, and I believe she knew it was going on. And she pretended to be too drunk or too sound asleep to hear anything going on because every time they would come over, my underwear would have rips and tears in them. There were stains of semen from grown men that used my hand to masturbate. The laundry and changing of bed linen were done by her only, and there is no way she could miss seeing semen stains on my sheets or the tears in my underwear and dried bloodstains. I was a six-year-old little girl when the molestation started. She never asked me a single question about why or what happened to me.

But she was all over it when Jeremiah began dating, trying to see if we were having sex. The semen stains you must have seen on my underwear should have made her curious and know that it was not from me but a male I had come into contact with; it was from my dirty old male relatives. These stains were in my underwear long before Jeremiah came into my life. I fought as hard as I could and screamed out loud for help long before the voices decided to take up the resident inside my head. No one has ever heard me or came to rescue me before or after Jeremiah. Perhaps this explains why I find it difficult to move on without him because of the promises we made to each other as kids. I hope to convince Jeremiah that we should honor those promises. I cried out for help by acting out as opposed to speaking out. I tried different things to bring attention to myself, like cutting my hair extremely short and uneven, hoping that I would not be attractive. There were occasions when I would take scissors and chop my hair off. I was hoping my dirty relatives would leave me alone. I had not met Jeremiah. A few years before, we met and interested one another. When Jeremiah and I began to have sex, it was my way of cleansing myself of the filthy older men who would touch me.

I remember when I went to school with a skirt that I had hemmed so short that you could see my panties when I stood up. And was sent home from school with one of my cousins to change, and that was not a pretty sight, but then nothing ever was when it came to my grandmother and me. Still, no one asked me what was wrong with me or only why I did these odd things. I think I had a mental breakdown or something at one time because my mind just went out of control as I was rambling and pacing back and forth about the house. According to my grandmother, I was just incoherent and making no sense. I do not recall the mental breakdown once, and I told later what had occurred. I think it was something that I said because some of my male relatives never molested me again. I wonder if I had remained mentally broken from being molested, my life would have turned out different. But then I quickly shook this thought from my mind because that would have meant that Jeremiah and Annie would never have existed. All the hell that I went through in my life, meeting and falling in love with Jeremiah, was worth it. He used to look deep into my eyes. I do not understand why he could not see the pain I was in, but then I always responded with nothing was wrong or on my mind when he would ask me to share my thoughts. I was sure that if I told him some adult men in my family were molesting me, he would change his opinion or perhaps even leave me. But something deep within was telling me that Jeremiah would love me more and hold me closer. I could not take the chance.

The Ghost that Haunts The Lie And me

Today, we are trying to sort out what went wrong with our relationship. I know that transferring schools became a big issue for us, and I was never big on writing letters, only reading them. I took all love letters and poems written by Jeremiah with me and read them repeatedly.

The molestation was over, I thought, but an uncle raped me. He had molested me when I was a little girl. The rape left me pregnant, and I was afraid and did not know how to tell Jeremiah. Jeremiah had earned an academic scholarship from a college in Dallas, so he was farther away. When he came home for the summer, and he visited me, I shunned away from him, trying to hide my pregnancy. I was very toward him, and I could see this treatment from me hurting him, but if Jeremiah knew I was pregnant by someone else, I felt this would have hurt him. It was fall, and he returned to school for the fall semester. I had labored and tormented how and when would I tell him I was pregnant. I remember writing him a letter asking him to call me on a specific day and a particular time. And being Jeremiah, he called me as I had asked him to. We chatted at first, and I just blurted out, Uncle Leonard raped me, and I am pregnant. He asked the strangest question. What are we going to do about it, and how are you doing? A few days later, I received a letter from Jeremiah telling me he would be transferring schools to be close to me when the baby was born. The typical Jeremiah kept his word and transferred to the local college and started down the street from where I lived in January.

After I gave birth to my daughter Lydia, I knew she would be a daily reminder of a terrible event already etched into my brain. The first time the uninvited visitors have visited me inside my head. I could hear the threatening words forcing me to comply, and I needed to choose life or death. Many think this child is Jeremiah's, but we both will know the truth. I felt anger toward Jeremiah for allowing this to happen and not protecting me. Amid my shame and hatred for my dirty uncle, I was faced with how I would love this baby born not of love and out of wedlock.

Jeremiah was there and developed a real loving relationship with her. I started to think that I wished Jeremiah would go away, and I wouldn't have to see his face either because it was causing me to feel guilty. And why won't he confront me or show any anger toward me? Instead, he seemed to concentrate more on holding Lydia in his arms than me. After the birth of Lydia, I was never embraced and loved by Jeremiah, the same as when we first fell in love. Lydia had replaced me, and I was jealous that he showed more love and care for her than me. I had felt shame that I would allow myself to become jealous of an innocent baby. I believe this was a cruel way for Jeremiah to punish me by not showing anger toward me but love for Lydia. This scenario fits perfectly because he never speaks when angry but gives you the silent treatment. Uncle Leonard had created a lifetime problem for me, and it was up to me to maneuver this minefield. The guilty party never showed remorse, and the bastard tried to rape me a second time. By this time, Jeremiah had departed my life again because my stepfather had issues with him. Jeremiah was not one to hang around where he felt he wasn't wanted. I needed him but did not know how to tell him or ask him to stay with me. I drove him away without saying thank you or even offering to share the full story of how I had ended in this situation.

Long after Lydia began to talk, she would ask who her father was? And later, not being able to tell her who her father was? I thought I had endured unbearable pains and embarrassment. But now, I am being asked who was the other half of creating a child.

If only I could turn back the time to where I could have told Jeremiah of the abuse I suffered when I was a child. Instead of telling him what was going on with me, I plotted to get pregnant for him so that I could leave my grandmother's house. I thought it would be a short time, and he would resurface with that grin on his face. But days, weeks, months, and years passed before I realized I had driven the one person who had stood by me through good and bad times. The one person that had bought me the most joy in my life was gone because of an evil deed done to me.

Where Did Jeremiah Go?

The chance to provide input in Collateral Damages, Kept Secrets and, I could not wait to tear into Jeremiah as I uttered the words, why did you leave me, and where have you been, Jeremiah. And I needed to get some things off my chest before sitting down at the table across from him. But this was just my mind tricking me into imagining how I would answer all of Jeremiah's questions. I had hidden some secrets I should have shared with Jeremiah when he was my high school sweetheart. These were secrets I kept hidden before dating back in high school. They were haunting me before we were a couple of hot-blooded teenagers proclaiming our love for one another. And I and I am tormented by them more today.

I lost the love and respect of my first boyfriend, and I am not aware of what happened. This loss of love also torments me, especially each October 25th. I hope to receive answers to my questions and provide answers, and I want to meet with Jeremiah and share some things that happened in my life before I met him and affected me.

These things continued while we were still in love because I kept silent. I did not know what to do, and I certainly did not want to lose him. I silently begged him not to pass me by and never leave me behind. Many nights I imagined his presence in my bedroom, every night protecting me. He made me feel protected and not dirty. Before our relationship, I was taunted each day of my life by the ghosts trafficking inside my head. They were reminders of how bad things were in my life, I needed him, and I needed all the love he could bestow upon me. Jeremiah played a significant role in my life. He was unaware of how much his coming into my life helped me cope with the secrets. I kept them hidden from everyone, including him and most other people in my life, by suppressing them subconsciously. I hope to use this opportunity to cleanse myself by sharing all the Collateral Damages, Kept Secrets I had withheld from him.

Hopefully, I will be able to shed light on some of the darkest moments of my life during our face-to-face meeting. He will probably see me as the ugliest and most vile person he has ever met. I believe he deserved better, and he deserved to know how those secrets affected us and have destroyed my life. He was my first boyfriend and the first man I ever trusted to touch me intimately. Jeremiah and I have not communicated for more than twenty-five years. In the past, whenever we met one another on the street, it would always end up with me verbally attacking you. I was angry with him because he did not stop the molestation by male relatives and my grandmother's harsh treatment. I have remained ticked and mad with him for going away, leaving me behind, and staying hidden for nearly twenty years.

When we finally went our separate ways, Jeremiah seemed to purposely make a point to avoid me and not meet with me one-on-one at all costs. I will take full advantage of this unexpected opportunity he is giving me to communicate with him in person. I want to know what has Jeremiah doing with himself nowadays and how life is going? He told me he was trying to write a book as one of his bucket list items. I thought to myself because it was on his bucket list. I hoped that he would share his entire bucket list with me in a sly and cunning sort of way. It was an excellent opportunity to unload all my guilt and wrong thoughts in his book. Reminiscing back when we talked as lovers in person and on the phone about everything we hope to accomplish in life together.

I am sure that Jeremiah probably did not tell me half of what he had planned on doing in his life when we were lovers. Anyway, he did not fall for the bait. He barely gave me a nibble. Same old Jeremiah is always playing it close to the vest, with that shit-eaten grin. That grin seems to say I know something, and you do not, or nothing you say or do will cause me to become angry. I once truly loved this man with the smile that pisses you off. And yet, I used to couldn't wait to see his face. I am mad with Jeremiah, and I cannot say why or how many things.

As for me health-wise, I am almost dying, but I notice Jeremiah never asked me how I have been doing? One of the things I always loved about him was his concern for other people. I do not think he knows or frankly even cares that I suffer from kidney, liver, and heart disease. One of the things that angered me the most was that he moved on with his life and gave up on ever attempting to rekindle our relationship. I hoped to help co-author this book with him because I need to tell my children some things about my past. And perhaps he would take a little interest in my pathetic life. Jeremiah made it clear it is a book he is writing for his benefit and is willing to include as much of his story as related to our past. But there is no future on the horizon for the two of us. He politely explains the rules; the book is about things that happened to him in his life and to learn why our relationship ended the way that it did. And after our meeting concludes, Jay will be moving on from me, one of his past demons. Although he gave me credit for having played a crucial role in his life at a pivotal time, Jeremiah made it abundantly clear. Still, he is NOT interested in any extra-marital activities.

Life Without Jeremiah

I became a mother of four children and the ex-wife of three husbands. Jeremiah knows my oldest daughter Lydia because she used to call him her daddy. Despite his repeated warning of why our face-to-face meeting would not bring Jeremiah and Annie's second sequel to fruition, I have a plot with evil intentions. But right from the start, Jeremiah senses my secret plan. He is quick to point out that nothing can or will go on between the two of us beyond being cordial to one another. And Jeremiah let me know how he deals with ex-girlfriends and ex-wife by waving his finger from side to side, suggesting no-no despite my failing health from the various medical conditions that could take me out anytime. I tell Jeremiah, I am not on my deathbed, and this is not a deathbed confession. He can rest assured there is still a lot more kick left in me.

I am curious and anxious to see Jeremiah's reaction when I share secrets I kept hidden from him. I could sense Jeremiah's present was a drive-by, and he was ready to get back to his happy life with his wife. You could practically see the sense of urgency is written all over his face. It indicated half of him was here in my present, but the most important piece of him was with his wife, which was his heart. Jeremiah seems excited to get on with our discussion to satisfy his quest to find out my reason for sharing this information with him years later.

Jeremiah's first question he asked me was, why not sit down and tell your children yourself we all have a past. Annie, no one has a perfect history, and we are not guaranteed a bumpy-free future either. I see how much he loves his wife because he has made it clear he did not have any feelings that I may have for him, but I still trust him. Those are easy words to say when you have escaped the things and people who tormented you for the hell of it. It is strange how you can remember that helped you through tricky times. For instance, I remember Jeremiah used to paint pictures with his words. I need him to paint me a picture of my life, the Annie he once loved. Still, I never overcame the ugly deeds I did with secrets, and I kept them hidden secretly inside my head.

I have one crucial question that I need Jeremiah to answer more than anything. This man standing before me, all grown up and mature, was my inspiration for the best years of my life. Where was "Jeremiah" when I needed him to rescue me again? It has already been abundantly clear; what we had was unique and authentic. That October night in 1969 is a memory that we both drained of usefulness. Yes, we both went on with our lives having families and making plans with someone else not named Annie and Jeremiah. I wanted to make it with Jeremiah, but circumstances arose and prevented that dream from ever becoming a reality. Both Jeremiah and I could never deny how much we were the inspiration we needed when we met in 1969. I loved Jeremiah, and he relented long enough to tell me he never stopped loving me. And he thanked me for helping him gain the freedom and courage he needed to face whatever demons were chasing him.

I want to share and reveal the things in Collateral Damages, Kept Secrets with twenty-twenty hindsight I wished I had let Jeremiah in on. But am I making the same mistake with my children by not sitting down with them and sharing my painful past? Instead, I want to rely on a chance in a million they will ever read a book titled Collateral Damages, Kept Secrets. But I place my hope. Someday I hope my children will read about the valley life I had to climb from the depth of despair. And perhaps they will understand that I wasn't the mean mother they perceived me to be but a caring and protective guardian that I wished I had when I was a young girl. I remember how Jeremiah always seemed unphased by anything I used to say to try and shock him. Perhaps when I finish telling my life story, it will upset this ever under control and calm demeanor. For whatever reason, I wanted and hoped he would feel pity enough for me that he would take me in his arms and tell me that everything would be alright. Jeremiah was a part of my past when I felt most loved and safest when he held me so close to his body. And while being held by him, it said, I would never let you go, and everything will be fine. Maybe the perfect moment to share with Jeremiah and tell him of the pains and agony I encountered as a young girl when he told me that everything would be alright. I cannot figure out why I chose to keep these secrets from him except that I was embarrassed just as I am today. I entertain company twenty-four hours inside my head, reminding me of what happened to me and one thing that I did wrong that will hurt Jeremiah.

How I Fell in Love with Jeremiah

Jeremiah became my first boyfriend because he was brave (crazy) enough to approach me. Because of the rumors about my Grandmother carrying a pistol in her apron pocket, she was mean. They were not stories but facts. We both thought our teenage love affair had a lot of promise and a bright future. For me, Jeremiah was a dream come true. He was mature, thoughtful, and focused on a sixteen-year-old boy. Jeremiah's letters and poems told me

everything I needed to hear from a lover, more importantly, a man.
I did not trust males because of the abuse from some men in my
family. Jeremiah stole my heart, soul, mind, and later body because
of his letters and poems. Jeremiah gave me a nickname I still use
today; "Ebonic Woman," his chocolate woman. We thought we
were the only two people on earth when we were together. That
ended when things went awry, and we separated because I
transferred to another school. It was an awakening time for both of
us. We discovered that love had boundaries, and we did not have
the final say over our lives. We then found out that life had a way
of making you stand at attention as the marchers in the parade
passed. I felt he left me sitting in the stands after the ceremony to
find my ride home. I waited and still hoped that the drum major
Jeremiah Ford marched on and out of my life. But I stayed and
perhaps too long waiting and hoping that the band would return
with Jeremiah bringing back happiness into my life.

One secret I kept from him stemmed from the pain I endured from
being molested as a child. I always wanted to share this painful
episode in my life with Jeremiah. The constant chatter in my mind
has haunted me that he will become empathetic, making it easier to
share my secrets. But why do I feel that my confessing is more like
an apology for my wrongdoings? I think the fact that I can share
with someone that helped one time made it easy to cope with my
childhood pains when he came into my life. Jeremiah has made it
clear that he seeks to get information for his book and not on a
crusade to save souls, least of all mine. But the voices inside my
head taunt me daily. The sounds I hear are the voices of all my
abusers, and there is one that I am afraid to tell Jeremiah about
because I feel it will hurt him the most. But he is the only one that I
think that I can identify the voices screaming inside of my head
endlessly, and I was only free of them when we were together. I
recognize all the voices except one of a child's crying. Sometimes I

think that this child is me, calling out to my mother and grandmother for help. But I also have another theory about who that child might be, and I must share with Jeremiah who that child could be crying out to me for help. The tormenters give me ultimatums to remain silent in my closet of secrets or face the consequences of my shameful past. I hope that if I come clean with Jeremiah, it will help me get over the painful past that has plagued me most of my life. I tell myself that everything happens for a reason to get through each day. But I cannot figure out why I had to bear such a heavy burden. I am obsessed with finding out from Jeremiah what he thinks went wrong to cause us to go our separate ways. I suspect that Jeremiah's response will either satisfy my anger or create a more deep-seated hatred for him. I believe his leaving me affected me more than when my mother left me raised by a grandmother. And then it is entirely possible it will be a wasted exercise, and I will not be satisfied with his response.

Perhaps I still will not be free of the voices that haunt me inside of my head. I know and believe that the relationship ended with one of us blessed and the other feeling cursed. One of us became an over-comer, and the other remained in a depressed state of mind. One was lucky at cards, and the other drew the wrong card from the life deck. When Jeremiah and I were together and in love with each other, we talked about everything. Still, somehow, I never got around to telling him about my hidden secrets because I was too embarrassed and believed I would lose him. I blamed a lack of time to gain the courage to overcome the fear of feeling ashamed and the possibility of Jeremiah rejecting me. The latter was my biggest fear. Even though I never shared my closet secrets with Jeremiah, I still lost him. So, I thought I was giving him something to write in his book, hoping it would make it easier to reveal the reasons for some of my odd behavior. Will the telling of my hurtful past help or hurt him. Just as I did not want to hurt him when we were kids, I am not in favor of seeing him hurting today, but I need him to feel something, and I supposed it is a pain. I feel compelled to give him excuses for not sharing my kept secrets. Although the truth is, I could never find the courage to allow the words to flow from my lips. Time has convinced me that if this was 1969. I told him about what was going on in my grandmother's home. Jeremiah would grab me and hold me tight, assuring me everything would be okay. When Jeremiah came into my life, the bad things stopped happening after I announced I had a boyfriend, and I enjoyed happiness. I was hoping my falling in love for the first time would frighten my abusers. All except one uncle who would ask me personal questions that would ask me questions about what kind of things we did when we were together and having sex? I told him we laughed and talked about a lot of things.

At least a thousand times, I have asked myself why I could not move past the worst part of my life. And I keep coming to the same conclusion. It was also the best time of my life. If I could convey to him how much he still means to me and could relive one day with the two of us in love again, I believe that I could make it through the rest of my life. I could tolerate and endure the company I kept inside my head. I would not be bothered by the noisy neighbors keeping me awake and afraid to daydream for one moment. The effect that Jeremiah loved me had exposed me to true love. I find myself more comfortable in the presence of total strangers than around family members and friends. I am sure the strangers would not know about my horrible past and the abuse I endured at the hands of some terrible people in my family. I do not remember when there were no occupants inside my head tormenting me. The demons roam about in my head, receiving free shelter. I hate and love Jeremiah simultaneously. I love him for the past joy but want to hate him because he chose to move on without bringing me along on his journey to happiness. I considered myself the villain instead of the victim because I refused to share the bad things that happened to me as a child and harbored them. Even though Jeremiah was there and talked about many things, I could not find the strength to tell the one person I loved and listened to me what was happening to me. I find myself pissed and confused, wondering how come Jeremiah claimed to have loved me the way he professed to have, but didn't they see my agony? I was robbed of my innocence when I was a child. Today I am permitting them to deny me peace of mind because I allow them to reside rent-free inside my head.

I felt helpless and hopeless because when I told my mother and grandmother what was being done to me by the men in our family, they ignored my cry. If only I could be as deaf as they were to my pain, I could perhaps deal with the voices regularly speaking inside my head. I was in a hopeless situation, fearing if I told Jeremiah that he would turn his back on me and walk away too. I was afraid to expose the evil deeds done to me because of the fear I would find myself in my darkroom all along, screaming for help, and no one would come to my aide. Only when Jeremiah Micah Ford came into my life did I stop yelling for help. Jay had brought hope and joy into my life.

The Lies I Kept Secret

Unlike all the other secrets I had kept from Jeremiah, I was going to have to give birth to a child conceived by rape and rear it as a happy mother. I told Jeremiah some of the circumstances that produced Lydia, but I still must come all the way clean with him. There were times when I would find myself hating my daughter while loving her simultaneously. The worse hurt that anyone can experience is love and hate at the same time for the same person.

The best description that I can give is what happens when hot and cold air meets. Stormy. Since my mother did not come to my rescue, why don't I tell my daughter what my grandmother told me? You were bought and paid for, and my mother can have you? Would I be the one to run away from my responsibilities this time? I remember Jeremiah coming to see me in the hospital and holding Lydia. He talked to her as if she was his child. I have so much respect for this man because he never mistreated my child conceived while we were supposed to be still in love with each other.

Years after being raped, I am still unable to move beyond that horrifying moment. Somehow I knew it was the beginning of the end of Jeremiah and me because I would not allow myself to tell him the entire story. I am trapped inside my mind because although I seek peace, I can never find it. Instead of being reared by a loving mother raised by my grandmother, I am starting to wear down. From the beginning, someone other than me has controlled my body and mind denying me the freedom to share them with whomever I desired. For more than forty years, it has been either the free renters who torment me or the memories when Jeremiah and I were together. One or the other will dictate whether my day will be good or bad. There are times I think about picking up the phone and telling someone about the kinds of things that have happened to me. But who would believe me? I would want to share and have shoulders to cry on is Jeremiah. Still, I chased him out of my life long ago in an abrupt manner. I have absolutely nobody to cry out aloud to. I have no one to share my pain; my Mama and Grandmother are dead, and Jeremiah lives a beautiful life with someone else I thought would be ours. I have never found that kind of courage. When Jeremiah left me, he was the only person that I ever felt I could trust to tell my secrets to, but time expired for that too.

Move and I Will Kill You

I felt worthless and started to sass my grandmother whenever we encountered one another. I learned that it was a bad idea because I said something to my grandmother that she did not like, causing her to call one of my mother's sisters, Aunt Bettie. When aunt Bettie arrived at my grandmother's house, it was to take care of business, and I was on the business end of the deal. Aunt Bettie reached into her purse and pulled a pistol on me. She placed it to my head and began to read me the riot act, all the while daring me to move or say anything; I will blow your (expletive) brains out. My mother was aware of what her sister had done to me, and she never confronted her for threatening to kill me. I was her daughter. She did or said anything to Aunt Bettie. She did not even threaten to come and take me from my Grandmother's house. When I turned fourteen, all the abuse seemed to all of a sudden stopped. But I was still not comfortable when my perpetrators would come around.

A Change Is Coming

Aunt Bettie's visit set me on the straight and narrow for a couple of years. And the next big event in my life occurred when I met and fell in love with my dream boy. Mr. Jeremiah Micah Ford was tall, skinny, handsome, and bow-legged. Jeremiah was a deep thinker for someone his age; I think that is why he could write long letters to me. The boy wrote me a continued letter for two weeks, which was funny and took my mind off my pathetic home life. Not long after we started dating, I fell head over heels for him because he respected me, especially my body. He never pressured me into wanting to have sex. I believe that the violation of my body caused me more worry than damage to my mind.

Now that Jeremiah has come into my life. And my mind stayed occupied with learning how to enjoy being loved for the first time in my life. Yes, we eventually had sex, but it was mutual, and Jeremiah did not pressure me into having sex. The truth is the first time we attempted to have sex. It was at my request. He might not remember, but before our first time having sex, he must have asked me a hundred times if this was what I wanted to do? *He said I do not want you to do something you are unsure about.* He was more afraid of having sex than he let on. We had practiced with each other bodies by touching and rubbing against each other. Although the men in my family were molesting me, I wasn't afraid of Jeremiah touching my body. I wanted to have sex with Jeremiah, despite my disdain for them. They used my hands to massage their private parts. They were evil and dirty men that my grandmother allowed me to use my hand to masturbate, leaving warm sticky junk for me to wipe off on anything that I could find.

I was in love with Jeremiah Micah Ford. Each time after these disgusting acts were perpetrated upon me, I rushed my mind to thinking of sex for real with someone I loved and wanted to touch me. I had become curious about what it would be like to have someone make love to me, and I participated. I grew even more interested when two of my best friends and I talked about how they felt after having sex with their boyfriends. Curiosity did not kill the cat; it only raised the level of my nosiness. I needed to overcome this fear caused by the sexual abuse I had to endure. If there is something more substantial than hate for bad things someone has done to you, I would like to have such a feeling for certain people. I hated the thought of sex at first because I did not know love and sex went together. My friends spoke about how much closer they were with their boyfriends after having sex with them. I suppose that I can be happy for one thing, and that is none of my male relatives penetrated my vagina with their penis. Their penetration was when they forced their fingers inside me. It was painful, and I suppose that the frantic look on my face did not make them feel sorry for hurting me and did not stop until these grown men were satisfied. I was not more than seven years old. Remembering one Monday morning, I did not want to go to school because one of my grown cousins had come over on a Sunday evening. Granny had fallen off to sleep from drinking. He left me so sore that I was afraid to pee from the burning pain. After this encounter, there were bloodstains in my underwear. Why didn't my grandmother realize that something was going on?

I was too young to be menstruating. Even today, I remember the pain from when their fingers would penetrate me. I was excited about having sex with Jeremiah the first time. I needed to know if sex would replace the fear and pain inflicted on me by the evil men I had been molested for too long. What kind of sick person am I to want to have sex with a boy, this means allowing him to touch and penetrate my vagina, but I am not afraid of Jeremiah's touch. I know he will be gentle with me because not once have he tried to force me to have sex with him. It has been the least talked about thing between us since we started dating. I love Jeremiah, so now it will be my turn to brag to my girlfriends that we had had sex with each other so that we could be closer to each other. Jeremiah had given me comforting love and a hopeful outlook on life, and maybe having sex with him would erase those other men's touches. Our first attempt did not go well because I was too tight and nervous. But then there was also Mr. Jeremiah had to share some of the blame. He did not have a pencil to write with either. When Jeremiah heard me groan and the painful look on my face, it was over. Sitting up and pulled me close to him, repeatedly telling me *I am sorry, I never want to hurt you.* He kissed me on my lips harder than ever before and held me tighter as if I were going to fall and break into pieces. I still felt closer to him and wanted to do everything I

could to please and keep him. Our first try at sex was unsuccessful.
I remember feeling like I had failed him, but he never stopped
trying to comfort me, saying everything would be alright. He said it
is no big deal; we still love one another. I needed to hear that from
him. I know that I have mentioned it before. Even as I look back, I
cannot get over how mature Jeremiah was about everything. I will
forever remember the love he displayed this night because he made
me feel like a valuable piece of collateral and not something
damaged. The boy presented love for me as if he had read a
manual on pleasing a woman. A few weeks had gone by, and we
found ourselves in a place and time where we did make love for the
very first time!

There are some things you remember as if it was yesterday. Like
Jeremiah entering me slowly and stroking me as if he intended to
make love to my whole body, he certainly was doing a job on my
mind. After this night, if we were together, I lost the fear and shame
of being molested. Is this why I never told him about what was
going on? I will use any excuse to explain why I refused to share
this damaging information with him. I remember thinking to myself
that I hope this never ends. It was an incredible feeling, and I
enjoyed every moment, and I wished I would never stop. When we
finished, I remember not ever wanting to leave his arms. But
Jeremiah making love to me always kept my mind free of all the
bad things that had happened to me earlier in life. I remember us
holding one another but holding me gentle, this time in his arms
instead of tight like when we failed at making love the first time.
And yet, I felt the same safeness and love as I did when he wrapped
me tightly in his arms. Crazy thought, I am no longer a virgin, and
glad that I did not lose my virginity to any of my molesters.
Remaining a virgin should have been a virtue, but I celebrated it as
a victory.

My grandmother started to plot and plan; I wanted to have Jeremiah's baby. Here we are, two sixteen-year-olds with no skills, no jobs, and I was foolish enough to think that adding a third person would make things better for us. It was selfish of me, but all I could think of was getting away from my Grandmother. A few days later, we talked on the phone; Jeremiah shared that this was his first time having sex and that he never wanted to love or make love to anyone other than me. Why, I asked, Jay? Because in you, I have all the things that I ever dreamed of in a girlfriend and hopefully one day a wife. I was curious how you seemed to know what I needed and wanted after we finished making love when you took me into your and held me close to your body? Jeremiah replies that it is from all the dreams and letters I wrote *to nobody before you came along. I decided how I wanted the woman I made love with to feel wanted and closer. And you forgot to notice that I held you close to my heart because that is where I will always want you.* What the hell? He said that *I never thought I would find someone to love me back, so I just enjoyed* imagining *how to show my love and compassion through dreaming. Your dream came true, and I wanted this to be perfect because you are the perfect girl for me.*

Lies are like chickens; they will come home to roost. A lie that I told Jeremiah I would never get over.

Poor Planning on My Part

To sit across the table from Jeremiah Micah and give my input to his book Collateral Damages, Kept Secrets. I will have to tell Jeremiah about the secret lies. I must tell him why in my desperation to get away from my grandmother. Jeremiah asked a serious question today about me. I don't know how I would have answered as a teenager. And uncertain as to how I should reply today. *Annie, was it just your desire to get away from your grandmother and that you didn't love me as much as you proclaimed? Was I a part of a ploy to help you escape your grandmother?* There is no doubt in my mind and heart that I loved Jeremiah, and yes, I wanted to get away from my grandmother's house too. I want to share the truth with this man so badly and who is no longer the boy I had hoped to get pregnant by him to help cover up a lie that I once told him. Thinking that this would make it easier for him to forgive me has my plan come to fruition. And he throws this question up in my face. Some of the things and tricks that I tried to be along with and I could get pregnant. I had no limits. I tried calling him to play hooky from school to have sex, hoping to get pregnant. For Jeremiah playing hooky was not on his list of things to do. If I could get pregnant by Jeremiah, all would be well, and he would find it easy to forgive me later when I confess to him what I had done when we were kids. Something about Jeremiah's persona made you know that he wanted to succeed in life. He was driven and focused but a complicated person to someone like me. After learning what occurred to him early in his life, I understand the drive to succeed. But I could never see past the next day because I struggled with trying to get through the present. I never told him I wanted to get pregnant because he looked at marriage and a family after finishing high school, college, and finding a good job. I was planning on derailing those plans without him knowing. I was intentionally trying to get pregnant by him. Was I wrong for trying to establish a trap and spoil his plans? I was selfish and did not want to wait because I felt the abuse would start again. My mind always goes back and wonders why my grandmother was never suspicious of my family's men that molested me. She worried about Jeremiah getting me pregnant but did not seem to care about me getting pregnant by a family member. I knew what to expect when she suspected Jeremiah and I had had sex. I would go through being humiliated by my grandmother would make me disrobe and then make me scrub my private area. She would go so far as to make me take off all my clothes and scrub me in a private area. My Grandmother knew exactly when my period was due. I believe she knew better than I did. When I was pregnant with Jeremiah's baby, I had missed my period for the first time. The menstruation watcher was all over me. She phoned my mother to tell her. I think this gal has got herself pregnant by that boy, and you need to come and take this gal to the doctor to check for sure. My mother shows up for this, but not for the other things that I told her were happening to me. My mother asked me if I was having sex with Jeremiah. Now I will say to her, yeah, I liked it, and I was the one to ask him to have sex with me. Right? I told him I would not be at school the next day because my mother would see a doctor to determine why I was late. I had to explain what late meant to the boy I had deemed bright, intelligent, and very mature. I finally found a book that he was a little slow to read, the books on the birds and the bees. I phoned Jeremiah that night, and we talked like always. I whispered that I was waiting for my grandmother to leave the room because she was so nosy. Then I told him that my late period was not because I was pregnant. It was a lie, but how could I say to him that I killed something we had made together from love? A strange statement from both my mother and grandmother was when they made it clear that they did not want me to get pregnant by Jeremiah. It was said they wanted nothing to do with any child from him. They got their wish because I became the mother of four children, and three of them know their father because I was married to him when they were born. My oldest daughter, Lydia, would often ask me who her father was? She wanted to know if "my Jeremiah" was her father, and I would tell her to ask him. He was always gracious by not hurting her feelings or telling her that no mother's uncle Leonard is your father. Deflect her question by asking how much she would pay him to be his daughter? Then the discussion became money, of which she had none. Lydia and Jeremiah had a great relationship. As she became a teenager and young adult, I heard her talking to Jeremiah on the phone. Her laughter reminded me of when I laughed at Jeremiah's jokes or comments. She listened to him and would go to him for advice and help whenever there was a problem in her life. And he always seemed to talk her through each situation. I became jealous of the two of them and accused them of having an affair. It probably was not the wisest thing I had ever done or said to Jeremiah. It was hurtful, mean, and vindictive because I am angry about why I never told him about my home problems. Not many things tick Jeremiah off or set him off; I just accomplished both by accusing him of having a romantic affair with my daughter. Someone I was trying to protect from ever learning that she was conceived by rape by a family member. When it comes to me saying or doing something hurtful to Lydia, it always turns him off. Usually, he becomes silent. But when that black man is mad, he does not talk, and you cannot make him, but you will feel his wrath somehow and soon. And he gets his point across in a nonverbal kind of way first, and then he places the icing on the cake verbally when he has calmed down. I remember Jeremiah once saying to me that Lydia got short-changed. I never asked what he meant by that statement and felt that he was saying something to make a point, but I was too shallow, and he was deep in his thoughts and way of thinking. Today I believe that meant if he were Lydia's father, she would be loved by him.

Uninvited Tenants Inside of My Head

All my abusers are dead, but I am still haunted and do not know how to evict them from my mind. I wished the adults responsible for protecting me would have shielded me by reporting the wicked men who abused me. I will always wonder why they refused to seek justice for me. As for my mother, I have not visited, nor have I wanted to see her gravesite because she never came to visit me when I needed her.

I asked Jeremiah if his wife knew we were collaborating on writing this book. He responded that he did not see it as collaboration, but input from his characters, meaning me. And I do not share what I am writing until I finish what I am writing or ask for feedback or point of view. That comment took my mind back to when we were in high school. The students in our school used to share all their secrets with Jeremiah. I think it was because he was trusting and comfortable talking with me about anything. He would not violate their trust in whatever they told him in secrecy. Our school should have provided him with a sofa because of his upper and lower clients. So, I think to myself, why was it so difficult for me to come and tell Jeremiah the things I was keeping secret from him? He was easy to talk to because of his easy trusting demeanor. I loved that about him. I feared that he would think or say something mean, but looking back, that was not him because he would always find positive things in people.

Jeremiah can scare you with his eyes because I think he used them to investigate your soul. When he talks to you or is talking to him, he looks you right into your eyes. At least that is how I felt, and the way he would ask you a question to get the correct answer by first relaxing you and causing you to have a slip of the tongue. After falling victim a couple of times, I became slower and more deliberate in my answers. I believe that he still knew I wasn't forthright with him when he would ask certain things but was too much of a southern gentleman to call me out on them. Like when he asked me why I wanted him to write a book about me? The first thing that came to my mind was, I trust you. After all these years, I believe that I can still trust you. Knowing that gave me hope that I still had a second shot at happiness that only he could bring into my life. Jeremiah forcefully reiterated, I will never violate my marriage vows to my wife, Ruth, just as you trust me, so neither does my wife. Oh no! He busted me and saw right through my ploy. A girl can dream, can't she? If Jeremiah could see through me, how is it possible that he could not see my pain in high school? There are days when I cry almost all day, wondering what I would have to do to hold on each day if Jeremiah had not come into my life? I may not have ever known or enjoyed true love. But Jeremiah put me in my place on multiple occasions; he is one man for one woman and has no room for any extras. And I have vowed (wink, wink) that there would be no more attempts on my part to try and revive our dead relationship. I have always wanted to tell all my secrets but was too ashamed. The fear of being embarrassed and labeled as a loose woman. The love Jeremiah gave me provided me the strength to escape my closet for a brief time; perhaps he will be able to help me to renew that strength for the rest of my life by allowing me to evict the tormenters inside of my head after years of living free on accommodations provided by me. I am nervous because I do not know his reactions to things. I feel compelled to tell him to write for the benefit of my children. Some are also for his interest. I won't tell my story without involving our past relationship. I hope he will not hate me for the wrong decisions as a teenager. I keep waiting for Jeremiah to say or show signs of hatred for me. Instead of saying that he was angry or hated me, he always expressed his disappointment with how our relationship ended and my failure to communicate with him. The bottom line, he has accepted the fate of our failed relationship and has moved on with his life. The need to confess to Jeremiah about matters that I never took the opportunity to explain or share with him before. How we separated has always stayed on my mind. We used to talk about everything when we were young lovers, except for what he needed to know about me and my home life. We never got around to discussing the kind of hell that I encountered while living with my grandmother. I believe that Jeremiah is happily married and committed to his wife. I fear what opinion he will have after telling him my story and answering why. Just as I want my children to know the secrets of my past, I want Jeremiah to know how much I loved him and still do for the happiness brought into my life. The love letters he wrote to me were pictures only with words. That is hard for a girl to get over, and I must say that I am jealous of his wife but can appreciate that she knew how to earn his love, trust, and respect. It is difficult to see and talk to a man I once profoundly adored. And even though I will never have him as my husband and lifetime soul mate, I am proud of the man he seems to have become and regret I was not patient enough with him. He is who he said he wanted to be when describing his aspirations in high school. When I was a young lady, my vision was always near and never looking far ahead. My ultimate hope is that we end as two friendly ex-lovers by burying the hatchet, I mean the past. After many years, I am nervous today, angry strangers blaming each other for how things ended for us instead of the beautiful love we had together.

CHAPTER FOURTEEN
As I Remember, Jeremiah

I fell in love with Jeremiah, and I was unaware as to what my love had done for him, that it was strong enough to free him from a closet of darkness; I never knew until this book. I think that he took the too-dark patrol best shot. I would love to see what that shy individual is like today, who was once shy and very reserved. I made the mistake of telling him that he does not seem to care about people's feelings and shows little concern about other people's opinions different than his. We find ourselves sitting and discussing what went wrong with our teenage relationship. And Jeremiah does not seem to care about my health or how I feel. I want that warm, caring Jeremiah that I used to know.

(**Jeremiah response**) Annie, just for the record, the last forty-plus years, all I seem to do is piss off people, and I do not understand why, and none of them have ever been able to tell me why. So, Annie, I refuse to try and live my life by what people cannot articulate—based upon who I once was perceived to be by trying to relive an experience that I have no interest in reliving. And their problems are not mine. The negative things were said to me by people growing up. Until now, it has been my choice to ignore the idle chatter and correct identified errors. Beyond that, I could give a flip. We are here to have a discuss get answers to two questions. You want to know my whereabouts, and I want to know what happened. I tried to explain to Jeremiah the collateral damage done to me was from the abuse, forcing me to deal with replaying them in my head all the time. Somehow, I must tell this man that I have not had any peace in such a long time.

Secrets are okay if they harm anyone, but they are equally wrong to destroy a human will to live. When I first met and fell in love with him. I have damaged collateral already; I did not tell him about my home life. I shared many things with him but could not find the strength to speak out and say that my home life is horrible living with my grandmother. I was mistreated and abused. When he came into my life, I finally enjoyed being loved and hoped it would ease or erase my pain forever. When we separated, that was the worst thing that could have happened to me. I would have run away with Jeremiah if he wanted me to, but we lost contact. I failed to write and respond to any of your letters. I reply to the last letter he wrote to me, too late and too little, more than forty years later. Today if I were to act out the way I did back when I was a child, someone would have recognized I was collateral damage from some form of abuse. There is only one victor between us, Jeremiah, because he decided to flee from his closet and never return. The loser is me because I surrendered by fighting when Jeremiah and I separated. I lost the strength to fight, and my attackers took full advantage.

I am annoyed by the screaming voices inside my head each day of my life. I wanted to meet another Jeremiah to help me cope with my past heartaches and pains. I can sit in a crowded room and cry without anyone noticing my tears. I do not know if I learned to mask my pain from childhood and adulthood by always disguising my hurt. I cannot explain the emotions tugging at my heart because of the constant visitors in my mind, just like those in my bedroom when I was a little girl. I screamed, and no one came to my rescue until you. I must get him to understand that no one comes to me when I cry out today. I have learned to live this double life for so long that seamless transitioning between the two. I have a motto that I repeat to myself many times throughout the day, life happens, and some things are just what they are. You cannot change them. But I know that Jeremiah believes something different because he thinks change happens when you take control of what is out of control in your life, so you say. But he alluded to the fact that I was all over the place. But I was trying to escape from my attackers. I attempted to avoid my abusers. I never exposed them because my mother and grandmother did not seem interested in preventing me from being molested. I just tried to fight for my freedom. I hope that by telling my story in Collateral Damages, Kept Secrets. I will find peace and not judge people who never experienced the abuse I encountered. My mother thought I was insane or suffered from mental illness. When I was a young girl, men in my family molested me, and everyone knew, yet they acted like I was born for such treatment. To have no one come to your rescue, or if they come, they do not believe your abuse claim. My grandmother forced me to sit in the company of the ones abusing you, seeing their wicked smiles. The feeling that they are sizing you up or plotting their next attack, and you are trying to find a way to counterattack as a child. With Jeremiah, I hope to develop a plan that will help me. I wonder if such a person still exists as Annie because I hardly recognize the Jeremiah I see today.

Because of my story, someone else will have a choice to decide which of these individuals would you like to be? The one that is physically seen every day and functioning as a loving mother and grandmother? I was the one too afraid to step outside of their soul. And as I was always screaming for love and the caressing of a compassionate person? The wanting of two physical arms to hold me close and a whispering voice assures me that everything will be alright. My tormenters' sounds live within my mind only because I am too afraid to confront them and demand that they leave. I have somehow managed to force myself to function and not allow the visitors inside my head to get to me. There are some days when I hate Jeremiah for no apparent reason. He loved me, but I feel like his leaving me was like my uncle who raped me. The person trapped inside my brain is hurting and crying. I cried so hard for many nights. It felt like my heart was about to come out of my chest. I see no, difference between the cry of a woman in her sixties and the cries of a six-year-old girl suffering at the hands of my abusers. Did I have a soul then, and did my abusers ever see me as more than something to satisfy their pleasures? They saw the fear and hurt in my eyes, staring back at them, saying no, and asking why. They saw no reason to show me compassion or concern about the collateral damages they could do to the child. Sharing my story with the only man I believed ever absolutely loved me and respected my body as my own to do with as I pleased. The key is that I feel that I can trust him. Will I find peace or more hell?

I Want to Get Next to You, Jeremiah

The first seven months of our relationship were surreal, and we seemed perfect for one another. We did a lot of hugging, kissing, and talking, but absent from all our conversations was the discussion of sex. We touched each other and were familiar with each other anatomies when things got a little heated between us.

We talked about a lot of things but never about sex. We spent a lot of time talking about love and showing love for one another. To say that making love to Annie had never crossed my mind during our first seven months would be a lie. I thought of what it would be like to make love for the first time with my first girlfriend. Still, I also had a tremendous amount of respect for Annie. I did not want to go back on the word I had given her at the beginning of our relationship.

CHAPTER FIFTEEN

ANNIE'S STERN TALKING

After I had received a stern warning from Annie the night, she escorted me off the football field after our homecoming game. This little black duck was in no way going to try and swim in that pond uninvited. I do not know if we would have ever had sex as soon as we did it, not for the Temptations' song *Cannot Get Next to You* because it must have moved Annie to want to have sex. I do not recall her exact words, but I remember asking if I wanted to get next to her. I was a little thick, so she had to simplify what she asked me. I feel close to you, more intimate than I have ever been with any girl because my response was—the fact. Annie was kind enough to break it down for me, and then it was more apparent to me what she was saying. I was playing dumb!!!! Right. She had already admonished me on what not to expect. I had a sweetheart of a deal, and I was not about to mess up without assuring she understood my real intentions were to love her, and having sex could wait. So, we decided to have sex one night at a school function. I believe it was an open house. We were about to do something that could change our opinions and possibly damage our relationship. I remember asking her if she was sure that she wanted this. I loved her, and she never gave me the impression that she was a loose girl. I chuckle to myself even today because I never thought she would become my girlfriend, let alone we would ever make love to me. For some reason, I always saw us married before this would ever happen and raising a family together. Truthfully, I did not see her being my girlfriend beyond homecoming night.

Because my thought was we would go back to being casual friends, and she would be the girl that I would admire from afar. Did I mention that I was timid? I always remained prepared for rejection by Annie, this beautiful girl I adored from within my mind and heart. Still, instead, I was accepted by her and became her lover. So, I protected myself by not putting my heart out in the open to be hurt. Thus, the night came when we would have sex with each other for the first time. I was nervous and did not want to mess up or do something crazy, also afraid because this was my first time trying to have sex.

Our first attempt to have sex did not go all that well because my thing did not fit in the doggone hole, or I did not know the code to get into the gated area. I do not know. After I struggled to drive the damn thing in without causing Annie any pain and with ease, I had failed, and I could see that it was causing Annie some pain. The one thing I never wanted to do was to hurt Annie or inflict unnecessary pain on her. I wanted to make love to her, but we could wait and try another day and time because we were building our relationship for the long haul. We eventually gave up on having sex this night, realizing that we did not know what the heck we were doing and needed to go back to the drawing board. We learned that it was much more to sex than two individuals lying down and humping each other. Another strange thing happened that night. A boy named Terry followed us around to see where we were going. I guess he wanted to be cut in on the action or just wanted to watch. Either way, he was not invited nor welcome. We were able to shake him by splitting up and losing him in a crowd of people. The maneuver confused his little pea brain, forcing him to think which of us to follow. Because as long as his feet were moving, he was incapable of such a feat that was too many things for him to accomplish at once. We arrived at our destination and struck out miserably on our first attempt. We did not discuss what went wrong, nor did we plan a second try at having. The second time seemed to happen spontaneously, we were together, and the moment was exactly right. We found ourselves making love to each other at that moment. Jeremiah helped me to understand why it was called making love altogether and not only having sex when two people were in love with each other. Annie receiving me inside of her just seemed like I belonged there, and what we had was just for us. I lost my virginity to the girl I thought would someday marry as my wife. We had consummated a relationship and not a marriage on our wedding night. We seemed to be even more committed to each other now that we had taken things to another level.

We had crossed over into the area where married adults reside, giving no thought to the consequences. We were two young dumb and full of desired kids involving ourselves in a dangerous situation. Our love for each other blinded us from creating another life because of our careless behavior. Two geniuses. I did not care because I wanted to be close to Annie and enjoy this moment of closeness with her. I knew that this was the woman for me. Perhaps it was because this was the first time making love that I was so excited and felt even more in love? The feeling was more exciting than I imagined. I had the feeling of someone genuinely loving me. Afterward, I thought of the risk of having unprotected sex. Still, because I felt genuinely wanted by someone, Annie had invited me into the most intimate space of her body. She allowed me in a place where she had never been passionate about before. I wanted to be the last man she would ever let into this space. On our second try at making love, we had no difficulty and had privacy. Another thing we did not discuss was the possibility of Annie getting pregnant but ignored those possibilities again.

CHAPTER SIXTEEN

MAMA HAD JOKES

Your Son Jeremiah Might be in Trouble

One day while lying across my bed, embracing my pillow, trying to take a growth nap, and hoping that I would not be disturbed by any of my siblings. My mother was the one person who could throw little subtle hints as if she knew something you were doing wrong without coming out and saying it directly. An example is when she strolled through my room out of nowhere and asked, what girl do you have pregnant out of the blue? Today I wonder what answer did she expect me to give to her. Anyway, I tried to dismiss her question but immediately started sweating because mothers know everything. I was surprised when my father, of all people, became concerned with my sexual behavior or misbehavior, telling me, *do not you knock that gal up*. Since when did he care if I got into trouble? All I know is that I was a sleepless and sweating young black man, worried that my girlfriend was pregnant. I did not know the first thing about raising a family, only dumb enough to do something that would get me a family sooner than later. Was this supposed to be the father-son talk about the birds and the bees? If so, too late. This bee had already tested, tasted, and enjoyed the honey.

Later that afternoon, as fate would have it, Annie called me to tell me that all the fun we had had the past couple of months that she was something had not come yet. I was there, and why wouldn't I know about the joy and pleasure we had together? Then she said, *Jeremiah, I think I am late this month.* Late for what? I did not realize we were meeting or doing anything together. Being the young dumb and stupid brainchild I was, she explained a chapter from the birds and bees. *I have not had my period, she replied.*

I knew what that meant because I had three older sisters, and that conversation came up a lot in the presence of my brothers and me. I think they felt we were too stupid to figure out the coded language. And they were correct.   For two weeks, I was praying, sweating, and afraid of not knowing if I was about to become a father at such a young age. How would I take care of a wife and baby? I had never had a job or been on my own, but I was naïve enough to think that our love would suffice and survive anything. Annie's mother, who lived in Harrison, came to Littlefield to take her to the doctor to determine pregnancy. The pregnancy test was negative, so it was a false alarm. Annie said on the way back to Littlefield, and her mother asked if we were having sex.

I lied to my father when he suggested Annie and I were having sex. I vehemently denied his accusation by saying nothing like that was going on with us. I wonder why parents ask such foolish questions when they know that kids are not likely, to be truthful. We both thought it was great that Annie was not pregnant; it called for a real celebration. And guess how we celebrated? We had unprotected sex again, and it never occurred to us that we had just gone through a couple of weeks worrying if she was pregnant. Talking about being stupid and parked in an idiot parking spot, I was the driver.

It was the end of the school year; Annie and I would be apart all summer. Annie would live with her mother in Harrison for the summer, meaning we would not see each other. After thinking about how long it would be before seeing each other again, we stocked on having sex. Once while her grandmother had gone down the street to visit one of her friends, we would engage in sex again and again. We often had it as married couples for two individuals who started a relationship to understand that it was not about sex. Maybe! We only saw each other twice all summer, which was exceedingly difficult for both of us. Still, we survived the absence of one another. In 1970, the schools became integrated, with no more predominant Black or White schools. We started the fall of 1970 at a new school together, learning new everything. I believe we began to separate and not be with each other as much as we had the previous year. I still loved her, and I think that she always loved me, but something was missing.

CHAPTER SEVENTEEN

FINDING MY WAY HOME

My best friend and I were caught in a bad situation that temporarily caused him to lose sight. There were two girls who, for some reason, like me and my best friend, Allister. And they understood we had girlfriends and were supposed to have been exclusive. So, I decided to try and set up a double date with them, and we were to hook up at a Junior Varsity football game. I only got too big for my pants and tried to explore having sex with another girl. Annie had gone to the dentist that day. She was out of school, so I convinced her to stay home because she had a tooth extraction, and I was not going to the football game, and I would call her later like always in the evenings. Allister had also convinced his girlfriend to stay home because he was not coming to the game either. Everything was a go for Allister and me, and we were going to meet the two girls at the game. Neither one of us would leave our girlfriends for these two young ladies. Still, we did want to conduct exploratory research in other areas. Annie decided to call my house, and my dear sweet loving mother told her that I had gone to the football game with Allister. Annie phoned and informed Allister's girlfriend, and they showed up at the football game without our knowing it. That is not the thing that got us in trouble, but some loudmouth shouted out of stands- there go Jeremiah and Allister with two girls. Now I wonder what low life would do something like that. I always believed my younger brother ratted us out because he enjoyed seeing his big brother in jams that could cause me embarrassment. For some sick reason, it gave him a real thrill and something to laugh about as I tried to wiggle my way out of the mess. In Texas, voices seem to carry at night. We were just about to step into darkness. Imagine me in the dark. And two voices were screaming at us, calling our names. Jeremiah!!! Allister!!! It was our girlfriends, and they were sprinting, not jogging, not trotting, not walking fast, toward us but sprinting. And they were not running with open arms either. Annie had picked up a big stick, and I guess it was a baton for the four-by-four relay races. The two girls disappeared like two thieves into the night, and our girlfriends were getting closer to us. Being the alpha male he thought he was, Allister rushed up to his girlfriend, asking her, what are you doing here? She responded with the question to him: Why would you cheat on me with another girl? He was my best friend, but he was not too bright in the head. His response was because I wanted something new. And his girlfriend drew back and slapped him so hard he went blind for a few moments, rolling around on cars and calling me to help him. Meanwhile, at my ranch, my girlfriend, with the big stick she had picked on her way to greet her sweetheart (me), started chasing me around a car, I guess to pass me the baton in the relay race. More than likely, upside my head instead of in my hand. She had the nerves to tell me to stop running! REALLY! I eventually tired her out and told her that I would come to you to talk if you put down the stick. Annie was tired anyway after chasing me around a car, so she dropped her weapon of choice, and I rushed to her, grabbing both wrists and saying I am sorry. Back to Allister, he eventually regained his sight long enough for his girlfriend to fire off another George Foreman upside his head. You could hear the laughter from the stands because everyone had stopped watching the football game, looked at the boxing match, and played the race. I knew what whippings were, so I had years of training trying to outrun a beat down from my mother. I asked Annie to walk with me for a minute as I explained to her (I lied) that Allister had convinced me that I needed another girlfriend and that she was not the right girl for me. Although, I was the one who set up this rendezvous. She forgave me but never forgave Allister, and he could never understand why she would give him the evil eye from that night.

My friend Allister recently passed away after a long battle with cancer; I miss hearing him laugh. But I am so happy that we could hang out near the end of his life and talk about some of our life experiences and the events, like the night his girlfriend slapped him blind. We must have laughed a good half hour about that alone while trying to describe what happened that night and giving our version of what happened. I guess he finally realized that I had come out unscathed from our minor indiscretion. His laughter stopped, and he asked, *Jay, why did Annie not slap or hit you with the stick she had in her hand*? I calmly said because I got her to settle down to talk. Then I told her that it was all her idea and advised her to dump her and find another girlfriend. I begged her to forgive me for listening to you, and she did. I promise never to let Allister talk me into anything like that again. Allister is not laughing anymore. *Is that why she would give me the evil eye and like she was growling at me? Yep, I said, smiling; he called me a rascal.*

I asked, Allister, where did you and your girlfriend go after the dust-up or, better yet, dust down? He said *I think she went home crying and would not talk to me anymore that night.* Then his inquiring mind wanted to know what about Annie and me? *So, where did you all go? Did he ask?* Oh! We just made up. Allister and I knew we were both sexually active with our girlfriends. We never told each other that having sex with our respective girlfriends was off-limit. Out of respect, the ones we had dedicated our hearts to were personal. Although we never discussed having such a pact, we never crossed that line.

 There was a previous incident where Annie had slapped me in public. The whack across my face was so hard that I saw stars and little birds circling my head.

Birds Watching and Stars Gazing

Annie and I were sitting in the stands watching a basketball game. The varsity team did not play on this night. Sitting behind us was a girl named Gertie. I think it was Gertrude for short. There was a big misunderstanding on her part concerning another girl. And I was not aware that Annie had issues with this girl, and she had never shown any sign of being the jealous type. Anyway, I was unaware that Gertie was trying to flirt with me by kneeing me in my back and getting my attention. I turned to tell her a couple of times to stop kneeing me in my back.

When I was nervous or angry, I smiled, and Annie was not aware of this because she thought I enjoyed Gertie flirting with me. But Annie had had enough, and the third time I turned to ask Gertie to stop kneeing me in my back. I did not see Annie's right hand, but I did feel it, and I do remember her slapping me so hard that I saw stars and little birds circling my head. She rocked me, and the slap had also stunned me. I was unaware that she was jealous of me. And that should have been the very last thing that she would worry about from me. No matter how green the grass was on the other side, I was not going anywhere, I was her man, and I sure wanted to keep her as my woman forever. And this incident occurred at the beginning stage of our relationship, and we had only kissed and fooled around at this time.

I loved this girl and would do anything to keep her shy of making a pest of myself by pursuing her if she had rejected me. I now had someone to write letters and poems to and give them to read other than myself. So, I could not hit her back physically. Still, I could emotionally by not having long conversations with her like we had become accustomed to every night and school. When she would call me at home, I would give one-word answers. I would hide out in my favorite place during lunch or recess in the library at school. After a few days, she asked me if it was over between us and that she was deeply sorry for slapping me in public. It was not the hitting me in front of a large group of people that bothered me as much as her thinking that I would be disrespectful in her face. I told her that I forgave her. And I think that she was ready to hear me say to her that I loved her also. I explained to her how much I loved and needed her in my life. But hitting me would not keep us together because I did not want to be in that relationship. I explained to Annie that I would never hit her and would not stay around for her to abuse me either. That incident reminded me too much of my parents, and I did not want a girlfriend that I could someday become my wife's punching bag. One of the many lessons that my father taught me about life and being a good husband. You see, everything he did, I learned to do the opposite. Annie and I continued our journey pursuing an incredibly loving relationship. So, I think she had some recall of the last time she struck me and what the outcome was, believing that I would not stay around to be a punching bag or be with a brawling woman.

Even though I was wrong for being with the other girl, it did not warrant getting hit with a stick. And indeed, it was not a tiny stick.

CHAPTER EIGHTEEN

TOO MUCH DRAMA

It was 1970, which turned out not to be a good year for Annie and me from September to December because something was missing. I do not think our love decreased for each other. Annie shared that her grandmother's health was not as good as it once was and started worse. When Annie talked to me on the phone one night, she began by saying, Jeremiah, I may have to move or do something drastic. I remember saying that I would do all I could to get her out of her grandmother's home after finishing high school. It was early in the school year, and she never mentioned it again.

It appeared as though my senior year would be challenging for both of us. A few days after our conversation, I played a basketball game, and Annie came to watch me play in the game. She had come with one of her male cousins who attended the same school and played on the team with me. The next day at school, one of my so-called friends, Reese, could not wait to tell me about an alleged trained (gang rape) pulled on Annie, my girlfriend, last night when her first cousin Walter and two of his friends drove her home. They threatened to put her out down a dark road and let her walk home. My so-called friend Reese was one heck of a buddy and seemed to have found joy in telling me that my girlfriend had been a victim of gang rape by her first cousin and his two friends. Reese had obtained this information from his brother, Arnold because he was one of the rapists. Another pinhead punk named Ralph always seemed to have had a burr under his saddle for me.

When Annie and I met for lunch later that day, I asked her to walk with me instead of going to the cafeteria to sit down to eat. Holding Annie's hand, I asked her if anything had happened last night when her cousin dropped her off at home after the game? Her response was not an immediate yes or no, but she wanted to know what and why? Without hesitation, I asked whether you had sex with three boys last night. Annie's demeanor was not her usually pleasant self; she seemed royally pissed at me for asking such a question. And I hated asking her because it was one of the most awkward moments in my life. I did not know whether to embrace her, as I usually do when she was hurting and upset. Is this when I should walk away and cut all ties with Annie? I could not tell if the tears were because something happened, and she was ashamed, or maybe nothing happened, and my asking had hurt her feelings. In hindsight, perhaps I should have approached those three butt heads and asked if they pulled a train on my girlfriend? Later that night, while on the telephone, she asked if I think that she was the kind of girl that would have sex with three boys and one of them, my first cousin? Jeremiah, why do you say you love me and think so little of me? Tell me now if you still want to be with me, Jay, because I have not had sex with but one boy. And not three. I have not had sex with anyone but you, and for the first time since we have been together, you hurt and angered me. I explained to Annie; I needed to ask her because your cousin and his two punk friends are the types of guys trying and pulling a stunt like this. I have overheard them going around bragging about some of the things they alleged to have done to other girls. And I needed to know if I needed to defend your honor by calling these three jerks out for an ass whipping party if they committed this cowardly act.

No Disrespect

I shared with Annie that I love and respect her, but my parents were adamant that my brothers respect all girls. Without sharing the names of a couple of girls that I could have taken advantage of, I will share that there was one time a girl I liked had consumed too much alcohol that she passed out. I was always the designated driver when my brother and friends went out. I put the girl in the car and took her home. I did not molest, fondle, or rape her because she was unconscious. I drove her home, helped one of her sisters carry her inside their house, and left. Then a second incident involved my brother Joseph and one of his friends. Three girls had attended a party at our house and did not have a ride home. My brother and I got into a heated conversation when he suggested we drive down a remote country road and force the girls to have sex with us. I was the driver, and my mother's instructions were to take the girls home and come directly back home. Mother knew how long that trip would take us, and I did not want to explain to her why it took us so long to return home. I was always a coward when mistreated or taking advantage of another person. If I had agreed to go along with my brother and his friend by forcing those three girls to have sex with us against their wills, I know it would have bothered me for quite a long time. I like to sleep sound at night. And if our parents had found out that we pulled such a cruel act, they both would have taken turns killing us for such a dirty and cowardly act. I can still hear my mother's voice telling my two brothers and me to treat girls the way you want your sisters treated. One lesson hit home with me because they made us consider how we would feel if a boy mistreated one of our sisters had come with a stern warning. Some boys would carry out these acts in the sixties and seventies, giving the girl three options, sex, fight or walk. Although her cousin was the driver, the bottom line is that I would not put it past him to be a party to such deviousness. She said it did not happen, and I had to believe her because I love her.

The Slow Fall from Happiness

To say that the first half of the school year was like a movie viewed in fast-forward mode. I could sense that some other issues involving Annie would come out later. Annie thought she was pregnant, and for some reason, she was not happy to tell me that it was a false alarm. We reached Christmas break, and school was out until after New Year in January 1971. Things came to an abrupt halt between Jeremiah and Annie. The relationship ended because her mother transferred to Harrison High School, twenty-five miles away. We did not know that this would happen and never got the opportunity to say our plan to keep in touch with each other.

In December 1970, Annie had walked out of my life as quickly as she had walked into my life. For all purposes, the transferring of schools was the first nail in our coffin. My heart's sadness was equal to the joy I experienced when she entered my life. We stopped being a couple of teenagers in love with two individuals trying to avoid going back into the closets that had trapped us, causing us to be collateral damages.

When I returned to school after the Christmas Holidays, I needed to find a new way to face each tomorrow without her by my side. I was faced with a fork in the road and had to decide to hold on, not knowing if Annie and I would continue being in love with each other or pursue other dreams. Before I met Annie, I wrote my thoughts in a notebook. I called it The Book "The Reality of a Man Revealed in A Dream," Annie was that revealed dream that came to the realization, but now I must face reality without her in my life. She was gone, and I needed to find something new to dream about without including her. My only choices were to rely on my first passion or return to the closet by allowing myself to get bullied back into shyness. She came, stayed awhile, and is now gone by writing my feelings and emotions on paper. And gone with her went my heart because she did not return it to me. I had three options. The first was to convince my parents to graduate from high school early since I had earned the necessary credits to graduate already. That turned out not to be an option because my parents insisted that I waste time going the entire school year. As part of my notes, I still have the last letter and poem I wrote Annie until I was out of high school and in my first year of college. I even had a copy of Annie's previous letter and poetry. The letter and poem reveal my loneliness, confusion, and some of the fear I would have to face alone forever without her. Annie now accuses me of abandoning her when she left me be involuntary; she moved away. She has repeated this untruth; I did not go off and leave Annie.

Annie left Littlefield; she hoped that she was running away from hell, just as I wanted to get away from East Texas, as fast as I could for basically the same reason. Annie came into my life, and I felt valued and loved by someone. I decided that I would not allow words to hurt me again, nor would I shy away from anyone when they commented about my dark skin. I had proven the Malign twins, Mrs. Louser, and others wrong my dark skin was not a problem; it was too complex for their simple-mindedness. One individual, I could never convince or feel satisfied that I had overcome their rejection and ridicule, and that was my idol, my father.

In Annie, I had lost my incentive and encourager. Still, her absence emboldened me to face bullies head-on. After I lost Annie, I found freedom and courage to accept myself and think of myself as deserving of whatever I desired to pursue in life. I attempted to reach out to Annie and hoped to return us. We were never the same together afterward. Finally, I came to realize that just like Annie, I needed to distance myself from painful memories of school and home. So basically, we became two individuals fleeing our closets of secrets, some people in our lives built with the intent of keeping us in bondage. But in our eagerness to escape together, we ran in opposite directions. When I ran out of my closet, Annie ran back into hers. I could feel the tug on my heart to go back and try and save her, but my strength was forcing me onward as I resisted the urge to get pulled back into where I had escaped. So, I continued running, trying to flee from my past as quickly and as I could. Ironically, the voice told me to keep walking. I never heard it say, go back and save Annie. In my mind, I ran as fast and far as I could, thinking that I would have a chance to go back and save Annie later. I also knew that I needed to seek refuge from my nemesis and protect myself. One of the few times or only times in my life that I was selfish by looking out only for myself. The route I chose to put my past behind me also denied me the chance to live my life and share my dreams with Annie. I wished our future would have turned out differently. For example, I never told her how to be a lawyer and defend people less fortunate or screwed by the wealthy. I never had the opportunity to say to her that someday, I wanted to write books about love and that she would be my inspiration. I never told her that I wanted to be a great husband and father. I never said to her that I wanted her to go away with me, and together we would create a whole new life not involving our families. She failed to respond to any of my letters. Because of her abrupt departure, I never told her I started loving my father and wanted to be his little boy. I wanted my father's approval. One day, I stopped caring if he supported me or not, and I resented him and wanted to be everything opposite him. She played a crucial role in getting past the hurt by my father, not loving me or showing that he was proud of me as his son. Because instead of caring more for my father, I learned to despise him more. She never knew that she replaced the hurt caused by the father I once idolized when she came into my life. I wanted her to someday be proud of me for excelling in life and being a decent provider and faithful husband to one woman. Annie never told me any of her dreams, goals, or aspirations. Like my father, I stopped caring about whether Annie loved it. I no longer cared whether Annie and I had a future together. I appreciate the letter; it explains that I did not know or understand her situation. It will suffice to fill blank spaces when she left me for greener pastures. And why she chose not to communicate with me. I received a letter year later and much too late to care for anyone. Annie tries to explain her silent behavior. It is not a love letter, but something that she has rarely done, and that is to express herself by writing.

She stated she did her best to leave all her heartaches behind in her letter. I assume that our togetherness was the cause of some of her pains in Littlefield. I believed it safe to say that staying close to me was not an option to ease some of her pain and agony.

There are many questions about her life in Littlefield. I won't answer that she never shared with me, even though we spent many days together, on the telephone, and at school. She never loved me enough to share with me or feel that my love was enough to help her cope with whatever she was going on in her life. I was disappointed because I did not meet all her needs as a lover. But she moved to Harrison seeking a better life, which meant leaving me behind for a better life. After writing to her but never receiving any responses. She knew that I still loved her and was waiting and hoping that she would return.

Jeremiah, I can best explain how much you meant to me then and how much I loved you in this letter. You are incredibly good at disappearing and not being seen or heard for long periods. Yes, I am doing what I'm not particularly eager to do because I probably will never get this opportunity again.

Dear Jeremiah, you know I (love) loved you so deeply that it hurt to breathe. And yes, for a long time, I refused to allow thoughts of you to leave my mind. At our happiest and most loving moments, I would cry at night because I loved you so much. I do not know what to say that will make you believe me. When I left Littlefield, I did my best to leave all my heartaches behind. They say we should be careful of what we ask for because we might receive them. I always wanted to live with my mother and other siblings. It was a bittersweet move when the time came, more bitter because I left the most loving person I had ever known. As far as us, I did not know what to do, so I learned to cope. I, on the other hand, do not like writing. I never have. I tend to communicate better by seeing a person. I waited for you a long time to visit me. I did not know you had joined the military and was happy when we started dating again. I got a letter in the mail with a receipt in it where you had purchased a ring, a surprise it was. But this was after I had not seen you in forever. You seemed to think I did not love you or was not as into us as much as you. Sorry, you felt that way. It was your letters and the memories of us when we were together that kept me going day-to-day and all that kept me from running away. When I ask where you were, I still want to know where you were? You found a way to go anywhere else you wanted to. The house I moved to in Harrison with my mother was just as wicked as I left in Littlefield. You could have come to me; I wanted to believe. I do not write in color, so to speak, as you do, I may not have that flare you have for that sort of thing, but my love, heart, and soul are filled with nothing but respect for you. Life was hell for me, and after a while, I just went with the flow, so if you feel that I did not live up to what you remember, I do not know what to say. I tried saving all your letters. A lot was lost in storage and at that house on Mather Street. My stepfather ensured that; he would go through the storage room, get drunk and ramble through my things, no one else but mine. He had read the letters you had written to me to start an argument with Loretta and me. My stepfather said awful things and accused me of meeting you at different places, not knowing that the letters were long ago. But there were times when I wished I could sit with you and tell you the life that I have never shared with anyone. It is the life that I put out of my mind, but it stayed in my head because periods of my past still haunt me. To deal with the things going on in my life, I had to block everything from memory, even our joyful moments together. Jeremiah, I used my mind as a coffin to bury the skeletons that seemed to roam freely inside my head. The loud chattering reminded me of the pain that most of the time replaced our love. I could not allow them to be near my heart because much love filled my soul and spirit when I think of days with you. Jeremiah, you say I gave you strength for many things. I am glad, but I want to tell you some things face-to-face, and then maybe we will finally become friends and lovers. Please understand that the last sentence is something that I will explain but only face-to-face. So, what is next for Jeremiah and Annie? Always remember, I loved you.

Annie Sims

Annie We Have No Future

Annie, I can appreciate your letter, but forty-five years later, if I had received this letter in 1971, I would have known that you still loved me. We cannot blame the postal service, or you could not mail the letter. It was due to your selfishness and self-pity. One small note would have given me such great hope and something to hold on to, knowing whether our relationship was not over. I was deeply in love with you and would have waited for you until you told me it was over; you never did. I had to find out from others that you had decided to go on without me. Like the time I surprised you when I lived in Missouri, and you had a guest. It crushed me, and never had I ever felt so empty. And not since then have such a feeling of helplessness overtaken me to the point that I just wanted to drive to the end of the earth. As I drove back to Missouri, Alone in my car were the shattered memories of a love I thought we had that would never come to an end. This night and the drive made me face the wall of reality. It is over, and I thought to myself as I accepted us as being over that night as I drove back to Missouri. None of my thoughts said I should allow you access to my heart ever again.

Yes, I have also had dreams that caused me to wrestle with the sudden unexplained ending. But I knew that would only leave me feeling miserable, so I decided to bury Jeremiah and Annie that night on my way driving from Texas. Annie, when I learned, you had moved on with your life. I accepted the hurt and appreciated the moments of happiness we had shared. I, too, moved on by establishing a new experience for myself. The walks that we used to take together seemed like so long ago. When you came into my life, I found an anxiousness to move forward without fear of life's consequences constantly. I understood and accepted that we had a love story that ended without any explanations given by either one of us. Two things I realized had happened in my life because of you, Annie. First, I overcame a lifetime stigma regarding my dark complexion. And second, you had given me the encouragement I needed to leave the closet that kept me safe from nemesis like the Malign twins.

Letter and poem to Annie on February 17, 1971.

Dear Annie,

Well, Ebonic lady of mine, how was your day, and how are things going in Harrison and your new school. Today, I missed you, and I hope that those days will not be forever nor too many in the future. I love you, and losing you is so extremely hard because we cannot talk every night anymore. I cannot see your smiling face every day. I watched the movie Valley of Dolls last night and cannot seem to get the theme song out of my head; it just keeps playing over and over in my head as she asks all the questions that are heavy on my heart. Annie, will you still be my lady and someday the wife I promise to love until death? My heart is hurting from the hole left in it when your mother moved you away. Was it because of me that she felt the need to take you out? I hope that you will not find another love, but if you do, nobody can love you like I do and will never love you as much as I do. I cannot forget how incredible this ride with you on our cloud has been. It was the smoothest ride that I have ever ridden. I still have two arms that miss holding you and two lips desiring to kiss you again and again, over and over. I am still in love with you, and even though I last heard from you looks like forever; I feel that we are slipping away from each other. Are you still the love of my life? Do you still love me as much as I love you? While I write this letter, I am listening to our song by The Friends of Distinctions <u>Going in Circles</u> Annie, I am strung out over you, and this merry-go-round that I am on will not stop to let me off so that my mind will stop spinning, just thinking only about you. You are my world, and it became empty and cold the day you left. I long to hear your voice call my name and see your beautiful smile. You remember how we talked forever, and I would play <u>going in Circles</u> over and over. I needed that song to tell you how much I loved you and encourage you to go on.

When will we see each other again, and will you still be mine? Annie, please come back and take my heart in your bosom and love me also; I need you, and I need you. You may not have heard, but I lost my oldest brother two weeks ago. The police killed him in Houston. I could have used your arms to comfort me and your voice to reassure me that everything would be alright. Well, I will close this brief letter, but my love for you is long and open forever. If you are not returning to me, it is not only a rainy night in Georgia but East Texas, too, because my eyes will be flooding with tears. I hope this letter finds you happy and missing me as much as I miss you. I wrote you a poem, like always when I lose you for a few moments, to keep you going until we are together again. Your absentee is nowadays. Your loving man forever,

Jeremiah Ford

The Moon Will Not Lie.

On this night, I lie awake thinking about which mask will I wear tomorrow?

Since you have gone away, I tell a different story each time someone asks where you are, and I explain why you are gone.

The quietness in my room makes me miss you most, filled with sorrow.

Curiously, I gently pulled back the curtain as I lay in bed to look up at the night sky filled with stars. I remind them that I am alone.

I look at the woods, and all I see is this one tree that seems friendly as it greets me with a wave.

Please, God, talk to me tonight and tell me that I will be alright.

This feeling weighs heavy on my chest. Am I free to continue to love, or am I to you a forever slave?

Today is a long time past, and tomorrow is still a long time to come. I am anxious to welcome it to end my lonely plight.

My love, we never said goodbye, but then neither did we ever say hello when we met.

The moon will not lie because it is faithful and true to rise and provide us a guiding light.

I played the fool and fell in love without knowing all the rules, and now it seems I have lost you like a bet.

The moon will be here tomorrow night, and I will look for it to shine where you are so bright.

Since you left, I am back to writing letters and poems to myself; again-but, it is you that I see.

Since you left, I am back to wishing that I had someone to hold and tell I love you too.

The moon will not lie because it does not just belong only to brokenhearted me.

The moon will not lie, for the moon was made to comfort lonely men who seek to know the truth by determining that my love is real.

The warm love that remains in my chest for you will never cease burning.

I am letting go of the curtain and losing sight of the moon, which shined so bright to show me you, the loveliest star in tonight's sky.

My closest friends and companion are pillows. I rest my weary head to absorb my watery tears and control my mind that is forever turning.

You were one of the million stars to land on the doorsteps of my heart one lonely day.

Closing the curtain, hiding the moon, and winking back at the twinkling star that is you, I say goodbye as I lay.

CHAPTER NINETEEN

Sleepless in Jeremiah's World

It seems ever since the first night Annie and I became a couple. I have had difficulty falling asleep at night because of the quiet and gentle whispering voice speaking to me, encouraging me to keep walking. I did not understand why that voice repeated those exact words to me, and always when I was trying to fall asleep. I did not know why I heard this voice whispering in my mind's ear, telling me to keep walking. One day Annie and I were together at the same school. When she transferred to another school, it bought me a fork in the road. Perhaps we had reached this juncture in our relationship because it was time for us to move on. I would still write letters to her, but I never received responses to any of them. I eventually learned to cope with her absence and hang out with Carl, Allister, and McArthur. Annie's best friend, Mandy, approached me, asking if I liked her and maybe we could start dating. I declined the invitation at that time, but we dated on several occasions after getting married and divorced. The thing that had troubled me most and kept me silent in my dark skin no longer bothered me. I did not even give one thought to returning to the individual who once was damage collateral hiding in a dark closet. Annie had served her purpose in my life and should earn a crown for helping someone falling and was near giving up. This time the quiet voice said to keep walking, and you will see an opened door. After the voice spoke to me this time, I no longer had difficulty falling asleep at night. Suddenly, I became bold, and my vision focused on the goals and dreams I imagined for my life. I think the voice told me that Annie would never be the person that would push me to become a relentlessly driven individual. Her role in my life was to draw me out of the closet I was hiding in and give me the courage and strength I needed to succeed. God guided me through some troubling times because the glitter from my first love had blinded me.

Thinking to myself today, I wonder if I would not have traveled to Dallas to attend college if Annie had communicated with me. If she had not transferred to another high school, would we have lost our closeness? Anyway, after I graduated from High School.

Were We Playing a Game of Dare?

I could feel the end of a chapter in my life had come, and I needed to seek a new path into the future. First, I found a summer job to help pay for school clothes and other items that I needed to start college in the fall. Before leaving home for the first time in my life, I will spend a night away from my family. Before leaving for college in Dallas, there were times that I would call Annie to talk with long-distance. She would be out on a double date with one of her sisters.

I learned of this from another one of her sisters. So, we were already slipping further apart.

If there is one thing that I cannot forgive or ever forget, Annie never felt the need to tell me that there was competition and that she had eyes for another. So, why didn't I ever confront her with this question? Trust, belief, and honesty were always important to me. They still are valuable qualities that I desire, especially in a woman. Sadly, I was trying to deal with this crisis without telling anyone that I was hurting. The hurt was caused by the one individual who told me she would love me forever. I had given my all to maintain the relationship that we had created. Yet, she walked away without an explanation or a kiss goodbye. I found another secret compartment to hide my hurt and a broken heart because of pride. I will never tell anyone that your leaving broke my heart. Yes, I was hurting that I had given my heart to her, and I thought she had given me her heart too. But that same heart she promised me now is shared with another.

I stopped trusting her, but I could not just stop loving her. It brought me to another crossroad in my life, one that I must move on with someone else or face the rest of my tomorrow without Annie. The times that I would call her long-distance, she was never home. When my friends asked me about our relationship, my response would be we moved on in different directions. I finished high school. We saw each other once or twice during the summer. I had no transportation of my own to go and visit Annie at her mother's home. I worked about forty miles east of where I lived. And seventy miles south of where Annie lived. I was trying to earn money for college and clothes. I soon realized that calling her was futile but tried reaching out through letters. That one-time chance meeting was not anything like I had dreamed it would be, and she wasn't the same girl that I had fallen so deeply in love with not long ago.

Our kisses seemed to be asking the question, have we met before? We had lost our magic and the excitement when we were in love, which looked like a long time ago.

When it was time for me to leave for College in Dallas, Texas, the gap widened between us. I still cared deeply for the girl that saved me by helping to lift my self-esteem. It was back to letter writing and a few phone calls.

CHAPTER TWENTY

ONE TRAIN, TOO MANY RIDERS

Lost My Way

I returned to college for my sophomore year. I started to feel a little more comfortable with college life after being away from home for the first time in 1971. Going off to college was the farthest I had ever been away from home and Annie at the same time. One was a place I always felt safe and comfortable and the other a person I felt loved and needed. I was obeying the voice that told me to keep walking, and I still thought that Annie would have been so much easier to adapt and transition with me. She was my comfort blanket whenever something did not go right in my life. I would find her in my corner. I still wanted to try and reconnect with Annie. The question that was never answered is, did we ever officially break up or just call it quits? Which of us made this decision, and it was me listening to the calm voice telling me to keep walking? When we saw each other over the summer or spoke by phone, there was no chemistry between us like us we had created.

Writing letters was a therapy for me because I could release emotions and contact my right side. Things went alright between us, and we made no commitment to each other except that we still had a love for one another. But like all the times after she transferred to the school, Annie seemed intent on distancing herself from me. I did not bother to ask why. I had finally begun to adjust to the shock of her transferring school, graduating high school, and going off to college; I was confident of meeting other girls without the fear I had before October 1969. And there were other young ladies on campus that I casually dated along the way. Since Annie and I were not communicating regularly, I assumed that she had moved on with her life with another guy.

I visited home just before the end of the school year and went by to see Annie, and she seemed surprised and preoccupied. I had had this experience before, not long ago, when Susan was pregnant. I did not want to think the worst, so I just brushed it off as if we needed time to find each other. Something was missing that I could not put my finger on precisely what it was. I could not get over how talkative Annie was but always made excuses for us not to be alone, still surrounded by her family. The voice and face were the same. Still, something was missing between us, and she thought that perhaps she was afraid that another boyfriend would show up while we were together. However, she had denied there being anyone else. I return to school just motoring along in my world with nothing but good things and getting ready to head back home for the summer so I can return to my summer job. I received a letter from Annie (surprise) asking me to call her at a specific time on a day. I thought she was ready to confess and announce that things were over between us, and she wanted to move on with her life without me. I called her just as she asked me to. The conversation was odd when she expressed many concerns about what I had been doing since school and if I would stick with it? Will you be coming home for the summer of staying in Dallas to attend summer school? Have you ever had this feeling that someone wants to tell you something difficult or ask you for a favor that may not be easy to grant?

One of my nicknames was Jay, and in mid-sentence, she said, Jay, I was raped by my uncle Leonard, and I am pregnant. Yikes, what the hell am I supposed to do or say about something like that? She just dropped it on me in such a cavalier way.

She tells me that her mother did not want her to press charges against her uncle because she did not believe her claim. I was never happier to get off the phone with Annie in my life than I was at that moment. I do not think I even tried to comfort her or say it would be alright. I was numb, and my mind right away blamed her. I thought this would damage our relationship forever. Now she was raped, a violent crime, and I am trying to include myself as a victim. The phone call finally ended, and I walked back down the hallway to my room. Walking from the phone was symbolic of me walking from her forever.

I could not understand how she would allow someone else into the sacred space that I thought she reserved only for me. I did not know what to do or say, but somehow. I found a way to make this horrible act seem like it had happened to me. I blamed the victim by making it look like she had violated me. I was confused and wondered, even today, why I did not want to love her anymore? She was damaged goods, I selfishly thought to myself. Who would allow themselves to get raped by her uncle, I am thinking quietly to myself? And how would I defend her honor now that her uncle, whom she knew was sexually interested in her, is her so-called rapist? And why did she wait three months to tell me what this may do to our relationship? If only I had heard her say what she meant by being alright, perhaps I could have had the right words to say to Annie and show her more compassion and understanding. I was downright selfish and thoughtless; this woman had had her life threatened, and her body violated. In hindsight, I was an idiot and worried more about my feelings than Annie's well-being. And I had the galls to think harshly of Annie and belittle her in my silent, angry thoughts about her. But I could not bring myself to say I hope you will be alright. Instead, I was thinking of ways to help her craft the false narrative that lives today. I am as much to blame for this monster lie as Annie because I did not encourage her to expose the truth.

I was complicit in keeping this lie a secret all these years. I never found peace or comfort after taking part in this lie. And would often find myself thinking about a conversation between Annie and me when we were dating back in high school. She told me about her uncle Leonard's comment about a photograph she showed him in my basketball uniform and his comment about boys with bow legs. But the jackass asked her about the size of my penis because men with bowlegs penises were big. What kind of uncle would ask their teenage niece a question like that? A pervert. I am starting to connect the dots because Annie once told me about Leonard's other questions about our sexual activities.

In hindsight, I now understand Annie's loud laughter masks the hurt from the abuse and molestation. I know now why she gave me the stern warning on our first night together, walking off the football field. The times we were together, and her eyes appeared as though she was staring into a far-away place. Should I have held her tighter and closer to me, perhaps squeezing the pains she was keeping inside out of her? Probably in my arms, she would have felt she had found safety from the abuse occurring in her grandmother's home. I did ask what was on her mind. I would ask why she was quiet? Her answers were always the same; nothing. I am merely happy you are holding me close to you. In the safety of my arms, she never shared the pain she endured from being trapped in a closet. And like me, she too was relegated to a place of fear. Something that we had in common and could have related to each other but never shared our concerns. Should I have told someone about my secret closet of pains?

I never once let her know it was because of the dark skin that I rarely approached her. Perhaps letting Annie know that my life was not easy either until she came into my life. If I knew she was being abused and possibly stalked by this sick uncle, I would have worked harder to help her get pregnant so that we could get her away from the abuse. In Hindsight, there are so many thoughts now that run through my mind and child abuse signs. Today, those same warning signs would be easy to recognize. And the only thing that I could think of was that she had betrayed me by allowing this to happen. I took Annie's raping hard emotionally to include chastising myself while thinking silently, you idiot. Jeremiah rape is not a voluntary sexual act; it is violent and violates another human being's body.

Annie helped to rescue me, and I could not allow her to go this alone without a friend that she could count on, not even if we were no longer going to be boyfriend and girlfriend. In January, I decided to transfer to College for the spring semester to a College in Harrison to be closer to her. But for some reason, her stepfather was not too pleased with me coming around. Not long after the semester started, I remember her sister Evelyn calling to tell me that Annie was in the hospital and had given birth to a baby girl (Lydia). I never knew. Perhaps it was because I was only looking at how having Annie in my life was solely for me and never once thinking about what I meant to her and her life. Maybe it was the tiny brain of her stepfather or Mrs. Loretta, Annie's mother, who believed I was the baby's father. I enjoyed holding her baby and feeding her. I have always been a sucker for babies and found myself getting sucked back into the notion of reconnecting with Annie.

I visited her at her family's home but never felt welcome as if there was some secret that I was not privy to know. Anyway, I rule that I do not feel comfortable about anything or place that I immediately remove myself. I left without expressing to Annie my concerns. They, along with others, were convinced I was the father of Lydia. When the semester ended, I went back home to East, Texas. I started refocusing on serving in my church and playing a lot of basketball. I could play three hundred and sixty-five days a year and in any weather. I gave Annie the freedom that I thought she and her family wanted and more so that she could sort out whether she wanted me in her life. And I also needed to clear my head because I was dealing with this and other weighty issues, like reestablishing and refocusing on my future education and relationships with other women. So less than two years, I found myself with two girlfriends, two rapes, and two pregnancies, and neither of the two children was ours together. Something is very fishy!!!!

CHAPTER TWENTY-ONE

VOICE FROM MY PAST

After returning home to be with Annie during her pregnancy and hoping to rekindle things between us, I dropped out of school and began working a full-time job. And the strangest thing happened.

Annie, out of the blue, married some guy. I felt like the BIGGEST FOOL in the world because here I was willing to abandon a college education, to which I had earned a full-ride scholarship. She showed me no compassion or care. I masqueraded my feelings as if we were done with each other. It would be a couple of years before we accidentally ran into each other on the street. One afternoon after work, I walked downtown Harrison, and I heard my name called. Annie and our chance meeting were awkward because it had been almost a while since we last spoke to each other. I was uncertain if this was a married or single woman. Proceeding with caution, I watched and listened for something to indicate which Annie was happy to see me. Why are we even talking to each other? We engaged in small talk, catching up on what each other had been doing, and of course, I asked how Lydia was doing? She is okay, Jay, growing and thinks that she is growing, trying to run the house. Annie insisted I go with her to the music store and buy a record that she liked a lot. I wish that I could remember the name of the song. Perhaps it would tell me where her mind and thoughts were at that time. We made plans to get together the following weekend to catch up on old times and see where things would go from there.

When I visited her at her parent's home the following weekend, I still did not feel welcomed, but I just tolerated those few moments and moved on. Our visit went okay but did not bring us closer together, so our once love train remained off the track. As was apparent at this time, I was in a rut and frustrated with myself that I could not get any traction as I pondered how I would get back in school. And my hopes of someday becoming a lawyer looked less likely. I still lived in East Texas, where I vowed not to return, so how would I move forward and remain in the same small town I dreamed of leaving forever? And Annie continued to be one of my many thoughts, and I wondered why we were no longer in love with each other the way we once were. We were not even showing any of the kind of love that we once shared. The temptation was swaying back and forth in my mind should I ask Annie to try and make a go at it again. I stayed in this stage of my life too long because I was afraid to move on out, encountering the kind of fear that had neutralized me, not knowing what direction I should take. I had not emptied my soul yet of what I felt for her and believed there was still enough love left in my heart to make me happy. Must I have a high threshold for pain, or do I genuinely love this woman? Did I wonder to myself? An unrecognizable Annie, I had allowed my mind to remain and remember her the last time we saw each other many years ago. I do not know, uncertain if I can trust her, and can I believe any of her words, especially if she tells me she loves me. If I do not feel sincere, it will cause me to hesitate to allow anyone to get too close to me.

Some days, it seems like nothing goes right, and you want a do-over. On this already lousy day, I received a call from a friend telling me that Annie had gotten married and had moved to another town. Yes, I was hurt, wondering why it was hard for her to tell me the truth. I am thankful for the uneasy feeling not to rush and trust Annie with how I felt about her. How flipping hard was it to say that she had found someone else and planned to get married? Once again, I am having second thoughts about the rape claim because nothing made sense to me. Why would she put herself through the pain and embarrassment of telling me that she was raped and yet have someone else in her life ready to marry so suddenly? If she did not love me anymore, why bother involving me in this lie. Was it rape? We had just spoken by phone the week before she married and not received a word about her impending marriage.

I decided to move on and give up on us ever being together. I work as a production manager for a blue jeans manufacturing company.

My workers were all women, and they were a headache to deal with daily. And having a tiny relationship with a couple of the ladies on the side was a bad idea. Still, I tried it and was severely defeated. They kicked my butt for trying to play the field. Heck, I almost burned it down with my black behind tied to a stake. But anyway, I digress to the most pivotal and vital decision I had ever made in my life to date.

Every year the entire company would go on vacation for a month. On my last day before the holiday started, I announced that I would join the military before returning to this job and going through the kind of hell I had just gone through. We were due back on July twenty-second, and I decided to join the Army on July 19th, tested, and left home on July 21st. I was on the run from more than just a lousy job. I wanted to bury Jeremiah Micah Ford so deep into my past. I needed to put so much distance between Annie and me this time so that I would never see or touch her or even bump into her accidentally. Her decision to get married destroyed any future we had. She would get an earful if she approached me as a married woman because I honor and value marriage. I did not know the individual she married, but I respected him because she was his wife. I needed to move on to have a future that did not involve Annie Sims. I had screwed up my full academic scholarship for college, thinking that I had a good enough reason for making the sacrifice to be near Annie and Lydia. I did not understand rape or the mind of a rape victim, but I tried to come to grips and understand how a woman may feel from this terrible act against her. After Annie had Lydia and based on the circumstances surrounding how she allegedly became pregnant, I wanted Lydia to know the love of having a father. Unfortunately, or fortunately, that never materialized. I needed to show empathy and not criticism, and Annie was not the kind of person I should be wasting it on.

Annie's marriage did not last long; somehow, we got back together briefly. I never told her that I needed to learn how to trust her again. I never told her things between us were not like before and for good reasons. I never expressed my concerns, and I never conveyed my suspicions about her.

When I joined the military, it was a decision based on us, and I had had enough. I was removing Annie permanently from the future I thought would involve her. Taking this step and my life into my own hands by changing my paths has put me back on track toward accomplishing my goals. This plan would put me in a much better position. I believe that I overcame my fear of bullies and faced them with force if I needed to. I was on-my-on, and I was alone to fend and decide for myself, and I do not recall feeling lonely for home or missing my family. It seemed like when I buried Jeremiah and Annie. I was trying to hide my family too. What was important to me was to focus on just one thing, one person, one day at a time. And not to become overly concerned with what I thought was a lifetime commitment to one girl.

Moving On Without Annie

Annie wasn't out of my system, but she had made some decisions that caused us to go in different directions. As much as I once loved her, I needed to move on for my sanity and test my faith. I believe she played a crucial role in my life and a pivotal time, but I didn't want to believe it was the end of the road for me. The sooner, the better I needed her out of my life and any plans I had for a brighter future. After having a reflective moment, I remember some of my life's sad and happy times. For instance, the first time, I fell in love with a girl that was so perfect for me at a time when I needed someone to come into my life at that very moment. I think about a sad moment in my life when that same girl I had fallen heads over heel for also caused me to put my life on hold because of a tragedy in her life. Sometimes I smile inwardly at happy times when I discover real happiness or enjoy writing and receiving love letters. And I could not have made it myself. I found it to be true when I realized my heart was collateral to offer in exchange for the love of my first girlfriend. I learned different evil acts that could cause collateral damage beyond repair in the wrong recipient's hand if they do not care adequately.

Annie once brought sunshine into my life and cast a veil of darkness on the face of a once-promising relationship. I believe I kept my sanity by joining the military. It is funny how, at first, she opposed joining the Army and chose a college. Would the latter have made any difference, and could I have prevented Annie from getting raped by her uncle? Am I taking too much blame and not accepting that life has ups and downs? I just needed not to be afraid to pick myself back up when I fell. I am away from home and Annie, and I hear a voice telling me to keep walking. Each time I tried to return to a point where I was comfortable with the dream, it became a nightmare. It will take a few more before I am frightened and awaken by reality.

I completed Basic Training in Louisiana and received orders for Missouri for my permanent duty station. I had a nine-day layover between basic training and Missouri. I never gave Annie a thought because I knew that she was married. And my decision to move on was the right one for me and my future.

Finally, my nine days were coming to an end, and I needed to board a bus to Missouri.

I was stationed in Missouri for nearly three years and saw my first real snow, the kind that comes up to your knees. I visited caverns. I climbed rocks and purchased my first car, a 1975 bright blue metallic Camaro. I was laughing, joking, and made a few new friends. I needed to clear my head and get away from people. I would go jogging for long distances because most people that wanted to hang around me and talk were not interested in running. I can remember writing my feelings and emotions for the first time was not a relief. It was running and playing sports. I left out of that closet running, and I supposed I had not run away far enough. Just getting free was the shortest part of the journey. Now I must deal with the collateral damages and not limit the number of ways I could express my emotions. I dreamed and thought of never going home again to live and what real, lasting love would feel like and if I would ever find it.

Annie, you love that person harder than you ever have anyone before. And ever will because you have no idea how powerful love can be. When you fall in love for the first time, it makes you feel like you are gasping for air or the next breath. And the lack of experience in how to pace and navigate day-to-day. I describe my passion and affection for you initially and through the struggles of eventually going on without you. Just as we started our first year of high school, we knew that we would eventually come to the end of our senior year and graduate. We both took full advantage of the other need for satisfaction to fill the voids that had eluded us before we met. I cannot speak for you, but I needed to get off the roller coaster our relationship had become by getting on with my life and venturing into a world without you. I needed to rid myself of the pain and uncertainty you were causing me in my life.

Taking Control of My Future

The day I enlisted into the military, I celebrate every year. It was the day I made the biggest and best decision of my life. I sold my life to serve my country and to have an opportunity to own a home, land, peace of mind, and lifetime security someday. I chose a future without Annie and decided to leave her in my past. And leaving her behind also were the dreams of someday that Annie and I would eventually get married and have children. I cannot say that I made this move to make things better to have a life together.

I did not confer with her in my haste or try to find out if she still wanted to have with me? I never thought she would not wait for me; if she felt that I left her behind. And in a way, I guess I did because I had nothing to give her except a promise. And no reason to stick around because it wasn't long after I joined the military I learned she had chosen other means and men to move her agenda. She later would accuse me of not telling her that I wanted to wait for marriage and children until I could afford to care for a family. That was not true because many of our late nights' conversations were about me finding a suitable job and place for us to live. I know that we had the conversation more than once because I referred to the house or the shack I grew up in and how I wanted my family better. I wanted more than to have someone to sleep with at night who would be proud of me. I didn't want to have to stare in the face of a wife and children in need. I sometimes wonder why I was so driven in the hell and focused on rising beyond where my parents landed. My comments were not to put down my parent while trying to puff up myself. Still, I always listened to my mother when it came to taking care of my wife's needs and becoming a good father to my children.

I desperately wanted a companion to climb the ladder to success by my side. I missed not having a familiar face to be my cheerleader and friend and someone who knew me before climbing the second rung on the ladder. Instead, I found myself celebrating alone whenever I accomplished or achieved something noteworthy. That is why I knew that a collaborative effort to write a book would never work between us because we had ended up in two different worlds. Annie seemed to have chosen to scheme and connive; I elected to work hard and thrive on securing a long-term future for myself. Marriage to the right woman was not out of the realm of possibilities. Annie is angry at me, but it is her that she is upset with because of where she has ended up in life. But that happens to haste and impatience when trying to prove a point to someone without a backup plan.

CHAPTER TWENTY-TWO

SHATTERED DREAMS

Is it possible to erase Annie Sims from all of my memories entirely? I must get behind the closed door of Annie's heart, where all the love I have remained. How am I going to get this love back? Because I am never going back and asking her to love me again ever in my life. To move on, I needed to become a thief and steal my love from behind Annie's closed and locked door to her heart without getting involved or falling back into her web of lies and deceits. I could see my unwanted love when I looked into the windows of her eyes; there was no passion as it lay lifeless on the floor and waiting to be picked up and held close when I took the attitude that I was no longer being used as collateral by Annie Sims. And I will no longer be a giver, but a taker then could regain possession of my love. In doing so, I proceeded to lift myself from feeling like one hundred buses had driven over me.

The enjoyment of running long distances to getaway in the middle of the day to think and relieve daily stresses was working. I knew that I had to rest in a bed at some point. It was always there when my mind would do the running, exhausting me to the extent that I felt tormented by the many thoughts that ran through my head. I had not yet freed myself.

Just Passing the Time

Playing in many pickup basketballs and softball games in Missouri also became a favorite pass. One evening with nothing to do, I decided to go and watch a lady's softball game. After scanning the players' field by observing their demeanor, I noticed one player's intenseness that caught my eye. I was fascinated by her, and for some reason, my mind put me back in 1969 when I first noticed Annie. It was not her playing ability, but there was just something about her that made me bold enough to go up to her after the game and introduce myself to her. Hello, I am Jeremiah Ford. Something that I had never done before in my life. I asked if she had a ride home or to her billets. She said, *no, why will you give me a ride*? I said yes, that is why I came to watch you play and so I could offer my chariot to take you home safe and sound.

On the way, we talked as if we had known each other for years, not a single word about the excellent game she had played. I am moving fast, where it took months for me to get up the nerve to approach Annie. In one evening, we learned a lot about each other. I knew that she had only been on the fort for about three months. Approximately the same amount of time that Annie had dumped me and put me on the prowl for newer, bigger, and better things in life. I chose the latter. Annie's action had pushed me to take back my heart from her forever. Annie and I were together as a couple briefly a few times. The time between our separations became more tumultuous and vicious. But I am feeling right about this young lady. Something draws me to her, and I move without hesitation or resistance.

This young lady's name was Dana Brooke, and for two years, she filled the void in my heart and life left by Annie that helped me regain my soul. From the beginning, we seemed to have created our world. While others existed but were not allowed to disrupt the high, we brought into each other's lives. No one ever asked how two individuals could live in their world and become so attracted to one another quickly? I know for me; I just needed a soft place to land with someone willing to allow me to lay my broken soul in their lap. I was exhausted and tired from trying to love Annie, and I needed rest. I could sense that Dana had experienced the same fallen relationship, and she, too, needed relief. Our needs were more like the perfect repair part necessary to get our engines running again like new. I hope Dana would show me how to move on without Annie by not allowing my past to interfere with my relationship with her. Annie had not only broken my heart; she had stolen my soul. Left with a void that needed filling, Dana was contoured, especially for that space. I no longer had any desire to give Annie another opportunity to break my heart. I had finally filled the void left by Annie, and there was no need for her anymore because Dana had come into my life to fill that once voided space.

I never asked Dana about her last relationship because I thought she would say something like rebounding from a bad breakup or getting married. She asked about my previous relationship once she asked me why a lovely, caring, and considerate guy is not married or has a girlfriend? That question meant the world to me because it told me that I was not junk, and I departed from my closet for good. I do have a girlfriend; I recall responding quickly, you. And that was the end of that conversation until it was time for me to leave Missouri. We just enjoyed being with each other daily without placing any expectations. Years later, I realized that I wanted to give Dana all my love but did not, and all she needed to do was ask me for it. I was not confident that the love in my heart was worth giving to anyone, let alone someone as beautiful as Dana.

Our relationship allowed us to do what we needed to get through the dark moments we kept hidden from one another. Throughout our relationship, we never questioned each other.

Dana never went on vacation with me. And I never went on vacation with her when she would go on military leave to visit her relatives in Alabama. When I went home on military holiday, I would see a young lady named Terri. For all I knew, she was going home to see another guy just as I was seeing another woman when I was in Texas. I did not care because committing to one person had proven fruitless, and I sensed the same for Dana. We were stationed together in Missouri and were exclusive to each other. And there was no doubt in either of our minds.

We both protected our hearts but gave intimacy willingly to each other unconditionally. We never told each other how we felt about one another throughout the entire time we were together; all I know is that I felt comfortable. Like me, I always believed Dana was getting over a bad situation or putting her heart affairs back in order. She was patient with me and seemed to know the right amount of space I needed and when I wanted it. As I reflect on it today, I am not sure it was her patient as cautious as not to continue making a bad situation worse. And likewise, I was the same with her. It was the strangest but most beautiful kind of relationship between two individuals. I wanted to assure Dana that her heart was not in danger of ever being broken or hurt by me. Because with her, I was willing to talk about anything, except my past, which would involve talking about Annie. I never wanted her to feel that she was catching someone on the rebound, but a survivor from a shipwreck of love that went under the sea and never resurfaced. It was necessary for me not to think that I was Dana's soft-landing spot. I never wanted on my resume that I broke a woman's heart, especially not the one that was beating in the chest of Dana Brooke.

I took two weeks to leave in 1975 to drop my car off at my mother 's house for my youngest sister to drive to school and work until she graduated high school. The relationship with Dana was a beautiful one. But I also needed to know whether I was over Annie forever. I needed to test my willpower to resist the glut for punishment by showing Jeremiah and Annie were a dead deal and no longer was alive. No matter how much Annie may still float in my soul, I never wanted her to be hurt, not even by the men that became her husbands. When Dana and I were together, if I went home, I would drive down the street where Annie's mother lived to see if I would see her but not be seen by her.

A Familiar Voice

While home on leave for my sister's high school graduation. One lovely sunny spring afternoon, I was driving with my windows down, just listening to the music playing on my car stereo. I heard someone shout my name, Jeremiah; I stopped and made a U-turn to go back and see who had called my name. As I approached a daycare and stood at the top of a hill was Annie. She seemed glad to see me, and I played it cool because she was a married woman, the last I heard. I was more hesitant than delighted to see; this is a married woman. I thought to myself. A woman that ditched me without telling me. So, I played it extraordinarily cautious and close to the vest. I was in town for a graduation and not a convention for stupid people, featuring Jeremiah Ford. I did not even consider the question of whether I should trust her or not. As soon as I finish what I came for, I will head to Missouri to Miss

Dana Brooke, where my heart is. Also, I had already auditioned and won the play's role (somebody got to play the fool), and it was not for me.

I asked about her husband and Lydia. No husband, but Lydia is doing fine and would be happy to see you; I do not think she would remember me, I said. Yeah, I think that she would, Annie replied. She asked me to stop by, but instead, I invited her to attend my sister Linda's high school graduation that night with me. Annie accepted my invitation, and we went to graduation together. As with every small town, many of the people we knew were there and seemed happy to see us together. Although they did not do that for me, it was a one-night stand, and I am off to Missouri back to Dana. After graduation, I asked Annie to drive back to her mother's house because I was tired. Annie, with her mischievous voice, Jeremiah, what would you do if I were to pull into a hotel? I cannot write my facial expression, but we stopped, I paid. We had sex. And more sex. And talked, but she seemed intent on trying to get me to commit again to her because she kept bringing up the subject of marriage and our promise to each other. Imagine the little old ultimate promise-breaker has the galls to talk about keeping promises. Too many men had invaded the territory that I thought I would be the sole dweller. I was not blaming Annie for being raped, but I wondered if there were no other men before and after our many breakups. Somehow my pride had crept in and was looming more considerable than the horrific tragedy. To pick up with her where we never left off would mean me leaving Dana, and that was not going to happen. She deserved much better, and I would not give her anything less. She had earned better than that from me, but I needed to know how far removed I was from wanting any kind of relationship with Annie. If I were to marry anyone, it would have to be the person I am going back to in a few days, Dana. I accepted I was over Annie, and I also had moved beyond her impromptu craziness. I wasn't called insane in my younger years but a smart ass. I guess I put it in today's vernacular and the Latin term caveat emptor (buyer beware). She was fire, and I had experienced getting burned by her flames too often. I really would have loved to have been a father to Lydia because I believe that her love was genuine and not swayed by her mother being a boob. I would have no problem loving a child that was not mine. My greatest worry and concern were possibly hating her mother. I did not trust, and borderline resented would not make for a suitable environment for a sweet innocent child.

I Want to Fly Again

Like a bird with a broken wing, I had lost my desire to fly before meeting Dana. The two years that Dana and I spent together had healed me, and I could again soar. I realized later that I had fallen as much in love with Dana as I had with Annie, with one exception. I was not afraid of losing her or leaving me for another man. Annie caused me to develop an arrogant attitude about myself. Because all of Annie's actions were od, she was not trusted. Being together with Dana had taught me to be prepared for anything. If things do not work out between us, we will not hold onto each other by holding promises and memories long past us. Instead, encourage them to move on so that you, too, can get on with your life. Fortunately, Dana and I did not have to experience a loss of love because of unfaithfulness or lost interest in one another. You must be versatile, agile, and mobile when serving in the military.

Time flies when you have fun and spend quality time with someone you enjoy immensely. I had become comfortable with Dana. I received orders for a permanent change of duty station, meaning I would have to leave Missouri soon and possibly Dana. My next permanent duty station will be in Oklahoma. But first, I needed to attend a school in San Antonio, Texas. Dana's relationship would be over, and I was unsure how either of us would react to the separation. Would I say or do something profound like asking her to marry me or request that we commit to one another forever?

My leaving Missouri was not going to be a surprise. I had not been successful with long-distance love affairs and was reluctant to try again. But I was less fearful of starting over or leaving someone I was fond of and had become comfortable sharing my life with for the past two years. Leaving Dana behind would create a void again in my life, and I wondered how I would deal with that void? Because Dana knows I am about to leave, we would get to say our goodbyes. Today, I wonder what I would have done if Dana was the one leaving me behind. Would I have made a more substantial commitment for us to remain together? Thank God I did not have to find out.

A reflection of when I graduated from high school and soon faced an unknown future with a different perspective on life. When I graduated high school, I was sure about Annie's relationship or how I would take college life. Dana and I had developed a unique but accommodating relationship. The time was still fast approaching for me to depart. We would soon be parting ways, possibly never to see each other again. I was prepared this time and believed things would be alright. I had learned how to deal with a girlfriend's loss and the empty feeling by now. I cared for Dana, and I believe she also cared about me. We had both enjoyed having someone to share full-time intimacy with without commitments. If I take one more step by adding, I love you, would it screw things up? I know I could not see myself opening myself up to the possibility of getting hurt again. Dana never placed any pressure on me or schemes to get me to commit to her. I believe that she had committed to someone before we got together and had realized the same fate as I had. The day finally came for my departure, and I missed Dana while we were in each other's presence. I held her close and very tight in my arms, kissing her like it was our first kiss, trying to impress her that I was the right guy for her, but this was one of our last kisses, and knowing that it was probably our last. We eventually left each other without ever saying goodbye. I think that we both had built such a fortress to protect our hearts from all the pain we endured from our previous heartbreaks. Our breakup was an amicable parting of ways, and the only thing that we were dividing was our memories of us. And we each received mended hearts full of love from our two years together. I was over Annie and Susan, and I would not allow another woman to hurt me by thinking she would be faithful to me once I was gone. The entire time Dana and I were together, we were free to see anyone else if we chose, but neither did.

I believe that we were enough in filling the spaces of each other hearts from voids left by two unknown individuals. I remember our last day together was how we said our final goodbyes. We did milk every moment out of that day that we could as we stayed close to each other. Standing near a window with the sun shining over my shoulders, I remember looking across the room at Dana standing near my suitcases. My heart wanted to say, Dana, I love you, and will you marry me? But my lips said I needed to shower and get dressed. I went in, took a shower, and got ready to leave my best friend for the past two years behind. During this shower, I was going to take a solo. It was a perfect time for me to cry, using the water from the showerhead to disguise my tears of sadness because I was about to leave someone who had come into my life at the perfect time. I could never figure it out except that I was going away from someone with a lot of appreciation for what she had meant to me in my life. That someone before her had freed me from my secret closet, and Dana freed and released me into a world I once feared.

The hour came when I needed to go and sign out from the post, and from there, I would be driving in Texas's direction. Dana accompanied me to the Charge-of-Quarter's office but would not allow me to go with her back to where we had enjoyed and accumulated two years of beautiful memories. She wanted to walk. Printed and signed on the line, and I officially signed out the post in Missouri. I laid down the pen. We immediately grabbed each other and kissed for the very last time. I have never seen or heard from Dana Brooke since that night. Instead of Dana saying goodbye, she handed me a letter. She told me to play The Commodore's song Easy on my way to my next destination. That is what you have been to me, Jeremiah, two years have made my life easy, so I am writing you this letter. The letter stated that loving you has been easy because you came into my life answered many of the questions I had about myself.

You made it easy for me to accept my losses, but more importantly, you kept me so close I never cried over my loss. After tonight I will only refer to Jeremiah as Easy because of the easiness I discovered loving you the past two years. I feel set free because you never made me feel unwanted but always needed. When the sun rises tomorrow, I hope you will think of our last sunset because when we met for the first time as the sun was setting, you walked into my life. Yes, you are leaving, but easy you will always be in my spirit. Again, we kissed and parted ways, both disappearing into the night, walking in opposite directions, knowing we would never see or talk to each other also. When I arrived back at my car, I sat in it for a moment, thinking about the two years I spent with Dana Brooke, a young white lady from Alabama who had healed me of my broken heart. Instead of rejecting me, she lifted this shy Black young man from Texas who once was too afraid to ask a girl to be his escort to a homecoming football game. She shared every part of being with me except her losses, but more importantly, she gave me more reasons to love again. The differences in our races never came up or discussed, and we never made it an issue. Dana impressed me the first time I met her, and I assumed she felt the same way about me. Thanks to Dana Brooke, I was able to move on. I transitioned from someone that had left me in a drunken love stupor too many times. Tonight, I am going away from someone special that had given me back my freedom. I began my drive out of the Ozarks, and I thought about how in 1969, I first discovered love as it did not have a color then, and for two years, it had no color. Instead, I found love to be colorless and boundless when caressing, caring, and fulfilling a need for a worthy of your trust. Annie was the first woman to take my hand and lead me out of the dark and fearful place I once found comforting. She not only taught me about love but also how to love. And many things about love, too, including making love, kissing, caressing, and caring genuinely for someone and giving me comfort outside of my dark skin and closet of fear. I am grateful to Annie for teaching me how to love. I am thankful to Dana for walking with me through the pains and disappointments—and showing me how to overcome the fear of falling or ever fear the likes of Mrs. Louser and the Malign twins again?

Although Annie and I never declared that it was over between us, for me, it was the moment I fell in love with Dana that signed our death certificate. Our last kiss ended, and we knew our love for each other was over also as we parted ways. I continued my drive to Texas, thinking I wished I would have had the opportunity to say goodbye to Annie's relationship. From Annie to Dana, I now have a benchmark of high and low. I was not afraid of leaving Dana behind because she had given me the strength to do so by affording me a second chance at love. I wonder what her response would have been if she said, I do not want to go without you, or if she had uttered, I need you because I want you in my life. The voice inside my head said, keep walking, and I guess neither of us got the short end of the stick.

We served the purpose needed to return hope in our lives. I do not understand why I was never curious enough to ask her for a commitment and why she never pressured me for one. Writing this book is the most I have spoken of Dana since we parted ways in 1977. The drive from Missouri to San Antonio was lonelier than I had expected. Dana crossed my mind more times than I thought she would. Despite the attempt to insulate my heart, I still felt sad leaving her behind. I guess I was afraid that I would have to find a new Dana because, like always in the past, we would be there for one another whenever things went wrong for either Annie or me. Since Annie was never an option again in my life, even though she would cross my mind, I wondered what if? They say you never forget your first love. Annie was the road I traveled in many events in my life, and getting over the cradle left by her was not easy. But loving Dana became the bridge that transported me across a sea of pain to safety and a bridge I gladly burned between Annie and me. I now knew how to deal with Annie and not be sucked in by her again.

This time I was the one to walk away from love, and I did not leave a broken heart behind me. I have been unable to describe my emotions adequately. I asked myself why I did not care enough about the person that was the balm that healed my broken heart by pursuing marrying her. Am I repaying all women because of one Annie by unintentionally hurting Dana? I believe that what I had to offer in emotional support was the balm needed to heal Dana's heart. I did hear the voice whispering again for me to keep walking. I guess what was so confusing was that Dana was a nice person, but then Annie and Susan were initially. I had always ignored that voice telling me to keep walking. By now, I am wondering how far I must walk. I found out why I needed to keep walking and decided to do something about it or continue walking alone, thinking to myself and chuckling inside my head. At the same time, this funny and kooky reflective notion passed through it. I wonder, will Dana call and tell me that she was raped and is pregnant now when I am gone?

CHAPTER TWENTY-THREE

THIS FUNNY FEELING
"Whispering Voice Says, Keep Walking"

Fort Sill, Oklahoma, finally, a new location to learn and meet new people. I played a lot of basketball and softball. We even won the Post Softball championship for one year. I still enjoyed spending a lot of time in the gym playing my favorite sport of all time, basketball. After leaving the gym from playing ball for hours, I would eat, and if I could find another open court for more basketball, it was just a circular routine.

One day I was sitting and eating dinner in the crowded dining hall, and up walked a private female soldier, her name tag read Lamare. She asked if I would mind if she sat at the table with me. Of course, the gentleman that I was replied, not concurring with her request. We did not say anything to each other; both just sat quietly and ate our meals, and went on our way, acknowledging each other as I left the table. Why wasn't I all into her like I was with Dana Brooke back in Missouri, puzzling me? I behaved the way I did again before Annie. The following day, I sat alone, eating breakfast, trying to get my head right for the long day ahead. My mind was in a world elsewhere, and I do not recall if anything were going on or that I would cause me to be in such deep thought. As I land back on earth, who comes and sits at my breakfast table? It was Denise Lamare. Trying not to be too forward or flip but somewhat kidding, I asked what time are we planning to eat lunch? I go to lunch at noon each day, replied Denise. She shut my big mouth, didn't she? Not to be outdone, I will see you at noon, and she was prompt as we both arrived at the dining facility simultaneously and went through the chow line together.

With my tray behind hers, we started a conversation and continued to a table. She was a recent graduate from the Medical Specialist course at Fort Sam Houston, Texas Academy of Health Science. There were thousands of soldiers going through various training. I left Ft. Sam Houston a month earlier before coming to Fort Sill. I learned that she was from Cincinnati, Ohio, and had a nursing degree but just wanted to join the military for travel. I found myself playing the role of initiating most of the conversations between us.

Denise was not a big talker, and I could sense that she was very cerebral and careful in her thoughts as if she were hiding something. She seemed to be hiding a secret and acted as if she said too much about herself. Anyone could quickly figure out the secret Denise wanted to keep hidden. She could give away some great mystery. We enjoyed being together and hanging out a lot together and did all the stuff dating men and women did back in the seventies. But nothing sexual ever took place between us. She had a car until it was wrecked and had to go into the shop for the period. But I would let her drive my car whenever she had appointments or needed to go to the commissary and stuff that she needed to do, like a hairdresser.

I had gone home for Christmas, but I think it was 1977 or 1978. I do not recall the precise year and do not care to remember. I know that it seems like I was always at home, but I earned thirty days a year and used them very liberally.

 While home, I learned that Annie was pregnant and married AGAIN. After her husband had severely beaten her in the hospital, she caused her to miscarry and lose her baby. How did she know I was home; I will never know because I never gave her my number in Oklahoma? I did not want to contact her because I was through with trying to restart a relationship I felt had died long ago. And was trying to work on trying to establish a meaningful relationship with Denise. But her sister Evelyn got in touch with me to tell me that Annie was in the hospital and wanted to know if I would come to see her. I had no business involving myself with Annie, and she was married, and it could be a chance that I could see Lydia's little pumpkin head. So, against my better judgment in a dicey situation, I found myself standing at Annie's bedside, hurting and in a lot of pain. She needed my help to make sure that Lydia had a wonderful Christmas. I think Annie was an excellent mother to Lydia. But I also witnessed her become bitter and resentful toward Lydia at times too. I am not sure if it had anything to do with Lydia's conception. I suppose she felt the need to confess to Father Jeremiah when collaborating on this book. Annie shared with me that she was jealous of Lydia and my relationship and believed that we had a romantic relationship going on between us. Anyway, once again, one of us was in a crisis and needed a shoulder to lean on. I could not give her my heart to hurt also. That was never going to be an option in the now or the future. But I would see that Lydia had something for Christmas, she was a loving little kid, and we enjoyed each other a lot. I was pleased to see Annie but sorry to see her in pain. But I was strong enough not to allow myself to fall victim to her wiles again. I had a life and a relationship going smooth back in Fort Sill; it had not reached the point of me, and Dana is, but I felt that it was moving in the right direction. And I saw no reason to upset this relationship I was trying to establish with Denise.

My leave was over, and I returned to my duty station on a Saturday evening. After getting settled in, I called Denise to let her know that I was back from leave, and perhaps we could get together later that night. She did not answer her phone, and I left her a message, unpacked, and did my laundry. A few hours had passed since I had called Denise, and I had not received a call back from her. I finished my chores and sat on my sofa to watch the ten o'clock news. The Newscaster's opening story was two Fort Sill female soldiers found in a Lawton hotel room murdered. The pictures of Shirleen Robinson and Denise Lamare appeared on the television screen. I was speechless, could not say anything, and did not know who to call and talk to about the situation. It was a long sleepless night of tossing and turning, wondering what happened and who did this? So, we were just in a man and woman relationship, and I was not the next kin for notification. All I knew was Denise was from

Cincinnati, Ohio, and I had never met her family. I feel good about finally getting Annie out of my system and walking away without feeling I wanted to give us another try. Denise's family had her body transferred back to Ohio for burial. They did not know me, and I did not know any of them. I never knew when Denise's funeral took place. They say we should not speak ill of the dead; I was so numb I could not talk and wouldn't know what to say if I could find the words.

For a moment, I began to second guess myself thinking perhaps if I had not walked away from my relationship with Dana, I would not be going through this agony.

The details surrounding Denise and Shirleen's deaths started to come out, and I felt deceived and like the world's biggest idiot. In the nineteen-seventies, individuals could be discharged from the military if discovered they were in a gay relationship. Shirleen and Denise were lesbian lovers. Shirleen, who was married and somehow her husband, found the affair, followed them to a Lawton Hotel, and stabbed them both to death. I now know the secret that I felt Denise had but could not figure out what it was, and she was using me as a shill to carry on this relationship with Shirleen. She borrowed my vehicle, she met Shirleen, and I could have been implicated in two different ways, as a man involved with another man's wife. Or a suspect in a double killing.

Perhaps becoming a priest would be the best career for me. My trying to pursue a relationship with Denise was futile from the beginning, and she knew it. And the time and effort that I invested would have never happened had I known Denise's secret; this was a waste of both of our time. We could have even still been friends, despite her chosen lifestyle. There never was any chance the relationship would go anywhere. Because eventually, it could have been me who could have discovered this nefarious affair and perhaps responded in the same manner as Shirleen's husband had reacted. I was shaken deeply by what just happened and placed many questions and doubts about my ability to judge people's characters. I thought that if you trusted everyone and not be suspicious because of a feeling, I was a fair-minded person. It was a colossal mistake because Denise was not around to explain or answer any of my questions. And the one problem was, why did you use me? You would think that I would have thought about returning to Dana and perhaps picking up where we had left off. But no, it was back to old familiar, not reliable, Annie. I would not return to Dana a second time, hoping she would again help me overcome another painful situation. I was not broken-hearted over Denise's death but disappointed that I did not vet her by trusting my suspicious feeling about her. We were not lovers, but I thought we had great respect for one another, which she did not have for me.

Another Wrong Turn

I needed someone to lean on and see me through this pain, and once again, I found myself back depending on Annie for companionship. I never shared with her why I had this sudden change of heart. What was the reason for risking my heart to her again, even though I was not all in just needing a soft-landing spot temporarily? Each time we got back together, there were always some differences in our emotions. I needed her to help ease the pain of Denise's death and deceit, but why in the heck would I want to turn to Annie, the queen of deception? I was back, and I was willing to give us another chance for Lydia's sake in exchange for her availability.

And I was attempting to be a father to a little girl that I adored. There had to be something else that kept us coming back to one another, was its destiny or just fear of going on without each other? Perhaps I just glutted for pain and abuse, being a battered lover. We took our relationship serious this time, and I started making plans to move Annie and Lydia to Oklahoma to become a family.

In my preparation, I forgot to make sure that Annie was honest this time and that there would be no more surprises. Stationed with me at Fort Sill was one of my cousins. My cousin had gone home for a few days. When he returned from vacation, he could not wait to come and tell me that Annie had gotten married. Again. I was always a relaxed, calm individual and never showed any emotions. Inside I was devastated. I had learned to mask my feelings. I lived alone; I would go to my quarters and think of how many ways to hate Annie equal to how much I once loved her. I had the perfect woman to move on with, Dana. Still, I chose to continue searching to end up with a dead lesbian and murdered by her lover's husband. Another disappointing attempt to make it with Annie. As always, the voice that kept encouraging me to keep walking this time, not back to Annie, I was initially too reluctant to move on.

CHAPTER TWENTY-FOUR

A FORK IN THE ROAD
"Keep Walking"

A man's heart plans his way, but the Lord determines his steps. Proverbs 16:8 Tragedy and bad decisions sometimes distort our judgment and ability to be reasonable by weighing heavily on us and putting us in a vulnerable position. The most important parts of my life dream had come to fruition except for one. I first wanted to find a job or career that would afford me the ability to take care of a family someday, meaning wife and children. Secondly, I wanted to travel and see the world and exhaust myself to where there would be no more desire to run or hang out with the fellas. Thirdly, I wanted a wife that we had both grown to love and respect before marriage. I was able to accomplish the first two relatively easily.

Jeremiah, Stranded at The Crossroads

I had come to a crossroads in my life when I needed to decide which direction to proceed at crossroads in life and was faced with a huge dilemma: do I wait, walk, or have a wedding. If I were to wait too long, what would I lose? If I should walk, will I miss out, and this become strike two after the failure of Annie and me. And if I wed anyone, will it be an attempt to fit a round peg into a square hole? Waiting on a crush that never manifested itself to catch up with my maturity will only create too much scrutiny and wrong assumptions. If I continue to walk, will I lose interest by becoming too content? Making this mistake could rob me of the pleasure of someday having children of my own to love and cherish? If I marry someone without knowing if their love for me is authentic, as they proclaim. Is it delusional thinking I can make them love me by showing them genuine love and kindness?

I grew up waiting for my opportunities to excel in life. I found no elevators or escalators to help me along my journey. But marrying someone you are not particular love is too big of a risk to take because of immediate loneliness or an unfilled part of a dream. The totality of thirteen years of infidelity, misguided trust, and lack of understanding and not the seven-year itch eventually did in my marriage to Sarah. But when marriage became the focal and missing link of my ambitions, I had failed, or fate failed me. And I do not have a steady girlfriend that I have grown to love and appreciate growing together. At this point in my life, I do not have an Annie, Dana, or even think at the moment, though of someone who may have a juvenile crush. I suppose I was looking for someone who could fill the void and emptiness in my soul created by the failing of my relationships with Annie and other young ladies. A question needs answering but will remain unanswered. Perhaps I should have been more patient and waited for the right woman to grow into my life, albeit a meeting by happenstance or a mature crush. These two individuals are like make-believe people, just as Annie was before becoming a natural person in my life. I never had a relationship with either of these two individuals. Our lips never kissed, and our arms never embraced. There were never any long walks have taken or silent moments with each other present. But none of the considerations were the right kind of woman I was seeking after. But in my feverish desire to throw away my freedom, I chose to rummage for one with the potential of possibly becoming a lifetime partner.

I decided to take an inventory of my life as going out to the Noncommissioned Officers Club was no longer fun. I spent most of my free time in the gym, playing basketball, or running long distances to avoid being around people. My other pastime was sitting in my bachelor's quarters, wondering what the next move would be in my life. I needed someone to be with when I was home. There was a girl, Sarah Dotson, that I would sometimes date when Annie was married. Sarah was an outstanding basketball player for a girl and funny at times. But she always looked like she weighed the world on her shoulders.

There would be times when I was home, and I would observe her sitting outside and looking like she was thinking of a far distant place. I knew that look because I purchased it a long time ago, and it is a profound look. After Denise's murder and learning that she was bi-sexual, I started to think about life more seriously, wondering if I should give marriage a try. I felt that marriage was more of a formality to say that someone else is wearing your last name. My parents influenced my impression of marriage based on what I saw from my parents and other married couples; the marriage was to have someone cheat on, argue, fuss, and fight. I was not seeing anyone, and I found myself staying in on weekends. I believe now that I was lonely, and instead of letting this emotion pass, I began to think about what it would be like to have a full-time mate. And I had my freedom and was not committed to anyone. After being on a roll of good relationships with women, I lost my joy until Denise's secret lifestyle and death had shaken me deeply. It did not upset me that Denise was a lesbian because I had encountered other individuals in college that were openly gay. I did not appreciate her involving me in a triangle love affair. And why include me in her lie. I began pondering the ladies I had dated or had a brief relationship with in the past. I started to believe that I was a lousy judge of character, or others could see that I was a real sucker. I had an enjoyable and fruitful relationship with Dana. I thought that I had found my way concerning relationships. And here it is, I have gone from two former girlfriends raped, and both ended up pregnant.

Did I mess up by not keeping my relationship with Dana going? Perhaps I should have committed to her and pursued a longer-term relationship. No, it would have meant that the relationship would have been long-distance, and I have had no success with those kinds of relationships. I cannot go back to Annie and Susan; they are both out of the question. What will I do with this aching emptiness, and how will I fill this emptiness? What do I want in a relationship, and how will I know when the person I meet is genuine and not with a hidden agenda? Denise shook me, and I am feeling gun shy of women? Why would I think about marriage in the world when I have not figured out how to have a meaningful and sustainable courtship? Marriage comes with a lifetime commitment to one person, someone I must love, trust, believe in, and rely on them to be accurate and faithful. I have no doubts about my willingness to be committed to one woman. What frightened me most was the mystery and unknown in the other person's heart. I did not want to get hurt again.

A Safe Haven

Whenever something would go wrong in either Annie or my life, we would seek out one another for comfort. It is human nature to either find someone to blame or fix our problem. I screwed up big time on both accounts. All my woes regarding relationships with women started with me. Those relationships eventually turned out to be also my fault. Sometimes we can try too hard to be a decent person for everyone but fail to consider our feelings. I have never wanted to be a selfish person. But if you keep screwing up and making the wrong decisions in your life because you cater to other people's desires for your life. I went too far and too long by allowing some family members to interfere in my personal life and affairs by letting them influence me or sway things their way. I would have gotten over Annie a lot sooner the summer leading up to leaving for college. I met a young lady named Willa, beautiful and fun-loving. Still, she did not fit one of my sisters' approval, and I shied away from her, even though I felt that we were pretty happy with each other. Then, the identical sister also tried to come between Annie and me by pushing another young lady off Michelle. There was nothing wrong with Michelle, and I had known her since we were young. We did not seem to have any chemistry between us; I wished we could have because she was an adorable young lady.

I believe that it was my way of rebellion against my family. And of course, Susan, the friend of my oldest sister, and it was not about the chocolate in this box. They interfered, but I made the mistake of listening and allowing their interference to dictate my life. Now I am pissed that nothing has gone right for me with any young ladies I dated or the ones preferred by my family. My next decision and every decision going forth will be of my choosing. If things do not work out, I can fix myself and whatever the outcome, but I am moving away from the tribe mentality. I am out on my own and have dealt with difficult situations without turning to drugs, alcohol, or going into a deep depression. I am alright, and I must be me and do me. My decision pissed off my family, but I thought of it as revenge for their interference in my life. I am one-hundred percent responsible for letting it happen.

I Messed Up and Missed Out

When Jeremiah and I first met and fell in love. October 25 is like an anniversary. I wonder if he ever thinks about this date and how much it means to me. When I found him, the object was shiny and without dents or dings to the exterior. He at least gave me a test drive before leaving me in the parking lot to be tested again and again by others. You turned the key to my heart and started my heart to love instantly. We both knew we were a perfect match. We thought we were made special for one another. How is it that two people so perfect for each other could not avoid a bad stretch of highway and avoid potholes that eventually threw our love so far out of line and into disrepair? The uneven pavement ended up in a ditch and totaled out the ride we both relied upon to transport us? On a clear day, our windshields were clean, and we did not see the end of the drop-off at the end of the road?   I remember you singing the _**Friends of Distinctions song, Going in Circles,**_ over the telephone. How did we end up outside the circle that kept us always coming back to each other? I remember because I can still hear your voice singing it to me. For a long time after I left to attend another school, I asked myself whether this would cause any damages. Two young people unfamiliar with the cruelty of humankind. We were two individuals who dared to venture outside of the world of protection they had created for themselves. Our love for one another was the collateral we planned our future on being together for a lifetime. The deposit we put down frees us from dysfunctional homes, families, and activities. When we lost control, there was no saving us from becoming a total loss. And our inability to navigate our way back into the circle of safety. After separating outside of our world, we faced many obstacles without a map back into each other's hearts and physical presence. Every aspect of that song describes our demise and calamity. There is a real tragedy in our story as two high school sweethearts both kept hurtful secret hurts and pains from one another throughout our brief love affair. We both had loved ones threaten our lives. We were the scapegoat because of their wrongdoings. And unwilling to accept the blame for their transgressions. When you found me and fell in love with one of me, I thought all my heartaches would go away. Had my life never experienced incest and eventual rape, I would have had a happy life. But instead, I fight for peace within my mind, soul, and body. But the voices inside my head are continuous throughout each day. It was because of ignorant people who saw black as a negative color. Your father's shame exposed him because you told confirming your mother's suspicions due to your unawareness. More than a million times, I have asked myself this one haunting question. Where would we be if I had not moved away from thinking that I was running away from harm? Instead, I caused permanent damage.

What I know and feel is this, I should be your best friend, lover, and wife, but I am not, and dealing with those three failures has somehow compounded my hurt. Jeremiah, I feel worthless and not needed partly because of your rejection after being molested, abused, raped. I think that losing out on you and me is a more considerable pain to my heart than all of those put together. I know that I could have overcome all of them with you because of how much we loved each other. My regrets are few because I spent most of my life trying to survive and provide for my unplanned child. When I see old school and classmates married for forty-plus years, I instantly become jealous and feel that what we had together would have lasted through the test of times. I say that because you never showed any dislike or meanness toward Lydia, a child that you knew for sure was not yours. You never made me feel guilty that I conceived Lydia from the violent rape of a monster. The music I hear lets me know the curtain has fallen on Annie, and Jeremiah has lowered long ago.

I notice neither of us has said to each other that I am sorry. And I am because being young and energetic will not always bring you to the victory circle. I am not happy speaking to you with so many restrictions because I have a lifetime of memories or thoughts that I wish to share. With my head on my pillow, you have been imagined you breathing into my face on lonely nights. Your imaginary arms have held me because I never forgot how tight you used to secure me with those bear hugs. I keep ever familiar in my mind you were kissing my lips. Jeremiah, I remember our first kiss.

That was a long passionate kiss, and I did not want to stop, and you showed no sign of wanting it to end either. Every day that I knew I would see you were a good day. Somehow, I feel that when we get to the end of Collateral Damages, Kept Secrets, it will be the end for us forever. I hope you feel some sadness that we conclude by saying goodbye instead of missing you and our past when we were together. You have shown me that you can move on and slam doors shut. Jeremiah, thanks for a lifetime of memories to help fill the lonely nights and days of the gloom of someone who will keep a part of you in my heart forever. What was shiny and reliable is now in a junk pile.

CHAPTER TWENTY-FIVE

I PRAYED BUT DIDN'T WAIT

I picked up the pieces when I dated a young lady named Sarah Dotson. She was someone I had dated a few times before and thought that we had a good rapport. She was a few years younger than me but more mature than some of the other young ladies I dated in the past. My mother and sisters did not like Sarah. But neither did other people in the neighborhood label her as loose and available for many guys. I never saw her in this way, and I never liked to assume someone to have a negative reputation without proof of my own. I had experienced being mischaracterized by some in the same neighborhood also. However, I was not cheating on my spouse, lying, and causing discord in the community. I would have appreciated the benefit of the doubt, and so I believed in giving others the same kind of respect. Another former girlfriend was Susan. Give her another chance? I think not because she had crossed the black line a long time ago, so she is out. Perhaps Theresa, no way because she violated my number one rule. Theresa lied to me by claiming to be single and married. It seemed like Sarah would be someone to consider in marriage since it appears strongly. We had no one, at least I thought so.

Today I think I made an even bigger mistake by not being patient and waiting for God to answer my prayer. I had already had experiences with these ladies, so why the rush? My haste by not taking enough time to reflect on all situations by assessing myself. I had not developed the **COMMON DENOMINATOR FACTOR** that I use in evaluating why things may have gone awry in my life today. Primarily it was identifying what role I played when the situation ended unfavorably. Most of my relationships did not end favorably, and the one thing that each of them had in common was me. More than likely, the problem was not the other individuals as much as it was me for not doing my due diligence.

As it turned out, Sarah surfaced as the best of them despite all the warnings given to me by everyone to my family and friends. The voice was telling me to keep walking repeated. Keep walking. I decided to pursue a more intensive relationship with Sarah because of conversations and communication. Out of all the girls I had dated, she was the only one with an equal back and forth discussion about our past relationship. Our relationship did not have to rely on me to discuss that we both would take turns. She appeared to me to be the kind of person that had had some awkward moments in her life and advised that she was not a worthwhile individual. Hello, this was my kind of person, someone to help fix other brokenness. Jeremiah and Annie's love boat could no longer sail in disrepair. And focusing on Sarah, I was able to ignore the sinking ship of love we sailed together had sunk. And I never wanted to recover it or rescue our lost memories. I never gave us another thought until Sarah and I had divorced, and you called me late one night. How did we get to the point of divorce?

Describing the tumultuous thirteen years of lies, deceit, and unfaithfulness would make a clearer understanding of why I believe that whatever God has for you, you will receive it. Still, sometimes it takes longer, and you may suffer a few bumps and bruises before you get it because of your hard-headedness. Sarah said the most profound thing to me when she said nobody wanted me. Unlike Annie, she was always available to go out and have enjoyed moments together. I intensified this relationship with Sarah despite everyone describing her as a sneak. And should not be trusted. Still, I chose to base our relationship on how she treated me and nothing else. She would write letters responding to phone calls. And when I was home on leave, we would go out. I became restless, and I needed to find out what was causing this anxiety in my life. I remember going down on my knees and praying to God for guidance to discern my emotions. What is it you want me to do? God, please tell me what I should do? I failed to listen to the calm voice, telling me to keep walking and be patient. I went ahead with my plans to ask Sarah to marry me. God never gave me such a reply or any indication that I should go down this path. I wanted to get back at my family and friends for constantly butting in my affairs. Revenge is never a good tactic without a solid plan to assure you victory. I eventually decided to get married and settle down. Thirteen years later, I found myself on my knees again, asking God to direct me. Keep walking.

I did not get married because 20/20 hindsight would have told me that God's answer to prayer is not always immediate. And God had the right woman to be my wife. I could not see her as my wife since she was not Annie. I realized and understood that Annie and I would never be husband and wife in this life, and possibly it was never to be. I believe we served as needed entities when both were at low points in our lives. When she helped me overcome the Malign twins and Mrs. Louser's suppression, our relationship was to free me from my collateral-damaged closet. A thought went through my head that I must have been the most thick-headed fool in the world to keep trying to put back together something broken, and no amount of glue was going to put it back together. None of the girls I dated in the past appealed to me. I had already eliminated each one starting with Susan, with the issue of my dark complexion. Jacquelyn was a freak, and I can only imagine what kind of a wife she would have been.

Cynthia was just a basket case, and I chose not to mention a couple of other names. So, after a few more months of dating, I asked Sarah to marry me. Although our marriage ended in divorce, I will always say that Sarah was a good-hearted person. Still, the issue was she could not be satisfied with giving her heart and body to just one man. The warnings I received about her were correct, but I had to learn the hard way. Years later, we apologized to each other for marriage failure and moved on. I screwed up and married the wrong woman when patience would have been a real virtue. It caused a tremendous uproar from my family and others. They did not like her because they would tell me that she had a negative reputation. In the East, Texas language, she slept around a lot. But to think of it seems like everyone in East Texas slept around with multiple partners, with other men, wives, or another woman husband. I never allowed anyone to tell me who to like and not like, so I ran right through all their warning signs, and for thirteen years, I got ticketed every day. I loved Sarah and was faithful to her for thirteen years that we were married. I thought any woman would appreciate a man dedicated to loving and caring for her, always putting her needs and wants ahead of his own.

Meanwhile, my focus was on making Sarah and my girls live happily. They were the love of my life. Together we had two beautiful daughters, and I enjoyed being a father. When Sarah gave birth to both of our daughters, I was privileged to witness their coming into the world. It was my mug that they saw, smiling down at them as I carefully walked them down to the Nursery for Newborns. And the first friendly voice to say I love you. I make this point because it is vital for men to know that there must be some love for a husband for a woman to go through the travail of having a baby. And I took this gesture as Sarah telling me that she loved me and was in it for the duration.

I will always appreciate her, and that is why I do not belittle or speak ill or allow anyone to trash her because of how she may have treated me. That is my ax to grind, and I choose not to be filled with hatred or have a vindictive attitude toward her. Because at the end of Sarah and my story, I came out alright. I have a beautiful wife, and we have a great marriage. Losing Annie and never wanting to give up the resentment kept me from meeting the right woman when I decided to ask Sarah to marry me. When my marriage to Sarah ended, I did what I was supposed to do. I would listen to the voice telling me to keep walking and obey it. And I found myself walking on the sandy beach of reality, a slight kick in the sand and a beautiful pearl was lying just beneath the surface. I found my wife waiting for me to pick her up and care for her the way a precious stone ought to be. Many well-to-do family members and friends had forewarned not to marry Sarah. And I needed to be a man by doing everything that I could to try and salvage a marriage, just like I had given Annie, and that is saying a lot.

CHAPTER TWENTY-SIX

THE UNWISE CHOICE

When two people decide to get married, they agree it will only be the two and no one else except God. Sarah was not happy at home because of her troubles with her father and other issues. Even after we were married, she never left home throughout the entire marriage because her mother could not seem to keep her damn nose to herself. When men paid more attention to other women, Sarah would go out of her way to get their attention. She would call her mother, seeking advice. When we were dating, we talked openly and freely about everything. Still, once we were married, she could no longer speak to me and tell me if I was doing or saying something wrong even though I said these words to her. If I am wrong, I expect you to say that I don't think I am right. She never did and started saying she was not smart enough to do or say what was on her mind. Like many women, she was not a great cook at first, but I made her a promise that if she took the time to cook it, I would eat it. And we had a lot of rice, fried chicken, and pork chops in the beginning. Although I did have to ask if we could have something other than rice almost every day? I was beginning to get burned out on rice, which was never a big favorite anyway. She became a good cook when she learned how to bake and make desserts. Dessert is my favorite part of every meal. We had our good moments, and we had more than our share of hard ones too.

Despite all the hostile intelligence I had received and ignored about Sarah before I asked her to marry me, I wanted our marriage to succeed. I dreamed of having a wife and kids; we would take trips across the county together. I never saw myself fathering more than two children, a boy, and a girl. But I also recall thinking that marriage was a waste of time and not for me. I had self-righteous hang-ups with people saying they were married and still cheated on one another. Marrying Sarah helped dispel a lot of myths that I created myself. First, if you treat a woman well and do not cheat on her, she will not stray. Sarah never strayed; she merely handed out her calling cards. I try to understand why a person feels the need to cheat on their spouses instead of telling them they want out of the marriage. I see it as selfish when you have a faithful spouse, cheating on them with another individual. Let them go and seek true love with someone that will return their love in kind.

All Sarah had to say and do is I want out and leave. Do not use the children as an excuse for staying because you cheated on them. The thirteen years was not a good investment of time or effort. As far as I know, she never married any of the men she cheated on me with and believed that she was getting a better deal. I later learned that she thought she was getting even with me because she thought I was cheating on her. But that never happened, and yes, the opportunities did present themselves. Still, I was not interested in being the husband, but one wife, Sarah.

Another thing to consider before marrying someone, you should be sure they are committed to the institution of marriage. Don't you know what you might get when you unwrap the gift you think you are getting? I should not have been so dismissive and heed what others were trying to alert me to beware.

My Regrets

The fact that I ran all around and away from the woman God had for me all the time. Hearing from a voice telling me to keep walking. My wife, Ruth, and I should have married a couple of years after graduating from high school. We crossed paths and were in the same city at the same time when I went off to college. I sold myself short because I accepted and believed the negative reasons I could never have a woman like her. These negative impressions of myself started before starting elementary school. I am surprised that I even got the nerve to ask her to be my third-grade girlfriend. Her dumping me was what I expected and validated that I was unworthy of such a jewel. Today, people think I am stubborn, bold, direct, and confident. I did not just realize these qualities, they were always there, and the people who were feeding negatively in my life saw them and tried to suppress them. Sarah came along when they were cranking up and did not want to deal with them. Encouraging her to reach for higher goals was a bad thing. In contrast, my wife today appreciates the encouragement and support.

Disappointed and Not Angry

After thirteen years of trying to hold together, a wrecked marriage totaled the first time infidelity reared its ugly head. We all want forgiveness when we make mistakes and hope that we, too, will be forgiven for our transgressions. I think of myself as strange when closing or shutting down relationships with some people. Especially those I allow get close to me, and I trust and learn to love. I had high hopes for Sarah, and I entered into marriage because of God-sanctioned marriages. But it is unfair to say that God is amid something that you ignored and decided to go ahead and do it your way. You must accept whatever the outcome of your decisions may turn out to be. I believe in being a loyal individual and committed to keeping my word even when hurting. There have been times in my life when I have remained committed to people who checked out on me a long time ago. The perception of me is that I am mean and impatient with people. Still, the reality is I tolerate people and situations longer than I should because I hate giving up on people. I think about where I would be if the people who saw potential in me when I was happy to hide because of those who never wanted me to realize that potential. I am abundantly grateful today for every individual that spoke positively into my life.

I don't talk or say anything when I am angry, and I smile uncontrollably if pushed to the point of anger. Then comes the end when I decide to move on with my life and allow people I once loved or trusted for a long time to vanish from my space. When Sarah and I got our divorce, I wasn't angry that we were leaving each other because she had totaled our marriage the first time she cheated on me. We should have gone our separate ways. When the union was finally over, I was disappointed that I could not sway someone to turn their lives around. It was something more than a failed marriage. I was disappointed that I wouldn't be a father only to my daughters. I praise God for allowing me to be a father that could raise my daughters as a single parent. But I am disappointed that I couldn't be just a father in their lives. I had given up on the marriage, but I never gave up on wanting to be a father to my girls. In trying to rear them the best that I could, I found myself making decisions that I wouldn't make if I could have just been their father and not serve in the role of being a mother. Today, I often apologize to my daughters for not being the father I wanted to be for them. We had a good father and daughter relationship before deciding that I needed to marry their mother. I wonder, could I have sacrificed a few more years for their sake and kept the family together?

Sarah didn't deceive me; I chose to ignore sound advice from those who knew her best, and she was not the kind of person I thought. I was forewarned by many people who must have cared enough about me, and they did not want me to make the type of mistake I was about to make. I ran all of the signs, stop-yield, and dangerous curves ahead. It wasn't until I found myself in a ditch that I could not get out of that I realized I had screwed up. And more importantly, I ignored God's instructions for me to keep walking. Like many parents, my mother used to say. A hard head will cause a sore behind.

I am disappointed that I will never know what it would have been like loving only one woman. Instead, I had to experience the pain of trying to love Annie Sims for too long. I am disappointed that Denise LeMare used me because I failed to trust my hunch and the voice that spoke to me to keep walking. I am disappointed with myself for not giving Ann and me a virgin a chance. Still, it was the crying and tears of my oldest daughter that kept me from chasing another possible dead end. Ann was as lovely as could be, but the voice did not permit me to pursue that relationship. I start to learn and heed by not following my heart but the familiar voice telling me to keep walking.

The disappointment made me feel I needed to misuse and abuse good women's trust. Because I thought I needed to get even with myself for being so stupid and falling for the wrong kind of woman to dedicate my love to her. I was disappointed with myself for the lack of patience. I should have waited on the right opportunity to pledge my love to Ruth Allen. Instead, I allowed myself to return to the closet because I doubted being good enough for Ruth. It was too dark, and ringing in my mind's ear was the voice of my father telling me that I would never be anything. To get someone like Ruth to love me and be my wife, I needed to have something to sell her. I recalled one day a guy asked me how did I get such a beautiful wife as Ruth? I didn't perceive myself as handsome enough for Ruth.

I responded by telling him my hump was in the shop to repair the day I met her, and she fell for me while it was still in the shop. I kept such quick responses at the tip of my tongue as deflectors and defenses. One of my disappointments is that I didn't get the opportunity to love my children as a father. As it stands today, they know half of what they consider a father. I missed the chance that I would have had to talk them through painful situations while they laid their heads on my shoulder. I would have loved more drives across the country, just the three of us having fun and acting crazy. When I returned from Korea, they were too big to ride on my back, and we didn't make the funny hats from the newspaper and march through the house like soldiers. One solace was that I got to take them to work with me as often as possible. The year in Korea turned everything upside down, mainly because of my selfishness to end a long overdue marriage.

I regret not finding a better way to end this troubled embarrassing relationship before going to Korea for a year. Before that moment in my life, I always put them first and foremost in front and center. I am disappointed in myself for not getting them out of a bad situation before deciding to force Sarah's final hand. I knew full well that my bluff would pay off, but perhaps I should have tried it differently. By writing Collateral Damages, Kept Secrets, I learned more about my many weaknesses. I realized that I do not have a sustainable evil or mean spirit. I can be very disappointed in someone, but I never totally give up on them or their worthiness in life. You can only use the right things and people fed into your life to erase the evil deeds and thoughts from your memory. I often ask myself, what would you change to get where you are today? I am disappointed, not angry, because anger would suggest that I am not happy with where I landed, and nothing could be farther from the truth. I would walk in the direction of the voice trying to guide and protect me. Keep walking. Because I chose not to obey the voice telling me to keep walking, I am disappointed and not angry.

The Breaking of Vows

It was October, which meant it was time for my semi-annual physical fitness test. I needed to be at the test site around six in the morning to take the test. Once I finished the test, I returned home to shower and dress for work. I left Sarah and the girls in bed because I did not want to wake them up. So, I decided it would be best to come through the back door to enter our house, not make as much noise. I tried to be quiet as I walked past the girl's bedroom to get to our bedroom. I heard their voices in our bedroom playing and overheard my wife's voice, telling someone on the phone that she missed them and loved him and could not wait to see them at work. All the warnings about Sarah have come to fruition; she has a weakness for men. I was shocked but should not be surprised. I did not know how to deal with this situation because I never found out until too late when Annie cheated. I confronted her, and you could see the embarrassing look on her face but not a glimpse of remorse. At first, she tried to lie and say I did not hear what I had heard.

Infidelity Rode Alone With Us

A few months later, I received orders reassigning me to Army Recruiter duty in Toledo, Ohio. After Sarah learned the land lay, it happened again, and Sarah and other men again. I cannot explain her, and I doubt if she could either. She would appear as being so loving, caring, and dedicated wife. But also equally as unfaithful. Any man who would show her the least little bit of interest was in hot pursuit of that man. After completing my recruiting duty, my next duty station was Army Medical Center, Washington, DC. They used to say DC is where young and old marriages divorce or find infidelity. At least I thought that he was my best friend in Toledo, started calling our home disguising his voice, wanting to talk to Sarah. They, too, were having an affair sexually and whatever. But of course, they both think that I never knew about their relationship. His wife alerted me because her husband felt guilty for cheating and betraying a friend. He should not have supposed guilty about it; to do what he did was not a friend. It was just a country dog. I received orders to return to a regular military post, and my next duty station was in Washington, DC.

The Chicken Comes Home to Roost

There was a saying that young couples come to Washington, DC, to get divorced. We will soon get tested because the woman I was married to will fall for any man that looks at her. One April, my name came up for Staff Duty, which meant I would go in at three in the evening and not be released until eight in the morning the next day. It was a cozy duty because I had a bed that I could sleep in a while my assistant would stay awake. I recall vividly speaking to Sarah before leaving for work and then to Staff Duty this morning. I looked Sarah in the eyes and asked if she was having an affair? If you want someone else, please go on and be with them, because if you bring it to our home, it will not be a good day for you and him. She denied having an affair and said that this was just my imagination. Suppose I could have only married my vision instead of the individual standing before me, telling me another lie. The time is 9:00 P.M. I had reported for Staff Duty seven hours ago. I called Sarah to see what she was doing. She said the girls wanted to spend the night with Alfredo at Nanny's tonight. Why not come and spend the night with me at the hospital? I have a room with a bed to rest in after midnight. No, I do not feel well, and I will bed early. Oh! Okay, I will talk to you later.

10:15 P.M. I called Sarah again to see if the kids were still spending the night with their little friend Alfredo. There was no answer. I phoned once again at 11:00 P.M. and no response.

It is now midnight, and I can go to my room and sleep until 3 a.m. before making rounds again. Still, I am going home because of my suspicions that Sarah said she was going to bed early but did not answer the phone. So, I put my assistant in charge while going out for a dinner break. But I am going home to validate my hunch that Sarah had lied about going to bed early and busting her. I suspected that she wouldn't be there and had gone out to a club or with her friend Becky. As I walked up to the door, I could hear soft music playing. I reached the door, placed my key into the lock, and turned the knob to open the door. A white man was streaking toward one of the back bedrooms, and Sarah was trying to get dressed while apologizing. You do not have to get dressed because of Sarah. I told you not to bring your mess to our home, didn't I? Sarah cries, I am sorry; I did not mean this to happen. I called for the streaking individual to come out, and he did reluctantly. Punching him once, Sarah jumped in between us and received some action. He fell to the floor near the front door as I went into the kitchen to retrieve one of the sharp knives for special occasions. I guess when you catch your wife and another screwing in your home, that could come under the headline of special events.

I intended to kill both Sarah and her lover right there in our home and go back to the hospital and finish out my staff duty detail. I will find them dead when I return home later in the morning and report to the police that I found my wife and another man dead in our home. I would use one of the sharp butcher knives I kept stored in one of the kitchen drawers to carry out my plot. But I could not find one in the kitchen drawer. I thought that Sarah had hidden them from me. But that will not keep me from killing them. I was determined to find a way to settle this matter once and for all, and I will not be a suspect because I was on staff duty. They both fled from our home, and I chased Sarah down as she tried to go where our daughters were spending the night. I was determined to let the last time she saw our daughters before sending them off to spend the night with our babysitter and her son. They were going to be motherless, but they would be okay. She pled for me not to hurt her and that she was sorry and did not intend to hurt me by cheating. No, what she did not expect to happen was getting caught in the act. I still could not find my sharp knives in the kitchen drawer. Finally, I decided to take her back to finish my staff duty tour because I did not want her to get to our daughters and try to run off with them. But then my mind gave me a second plan. While riding back to my place of duty, I would accelerate my car at a high-speed rate and force her to jump from my automobile, thinking that the jump would kill her. She cried and wanted to know what I would do to her as we drove back to the hospital.

My anger had subsided some, and I was able to finish my tour of staff duty. But I screwed my plot when I made her call her mother in the middle of the night and tell her that I just caught her screwing another man in our home. She always sought advice from her mother and her butting into our affairs. I wanted her to know that she had a slut for a daughter. I couldn't stop thinking about my missing knives from the kitchen drawer. Where in the hell were they, and who had moved them? When we arrived back home, I went looking for my knives again, and they were both in the kitchen drawer, where I had always kept them side-by-side. Who came to our home while we were out?

What angered me most was not that she was screwing another man, but she disrespected our home. I was not happy with the cheating; when I caught her in the act, it showed the level of disrespect for me, our children, and the marriage. I recalled our last conversation before leaving home for work that morning. And I asked Sarah directly to her face, are you having an affair. Her reply was no; I am not, Jeremiah. Sarah, whatever you are doing, do not bring it to our home. I proceeded to walk out the door heading for work. God had a way out for me, and killing two worthless individuals was not how he wanted me to dissolve this marriage. Sarah tried to change by going to church and even joining the church. But that did not change her from being the lizard that she was.

I Got This Funny Feeling

A few days later, I came home one evening and found a note on the refrigerator. It read Jeremiah; you know me so well when you looked at me this morning and asked what you up to now? I thought for sure you knew that I was leaving with the girls. She just hit me where it hurt now by running off with the girls and taking them back to Texas to live with her parents of all places. Why would I keep giving this woman a chance after chance?

For one thing, I did not believe in divorce, and I did not want to be a failure by letting my family tell me we told you so. I was someone who would take a dare and challenge you. By the way, Sarah's family and mine lived next door to one another. Of course, my nosy mother, not caring for Sarah, wanted to know what happened. Believe it or not, Sarah decided to say it was because I did not take care of her and the kids, and they were always going hungry without food. I was abusive and ran around with other women. That lie stuck, and people in our old community believed it. My mother wanted to put her two cents in, tried to defend me, and asked that my family not get involved in my and Sarah's affair. We would work things out. I would not talk to my family about what was going on; Sarah created her false narrative.

Sarah's older sister called and asked me what happened between you, and I just told her to ask her sister. But she went a step farther by lying to a couple of her male cousins that I had jumped on her and beat her up because I thought she was cheating on me. So, the two cousins would confront me, and I guess to try and jump me, and they told Sarah's sister their plan. When Sarah's sister told them that was not the truth and that I had walked into our home and found Sarah in bed with a white guy, they turned on her. That might have been a good stress reliever with all the frustration inside me. She does the wrong and places the blame on me. I had God on my side and people in the community who knew me and knew Sarah. Something was not adding up.

I was on leave once and went home to see my girls and spend time with them. I lived in a hotel to not deal with my family's interference. The pursuit of divorce was my affair, and I am adult enough to deal with it in my way. Sarah left for about four months, and the girls. One evening after I had returned home to Maryland, I received a phone call from Sarah, telling me she and the girls were ready to return to Maryland. I also explained that the girls always had a home to come to, but Sarah did not have to and could remain living with her family. But insisting she wanted to return and start over again. There was no more starting over again as far as I was concerned. I had lost all trust in her and hoped to find a way to descend from this marriage that I had high hopes to succeed. That comment probably makes little sense to most because cheating is cheating. Hearing that your spouse is cheating is different from seeing them in action with another man. It was a visual that I could not seem to get out of my head for a long time. A couple of years went by, and we existed, but I was not feeling her. She told me once that when I looked at her, it was like I had x-ray eyes looking clear through her saw me as nothing. That was a good observation and accurate, for the most part.

CHAPTER TWENTY-SEVEN

WARNING
"Whispering Voice Says Keep Walking."

I did my daily Bible reading in my makeshift study closet in my little space one morning. When you love and trust God, you also know that He will never allow you to be harmed by your enemies and those who proclaim love you. He even prepares you for battles ahead of time without you knowing it. If I knew what was on like most, I probably would have attempted to find a way to interfere and mess it up. But trusting God and letting him lay out the battle plan for you is always a better idea. I went through a divorce that I found very painful, but I learned a lot about my relationship with God. Somehow, I kept calm while going through the divorce and custody battle. Everyone believed that I was on the losing side and that the giant, on the other hand, was too great for me to come out victoriously. A message was given to my nine-year-old daughter Dominique warning me how to respond to my enemies. In June of 1989, my daughter Dominique came to me and asked if there was a book in the Bible called James 1:19? I replied that there was a book in the Bible named James. She remained quiet, standing behind me to see if I would read the scripture. I went back to reading the Bible, picking up where I left off before she entered the room. Dominique interrupts me again by asking, daddy, will you read it? So, I turned the pages over to *James 1:19 Wherefore, my beloved brethren, let every man be swift to hear, slow to speak, slow to wrath.* After reading the scripture, I looked at her and asked if I had done or said something to her that would make her think I was angry or upset with her? She said no, someone told me to tell you to read it and turned left the room without saying another word.

Whenever someone brought up Sarah's infidelity during our marriage, I thought it humorous and strange that Sarah and I had

friends who considered themselves our friends, proclaimed to care
a lot about our daughters, helped her go out, and cheated. After
our divorce was over, they all seemed compelled to tell me about
how she used to cheat on me. I was aware of Sarah having affairs. I
didn't have all of the names and places, but I knew she was
unfaithful and thought she would get away with it and never get
caught. Eventually, given enough rope, she would hang herself. I
ask, why in the hell do you think that I care about her cheating after
we have divorced and gone on with our lives?

Joy Is on the Way

It had become a little tradition to take my daughters riding to see
the pretty Christmas lights throughout DC and Maryland. I would
do this while Sarah would be home wrapping Christmas presents
until the girls fell asleep from riding. Also, it meant I had to haul
both into the house when we returned and put them to bed.
Christmas of 1989, and we were out driving around. Like clockwork
and right on time, I could see that my youngest daughter Haleigh
had fallen asleep. Staring back at me in the rearview mirror were
two bright eyes. They belonged to my oldest daughter Dominique. I
asked, what is on your mind, Dominique. Daddy, do you know the
story about Dry Bones in the Bible? She gave me her rendition of
Ezekiel and the valley of dry bones. She explained how the valley
was full of bones and that they were dry, and they reconnected,
from the toe bone to the foot bone to the ankle bone, and so on. Her
version concludes that when all the bones rejoined, they came to life,
made happy sounds, and lived forever.

To the Land Called Morning Calm

We existed until I received orders reassigning me to Korea for a one-year hardship tour. When I received the Official Military Orders for Korea, I was so ready to go where, in the past, I would try and get out of leaving my children. A Colonel I worked for wanted to get me out of the assignment by convincing my branch manager to cancel my orders. The colonel was messing with my plans to suit his schedule, and I wanted to finish Sarah Ford's test. When I learned of him behind the back scheme, I went back and put my name back on the readily available for a permanent change of station list. I wanted to go and get away from Sarah because seeing her each day made my heart fill up with hatred. I said I had forgiven her for the last time I caught her cheating on me, but I think this one stuck in my heart to the point I could think of little else but how much I hated her. And if we were together, I believed the harder it was to forgive her and move on with my life. I did not want to hold hatred in my heart for the mother of my children because I served a better God than to allow myself to be a bitter person. I believed that this would prove whether our marriage had a chance or not to make it. I did not think so for my money, and the sad part was our daughters were caught up in the middle of this mess. Leaving my girls for a year indeed would be a real hardship and painful to endure. I needed to move on for the sake of saving my soul. I needed to forgive my enemy. I needed to settle this matter once and for all.

I left for Korea in February, and our marriage was over in June. I had already been alerted by the Holy Spirit in a message delivered by my daughter Dominique. It prepared me for the outcome without either knowing she informed me of the things to come and how I should respond in James 1:19. Before receiving orders for Korea, I never wanted to leave my children. I was excited to be going for some odd reason. And I wanted to be free of Sarah by ridding myself of this embarrassing blunder that I had made by marrying her. I knew that she could not handle being open and with me ten thousand miles away. This rat was going to play while the cat was away. The idea that everyone has some good in them did not apply to her in my eyes. And yet, I believed that she was a decent person in heart, just not for me as a wife. After that April night affair, she had finally reached a breaking point with me. This move is far better than catching her again and plotting how to kill her and her lover. I am happy I did not kill her the night I witnessed her in the act of adultery. Today I enjoy freedom and happiness at the same time by getting rid of her through a divorce. I have a clean conscience, liberty, and the opportunity to rear my daughters alone. I believe because of my faithfulness and obedience to God.

I received the kind of blessing and peace of mind that God had in store for me.

I never wanted to get so angry again that I would like to kill another human being for cheating or being unfaithful in marriage. I would have been surprised if Sarah remained faithful to our family while serving overseas. And on cue, Sarah could not contain herself. Less than six months after I was in Korea, I phoned her to ask if she loved me. Her response was I love you, but I am not in love with you. My advice was to start divorce proceedings sign the papers without contesting the divorce. When I came home for my mid-tour leave, she had not filed for the divorce but had managed to get both cars repossessed, overdrew our bank account, lost our home, and messed up the minds of two very loving little girls.

I am proud of myself, but more importantly, I thank God for giving me the strength to resist the temptations I faced in Korea. Despite my freedom and knowing the kind of wife I had left back in the

United States, I still did not violate my marriage vows by having an affair. A whole year in Korea, I remained faithful to God and the institution of marriage. I continued to stay committed to the institution of marriage until we were officially divorced.

I remember receiving a letter from my nine-year-old daughter once while stationed in Korea. She begged me to let her come and live with me in Korea. And I could not understand this at all. Our daughters loved us equally and would not mind staying with their mother. At the same time, I completed my overseas military tour. She wrote the entire lyrics to Bobby McFarren's song in the letter. *Do not Worry; Be Happy.* My wife, her mother, had moved another man into our home and told my girls that I had abandoned them and was not coming back. I thought it was because she just liked the song. How does one leave someone, and you said you watched their plane take off from Reagan International Airport? Things are starting to make sense to me now. I wanted to do something, but I was not allowed to because I finally realized that I was in Korea to watch God do his work without interfering. He will tell you what you need to know when he wants you to understand it.

1.   My first warning came when Dominique asked me to read James 1:19 and that somebody had told her to tell me to read it. Things were going to go wrong. The Holy Spirit forewarned me through my daughter not to get angry or seek to take matters into my own hands by striking back.

2.   Secondly, I have assured the victory and that God would rejoin my daughters and me. It was over between their mother and me. When the war is over, I will celebrate the side after the battle.

3.   And third, let God use whomever and whatever to get word to you to protect you from the incoming rounds. I lost my bed, wife, and money, but I needed to be happy and not worry.

I Allowed God to Destroy my Enemies

Early one evening, I had fallen asleep. I had one of the weirdest dreams involving me, a large white dog trying to attack me. I could see myself walking in a deep ravine. Still, I could also see Sarah and my two daughters sitting on a giant tree stump, hugging each other coldly and afraid. The girls hugged her tight, saying no one would find us before freezing to death. The sun was starting to set, and their mother said, do not worry, your father will come and save them. I continued walking along the ravine, crying and praying to God to help me find my children. But each time I attempted to come out, the white dog would charge toward me with his mouth wide open to attack me. I continued walking, praying, and crying to God, asking him to save my children. And lying on the ground in front of me were two brand new handles on the push broom. Picking one up, I tried to leave the ravine again, and the dog charged for attacking me again. When I raised the handle to strike the dog, he retreated but started to walk upright like a man. I could see a smile on his face even though I was chasing him from behind. As he walked away from me-I attempted to strike him with the handle. Still, he slithered back and forth between the trees with the movement of a snake, taunting me by saying, you cannot hit me, and I got your wife, and you will never get her back. At this time, I had awakened from the dream and decided to call my wife.

I needed to ask one question and only required one answer. Sarah uttered I love you with a long pause if she still loved me, but I am not in love with you. I advised her to start divorce proceedings and sign the divorce papers without any problem. She did not, and I suspect that drugs had something to with her not filing for the divorce. And perhaps she figured that she had money to support her drug habit and her new lover if we were married. I never understood why she would move another man into our home drive our cars by parading this so-called man over our daughters. In September, I went home on my mid-tour leave to get things started after the divorce. I suffered from jet lag for most of the time I was there; she was asleep when I was awake and vice-versa. Still, she was not interested, yet I did not know that a man was lying in my bed while I was away serving my country. So, I did not want to spend all my time with a lawyer because I wanted to spend time with my girls and have a little crazy fun like we did before I left. Nothing got accomplished, and I returned to Korea and started my short-timer calendar.

I wrote my girls' letters and called to speak to them only. It became unbearable was when communications between my girls and me were cut off. I wanted to hear their voices on Christmas day since this was the first time I would not see their excited little faces on a Christmas morning. I phoned home to wish them a Merry Christmas, and I got the message that the telephone was not in service. Thinking that I had possibly misdialed the number, I tried again. I got the same result after wondering how I would get the chance to speak with my daughters at Christmas. I called my neighbor Tommie Winston and asked if he knew what was happening at my home? I tried to reach my house phone but received a message that our phone was no longer in service. With a deep sigh, Tommie says to me, Jeremiah, of all the days for you to call, that woman packed up and moved out the day after Thanksgiving and has not been seen since by anyone.

I explained to my First Sergeant, and there was a situation at home. And I needed to request emergency leave to fly home to Temple Hills, Maryland, outside of Washington, DC. I had left my family before the permanent change of duty to Korea. Ten thousand miles away from my daughters, and it was very troubling not knowing how they were doing. While sitting on the plane at Kimpo Airport in Seoul, waiting for the flight to take off, nothing but the worst things floated through my mind, not about Sarah but our children. I recalled a gentleman sitting on the seat next to me, and I guess that he sensed my anxiousness for the flight to start. I would open my Bible, read scriptures, and pray that nothing had happened to my children. The gentleman spoke to me calmly and said, you look worried. I replied that it was just something at home that I needed to check on their well-being. He said, matter-of-factly, everything will be alright when you get home. It was a thirteen-hour flight, and we said absolutely nothing else to each other the rest of the plane ride. My prayer to God was that I do nothing that would not reflect him, and if he leads, I will follow.

Finally, the plane lands at Reagan International Airport in DC. I have not experienced such a lonely feeling since Annie transferred to school during our senior year of high school. Something hit me as I started to walk through the tunnel. I realized that no one was waiting to meet me at the end of the tunnel. I have no home to go to because she has lost our home. I have no car to drive me because she has let both of our cars get repossessed. Before leaving Korea, I tried to get money from my bank account, but none. I had to borrow airline fare from a friend. All these feelings and anxieties I was having were identical to when Annie betrayed me by breaking my heart multiple times. I will be all right because I have a doctorate in broken hearts. I am battle-ready and war-tested for the fights ahead. The first fight was finding my daughters and knowing that they were alright.

Sarah knew how much I loved my girls and would die for them so that she could not have picked a worse! I was okay with us going our separate ways. Our wedding was dead before leaving for Korea. Sarah would have had to make a complete turn-around in her life for us to continue the sham of a marriage. I was not afraid of being alone or feeling lost. I had this happy and anxious feeling of wanting to move on as fast as possible and put the past thirteen years behind me. She could not care about me or my marriage based on her history, and our children did not matter. Just keep walking. The past attempts to save the union with Sarah was ending. I finally realized that the energy wasted trying to continue in a sham marriage was all for nothing. So, I would only be fighting for what I loved and wanted. That was to get full custody of my daughters Haleigh and Dominque, a final divorce from a miserable person to herself and others.

I called a couple of my friends who were still living in the area and told them that I was back in the country and looking for Sarah and my daughters. The next day I visited my children's last school to see if they were still attending. When I learned they were no longer enrolled in school, their mother said they were moving back to Texas, but I did not believe that for a moment. I contacted her closest friend to see if she knew where Sarah was living. She denied knowing exactly, but Sarah had mentioned something about moving into an apartment across from Air Force Base. So, my friend John, whose wife sent him to stay with me and not allow me out of his sight, drove down a side street, and we spotted Sarah and my two girls walking down the sidewalk. We rolled up beside them, and I got out wanting to hug my daughters, and they took off at a full sprint as if they were racing Jessie Owens, running away from me. What the hell? As if I was some evil man that was going to harm them. They eventually returned and waited for their mother to tell them to hug their dad. I informed Sarah I would give her the freedom she wanted and seek custody of our daughters and out of her life. For some reason, she thought that I was pursuing her instead of realizing I needed to know my daughters were safe. I left my girls with this crackpot (no pun intended) for almost a year to get away from her.

I lived with John and Martha for a short time. The girls would come by to visit me. I asked them why they ran from me when they first saw me. They responded that Mama told us you would kill us when you see us again. That was a real kick in the family jewels, and I loved those girls way too much to hurt them. Even if they turned their backs on me, I would not stop loving them. Now it is personal. She tried turning my children against me so that she could be free of me, and that was not necessary. It was not about us being bad parents. It was about us being in a lousy marriage that needed dissolving.

Proverbs 25:21-22 If the enemy is hungry, give him bread to eat; and if he is thirsty, give him water to drink. 22. For thou shalt heap coals of fire upon his head, and the Lord shall reward thee.

CHAPTER TWENTY-EIGHT

GOD SENT HIS ANGELS

Many kind people helped me throughout this ordeal, including my pastor, teachers, friends, taxi drivers, and total strangers. After finding Sarah and the girls, she ups and moved from that location, going into hiding again.

IT WAS A MIRACLE when I told people that I was homeless but never slept on the street. I did not have a car, and I did not have to walk. I had no money but was not broke before leaving the United States, departing Korea. I was back in the country, I needed to talk to my spiritual leader, so I visited with my pastor. After we had talked for quite a while, he prayed for me. He gave me some spiritual advice on how to handle Sarah. He even suggested that this could be like Hosea and Gomer's situation. He said you know God instructed him to get her and bring her home. I told my pastor I sure hope God does not ask me to do that because I do not want her back. We chuckled for a moment at my response. Pastor Williams reaches into his desk drawer, hands me a check, takes this, and finds you a place to stay. He picked up some car keys from his desk to the church van, used them if you needed to, and got back on your feet. I was able to take out a loan to cover the bad checks Sarah had written and put into my bank account from my pay. Of course, we no longer had a joint bank account because I had her removed.

Meanwhile, more blessings and God put the right people around me; I discovered that she had placed the girls in a school in Capitol Heights, Maryland. One of my church members, a superintendent, explained that it was a law in Maryland that kids could not be out of school for days. If she places your girls in a Prince Georges County school, I will know it and let you know which school. I showed up at my daughters' school, and a confrontation took place where the police came onto the scene. I followed all the directions from my superintendent friend. I went to the school with specific instructions not to cause a stir if the principal refused to allow me to see my daughters. If this happens, she advised me to go to the payphone in the lobby and call her, and she would call and explain the situation to the principal. The principal had lied through his teeth by repeating Sarah's lies. First, the girls were not in school. Then he checked closer and told me that they did attend the school, but I could not see them because I had abandoned them, and their mother was trying to protect them from me. I left the principal's office and called the superintendent as instructed me. She said Deacon Ford, wait there, and get this straightened out immediately. From his office, the principal came running after me. Your children are here and about to get out of school, are picked up on the north end of the building, you can meet them there, yeah!

He received a call from my superintendent friend, I thought to myself. A sign hanging behind the secretary's desk caught my eye in that school. It said *a mistake is not a mistake unless you refuse to erase it.* Keep walking. Despite all the cheating, I do not blame Sarah for our marriage failure. I hate that she allowed her family to tear me down by telling lies that she knew were untrue. And anyone that knew me would have said he loves and care for his wife and daughters, and he would never hurt them. We had a few other run-ins and heated discussions about our daughters before she realized that it was not about me wanting her back. She could not seem to get into her little pea brain that my chase was about knowing our daughters' whereabouts and not about her.

I never asked her to come back to me, nor did I want her again. I just wanted two individuals, my girls. One argument involved the police coming onto the scene. She was acting a natural fool, talking about I was harassing and stalking her. I think she hoped her new beau would intervene, and we ended up in a fight. Lord, if only that could have happened. At this point in our relationship, I would never fight for nor over her. I was going to fight for my girls. Anyone that thought so little of them that they would allow a mother to spend money on drugs their father worked and earned for their health and welfare. At this incident, she told me that the girls I watched being born into this world and had cared for all their lives were not my children.

I was stunned for a moment but rebounded and said that they are my dependents, and I need to know where they are, and their well-being will always be of utmost importance to me. When the officers asked who had custody of the girls, she lied and said she had it. The officer asked for the custody papers. Then she decided to change the lie by saying I abandoned her and the girls. Slight problem: she forgot to tell the officer that she and our daughters drove me to the airport and left for Korea. I did not run out on them; I had orders for Korea for one year. The officers realized Sarah was not truthful. I was escorted off to the side by one of the police officers. He suggested I go to Upper Marlboro to see a judge getting a Pendente Lite Custody Order to get my daughters' temporary custody. The following day, I could not seem to get out of my apartment without forgetting something and going back inside several times.

The third time I went back in, my telephone rang, and it was Sarah. I had given the girls my phone number if they ever needed to call me. Hey Jeremiah, this is Sarah. The girls want to know, can they come and spend the weekend with you? What girls, I asked?

Dominique and Haleigh, she replied. I reminded her that she stated they were not my children, so why would I keep someone else's children? You know that they are your children. I just wanted to hurt you. Well, damn, running off and hiding out with them was not hurtful enough. Losing our cars and home and overdrawing our bank account to the tune of $5000.00 plus fees was not enough. Oh! And by the way, she was writing hot checks on base as well, stuff that could have very easily ended my military career.

February 1, 1991, Sarah dropped off Dominque and Haleigh and never returned to pick them up. When those two girls jumped out of the car she was driving, they flew into my arms through the opened patio door on the apartment, and we hugged and kissed as we used to. She left them and did not return to pick them up. It did not take long for them to become their old selves, raiding the refrigerator and eating all the junk food their stomach could hold. It broke my heart when Haleigh, my youngest daughter, told me that they could not eat food from the refrigerator where Sarah lived. Everyone wrote their names on the food containers. They had never had those kinds of restrictions placed on them before, and it saddened my heart that Sarah would allow them to live in unsafe conditions.

I called my lawyer and informed him that she had dropped the kids off a week ago and never returned to pick them up. He advised not to pressure her about not returning to pick up our daughters. He instructed me to keep them and then my daily business. And after six months, we would file abandonment with the court on my behalf. I lived on pins and needles, hoping that she would not come back, upsetting the girls' lives. She did not return to pick them up. She would ask to see them during this time, and I had no problem. She attempted to drag our children into the middle of the mess. Still, it was between the two of us moving on and fighting for the best opportunity for our children going forward.

The Raising of Latch Key Kids

I lived in Suitland, Maryland. She had enrolled them in a school in Capitol Heights, Maryland, two different school districts, and February 1991. The school year ended in June. Again, one of my superintendent friends advised me to petition the Capital Heights school district superintendent to allow my daughters to finish out the school year. I would be responsible for dropping them off and picking them up every day. Another angel appears; Mrs. Vincent, son, and husband were on the Deacon Board with me. She had an office down the street from the school. Renae and Chuck volunteered to pick the girls up for me in the evening and allow them to stay at her office until I got off work. If she were not available, she would get the son's wife, Renae, to pick them up for me. Because I had to go to work early in the morning, Renae agreed to pick them up in the morning for me at my apartment. They were latchkey kids with some guidelines that they must follow. I explained that I had to trust them to do what I told them to be safe. We had strict rules. 1. Call me when you are leaving for school. 2. Make sure the security alarm is on. 3. Call me when you get in from school. 4. Set the security alarm, and I will see you in about an hour.

Whenever I had staff duty overnight at Walter Reed, Mrs. Alston, my secretary, would take the girls home with her to spend the night. I would take them to school the following day. When they were out of school, I would bring them to work, and we would also have a blast there.

I was able to attend field trips and school outings with my girls. One time I wanted to see how my oldest daughter was behaving. I put them on the bus. I then rushed to her school to sit in the classroom when she walked through the door because I wanted to know how my kids behaved when they were out of sight. My youngest daughter was more like me and just wanted to be left alone. While school was out for the summer, I needed to enroll in Suitland before the next school year. We now needed to set up our latchkey guidelines for the summer and start school again.

I needed to get divorce papers served to her. My attorney and I put a plan together to get the documents in her warm little hands. Although she acted like everything was alright between us, I remained calm. After a few attempts by the processor failed previously, I was determined to rid myself of this mistake by marrying her. I never refused to allow Sarah to talk to the girls, so I put a phone line in their room so that I did not have to speak to her, and if she wanted to call them or phone her, they were free to do so. My only objection was that whatever went on in my home was none of their mother's business. And whatever went on where Sarah was living was none of my business, unless someone harms or touches them, then I do not want to know about it.

When it was clear that the girls would be staying with me, I promised them that the home we were living in was just for the three of us. This promise I kept until Ruth and I got married in 1996. I will never have another woman living with whom I am not married.

Anyway, Sarah had asked to pick the girls up on a Saturday, and I agreed. The plan was my lawyer would have the server wait at my apartment until Sarah returned later that night with the girls and serve divorce papers to her at that time. Finally, she returned with the girls, and the server walked out with me to her car. I asked

Sarah if she remembered him. She replied no, and he said, yes, you do, and I had something for you and handed the papers to her. When the processor gave her the documents, she looked at them and realized I was finally going to get my day in court so that I would rid myself of her for good. Her response was, *I do not want this,* and she threw the paper to the ground while calling me a couple of nasty names. I was so happy, and I could not sleep that night; this kind of joy was right up there with the night Annie and I fell in love with each other. How ironic this time it was because I had fallen out of love. Finally, in April of 1992, we appeared in court for our divorce and child custody hearing. When we eventually appeared in court, the judge granted our divorce petition. But he saw fit to give Sarah more time to seek counsel and respond to the court why she had not responded to any of its notices.

I had to travel to San Antonio, Texas, for a course from May through July, which meant the girls would have to go with me as well. The judge granted me the authority to take the girls out of state. While there, I received a note to call my attorney when I returned from class. I made the call expecting something terrible like the judge had decided to grant Sarah custody of the girls. Instead, he said, Mr. Ford, and I have a great Father's Day gift for you. *You were given full guardianship of your daughters by the judge, with no rights or visitation to the mother.* God, I was so happy, and now I can start working on the next phase of my life – raising my daughters as a single parent. I am free from loving someone I could not trust and who used me more years than she loved me, not that she ever cared about me. I do not have to deal with the lie. I caused her to become a cheater and a liar — funeral Arrangements for Jeremiah & Sarah, Sunrise May 5, 1979 – Sunset April 14, 1992. I do not have to see her anymore to remind me of the night I walked in on her and another man in our home having sex. I can now bury all Sarah had cheated on me from Oklahoma to Maryland. It appears no one was off-limits because she did my so-called good friend that lived in our home when we lived in Ohio. Distancing myself from this nightmare of thirteen years will be a pleasure. I think the craziest question ever asked me regarding rearing my daughters was, how will you raise two girls by yourself? My response was simple; anything you make, love, and care about, you should not have a problem taking care of your children. Still, I love my babies the same as when they were little girls.

CHAPTER TWENTY-NINE

THE TALK

As a father, if you have sons, you look forward to having a particular talk with them about growing up and the changes their bodies will go through and into manhood. I raised two girls as a single dad, and there are some challenging talks I had to have with my daughters about the changes their bodies would go through and on into womanhood. One such conversation involved talking with my daughter during her first period. But I must say that I was more relaxed than when I tried to explain death to her. Their self-adopted sister Precious and nickname Putt-Putt passed when she was incredibly young. It was a tough time for the girls and the grownups who knew Precious. They loved this little girl, and she loved them as well. Precious had some medical problems and eventually succumbed to them. Our first mistake was telling them that Putt-Putt was asleep and would live in Heaven. Their central question was, will she still be able to visit Putt-Putt when she goes to Heaven? They were alright throughout the funeral services. And one of Precious's uncles and I served as pallbearers and carried her out to the gravesite. They saw Precious in her tiny casket asleep. Things became a problem when they lowered Putt-Putt's coffin into the grave, throwing dirt in on the grave. Trying to keep them composed did not become a problem until her Putt-Putt started to shovel in the soil. My daughters came unglued, especially my youngest daughter; she did not want dirt thrown on top of Putt-Putt. She was emphatic when saying, *do not throw that dirt on our baby, do not put that dirt on my Putt-Putt.* I loved the little lady, also. She enjoyed me raising her leg and dropping it, as she would lift it over and over to let me know to do it again. You get the message. Finally, tell them about death, and Precious's sleep was called death. Putt-Putt was going to a much better place so that she would never hurt or be sick again. I asked which would rather, Putt-Putt be in pain or no pain? They both agreed and said, we do not want our baby hurting. So, Precious dying, all her problems will go away forever. They never forgot Precious, and even today, they still talk about their Putt-Putt.

Rearing Girls

I wanted to finish allowing my girls to be reared in a loving home without hatred in my heart for their mother. When you say the moments will come, things begin to happen if you are a male. There is no manual or hotline for you to refer to or use when faced with the mother's side questions. I cannot count the number of times when one of my daughters would come into my bedroom crying from a nightmare. I would place a blanket or quilt beside my bed and lay on the floor, giving up my bed to assure them that I was near. There were a couple of awkward moments for me that I remember. One situation I recall vividly, like when my oldest daughter started her period. I think it was more embarrassing for her than it was for me because I knew that time would eventually come and had read a couple of little pamphlets about it. I remember her calling me at work, and I could tell something was going on or had happened because there was a different sound in her voice. I knew something was bothering her, not in the wrong way, but as if she needed to ask a question. I was at work when she called. Daddy, I started my school period today, and the school nurse told me I needed to let you know. I interrupted her briefly to say, go into my bedroom and look on the shelf in the back of my closet, you will find what you need, and we will talk when I get home this evening. Okay? She replied, thank you, daddy. Later that evening, after I arrived at the apartment the three of us shared, we did talk about becoming a woman. I was now serving in both capacities and doing what I thought I knew about girls coming into womanhood. I do not know whether the talk was as thorough and correctly stated, but we talked. I explained that this was a natural part of growing up and becoming a young lady and never feeling ashamed and afraid to come and speak to me about anything. Daddy will try and find the answers to the questions that I do not know the answer to. Thank you, daddy; I love you.

Another Broken Promise

Now that I am free, I must try and get the girls accustomed to our new life, so everyone would know their responsibilities and how things will be going forward. I learned to accept Sarah's inability to be faithful and dependable. I feel that I never went out of my way to put her in a negative light before our girls. No matter how much I despised her for wasting thirteen years of my life, I failed to promise the girls or disappoint them. I needed a lot of prayer and restraint to refrain from just lambasting her. There were a few occasions when Sarah would cross the line for some reason. And one time, Sarah tried to dictate how I raised the girls and did not provide any support. It would be an understatement to say that Sarah and I had a different perspective on the value of getting a good education.

I could not accept the girls just saying they could not do something without putting forth their best effort. Sarah, the carefree mother, told the girls they did not have to work hard in school if they did not want to. And she was going to come and get them to live with her. I asked if they wanted to go and live with their mother. They each said yes. I was both hurt and disappointed that they would like to go back to live under the conditions described. I refused to show hurt or anger for their decision. I did show arrogance because I knew Sarah would find a way to disappoint them, but I would not stand in their way of living with their mother. They packed all their clothes, including putting some of them in trash bags because their mother was coming to get them that evening. With their clothes in the plastic trash bags, they waited for days for their mother to show up. She never showed up, and I could see the hurt look on their faces.

Candy Parent versus the Vegetable Parent

Finally, after a week, I sat them down and shared with them how much they meant to me and that I would never let them down, and all that I wanted for them was the best. With that said, I won't accept less than the best effort in school. You can continue calling this your home, or you can continue to wait for your mother to come and get you. Your clothes are still in the trash bags in the living room; you have a choice of homes and parents. You can place your clothes back in your rooms and in drawers and closets where they belong. We also discussed our living arrangement and why a woman would never live with us if not married. I respect both of you, and this is the home for three people. I intentionally never involved our children in what was going on between their mother and me. I never used them to hurt Sarah, like refusing to see or talk to them. And to this day, twenty-five-plus years after Sarah and I divorced, I have yet to put down the mother of my daughters or even accuse her of ruining our family. All I ever said to them is, if you ever want to know what I think happened to cause your mother and me to get a divorce, you can talk to me, and I will tell you my side of the story. Your mother will have to speak for herself.

I attempted to use the analysis of candy and vegetables. I will insist that you eat more vegetables than candy because I am looking out for your good health to sustain you a lifetime. And mom is the candy parent, a short-time satisfaction but could have long-term detriment. My daughter received the lesson when she became a single mother after a divorce. She told me that she explained that she was the vegetable parent and not the candy one. We have never talked about why their mother and I divorced because they never asked me about what happened. So, it was not that important to them and me anyway, and for what? We both got what we wanted, one thing, and that was freedom. I got the better end of the deal; I could rear my daughters and know they were safe. That meant all the world to me.

CHAPTER THIRTY

FORGIVE, AND MOVE ON

Since my and Sarah's divorce, we have apologized to each other. I apologized to her for whatever I did to her that would make her think that I did not love her or wanted her in my life, I was sorry, and I asked Sarah for forgiveness. She apologized and said that she was relieved because she wondered if *I would forgive her or if she would ever get a chance to apologize*. It is always cordial when we cross paths, and I wish her well. Even after things went awry between us, I still defend her against friends and family when they speak ill of her in a way that will hurt my daughter's feelings. I try and explain that she is the mother of my children. Even for me, to say hurtful things about their mother would hurt them, and I would never want them hurt from mean things said about their mother by me or anyone. I have gone out of my way to do so. But the same wasn't accorded me by members of Sarah's family. I never cheated on her, not even when we were apart. During my entire stationed in Korea, I remained faithful despite having many opportunities and reasons. I respected God, her, and the institution of marriage. I focused on myself when things ended between Annie and me; she had created the blueprint for moving on and making lemonade when given lemons. Unlike all the times that I repeatedly tried to revive the dead relationship between Annie and me. I would not try to restore a marriage that had run its entire course because we both had worn out our welcome.

I do blame Sarah for the demise of our marriage. But I placed more of the blame on me because she tried hard to show herself by revealing who she was, and I refused to accept that person. I will always believe that she was a decent person. Still, we should not have been much more than platonic friends with occasional benefits. Good conversations do not make a good marriage. History was bound to repeat itself because I did not learn from Annie's first lesson. The erratic behavior was telling me that she was not mine to keep. Sarah confirmed who she was from the beginning to the end of our marriage; I did not want to believe her. The end.

The role of being a single parent meant I had to go on field trips and school outings with my girls. I visited my oldest daughter's school because I wanted to see how she behaved entering the classroom. I wanted to know how my kids behaved when they were out of my sight. I saw them on the bus and rushed to her school so that I could be sitting in her class when she walked through the door. My youngest daughter is more like me and wants to be left the hell alone, and we will get along merely okay.

The Result of a Hard Head

My grandmother had a saying, *"there are two things that you should never argue with, one a posted sign and the other a fool."* forewarned that Sarah was a bad character and would not be a wife that I could trust. When Sarah and I were married, one of the things that we disagreed about was that she hung out with single women and went to the club. She had friends that made house calls, job visits, and obscene phone calls. I said to her that her friends wanted what you have got. And her response was none of my friends wants you; nobody wants you. I was not talking about them wanting me, but they were looking for a husband to love them, provide for them, and do the kinds of things that I did for her. So, once our divorce was final, I was officially free to date whomever I wanted.

One night I attended a church meeting, one of the ladies stopped me; Deacon Ford, can I talk briefly. I did not know what we must speak of, but I agreed to talk with her. She started her sentence by saying that this lady here at the church wants to talk to you badly. Can I have your telephone number to give to her? She is a lovely lady. Well, I do not know who she is, and are you sure she meant me? Yes. I was having a problem with another female church member who was harassing my girls and me. She even had the nerves to hold my kids captive after church one Sunday so that I would have to go through her to get my children. I almost lost my religion on that one but tried explaining to her once again that I was not interested. Of course, it must be my daughters that I want as girlfriends.

Are we going to go there? I just was not into her and did not want to mislead her to think that there was a chance of us ever getting together. It was awkward explaining that I was not interested and please leave my daughters and me alone. But, back to the other lady, I finally relented and agreed to give my phone number to pass on to her friend. The lady called me that night; we had a pleasant conversation. She was lovely, and by now, after being divorced for about a year. I decided that I was ready for a relationship I had not had in thirteen years. We dated for about two months, and I could not go further. Nothing wrong with her; it was me. Whenever the girls spent the weekend with their mother, Evelyn, or whomever, I spent weekends and nights together at my home or theirs counting sheet threads. During pillow talk, Evelyn shared that other women in the church were interested in me before knowing I was married to Sarah. They wondered why I was married to Sarah. At first, I attended church alone, and when she appeared, she said they were disappointed. Anyway, Evelyn and I could not make or did not make it to the next level. She was a lovely lady but a no-go. The time must have been up because the voice telling me to keep walking was heard loud and clear. And this was one of Sarah's friends that did not want me.

Then, the next one was someone I liked for a moment until she lied to me, and I saw her do something that disgusted me. She publicly belittled her ex-husband before their sons and did not seem to care; it upset them. She tried to influence me to stay in the relationship by bribing sex. One night I was relaxing watching television and heard this banging on my door. It sounded like the cops! I looked out the peephole to see who it was, and she was not going away. Fortunately, my girls were not home and spent the weekend with their mother. But I thought it odd that she was wearing a raincoat in the summertime and it was not raining or cold. A lot of strange thoughts ran through my mind. I wondered if she was carrying a weapon or something? I knew her from the church, and we have always been cordial and friendly toward one another. So, finally, I decided to open the door. Immediately upon her stepping in, slamming the door behind her, the overcoat dropped. Oh, mama. She had a weapon alright and was fully loaded and cocked. I guess this must be her birthday because mine was not until January. She demanded satisfaction and refused to leave until I met her demands. Since I am no longer married, I now take walk-ins. It just so happened, I had an opening, and so I could see this walk-in. This relationship lasted all about two months. Keep walking is starting to sound like a theme song.

Next was CJ, who lived in Washington and worked for a radio station. We talked long distance, mostly, which was nice because I was not searching for anyone to marry or go steady. So, I wanted to see her for Christmas before moving to Massachusetts in January. This was the worst of all the relationships I was involved in after Sarah divorced. This woman was a phony and the worst sexual partner I **EVER** had in my life. Blah! I will say no more except that when she boarded the plane back to California, bye-bye birdie as far as I was concerned, forever.

When I was in Korea, I met Ann, a single woman, a virgin, and wanted to marry and have children someday. I was married, and Ann and I were only talking friends, intellectual with absolutely no benefits. She seemed intent on sharing many of her dreams with me about her future. I was going through a rough time and tried to bide my time in Korea to end my marriage with Sarah. I regretted not driving up to North Carolina and enjoying Christmas with Ann and her family against my better judgment. I never shared this with Ann because I did not want any influence or encouragement. Not that she would have attempted to do so. Ann's new duty station was in Virginia when we returned to the United States. I was back at Walter Reed in DC. Now we hooked up again, and we have become a regular couple. She would drive down to Maryland some weekends, and I finally introduced her to my girls, which I was always against doing. They seemed to like her vice-versa. I needed to come clean with her about something that affected her plans in life. I did not want any more children, and I would not get into something through pretense. We drove to Canada and had a lovely time.

I was getting reassigned to Massachusetts in January. She was about to be shipped to Germany about two weeks prior. I headed to Massachusetts for my third Special Duty Assignment when I should have only had one during my entire military career. I asked not to be reassigned to another Special Assignment since this was my third assignment. Nine months later, I retired from the military and moved back to Texas. Ann wanted me to visit her in Germany, but I could not because my girls were raised and cared for. Then, how about you and the girls moving to Germany? That will not work, and I finally had to come clean with her about my feelings for her, which were genuine.

Still, I did not want any more children. It would be unfair to her to be in a relationship with someone who did not share her dreams, and having children was something that she wanted. My daughters had gone through enough already, and I was not about to uproot them again, even though I would have enjoyed being with Ann in Germany. I regret not telling her when we had the opportunity to talk face-to-face; she was deserving of better. She was a beautiful person whose situation had been different, and I had not gained custody of my daughters, who knows. Besides, nothing was going to make me break a promise to my oldest daughter. In the military, you move a lot. She had never graduated with a single class she started from kindergarten through the eighth grade. I promised that she would get the opportunity to begin her first year with the kids she would graduate with her senior year. I kept that promise.

In 1978-1979, I struggled with loneliness and wanted to have someone in my life full-time. I did not just contemplate marriage; I entered matrimony. Thirteen years later, I was free of the worst mistake in my life. My punishment was for being stupid enough to believe that I could change someone just by being kind to them and placing their needs and wants ahead of all of yours. This time I was happiest at home alone. I had come full circle. This time I would not look to Annie for comfort because I understood that we were not suitable for each other as we thought. I was not looking for love and was not looking ever to marry again. I remember a conversation that I once had with my friend Peter. I shared with him that I had found something that I had lost and did not realize. I found my smile again; I saw reasons for laughter and was free of being embarrassed and laughed at behind my back. I pledge that no one else would ever break my heart because I will always keep a corner for a safe escape. I was never getting married again; my friend Peter admonished me. He shared something with me that I was unaware of, Jeremiah if you do not marry again. That would be unfair to God and some woman who deserves a man like you. Let me tell you, Jeremiah, all the husbands in the community admired you, looked up to you, and how you took great care of your family. Sarah was a fool, and we all disliked her for what she did to you. But my brother, let me tell you what I am impressed by how you remained calm throughout all that you went through, and we are afraid that you would snap and hurt someone. But instead, you live a testimony that you can share, and we can tell others who might have this kind of difficulty. Do not shut that door without God telling you to do so. Then I had the girls worrying about me, and this had gone on a long time, back when we were still living in Maryland, and they spent the weekend with their mother. Sometimes, the girls would tell me, daddy. We hate to leave you here alone by yourself, thinking that I did not have a social life. But I was happy and content; I had my entertainment when they were away and never while they were in the home. It was important not to shack or parade women in and out of our house. I knew that I was not ready to commit to anyone fully, and I needed to learn how to trust again. I did not want a repeat of Annie and Sarah's scenarios.

Because I have two more individuals involved in any future relationships, I may get involved. I knew what I wanted in a woman where, in the past, I had no standards, only imaginations. I knew that I needed to unpack old baggage by not lumping all women into one category. I created a **STANDARD CHART** to identify my standards, and I graded women by observing them. Again, I was not going to make a mistake by giving my heart to someone who was flakey initially. When my daughters were away, I conducted interviews and gave interviews, so I was not lonely as they may have thought. The moral of the story is I tried to win an argument with a posted sign only proved that I was a fool.

CHAPTER THIRTY-ONE

REPAIR AND PREPARE TO REBUILD

My divorce from Sarah was more than a year old, and I had had my run of catching up on a few things, and I was in the right place as far as relationships. I could take or leave them because they were not a priority, only my daughters. If things were not working or I felt the least bit uneasy about the person I was in the relationship with, I moved on. I did not waste time trying to figure out if we could coexist. After my divorce, I believed all my involvement with women to be flexible and non-committal. And they allowed for compromises that could easily withdraw on a whim and only served to help one or both parties to move. It was essential for me to stop using Annie as a revenge factor or a motivational reason to hurt others. I may have damaged some of the ladies I dated before reaching the Promised Land in a wife. When people asked me about my marriage today versus my marriage to Sarah, I merely say that I got rid of a booby prize for a grand prize.

I did what any man should do if he sought to find a pearl. I dug beneath the surface and was not afraid to knock off the sand to see the shiny object beneath the surface. In Ruth, I did just that. Just as I did by digging beneath each ladies' character, I would have had to drill to China to find that pearl in them. Ruth was an easy find; I was just too slow. And I thank God that he kept her for me. All the other ladies had one thing in common; they each had a hidden agenda and told me so without them knowing. It says you are not interested in considering my opinion. It does not matter because it is all about you. If I dated a woman with children, she struggled to make ends meet but spent money on me. I automatically eliminated her, gone-gone, and fast. Women should always place their children's welfare first, not make me happy or a higher priority. I felt something was wrong with her spending money on me instead of her children. I am old-fashioned, not the kind of man who enjoys women purchasing gifts for me. I would never want to be that important to a woman that she needs to feel like her children should be neglected or made second.

After my divorce, every relationship I entered would last only a couple of months. For whatever reason, I could not stay much longer. I did so as a friend, and although we did more than friend things, from my (perspective, I never changed from being friends, although theirs did). Annie had left me hurting and empty so many times, and it was not that I was on a revenge crusade. The voice just kept telling me to keep walking, never allowing me to feel at ease with any of those women.

How far am I to keep walking? I was lazy and had no problem settling down with women like Annie, Susan, Jacqueline, and the like. I remember telling myself that I could deal with every woman I dated after my and Sarah's divorce because I would not give myself up for them. If they wanted to be with me, it had to be ninety percent me and ten percent them. It would come at a hefty price. Yes, I would take good care of them and treat them like a lady and wife if we had gotten that far. Still, the nice guy is stranded on the side of the road holding an empty gas can because he has no more to give in being Mr. Nice Guy. And I could not understand, although the women I dated post-Sarah, were lovely professional women and some Christian ladies. They were all on Jeremiah's short order list of two months to audition and prove worthy of my time, effort, and attention. If they were unable to impress, it was over, done, and I was gone. I would use the friend clause. We always started as friends, then friends with benefits and friends more services. I would tell them that I don't see us going anywhere together beyond being friends. But I thought we were more than friends, they would say. I do not remember us ever saying that we were more than friends. If there is a piece of my past that I dislike or hate, it would be during this time. I had not finished walking, and I needed to get to stepping. And ease on down the road.

Was I being vindictive and trying to punish these women because of a deceitful Denise? Was it because of lying and cheating, Sarah? Was it unfaithful, Annie? But what about loving Dana? My lousy acting has no justification. I do not like myself because I see myself as no better than the women who betrayed my love and trust. But I wanted to display Dana Jeremiah. So, I am back on the beach of life again, still digging for an oyster for my pearl.

CHAPTER THIRTY-TWO

NOT THE WINNING PRIZE

Can I pick them? I do not advise anyone to rely on me, choosing the door with the grand prize behind it. So far, I have a success rate of point zero points, nothing regarding finding the right woman. However, the continued picking booby prizes did not discourage me from trying. The voice that told me to keep walking told me to continue digging beneath the sand, that there were many pearls. Because I keep uncovering them, there is one better, prettier, and more to your taste if you keep digging. I found her in the third grade, but she had not fully matured at that time, and God just wanted me to remember to stay faithful to him and patient in his word. He would bring my dream to fruition. I dug too long and on the wrong beach.

The Beginning of a Long Ending

One October morning, I had to leave early to take my annual physical fitness test. Once I finished the test, I returned home but did not want to wake Sarah and the girls up, and I decided best to come through the back door to enter our house, thinking they were still asleep. I tipped past the girl's bedroom and was about to go into our bedroom when I heard my wife's voice, and she was on the phone telling another man that she missed him and loved him and could not wait to see him at work. I am shocked and do not know how to deal with this because I never found out until too late when Annie cheated. I confronted her, and you could see the embarrassing look on her face but not a glimpse of remorse. At first, she tried to lie and say I did not hear what I had heard. She could not hang the phone up before I stepped between her and the receiver. The person on the other end was not too bright either; he did not hang up the phone. When did I say hello? He dared to ask, who is this? I am Sarah, husband, click. She informed him that she was separated and living alone.

My Way Was A Painful Lesson to Learn

No doubt, the warnings people had given me about Sarah were correct, and perhaps I should have listened to them. We transferred to Toledo, Ohio. A few months later, I received orders reassigning me to the Army Recruiting Command as an Army Recruiter. Shortly after Sarah learned the lay of the land, it happened again, Sarah and other men. I cannot explain to her, and I doubt if she could either.

On the one hand, she would appear as loving, caring, and dedicated to our marriage, but also equally unfaithful. Any man that would show her interest, she was in pursuit of that man. After completing my recruiting duty, my duty station was Army Medical Center, Washington, DC. At least I thought that he was my best friend in Toledo, started calling our home disguising his voice, wanting to talk to Sarah. They, too, were having an affair. I was ready for a new life and was genuinely sorry for not trying to understand the voice that kept telling me to keep walking. Married to Sarah was like one of my dad's whoopings. If that voice had said, keep running, I would have broken out in a Jesse Owens sprint until I dropped. I would not stop where I was if the voice told me to keep walking.

CHAPTER THIRTY-THREE

MEETING IN SESSION

There is always someone to remind you of the good times and the bad times. I am still waiting for Annie to provide me with some more input in the book we are writing, and she goes way back to a happier and more loving moment. So, she brings back a happy moment from when we were happy together, and it seemed to be a lifetime ago.

Annie: Recently, I saw an AVON book. I have not seen an AVON book in years. As I looked through the book, I smelled Wild Country. I wish you could have seen the smile on my face and been able to read my mind. You would have asked, why was I so happy? It would have said I am so in love because it was a happy time when I shared the same space as you; I was in a safe place. The Wild Country reminded me of when I used to buy this cologne for you. I could imagine hearing your voice thanking me as if I had given you the world. Jeremiah, you were my world, and I can try to explain or unwind the ball of confusion another lifetime. I would not be able to tell it explicitly. All I know is that I loved you and still do, but not in the way you might think.

Along with you being you, I also adored your voice. I fell in love with it because of the calm it would give me. Just hearing it was always reassuring to me. The letters you wrote to me brought so much joy and happiness into my life; you will never know and probably could never imagine how much. I kept them to read repeatedly, mostly when I felt down, lost, and unloved, and they are my reminders that somebody once loved me. I thought marrying other men on a whim would duplicate that love we discovered in 1969. Jeremiah, I do not know a day when I don't cry silently. It is daily I ask myself why I cannot have a love like that again. When I had your love, it silenced the chattering that was going on inside my head and made my heart happy with joy. It was the love you gave me unconditionally, and somehow, I managed to repay that love by destroying us. But Jeremiah, I was empty inside. I was decaying long before you and I met. You could only find the right part of me and never the whole person. I know you keep saying, *Annie, no broken chain is ever the same again, even if you weld it back together*. It is a fight not to love you because I know when this venture is over, I will return to the experience of feeling unloved. Also, when you gave me your word, I learned it was a bond, which meant a lot when you said that you would provide me with all the love in your heart. I trusted you with my heart; I wish now that I had dared to believe I could trust you with the secrets I was too ashamed and afraid to share. I have often asked myself why I did not allow you access into space where I was hurting? Because you had made my life so much better. It is easier to talk about my past today than when I was a teenager and in love with Annie. Was it shame or the fear that I would lose you? The evil entity residing there, and I did not want to be subject to the evilness that controlled half of my emotions. I am doing what I should have done today when we were in love by sharing that piece of me that I withheld. I finally told you the painful truth by filling in the blanks in my life and why I ran away from you but could not pull away for good. I see today the kind of man I believed would have fought to help free me from the prison I lived in growing up in Littlefield. Jeremiah, I need you to see my face since I hid some truths from you, and maybe you will know the pain of my confession. Annie, I am not here today to judge you, I want to know whatever you feel necessary to tell me, and if it hurts, I have had pain before. Thank you for telling me that I need not feel like I need to punish myself for my past, but I wonder what your opinion will be after I have finished confessing.

No Love Child with Jeremiah

Finally, I got my wish to go live with my mother and other siblings. It was not a good time for the move; neither did it turn out to be the right move. I must have had a brain fart for a moment because I did not care or think about leaving Jeremiah behind if I were to make such a move. After arriving at my new home, I soon realized that it was worse than when I lived in the country with my grandmother. Alvin Jones, my stepfather, was an alcoholic. After dealing with my grandmother, I must deal with an alcoholic stepfather who enjoyed picking fights with me. Alvin would put me out of the house every time we butted head about anything. And wouldn't you know the one thing he would always bring up is you, Jeremiah, the one person I missed more than anything?

I could not call, write, or see you because Alvin would secretly accuse me of meeting you to have sex. Though he was falsely accusing me, I wished those lies were the truth; I missed you, Jeremiah. Alvin never expressed to me his dislike for you. He never made you feel welcome when you came around — having all my sisters and brothers present and close by to ensure that they would be a part of all our conversations. I understand that you did not have a car or a driver's license to come and see me. Alvin's imagination was the two of us meeting secretly, but something I hoped could be a reality. I had to accept that the best we could do was write me letters. I never answered any of them, a lifelong regret, because I realized the message. I was sending a notice that I no longer loved you. I tried to protect you from the cold treatment by Alvin.

I regret not telling you what I will reveal when it happens. Jeremiah, I terminated a pregnancy by having an abortion, a baby that you and I conceived. I am sure that I had an abortion to do away with the child we made together. A child that I know how you would have wanted to be a part of its life. Jeremiah, I am sure that you cared for Lydia, how the two of you got along, and still do. I heard her calling you daddy, and I got angry because you are not her father. Before the abortion, I was already dealing with a lot of shame. Now I have another secret of dealing with inside my head that I could not tell anyone. My life was a mess, and the only thing that was holding me together was your love, Jeremiah, and I betrayed that also.

I own up to my part for ruining our relationship, first by not telling you the truth that I was pregnant and had an abortion. Secondly, never respond to any of your letters. I know, and you have affirmed that if I had just replied or shared with you the kind of conditions I was living in before living with my mother. Keeping the secret about the molestation was challenging enough. Then I had to lie to you that my pregnancy was a false alarm when, in fact, it was the opposite. I do not know why I allowed my mother and grandmother to convince me to get rid of your child. I cannot count the number of times I wanted to yell it out to you just as I did when I told you that I had been raped and was pregnant. My mother and sister knew Lydia's father was that I was carrying inside my belly. They never suggested anything about me having an abortion. I am happy I did not repeat the same mistake forty-five years ago, but sadder because I made something with someone. I did not love the way I cared for and loved you. I am not comfortable telling you about all the abuse I suffered sitting face to face today like I thought I would be looking at your face. I can see the astonishment on your face. When you speak, I can only imagine your voice having a tone—asking why I did not tell you to tell him that I had an abortion. And it was a baby we made together. You seem disinterested in sexual, physical, and verbal abuse. Perhaps you are numb as I have been most of my life. I just shared a secret with the man that used to love me so much, and now all I can feel is your hatred for me. Jay can be a cold person without saying a word or just a few words whenever you feel hurt or betrayed. I just did both, and why would I expect anything more of you? Jeremiah, when I got my head straight, I no longer tried to find happiness with other men. This one secret, I have lost all chances of achieving the one thing I thought that I had a slim and a bit of hope to warm my body next to yours if only one of your bear hugs. Believe it or not, I found the courage to tell you Jeremiah about this secret in 1978. Still, you had disappeared, and I did not see anyone that knew of your whereabouts. I want to know where was he when I needed you the most at a crucial time in my life?

CHAPTER THIRTY-FOUR

ASHAMED AND AFRAID

Jeremiah, I prolonged telling you the whole story because of the pain from my past guilt. I agree I have hurt you in the past, Jeremiah. I do not want to hurt you anymore or lose a possible future opportunity to continue to talk to each other on occasion as friends. The pain was too hard for me to tell anyone or even talk about when we were lovers. Every time I said that I loved you after the abortion, I wanted to say I love you and the baby I once carried inside me; we made that. My love for you was sincere then, and I know it could be again today. I never stopped loving you until 1994, when you rejected me and accepted my daughter Lydia. I always remember you telling me why you loved Lydia. *Lydia had nothing to do with how she came into this world, and I cared about her. I hoped that care would overshadow the hate and disdain for your uncle, Leonard.* Jeremiah, you must understand that the kind of man you are and the person you were will never be easy for me, not always to want to love you.

At one time, I thought about giving Lydia up for adoption, and as crazy as it sounds, I was hoping that giving my child away would have hurt you somehow. And each time that I would consider doing it, your words would convict me. Jeremiah finally opened his mouth and uttered something that made no damn sense. (**Jeremiah**) *I respect you for telling me that we can never be any more than two ships that have already passed in the night. And I must accept this painful event in your life just as I would with anyone, but this hurts me today as if it just happened. It probably would have been worse if you had told me back when the abortion occurred. So, having this conversation with you does not change my opinion of you, and all I can say is, I forgive you because I must. You could have written this in a letter and taken the coward's way* *out. Telling me to see face and reaction is disturbing, and I will not utter a few expletives. Is it the pain on my face that you wanted to see or one more scheme up your sleeve for Jeremiah?*

You know about the voices screaming and tormenting me mercilessly inside my head, and one of those voices is our baby. I do not know of a day I have not cried since I was young. Screaming for help from anyone and after punishing myself by marrying the wrong men, it was too late for us because you disappeared into thin air. I asked you about writing a book. I wanted to tell my life story because I wanted my children to know more about me. It was so that I could finally share the things I had lied about with you. I want my children to know until after my death, but if they learn the truth before my demise, I want you to write it because I know it will be the truth. You are an essential piece of my life, especially being the first to love me and make love to me. I know that it appears I am stalling, and perhaps I am more nervous than I thought I would be. Could you hold me? I understand why you are continuing to deny the request. As we speak, the voices inside my head tell me I should not tell you about the abortion. When those same voices urge me to do so, Jeremiah, I need rest, what I would do for a clear conscience, if only for one hour. I hope you will see why and understand me more, not that it will matter. I could go on forever.

So precisely, what is the whole story, Annie? I want to know all the details. Jeremiah, where do I start? Do you remember when we thought I was pregnant when we were still in high school, and my mother carried me to the doctor? My grandmother thought I was pregnant also. You seemed intent on knowing if I was ever pregnant by you, and I know I told you that we never conceived a baby together, but that was not true. Another lie gnawed at me because I would not share with you. But I was pregnant after we had sex the second time, and I would hide it from my grandmother if I could. But she knew when my period was due and when it did not come that month. She called my mother, *"I think this gal has got herself pregnant by that boy she's been messing with that boy."* My mother came to take me to see a doctor. I wanted your baby and would have never had an abortion if I could have controlled the matter. I was frightened to be pregnant and happy simultaneously; it was ours but helpless when deciding to abort the pregnancy. My mother and grandmother told me never to say to you. It seemed everyone was in on it except you. When your father told you not to get me pregnant, he knew that I was pregnant because he and my grandmother had talked about it. Had I been allowed to go through with that pregnancy, you would have been a father, and I would have been a mother. I see that smile on your face, but I know that not all your smiles are because you are happy but sometimes upset. I used to hate that I could not read your facial expressions. I cannot read if you are angry, disappointed, or hurt. I loved you and would have enjoyed having your baby, but I had no say-so over my body. My grandmother bought and paid for me, owned by her from birth. I often wonder if I was part of some business deal for future consideration. I was someone's property, and I felt I had no say in my own body. Therefore, I never believed that I had a soul filled with emotions. Jeremiah, I have been in a prison of some kind all my life. Falling in love with you was the only time I felt free. There is no doubt in my mind that I loved you, but I found a way to resent you, just as I dislike my mother, who left me with my grandmother. She never attempted to protect me from my abusers, even when I told her of the bad things that they were doing. When she asked me what they did, I illustrated how my cousin Clyde would rub me with one hand while playing with his private. Her response was, oh! That was the end of the conversation. I never believed that my grandmother was fast asleep drinking too much alcohol when she pretended not to hear me. My voice for help was loud when I tried to get her attention by telling those men to stop touching me get off me. I would cry out. The only time she would speak to me in a kind voice was when I asked if she heard me? You must have been having a nightmare, she replied. No, I was fully awake. She never asked me what the so-called dreams were about because that would mean she had to admit she knew what was going on. Is this what she said when she told my mother that by bought and paid for by her? To be abused and used by the men in my family? Was she receiving payment from these men who seemed to enjoy pleasuring themselves when using me to satisfy their sexual desires? They were my grandmother's age, except my uncle, Leonard, was my mother's age. Today I consider all of them as old, sick perverts. I was overly protective of Lydia and her daughter Rylan, suspicious of all men. Jeremiah, I even had my doubts about you because you and Lydia were too close, and you were not her father. It was not until Lydia asked me if you were her daddy and loved her daddy Jeremiah. I asked her why she liked you so much, and she replied that he loved me.

Was It Revenge against My Aunt Bettie?

There are times when I do not call what my Uncle Leonard did to me rape or a sexual encounter of revenge. I convinced myself that it was a moment of weakness. Then I tried to justify it by thinking it was a chance to get even with my Aunt Bettie, his wife, for putting a pistol to my head when I was a teenager for the time. She felt that I had sassed Grandma Maggie. I have flashbacks of her daring me to blink an eye, threatening to blow my brains out. Jeremiah, it seems like ever since I knew I had a vagina, men in my family have touched me against my will. The first time this happened, I got this exciting feeling but did not know what it meant. But because

Grandmother Maggie told me not to let little boys touch me there, I knew something was wrong with a grown man feeling on my body in my private area. When you and I first engaged in sex, it was the first time I had been penetrated vaginally by a man's penis.

I loved each time we made love, and I cannot tell you how many times I wished we were still doing it together. After that first encounter, it seemed like Uncle Leonard intensified his advances toward me. He would allow me to drive his Road Runner, it was a four-speed stick shift on the floor, and I would have to sit on his lap with a pillow until we were down the road away from my grandmother's house and were alone. He would remove the cushion that separated us from touching. I could feel him gratifying himself through my clothes. I was happy that someone in my family showed interest in me, and I thought it was just because he wanted to be kind to me. Instead, he was getting himself off by having me sitting on his lap. Once, he ejaculated in his hand and made me pull the car over to the side of the road. This wait was until he adjusted himself before having me turn the car around and head back to my grandmother's home. I never saw his private part and never touched it with my hands during these drives. I felt ashamed afterward and did not know what to say or do, except to internalize for myself what was going on. I never figured it out, not even today at more than sixty years of age. When I asked you if you wanted to get next to me, it was after driving Uncle Leonard's car that made me want to have sex with you. Sex was never explained to me by my grandmother or mother, only I better not get pregnant with my mannish behind. And every month, I was asked about my period.

I never accepted advances because he never touched me inside of my panties. He seemed to enjoy getting erections with me sitting on his lap when perched on his lap, driving his car. I know telling you this now will not matter, but you were on my mind when these things happened. I always believed that I was cheating on you, although I was not having sex with my Uncle Leonard. I never felt good about myself, and it took a long time for me to look you in your eyes. Because I was hiding a lie to protect myself, it took a long time to look you in your eyes because of the deception I hid to protect myself. I so found lying my head on your chest and shoulders comforting.

IF YOU MOVE

Jeremiah seems like I have heard similar words before, someone threatening my life and warning me not to move. This time I lost my dignity, and my life was spared. Perhaps losing my life would have been better. At least I would not be facing you today as if you were my judge. I identify with the bums on the street because I have been without and cast aside by family and society. I have been that all men saw my vagina and not me as a person. I am unhappy because I thought that was the only valuable and worthwhile thing I had. I fought and screamed to keep private as a little girl. I was now making it available to the public at a price. I never made it out of the dark closet like you, Jeremiah. In the past, the collateral damages done to me are a constant companion and will be until I die. My heart was medically damaged, but it was broken and torn into many pieces before that. My liver does not function properly, yet I lied about telling you that everything works fine. I have had a heart attack and am not in the best of health, but willing to risk making love to you one more time, not for old-time sake, but for the feeling of once again being loved the way you loved me, Jeremiah. The day Lydia was conceived from a dream while making mad passionate love. Jeremiah, if you were ever to touch me there, I do not think it would be easy for you to get out because I would wrap my legs around your body as tight as handcuffs. You just asked me what I miss the most about my past, good or bad.

Many truths need exposing while we are cordial, open, and honest. But since we are friendly with each other. It gives me hope I will get to know Jeremiah, the man, father, and husband. In speaking with him briefly and seeing him once since he returned to Texas, he appears to be the man I wanted to marry and grow old together. However, I will only experience one of those aspects of you. And for some reason, I want to start by asking you to imagine a young girl facing the trauma of having a gun put to her head, someone threatening to kill her. And later, I felt justified for doing something so hideous and wrong, revenge I thought, would be the best reason. I am telling you what is inside my heart and soul. I cannot get out of my mind, and I hope you will see why I chose darkness over light and understand how shame I am of my life and afraid for my life. I could go on forever now that we are talking face-to-face. I am not seeking sympathy but hope for empathy when you finally know the entire story behind my pain. There was joy in my life when you were in it and after I married and had children with my husband. But like most of my life, I was left alone to fend for myself and now four children later. I did some horrible and scary things to survive. I would tell my children that I needed to make something happen to eat and have a roof over our heads. There was a time when I accompanied a friend to rob an older man, and we were successful. I was nearly caught up in a prostitution sting because I was in the wrong place at the wrong time. One of my friends attempted to spike a man's drink; we almost got me and her killed. He had a gun and fired it at us as we fled away on foot. I regretted allowing someone to touch me that I did not love, and they did not like me. But my body had been such an abuse magnet for perverts; I felt that I should get paid for the privilege of being touched. It became easy for me because I was not in mind, only in the body, making things happen for my children and me. I learned how to use social services and even schooled Lydia to get into the system and get what she needed to take care of her children. I have been out of contact with reality for such a long time until I felt you owed me something when you returned in 1994. Like always, Jeremiah, you were accurate in your assessment of me. Yes, my heart was not into loving you or anyone else. I just needed someone to take some of the pressure off me because I needed a break. Between you and me, I do not think that I could have loved you again because you were a different Jeremiah than the one I first fell in love with years ago. I wanted to know your whereabouts and why you decided I was not worth your time and effort anymore?

I overcame my mother, leaving me never protecting me. I endured my grandmother treating me like a piece of property. I found a way to suppress the molestation by family members to the point I could turn off those moments but not the voices inside my head. I could not get over you are casting me aside. And the way you disappeared into thin air. Jeremiah, I was dealing with so many issues. I did not know how to articulate them to the only person that had shown me, love. I see your reactions and responses, and they are just as I thought they would be before you knew these things that I am sharing with you now. After this talk, any thoughts or words spoken by you about me, you may want to change some of them. You do not realize how much I still trust you after many years. I want to say what I believe but respect your wishes to not make this about trying to rekindle a burned-out flame as you so politely have put it.

A Dream that Became a Nightmare

I was in a sexual mood but in a lousy place to have a sex dream. I was pleasuring myself while dreaming that you and I were making love. I had fallen asleep on the sofa in the den, which was in the back part of my mother's house. I thought that everyone was gone, and I decided to nap. Jeremiah, have you ever closed your eyes? You thought of how lovemaking would have been. While you are thinking to yourself, you could feel the hugging, the warmth of a body touching you, trembling from satisfaction? Please do not take this the wrong way. You were there, and I could feel your hands rubbing down the mold of my back like you always did, and it made me feel relaxed and safe in your arms. I felt someone removing my underwear; someone softly rubbed me between my legs like you would touch me in that spot and the moments leading up to having sex. This dream was real, and I wanted nothing but you to screw me like the afternoon when we made a baby that I could not deliver to you. I never wanted to wake up from what I knew was a dream, but these feelings I was having were real, and I never wanted it to stop. I could feel my legs spread apart to receive you. I could feel myself hugging and holding you tight, and just as I felt myself nearing climax. At that moment, I woke up and was stunned that Uncle Leonard was screwing me as if we were lovers in your place. I told him no and to stop getting off me, trying to get from beneath him. Still, I was pinned down on the sofa from his weight, unable to separate myself from him as I could feel him ejaculating inside of me. *I have been waiting a long time to tag your ass, and I am going to enjoy fucking your eyes out your damn head.* Then he began to try and force himself inside of me a second time, and I fought him as hard as I could and kept telling him to stop. I resisted him as vigorously as I could. I repeatedly told him I was not trying to have sex with him initially; he raped me. He just laughed in my *face, s--t, you wanted it, and I gave it to you, and you know f--king well I was going to one day stick my dick in you I was waiting for your invitation. And if you think about telling anyone, as he lifted a knife from the floor and placed it to my throat, you will f--k me or die. So just lay here and give me some more satisfaction.* I was too afraid to try and push him away because he was threatening to kill me with the knife he held to my throat. As he proceeded to try and rape me with the knife at my throat the second time, my mother and Aunt Bettie, his wife, walked in on us half-dressed and my uncle with a knife to my throat. I remember hearing their voices calling me all kinds of names, but they never confronted Uncle Leonard or asked him why he had a knife? What was he doing? All those rides along within him and me sitting on his lap. And the fact that I just ignored it and let him sexually gratify himself through my clothes, I was telling him it was okay. But then why didn't my grandmother aggressively scrub and wash my body after each encounter that I had with Leonard and other male family members? Why wouldn't my mother believe me when I told her Uncle Leonard raped me? Had I acted too much like a brat by always complaining about living with my grandmother? Was this punishment for leaving Littlefield and moving to Harrison to live with my mother and siblings? Sitting in my room, I thought of death, and how would I end this day? Will I lose Jeremiah, and will he ever see me as his Ebonic Woman again? I never wanted to have sex with my Uncle and never wanted to leave you, Jeremiah. What am I going to do, and who can I turn to for help? It was not long before I knew that I was pregnant. Still, it took me at least two months to get up the nerve to tell you, Jeremiah. It was because I knew that you would soon be coming home for the summer that I decided to tell you. I am thinking to myself. My mother knows I am pregnant. Why will my grandmother not do what they advised me when it was Jeremiah's baby by insisting that I have an abortion? Is this what my grandmother meant when she said she bought and paid for when she refused to allow my mother to take me? Was it to sexually service or satisfy men in my family so they could pleasure themselves? Whenever you and I had sex, my undergarments never were torn darn near off me. I invited you to have sex, and any stains that she claimed to discover were there voluntarily. It was you that I was having sex with Jeremiah in my dream that resulted in forty-five years of torment and a nightmare. It is the most confusing part of my life, and I feel it is where I feel guilty. Jeremiah, I did not want to be raped or have sex with my uncle Leonard. A dream where you and I were making love turned into a nightmare that I have relived every day of my life. I just wanted to be sexually satisfied and make love to you. It has been a struggle since I received all the blame and no family support. I have never been able to keep a man because of my feelings about lovemaking. There have been only five men in my life that I allowed to try and satisfy me since you, and you may think that is a lot, but out of those five, I have yet to find but one that made me happy. FOR INSTANCE, when I think of lovemaking, I called your name during intimate moments with my husband on more than one occasion. Thinking about you also helped me get through my wifely duties and sex with other men.

I believe my life was that of someone doomed from the beginning. Jeremiah, by you coming into my life was parole from hell. And never getting a full pardon has been a big downfall in my life, but hell, life goes on, and so do the voices inside my head. Leonard's laughter seems to haunt me the greatest because it was at that moment that I felt I lost you forever. You tried to be there, but it was not you that I needed. It was my mother to believe me and loved me. I needed a family that was never there for me. The only sense that I belonged to anyone and was made to feel special was 1969 to 1973 before the rape. Although we were not in close communication as we used to be, I never stopped loving you, and I still do. I hate you for leaving me and never coming back into my life until now. I know that I messed up some things, but you could have stuck it out with me as you had for so long. I was not running away or intentionally trying to hurt you because I loved and never stopped loving you. Many issues were going on in my life that I felt too ashamed to share with you. I needed to find the best Annie to give you, and when I thought that I had discovered her, that someone who would love me for the rest of my life, you were gone and had disappeared into the world. Question for today: Have you ever closed your eyes and thought of how lovemaking would have been. While you were thinking to yourself, you could feel the hugging, the warmth as if your body were trembling from satisfaction?

I will talk about other things you might see something wrong with, but you are the writer. I am the teller, so fix it. Years gone past that can never be retrieved. So really blame, I think not, unless you care not to hear what I have to say, I am sure somewhere in this tell-all, there will be some toes stepped on, but I look at it like it is a roll with it or gets rolled over so to speak. So, what is it going to be? I am okay; there is nothing to blame. I do not know many big words, so I do not understand what an exercise in futility means.

From what I can see, you were dating as many as you could, and I did not see you trying to find me, so where is the beef. Mistreat, no pissed as hell yes because you had claimed so much love and devotion to what we had, and you dropped off the face of the earth, and when you did resurface, you had a wife. I am not jealous but pissed because I felt like you were a fraud to the cause. There is no way on the green earth that I would not have contacted you if I knew where you were. If I had not been in Shreveport one night and saw Joyce Young, I still might not know where you were.

Jeremiah: Annie, if you had gotten in touch with me between 1977 and 1992, I would have rejected you. First, you had gotten married, again, without telling me that there was someone else. I do not understand why the hell you feel that I should have just stood still forever while you were doing all the dumb junk you were doing with your life. I was a man with goals, and until you decided to take yourself out of becoming a part of those goals, you were significant. Annie, this is the third time that you have alluded to the fact that I did not come to find you; for what? Einstein said *the sign of insanity is doing the same thing and getting the same results*. DAH!!! You can stay as late, and if you want at this pity party that you have thrown for yourself, I choose to decline your invitation. I prepared my life, hoping you would be a part of it, but that was contingent upon your wanting to live your life with me. ALL your actions said no. And you lied from the jump, rape that now accidental incest. Why in the hell cannot you tell me the truth even now about things in your past? I do not give a darn, and the fact that now you think that you will con me to believe anything that you tell me today will somehow change how I feel about you. You should tell Lydia the truth. You are not at fault for what happened to you but guilty for not exposing it.

Annie: Jeremiah, Lydia was not conceived by rape but incest. It is too bad that you are married because I would enjoy illustrating a nightmare with you. I believe it would better explain what went wrong at an inopportune time. Please do not take this the wrong way. I have not been hugged, kissed, or anything in as many as twelve years. And it has been even longer since sex; there has been no man in my life since my husband makes me feel safe. I have never been able to keep a man because of my feelings about lovemaking. There have been only five men in my life that I have tried to love since you. And you may think that is a lot, but out of those five, I have yet to find one that made me happy when I think of love, and that has been a big downfall in my life, but hell, life goes on. Jeremiah, you asked me *how much of yourself have you given to have a relationship with a man?* I have nothing, Jeremiah. So, I received nothing and cannot pursue anything because my life has gone to hell in a handbasket. I am good. We must change this kind of thinking and mindset. Was there a terrible experience that turned you off from intimacy with a man, and you elect not even to try?

Thanks, I lost my happiness in this struggle, and I want it back anyway. What can I do to help you? Again, I believe that you are a valuable human being and should not deny a worthy man the pleasure of having you as a life partner. I am okay, like I said, just venting. Thanks, but life goes on, and I will not be jumping off buildings. Being my friend and not judging me. I value your opinion a lot. And trusting someone has always been important to Jeremiah and me if there is one thing that I can say about you. I have never found myself not believing you.

If God creates another Jeremiah and Annie, I hope their love will have a much happier ending than ours. Our intentions to love and care for each other were innocent, and I could feel your determination to sustain the test of time. We failed to make it about both the heart and mind. Because I bought negative baggage into our relationship and was blinded by the shiny object before me, someone loving, turning a blind eye to what was in my attic (mind). I was hoping that I would see the hurt on your face, but it seemed to have backfired, and I am the one hurting because I never planned on mentioning incest to you. But once again, your eyes and the way you questioned me prompted me to come clean.

CHAPTER THIRTY-FIVE

OUR LAST CONVERSATION

Jeremiah: When we were Jeremiah and Annie from start to finish, I gave you my entire heart filled with love. And I even tried to pull you out of the situation that you just finished describing. All sins are forgivable except for one. The question I have for you is if you used twenty-twenty hindsight. How could you say that you loved me and destroyed something that would have connected us for a lifetime but not see the need to abort in case of rape? Today, I am convinced of the rape I could have overcome and lived a happy life together. But the other deceitful things you did and kept me aware of are all unforgivable.

I thought that we loved each other, and no, I did not tell you of my fear of being rejected by you because of my dark skin. I never kept any of my love from you.

Why did you lie to me proclaiming rape instead of telling me that you got caught up in a moment? And what was a dream turned into reality, and now you want to call it a lifetime nightmare? Why wouldn't you tell how you conceived Lydia? Were you raped or incest? Why wouldn't you report it to the police? My questions are why, just as yours are where. I was where you needed me to be when you were not running off and getting married behind my back. Was there something going on between you and Alvin? And he did not like me cutting in on you all actions. I mean, I do not mean to sound harsh or rude, but you are like my ex-wife, do not seem to know the truth unless it benefits you. Disappointed about abortion, yes, but that is not the only thing. How about all the things that you kept hidden from me? You could have cried out to me, and I would have heard from you. Do you want to change your story? Was a sex train pulled on you by your cousin and his two friends? Let us just put it all out there so we can wrap up "These are the Lies of Annie."

Annie: Man, I have been in survival mode most of my life, primarily when I was a young girl. Please try and understand by imagining how to protect your body before knowing your body parts' names. There was nothing between Alvin and me, and no, I never had a train pulled on me as you now seem to think I did. Put yourself in the place of someone rejected, denied, and misused by those who are supposed to love you and protect you. When I felt loved was when we were together. It was only for a short time that we were together and in love. Every day that I came to school, and you were there, I knew that I would have a great day. Weekends interrupted my happiness; little did I know that transferring school would end that happiness. I believe that my uncle, the rapist, had intentions of raping me from when I was a young girl sitting on his lap. I told you that he asked if we were having sex and alluded that men with bowlegs had the bigger penis. My uncle was a vile-speaking adult when we were alone, and no other adults were around.

I did not have the good sense to tell my mother and grandmother about these conversations. I had no confidence that they would have believed me because of their low opinion assuming I asked for it because you and I were having sex. Uncle Leonard's voice has dominated my daily thoughts that go through my mind. I hear his voice and remember all his words while raping me yesterday. They stay fresh in my mind. I think about his questioning your bowlegs and comment telling me that boys with bowlegs and a man's penis size. Based on my mother and Aunt's Bettie reaction, I was to blame for what happened.

Jeremiah, you say we were playing checkers. And it was me who was always leaping and making the wrong moves, preventing us from getting back together before you decided to move on with your life. I was trying to survive and provide for my child and me. When Lydia was born, you became a lesser priority, but I felt it necessary in my life. You never told me to love you more than Lydia, but you never told me what your plans were for us, either. You never told me that the moves you made were plans for Lydia and me to be with you. My movements were survival and escape. Ultimately, we kept canceling out each other plans for our future due to a lack of communication. Jeremiah, I cannot take total blame for our failure because, just as I should have told you all that was going on in my life, you should have shared your goals with me also.

I never felt safe around Uncle Leonard after this incident, even if we were among a group of family members. His evil act turned a dream that I enjoyed into a lifetime nightmare and permanent residents inside of my mind. Uncle Leonard's second attempt to rape me was interrupted by my mother and aunt. They thought I consented to have sex with Leonard. I told you rape because I hoped that you would still love me. He was someone who had molested other girls in the family. His evil deeds also included the daughters of women he was messing around with behind aunt Bettie's back. Besides feeling dirty and worthless, I still needed to know that someone loved me.

I would not have to ask you to forgive me for something that was not my fault or intended, so I said it was rape, and I believe it to be rape even today. I wonder if I had told you what I am sharing with you today, how it would have made a difference in our lives. Would you have wanted to marry me and raise someone else's child even though it could appear as though I was the blame? Jeremiah, I need to know. I want to see if we could have gone on with our lives together as planned. If you were present at that moment, Lydia would have been would have had our baby together. And maybe

telling you that I had aborted our child would be easier to accept by
you. I do not think I would have ever informed you about the
abortion had we made Lydia. Jeremiah, I love reading the things
you write and how you seem to paint pictures with words. I do not
want to read the images you have of me. You tend to paint pictures
that you know are a hurtful truth. I do not think that my family
disliked you. I believe you, scared people, because of your mature
way of going about things. My grandmother told me that you were
a very respectful and polite young man. She must have trusted you
because she left us at the house alone, knowing that we had been
having sex, but then that was one of my inspections and scrubbed
downs Saturdays too. Do not judge me; I am asking your help to
stop this constant chatter inside my head.

Jeremiah: Annie, I hear your words. I can never imagine what it is
like to be raped, especially by a family member. I know that, out of
that bad, someone excellent and loving came into my life for a
moment, and that was Lydia. I could accept her more than I could
trust, loving you as much as I once did. I know you claim it as rape,
but you have altered that story a few times. I was a young man
without much sense or knowledge about rape, incest, molestation,
and other acts of abuse. I acted out of character by behaving as if I
was the victim. There was something stolen from me, and I could
not handle it. I was wrong and had no right to think about the
intimate space you shared with me and deem it mine. It was on
your body to allow whomever you saw fit at your pleasure. I
enjoyed and loved each of the special moments we spent together. I
apologize for letting such a selfish emotion overtake the sense of
compassion and care I had for you. In a way, I felt as if your Uncle
Leonard raped me, too, by taking a liberty that was never his. Still, I
am fifty-fifty because some parts of me want to believe that you

enjoyed his attention, which ended up going too far. Perhaps I would have had a different outlook today if no intro led up to this act. I must live with what you tell me to sway my opinion that it was rape, maybe. But the fact that you would not even tell me about the molestation by other family members makes it harder for me to paint anything but a portrayal picture. Annie, do you remember one night we talked on the phone? I was doing most of the talking. I said I would not hang up the phone tonight without telling me all your thoughts for that day from the time you awakened to the present. There was silence on the phone for a period, and all that we could hear was each other breathing?

Annie: It is not the same, Jeremiah; you make it seem like walking into a candy store and asking for a piece of candy. I turned to only you when this attack occurred; this was my way of reaching out to you for help, Jeremiah. You stayed around and tried to make me feel still loved. And I appreciate how you loved and cared for Lydia. I believe you checked out the night Uncle Leonard raped me. Secretly I was hoping that you would come and confront him. Oh! How I wished you would have been my knight in shining armor again. You never asked me where it took place. How did it happen? Besides my mother and Aunt Bettie, you are the only person who knows and treats me the same. You refuse to get the picture, I was not okay then, and I am not okay now either. I have told you everything. As I said before, you are the writer; fix this by explaining my words to me to understand that this was not incest as you are calling it. I am not a liar, as you aptly describe me as such. I need you, Jeremiah, not to judge me so harshly. I have been confused about what happened because I tried to find the best way not to lose you then and today's best opinion.

Was It Rape or Incest

I Lost Jeremiah

Jeremiah, the rape of a woman, is one of the most demeaning and horrible things that could ever happen to her. She is expected to move on with her life and forgive the man. The victim can forgive a rapist. And raping someone is a crime punishable by law. But nothing erases the pain and stain from the victim; it is a life sentence that comes and goes. Every time it comes into your head, you feel the violation again all over. When the perpetrator finishes violating your body, he leaves a lifetime memory. You pray and hope that time will heal this wound, but it never does. As for me, it gets worse each damn second of my life. I have tried fooling myself so many times into believing that my pain was finally gone forever.

Jeremiah's rape is not like making love because there is only one willing participant in a rape transaction. It is a crime because the victim unwillingly obeys the criminal as they violate both your physical and mental space, with the latter being a lifetime. On the day of my rape, I could feel myself losing you, Jeremiah, a chance to overcome the early child molestation and the opportunity of forgiving ever wanting to forgive my mother and grandmother. I was over the physical pain almost immediately because I needed to survive tomorrow. Then I needed to live so that I could love you. If Lydia were not a part of the transaction, you would not have known what happened to me. Including me being violated by men in my family. I had often been placed in a helpless situation, fearful of getting hurt physically from the pain inflicted on me by men, getting raped. He told me I asked for it made no sense at all to me. I certainly would not have run off with all the men I did and married as many times as I did. You can wash away the semen stains from your body and clothes. Still, nothing can ever erase the voice commands given by your rapist as they force you to consent to them violating you. Although it was long, Jeremiah seems like every thought went through my mind. Jeremiah, I kept repeating your name over and over in my mind as if this would wash away the guilt and shame. I never felt that I deserved to have you or any happiness from that day. I have attempted to punish myself so that you would not have to. I still wake up from cold sweats with you asking me, Annie, why you hurt me? As strange as this may sound, I was more afraid of what this would do to us than the brandished weapon used to force me to comply with the violent act of nonconsensual sex. It happened between a relative and me, not a stranger or an acquaintance.

Rape is like the prey being tracked and cornered by the hunter. The only way out of their trap is to comply and hope that the perpetrator will spare your life. You use the only weapon you have, a plea for mercy, as you try and fight your way out of the control of your attacker. When you are finally free of the perpetrator's control unharmed, you are thankful for your life, all while you believe your life is over. Who would want a rape victim? Jeremiah, since that day, I have been a two-time loser every day. I lost my sanity and love simultaneously, and nothing is redeemable about me. All I had to give you, Jay, was damaged collateral beyond repair. I have never found the freedom I once had—a part of me as taken from me that I can never get back. To never know the peace of mind, I enjoyed it long ago. When we had sex after the rape, I worried you would pull a weapon on me by seeking revenge against me. I cannot escape Uncle Leonard raping me. It is an act I cannot erase from my mind, and it is impossible to escape. Jeremiah, when you moved out, I started hosting visitors inside my head. I imagined your voice, along with uninvited residents, always saying unkind and uncaring words. The victim of rape, my every thought, brings me back to that moment when my body and life belonged to someone else.

It is not a blessing when something happens to you so nasty and becomes a lifetime reminder of a rape. I was impregnated by someone I am not fond of today and cannot find forgiveness in my heart. I was a participant by force in creating a masterpiece for a devil to admire his work. Yes, Jeremiah, I love my daughter, but I hate the canvas used to paint her as a lifetime reminder. My reward for the devious act. I was forced to put on full display a creation created from an act of violence to pleasure my attacker instead of the gentleness I experience when making love with you. My body was not hired out or on loan but forcibly made to participate.

Jeremiah: I was not keen on the idea that we needed to meet and talk face-to-face to share our stories. Annie, I tried the best way that I knew how to come to your rescue. It was like I came to your house but could not force myself to enter. And Annie, I sincerely apologize for making it more about something taken from me, which never belonged to me in the first place. I was young and did not know what to do or say. Instead of helping you heal, I looked at it as if Leonard wronged me. I was inexperienced in what to do and say — and devastated by what had happened. But I did try to come through for you. Because you would not tell anyone, I could not talk to anyone because I did not want you labeled as something or someone undesirable. That was not your fault. Annie, it was you who shut me out and repeatedly. Annie, you broke me into pieces until there were no more pieces. I became collateral damage from the brokenness and pain you caused me and my knowledge of a kept secret. Before you, I had never loved anyone as hard and much as I had you. When you came into my life, I was able to empty my never-ending cup of loving affection into your heart.

Perhaps if I were home in East Texas when you shared this information with me, and I could have come to you right away, we could have combined our strength to do the right thing. I lost a significant person from life and a future that I dreamed of living with for the rest of my life; that person was you, Annie. You getting raped caused me to struggle; I decided my love for Lydia was far more important than my pride because someone had invaded what I believed was reserved space only for me. But you proved that area was not specifically for me by marrying other men. I lost you, Annie, without you ever giving me a chance to fight for you. Why wouldn't you tell me about the molestation that had occurred before our relationship? All the nights we spent on the phone talking, couldn't you have just blurted it out just as you did about your Uncle Leonard's raping you?

Annie: The face-to-face was essential because your writing tone seems cold and uncaring, and I need to see if this is Jeremiah Micah Ford communicating with me. Jeremiah, it may be hard for you to understand what I missed in less than two or three minutes. The loss of your love and respect ranks up there with the day of the rape. And from there, I lost my peace of mind. I lost the man I wanted forever to love; you, Jeremiah, and no one else. I put the molesting in a dormant state; the rape returned all those memories. I no longer trusted myself to love another man without hesitation as I did you. Jeremiah, out of fear that I could awaken my partner from the nightmare of being raped by Uncle Leonard almost daily since it happened.

Marrying other men was my way of punishing myself, believing that I deserved a Jeremiah Ford. Jay, strange, I was not as fearful of losing my life as much as I was worried about losing you. You were my life, Jeremiah. And I could never move on from when we were, even though you have made it abundantly clear you have moved on and enjoying the kind of married life that we had hoped for together. I could not explain to you what was going on inside of me, Jeremiah. I am incapable of telling you how I felt. Therefore, I suppose I could not expect you to understand my feelings — three times married because I could not cope with what was going on inside my head and heart at the same time. My marriages were all destroyed because of the lack of trust. And the inability to cope with the intimate part of being married; I needed to prepare for the touching and lovemaking. I cheated on all three of my spouses because I was always in two places, the lover I lost and the nightmare I encountered from the rape. They had the pleasure of my body and the loan of my vagina to relieve themselves, but not my heart and soul. They were always elsewhere. I tried to overcome the rape by forcing myself to become intimate with my husband; I am sure they could feel that they were making love to a blow-up doll. The only difference is I was a living person with a dead soul inside. For the past forty-five years, I have functioned like a reasonable person on the outside. But on the inside, there is a constant battle with insensitive chatter inside my head.

Annie: I know it is hard for you to believe me when I say that I never loved anyone but you. But you left me. I felt you going long before I married my first husband because you did not rescue me right away from all the pain. Before the rape, you had already left me. I became lost when you stopped welcoming me into your world each day. When I transferred to Harrison, I felt starved due to the lack of your love. And I was, I was not getting your love. You should have figured something out and made us work. You have every right to hate me, belittle me, and say as many awful things as possible about me that you want, but I will always hold that against you for leaving me. Then you marry my cousin and live happily ever after. That is some actual bulls--t.

Jeremiah: Hold on, Annie, from the outset, I have told you that my wife is off-limits, and she is now and will be the love of my life after we finish doing whatever it is that we are trying to do. I was not going around looking for your relative to marry. I knew Ruth long before I knew you, and if I had half a brain in my head, you would have never existed in my life. But due to my lack of courage and confidence, I delayed my intentions toward her. Ruth is and never will be someone that I will allow you to attack as if she did you some injustice. Now that is bulls—t. So, let us get it straight and keep it upfront. I am in love with my wife Ruth, and she is my friend, lover, and someone I trust, my entire world in her hand. Likewise, she can believe the same in me; our love for one another is no different from anyone else's; we love and appreciate each other. **YOU ARE NO THREAT TO HER OR OUR MARRIAGE.** It is secure because we genuinely care for each other. It appears we have disconnected when having conversations about my wife. Attack me all you want, but Ruth better never becomes a problem for you. I will be a bigger asshole than you already feel because I won't jeopardize my marriage to entertain a never-to-be relationship. We are NOT working on this project to get back together or rekindle a relationship that died long ago. You have accused me of going with your very own daughter. You are right; you do have a heart condition. It is called the absence of a heart. I believe I have thoroughly addressed this matter to understand and get through your seemingly very skull?

Annie: He, Jeremiah, you want to know what is crazy? I have never looked at myself in the mirror to say it is alright and I will be okay. I guess I had longed to hear you tell me that everything is OK between us. I hoped to face you when I shared my entire story. You are the kind of man that I dreamed you would someday become. Unfortunately, I never married one like you.

Jeremiah: Do we have an understanding that my wife, marriage, and my heart are all off-limits before we go any further?

Annie: Yes, sir, Mr. Jeremiah Micah Ford, it is clear, and I know that you hate me for what I may have put you through. In the end, I lost every chance of ever gaining your love back. I feel that I lost all when you stopped communicating with me, and I learned that you had married Sarah and had disappeared into thin air. Your whereabouts were like some top secret because everyone I asked about your location said they did not know.

Jeremiah: So, I ask you again what beef you have with my wife and me? I sense hostility. We had our run at trying to make a future together.

Annie: I do apologize. No beef, just feeling jealous that she got what I wanted. I sincerely do.

Jeremiah: Perhaps that is the biggest problem, Ruth needs me, and I need her to make us a whole. I am not a want. I thought that the rape was a problem but would have never taken me away from you because you made my life complete. Still, when you left, you severely ripped the very fabric off a heart that would never get mended back together again. I laid down at night, believing that you would be in all my dreams. Each morning, I awaken that you would make my day just by seeing your face and smile. Moments away from seeing you, filled with thoughts of a future day when we could be together as husband and wife. I could never repair the rip that you tore in my heart. I had to destroy that clothing because it only bought back bad memories. I stumbled about looking for that person to replace you, and that person never appeared. That place you once occupied in my heart; no one ever filled that void. That empty room still exists, just like the day you went away, the empty chair where you used to sit telling me how much you loved me. But it is just a reminder that we once existed. The dinner table and dishes still reflect the last meal we had together. I even left the key in the door, hoping that you would someday walk back through the door of my heart. And so did I keep opening the arms; you always said you felt safe and secure when wrapped around you. Love begged me to move on but never said I had to move your memories out as well. The door my heart was never nailed shut; neither was the key thrown away until you threw me away. The house that we built burned down in 1979, and I moved to another neighborhood. You never returned after eight years, and I decided in 1974 to go on with my life. And in 1996, I moved to a better home and neighborhood that Ruth and I built.

Annie: It does not matter to me when you got married or to whom. That is water under the bridge. Our past is a memory that a girl like me needs to get through the night and most days. It still breaks my heart how I betrayed you. But you never ask me how I survived. Or are you well? How is your family? It hurts that you do not show that you care about me or how I am doing. I became accustomed to another Jeremiah who cared about everyone and made them feel special. I realize writing this book is a transaction. However, I am still a human being deserving of concern and compassion. I get that you want your question answered and moved on with your life. After hearing you tell me how much I meant to you in the past, I understand and accept that nothing is left on the table. I know I was not truthful and faithful to us, but I want to amend by saying sorry. Can I be your long-lost friend?

Jeremiah: Annie, if you have gasoline on your hand and a bucket of water on one side and a blazing fire on the other side. Which one are you going to use? I know how a bucket of water can save me. I also understand how a blazing fire and gasoline can destroy me. You are gas on my hand, and I am not about to walk toward the burning fire. You will figure it out someday, hopefully. You were not considered a friend to me, Annie; if that is who you thought you were, it would be easy to pick up the pieces of a broken friendship.

I cannot do that, and I think you need to check yourself and replay the start of our conversations. Annie, I do not meet a stranger on the street, that if we speak, I will not ask them how they are doing? If you ask me to individualize a greeting just for you, that will never happen. We are strangers to one another, and I understand that; why do not you. I am not coming home to a wife after leaving a girlfriend. We are talking because you have decided to clear your conscience about some things and get them out and off your chest.

Is something that you want me to know about you or your family? Then it will get revealed by you voluntarily. Appreciate me for trying to be a man for telling you the truth upfront and not misleading you to some false hope.

Annie: Jeremiah, I did not want that to sound like I was trying to get you to feel sympathetic or anything for me. But it would be nice to think that you cared a little more about me than what you have shown. I guess I am still looking for someone who wrote kind words and showed love and compassion when I needed it most. I need those things now, and I understand what you are saying that this will not come from you because it is a business deal and not a booty call from the past. I hear you, and I appreciate your telling me that you would not cross the line and cheat on me if we were married. I should not expect you to become weak or caught up in a moment, causing you to violate your marriage vows with Ruth. I get that, and you do not need to continue reminding me.

Jeremiah: I know that you remember how I used to be and how I was, but precisely who do you think I am today the question. I am who I keep telling you and trying to show you. Perhaps you believe that I also remained stuck in the past that will never come to fruition for us. We had our run, and there were too many stones for us to turn over with the amount of time we had left to live. Allow me to break it down for you. If I were married to you, and Ruth was in your position, I would not violate my vow to you for her, either. Marriage means something to God and me.

Annie: There will be other things I talk about that you might see wrong, but you are the writer; I am the storyteller, so fix it. Years gone past that can never be retrieved. I blame it not unless you want to hear what I got to say. I am sure somewhere in this tell-all book. Some toes are going to get stepped on. But I look at it like this. Either you roll with the punches or get rolled over by the punchers' sort to speak.

Jeremiah: I am sure you expect me to believe everything you say to me today is real. And I am a big boy and can take it if you are willing to sling it my way. I suggest that you keep a catcher's mitt handy. If I need to return a fastball, I will aim at your head and not your heart because I believe you lost all feelings for me long ago. I seem to get a rise out of you when I do not express or say what I used to communicate. No, Annie, I cannot respond to your words of sweet nothings in the same way as in past years because I heard them before. Annie, I am sure that if the shoe was on the other foot and you were married. I would not expect anything beyond cordial from you because whether I knew your husband or not, I would respect your husband. Think about it; when you were married, I never once tried to contact you or get you to betray your husband.

Annie: I do not understand what that means.

Jeremiah: You know your question of my whereabouts. Annie, for some reason, you act as if I was a lifetime subscription you had signed up for, and I owed you a lifetime of waiting. Are you suggesting that I should not have moved on with my life? Because you certainly were doing your thing by getting married, leaving me to look like the world's biggest fool. I gave up a lot each time that you would come and go. Annie, you empty my soul for you. I see you as another human being with whom I had a past intimate relationship. I remember you as the girl that brought out the shyness in me. Still, I do not owe the woman Annie Sims anything more than thanks. I already gave everything, and you were taking everything and taking everything. You forget I transferred from one college to another to be closer to you when you told me you were raped and pregnant. Only, now to find out that you lied and had made me complicit to a forty-five-year-old lie. I kept this a secret, thinking that I was protecting you and a little girl that I would have loved and accepted as my daughter had you not married all those times. I wanted Lydia to be mine because you gave birth to her. I was that much in love with you, Annie, so much so I was willing to raise a rapist child as my own to be with you.

Annie: Jeremiah, you have every right to speak to me in an angry tone. I am asking you to explain that I was on the run from me each time I married suddenly and because I had Lydia, I could never break free from the chain of my past. I toiled a long time on whether to give Lydia up for adoption. Jeremiah, half of me wanted to protect you and not allow you to help me in the mess I had gotten myself? When my uncle Leonard learned that you were back in my and Lydia's life, he tried raping me again. Lydia was two years old. I could take him hurting the other men that I allowed in my life, but not my Jeremiah, the man that gave me the nickname Ebonic Woman.

He had abused me once and believed that I would be an easy target a second time. He threatened everyone that meant so much to me that first time. I was scared and shaken up by a messed and confused woman, and my mother was no help. If I could relive that dream and physically put you into that moment, I would in a second. When we talk, you make it seem like you do not make mistakes. You are not perfect.

Jeremiah: True, Annie, I am not perfect and have made some mistakes in my life and still make them. I do not want you to make another mistake by allowing yourself to get involved with a man from your past. Because that is who we are to each other memories, dreams, and failed aspirations. I would make a lousy boyfriend for you today because you would be so low down on the totem pole of priorities it would be like I do not care about you. I am not into convenience relationships where I must see someone who will never be more than a hotel room guest. The problem with you is that you have never said I am sorry for what you did and did not tell me. Annie, I can feel your pain, but there is no remorse where you deceived me and involved me in a lie and a crime. What ruined our relationship is that you failed to trust me enough by deciding what was best for Jeremiah Micah Ford. I have not seen contrition once, or thank you, Jeremiah, for your efforts and trust. Many friends believed Lydia was my daughter because I never denied or affirmed. Yes, Annie, I make mistakes, but I will not make them the first time. And that is, I will not betray the love and trust of my wife, whom I love. Annie, here is something that will support what I am saying.

Sarah and I stayed married for thirteen years, and she cheated on me most of those years throughout our marriage. I caught her in the act, and I never violated my vow to our wedding. That is how you know that this nut will not crack. Trying and drawing me into your world of confusion is an exercise in futility. And if I were you, Annie, I would start working out at a different gym. As for your uncle, Leonard, we could have whooped his behind in court had you agreed to do so; not telling me of his threats was not a position of love but an excuse that you now want to spring on me. I am supposed to believe that you were concerned about me. Hell, I am a Ford. We drive over scum that chooses to get in our path. Today, if I thought it would do any good, I would go to Leonard's grave and dig his crusty ass up, dust him off and whip his butt until Lydia is satisfied for cheating her out of a daddy.

Annie: So, what is it going to be? According to you, I am okay with being blamed for everything, Jeremiah Ford. I do not know many big words, so I do not understand what an exercise in futility means. Jay, all I can sense is that you are angry at me, and I messed up anything? Will it allow you to open your arms and hold me just once like you used to? Can you place your hands into my hands, stare down into my eyes, and tell me that you do not hate me? Jeremiah, you were real to me and not a myth. With your hugs, kisses, and making love to me, I still have those dreams. Uncle Leonard interrupted a moment of passion that I enjoyed taking your time, caressing but moving to the spot that would eventually bring me the pleasure of making love to a lover and not a rapist. I spent three marriages hoping that I could climax just once like we used to make love to one another.

Jeremiah: Damn! No, Annie, I am frustrated that you seem to be in a loop and stuck in a holding pattern. Perhaps I should purchase you a gerbil and a cage with an exercise wheel. Maybe then you would understand. I am offended that you are pissed that I decided to go on with my life. In doing so, I found a faithful and loving wife. Think about this for a moment. Had your husband not gotten involved with drugs, would you have still been happily married to him? Probably yes, one big happy family. I think eight years is more than long enough to wait for someone to get their act together. The number seven is the number of completions, and eight is the number of a new beginning. That is what I sought to do, start a new life, and erase you from my past. Annie, as sorry as my marriage was with Sarah, I never sought to try and rekindle our relationship. I got over you because I fell in love with the married life, trying to be a faithful husband and a loving father to my two daughters. It is unfair for you to place all your failed relationships at my feet. I did not come out of that marriage bitter but better because I found how strong I could be, and I could be a value to someone worthy of all I have to offer. There I was living in another country without a wife for more than a year. I never relented to violating a marriage vow that, for all, was over and a wife living with another man. That was me, and I developed and had platonic relationships without benefits. When the court declared the marriage was over, I could roam again. The dreams I had where we were making love never ended. We just held each other so tight that we found ourselves trembling as if we were afraid to separate ourselves.

Annie, I never wanted to leave you then, but today I cannot wait for us to finish our collaboration on this book, and I cannot see me ever wanting to come back and kiss, nor take your hands. Ruth's hand suits me fine. Thank you very much. Annie, I will extend my hand out to shake yours, but the arms are for members only, Ruth Ford. Annie Sims and a cast of a few others did a job on Jeremiah, and I am the better for having known someone like you. But we are discussing the where and the why. I had to take myself where I would not have access to you, returning to you every time things went wrong in my life. I am happy and in a perfect place. I have a woman that I believe that I love ten times more than I could have ever loved you.

Annie: Jeremiah, when my uncle raped me, I lost my desire to love and be loved. I did not feel that I deserved it, and I went through long periods of deep depression. I was going through the motions of being a mother, wife, and whatever else there was. I even tried to relate everything to get me through each romance episode when we were together. That event, or whatever you want to call it, stopped my world and it has remained standing still. I keep waiting for the next Jeremiah to come along. I cannot tell you how many times I have tried to remake you, your gentleness, and loving-kindness. You made me angry because you were the right man to and for me. Jeremiah, is there an iota of a vacant spot in your heart for me, anywhere? Yes, I did some messed up things and hurtful things to you, but it was not intentional but protective, as I tried to explain. It seemed like every time I was ready to come clean and tell you, the entire story was when I needed you most, and you were never there. Why weren't you the real man in that one dream? It is a nightmare that I cannot forget. There are days I hate hearing my daughter's voice; I would welcome your voice more. I appreciate you for trying to love her, and I am sorry that I made you feel like you and she were lovers. But then you could always get her to do things by just talking to her as if you two were buddies. Thanks for finally asking whether I can give an easy answer. I lost my happiness in this struggle, and I want it back. Thanks.

Jeremiah: So, we are back to rape. Maybe if you decide on whether it was rape or incest, you can untangle your brain. Annie, I believe that everyone is worthy of someone in their life to share their love with, and I do not understand why you have not given love another chance. I sincerely hope you will give love another chance with someone who will love you back the way you deserve. I would give you a recommendation. Annie Sims was a good, fun-loving woman back in the day; you should kick her tires and give her a try. Signed, I rode on her tires.

Annie: Still got jokes and that smile, don't you? I remember how I used to get confused when you would smile. You said that sometimes your smile signifies that you are angry, which is not good for the receiving end. Your smile today, which one has been displaying the most? I am good. I have nothing to give, so I expect to receive nothing, cannot pursue something or anyone because my life will be hell in a handbasket.

Jeremiah: Therefore, I have difficulty dealing with you because of your negative outlook on life. I am a half-glass whole kind of person. The negative thinking, I hope you will change that mindset. I am sorry for my non-caring attitude now; what can I help you with? No matter what you have done and what I may think of you. You are valuable collateral, so you should not deny a worthy man the pleasure of having you as a life partner.

Annie: I am okay, like I said, just venting. Thanks, but life goes on, and I will not be jumping off buildings. Be my friend, and not judge me. If given only one wish, it would be that we go back to October of 1969, as Jeremiah and Annie, and fall in love with you all over again. Every relationship I have had since you, I imagine that I am falling in love with that bow-leg boy with that shit-eating grin. Jeremiah, you are a person I can trust, and having someone to trust is so important to me. If you were mine today, I could imagine falling asleep and not being afraid of the nightmare I always have.

 Jeremiah: You vex my heart each time you come at me in that manner. I do not mean to sound cruel, but I genuinely love Ruth. I used to hear a voice telling me to keep walking. I have not listened to that voice telling me to keep walking in over twenty years. I prayed for your peace and hoped we would resolve some things while writing this book. You opened many old wounds, and it will take some time for me to get over all the hurt and pain you have caused in my life. Instead, you hid and denied me the opportunity to be a part of it for one second by electing to abort our child for no sensible reason. We made a mistake, but this only exasperated me. I would not have left you and that child to fend for yourselves; you denied me the opportunity to be a man and father to a child that I would have loved and adored.

Annie: I am sorry, and I can offer no other words regarding this situation. You grew up having your mother always there for you. A million times, I wished that I had the comforting and soothing voice of a mother. I needed her strength to fight the evil uncle who raped and impregnated me instead of condemning me. I did not deserve to be shamed and labeled as loose and fast.

Along with the pain, I suffered from incest. I felt forced by guilt and society to hide my pain and shame in my mind. Since I cannot erase this nightmare, not even by you, I must deal with a brain that will not cease playing the act repeatedly inside my head. I have had to contend with the screaming voices of my belittling companions inside my head. When you came into my life, I fell in love with you. And I had convinced myself I was unwanted by anyone, especially my mother. Because she did not fight to take me with her, I was not worth fighting for her.

Jeremiah: My father died without me ever knowing why he hated me. You think I just left you by writing you off and moving on. I did the same with my father. He hurt me deeply, but I still loved him, and, in the end, I tried to make amends with him, only to learn that he had moved, and before I could get a second run at getting with him, he died. Life did not start or stop because my father's relationship never existed when I became an adult. You made your choices the same applies to us, and you should put on your big girl drawers and woman up.

Annie: I like it when you talk dirty. Jeremiah, you are a fraud because you went on off and lived a good life. You did not look too hard for me, and from what I can see, you were busy getting with as many women as you wanted. You were going all over the place, but you could not find me and see if I wanted to go along. There was not anyone there to fill the void you left in my life.

Jeremiah: I would use a three-letter word, but you said you do not know any big words. Now, Annie, I will accept what you just said by calling me a fraud because I believe that is your area of expertise. You are calling me a fake because I went on with my life. I got tired of the surprise marriages you just so happened never bothered to share with me that you were in relationships with other men. Yes, I am a fraud because you made me one for believing that Leonard raped you instead of telling me that this was an incestuous affair. I guess this would fall under the category of doing whatever I could to survive. And the reward from this deed was you ended up pregnant and had to cry rape to me but not to the local authorities. This rape excuse you have given me bothers me, and I cannot get over your stacking lies upon lies.

Annie: Please stop calling this terrible mistake an affair of incest. I admit to making a mistake, but I am human, and having you look down on me for lying about the circumstances surrounding how I got pregnant is severe enough.

Jeremiah: My opinion of you changed because of the incest and the fact that you were willing to allow me to continue believing a lie by helping you live that lie. To think that when the alleged rape happened, I was obliged to step up and take the responsibilities of being a father based on a lie. Secondly, you kept a child that most would have aborted but saw fit to get rid of a child we conceived in love. Things are not adding up, and you are not doing anything to subtract from my suspicious thoughts.

Jeremiah: The tiny antennas keep going up inside my head. I told myself that I was being played or attempted to be manipulated by the 2018 Annie. So, I decided to test my suspicions in a poem, and she flat out rejected it. As you like to say, Jeremiah, you have a way of asking questions that trip up a person. We have come to the end of our collaborative writing a book. I want to be truly clear about how I express myself. I want it to be understood and direct; violating my marriage with you or anyone else will never be on the table. I need this understood before we start to stroll down this little memory. I do not particularly appreciate being played or having my wishes ignored. The possibility of me changing my mind was never an option. If I did not cheat on a wife who cheated on me, what would make you think I would cheat on one who does not cheat? There would never be anything beyond us, just trying to write a book about two kids that fell in love over forty-five years ago. We both agreed to put everything out on the table and tell all. Still, you opted to withhold information that you believed would reflect unfavorably on you in my eye. I need the truth; I'm not trying to fix what happened forty-five years ago.

Annie: I understand your position, but for the years I have left on this earth, I will pursue my Jeremiah, although he will not be the original Jeremiah Micah Ford.

Jeremiah: Now that we have had our face-to-face and telling each other off sessions. I would have preferred that we communicated solely through Messenger and email. Still, you stated that you wanted to see my face when you told your life story after us for some morbid reason. I feel that it was more of a ploy to catch me in a weak moment and that I would succumb to the advances. You delivered some blows that hurt me but were not hard enough to get me to concede deceiving my wife. I do feel sorry for you, Annie. First, you lied to me about being raped. I am mad as hell about the abortion. To think I transferred colleges and even put my college education on hold to support you with taking care of another man's baby. I do not remember you giving me a chance to do so on my own because you aborted it. You are welcome for wasting my time and delaying me from moving on with my life.

When I returned to Texas in 1994 and saw you for the first time in over twenty years, I saw a woman consumed by hard times, hate, and schemes. It did not take me long to discover that you had become a taker, using any means to get over on people. The person I used to know had devised a system fixated on using and abusing people. I can only surmise that this was your way of seeking revenge because you, too, were abused. The problem is not everyone beats you that crossed your path.

People I feel have been impactful in my life, and I do not see or talk with them for a long time, and I tend to freeze them in my mind when we last saw each other. It is difficult for me to visit terminally ill patients in the hospital. The person I will visit is not the person I want to remember as I once knew them full of life. I do not deal with good-bye very well. The people that I have loved and were close to me. I had them fixed in my mind when the days were sunny. I left our relationship. It is differently set in my mind when I drove to Texas and back to Missouri in one night. Although we made other attempts, I never moved past that moment. I saw you as a cheat and in bed with another man. That encouraged me to never trust you again with my heart. Standing at the top of your balcony in 1994, I did not see the Annie I once loved and adored. I saw evil and not love. In my mind, you are the only person that I once loved that I see in a good light, and we parted on good terms. You are a horrible person who desires to desire others around you or feel you have wronged you somehow.

Of all the people in your past, Annie, I bet I am the only one that did not hurt you but by you. I suggest you put on your big girl's drawers and accept your responsibility for some of the wrongs in your life. The rape, incest, and molestation were all terrible acts against you, and I did none of those things to you. You must stop hating me and wanting to relive what died long ago. Jeremiah Micah Ford and Annie Marie Sims died when you lied. Just as you were my first love, you would be the last someone that I would ever think of trusting my heart. You are attempting to avenge your abuses by taking it out on everyone. I have yet to declare you as anything but the victim, not taking responsibility for you and a friend who decided to rob a man of his money and other valuables.

You need to feed your children does not excuse your willing participation. So, you sold blood, and you led a married man on by having an illicit affair with him because he took care of you and your children. All that I have heard is, Oh! Why me? Annie, allow me to share with you that I was homeless for a brief time, without a vehicle and no money, but robbing another person of their belongings was never an option. You talk about how your husband became a drug user without your knowledge. Well, my wife was a whore, and I knew it but dealt with it not by joining her in illicit affairs but through prayer and faith in God. You have always known where your children were. I did not know where my children were or whether they were safe. And one I will never know. You cry about how your mother did not love you and support you. My father did not like me and made it clear that he would not give me one cent to overcome my growing conditions. When you came into my life, it lifted my spirit. It encouraged me to be better than the worthlessness some people believed, including my father. The positive of falling in love with you was that so many others inspired me. Today, I am wiser and mature enough to know that what made the difference in my life was taking the positive to silence the negative.

You suggest that I stand on from the holy perch, you choose to remain seated at the pity table with **BLAMES**, **COMPLAINTS,** and **EXCUSES** is **LAME.** What brought us together was the color black. I was trying to hide my blackness in plain sight, and you were hiding your blackness from plain view. Keeping secrets from someone you love is not always a great idea, and if it blows up in your face, you must accept the consequences.

You invited yourself to participate in writing this book with me. One of my bucket lists is writing and publishing a book about our relationship and how it propelled me negatively to a positive person. Then, I would include us in my book. I would have been writing and believing a lie when the truth was consensual intercourse between you and your uncle Leonard and not rape. The book will not end like a fairy tale where we both found happiness in life with that special someone. You have held on to two useless things for a long time. One thought that I would wait forever for you, and someday we would be together to live out the remaining years of our lives. Secondly, the anger you have for me is misguided, and I should be more at you for not letting go of the notion that I would again walk back through that door of stupidity. You had dismissed me like I never meant anything to you. You made me vow never to rekindle a relationship with a past lover because it usually meant too much pain and a lack of trust. Before you say, well, you married Ruth, yes, and we were two nine-year-old kids. I will always think it necessary for both of us to air our differences out in a civil manner about a teenage love affair that went awry. I am still thinking of others and was hoping that it would bring freedom from the secrets that torment you daily. The trust problem I felt I had is not that extra sense that God gives us to warn of dangerous snares and nets. You lied to me while we were in a relationship that would last forever. You later solicited me to assist in a lie. You did not have to lie. After all, I would have eventually forgiven you because I wanted to love Lydia as my own, which meant I had to accept her mother's shortcomings. You never gave me a choice in two critical situations to make the right decision.

Annie: I think you have held more anger in your heart against me than I have for you. The fact that you now know you were not the only collaterally damaged person in our relationship.

Jeremiah: I learned to deal with the pains from you when my marriage failed and was HAPPY to move on. You complained about how hard you had it and the trials you had to endure to provide for your family. I have faced the same fate as you, but I chose never to give up on God, knowing that it was he who had brought me through so many stressful situations. I feel good that I could rear my two daughters alone without a live-in girlfriend or family members taking care of them for me. And I never spent time whining about how hard it was to the point that I just gave up on life and became a better man as you have become a bitter woman filled with hatred and jealousy. I just learned that my first love was molested and that our failure was not what I thought, like transferring school and later an alleged rape. You denied me a voice in having the baby we made and all the other lies you withheld from me telling me that you loved me. I hope that one of the sounds speaking inside your head is the baby that wanted to be enjoyed by a father who would have never disappointed it. I am sure you can remember Leonard's words and your own words during that passionate moment between you. However, you cannot come completely clean and tell the entire truth even now. We cannot go back and erase the past, but we should be honest enough to wipe the wrong that we can and make it right.

Annie: You speak the truth, but I am a human with feelings, emotions, and needs. I understand that you will not oblige me, but I am right never to give up hope. I am not going to hide any of my feelings and emotions. The look on your face and the hurt you must feel in your heart because you learned that I aborted our child with a word to you. Jeremiah, this is the same feeling I got when I realized that you had terminated our relationship without telling me it was over.

Jeremiah: Was there some disconnect in your brain, Annie? What was happening that you kept running off and marrying other men? What in the hell did you want me to do? Were you expecting me to wait until we are in our sixties for you to decide to settle down? We are talking about apples and oranges. What you did is difficult for me to want to forgive you. It was wrong but continue with the rest of your truth of what happened. I was too young to know what I was getting involved in at that time. You never shared with me as a girl, and you were being molested by male relatives. But what you did share with me was a lie, and it numbs me today. Instead of sharing the truth and helping me understand what I should do when the girl I thought I would live the rest of my life with tells me that she was raped and pregnant — a lie.

Annie: I suppose you could not tell me because you knew the lie, and as I said, Jeremiah, you know how to ask questions that will trip up a person. Was this fear? A kind of fear that you could say I love you, but not trust or forgive me for a mistake I was guilty of by force participation.

Jeremiah: I never told you this, but I had gone through the ordeal of another girlfriend getting raped before you lied about it. It occurred after you and I separated during my first year of college. You and I were not communicating with each other. One of her brother's friends raped her. I experienced a girlfriend getting murdered. I endured thirteen years of a lousy marriage with more years of infidelity than faithfulness. Losing everything except my faith in God, I learned how to walk blindly during the darkest times of my life. When Ruth came into my life, I would not give her a broken man weighted down, carrying old baggage from my past. That meant we would get buried from 1969 until 1995, saying we only existed but never lasted. Annie, I had no plans for us to have a future together, and I think it was wrong for you to tell your friends that we would get married in 1994. A chance like that was never going to happen. I never anyone who hurts me a second chance close to my heart. Both of you cheated on me and wasted my time, so you became history the night I drove back to Missouri, and you were in bed with another man. I grew tired of getting embarrassed by your antics. And felt the need to go on with my life without you. I knew I was totally over you and Sarah when I opened the book to my life to Ruth to ask me anything that she wanted to about my past, my present, or anything that caused her concern about me. I gained wisdom from having loved you and Sarah because I did not ask for openness about your past, present, and expectations for tomorrow. I now enjoy living a life without you.

Jeremiah's Prescription for Annie

Annie, I can feel the anger you hold in your heart for me because I did not come back and get you. Annie, there was no you for me if I had returned. You were married at least twice before I was married once. Might I also say that your marriages were all done in secret? I left because you chose other men over me. By refusing to accept the fact, my decisions responded to your dishonesty. I am trying to assess your behavior today. I see a bitter and vindictive person too reluctant to move on with her life by accepting that we both made wrong decisions by not being open and honest about our secret closets. We were two young kids who fell in love, but unknowingly to each other was too afraid to share our fears. Who we are today, two people who were once madly in love with each other, are now hostile enemies? I waited a long time for this opportunity to express the complicated feelings that derived from your deceit and outright lies. A question I have is, when will you take some responsibility for your actions? And what have you done besides having pity parties for forty-five years? The hell you claim to have had to deal with inside your head remains because you want to continue living a lie while keeping the truth hidden? Allow me to share how I keep myself from being holier than thou and always the victim. The Common Denominator Factor: Three things go wrong in my life, involving three different individuals. None of the three know one another. I believe it is all the other individuals' fault, and I am the victim. I refuse to realize I must. It is always the other person's fault, and you take no blame. The three fingers pointing back at me are the Common Denominator Factor, more your fault than someone else.

Perhaps if you were to visit your mother's grave and forgave her for not protecting you from incest, molestation, the impregnation by your Uncle Leonard, it would free your mind of the voices inside your head. You need to stop with the love-hate relationship with Lydia, a product of the incest/rape that has reminded you since it happened. Your stepfather's abuse and the loss of a child, an abusive husband, and the mistreatment by your grandmother. Three words can set you free; I forgive everyone and then take a little for yourself by seeking to love someone that will love you for who you are today. The voices inside your head may be individuals. You refuse to forgive them and yourself. But instead, you are the one who is giving this refuge inside the mind.

Your choice allows the abusers' voices you live rent-free inside your head. Until then, chatter in your head will continue. Your abusers refuse to leave because you will not evict them by holding the door shut inside instead of opening it and setting you and the demons free. Your guilty conscience from your past is the padlock keeping them hidden, locked inside your mind, and failing to tell the truth. The oppressors will leave the closet when you free Annie by letting go of the past and moving on in life. You have hinted on a couple of occasions that you are hoping that the two of us will make a comeback. Annie, let me state we have run our course long ago. The life we hoped for as young teenagers never had a chance because we screwed up by taking each other for granted and not being truthful. I understand what you were trying to do back when and how you went about fulfilling your responsibilities as a mother. You said you could talk forever, and I could have questions forever. There are only two critical questions that haunt me the most. 1. Why do you never file charges against Leonard if it was rape? 2. Why did you never file for child support through the courts? By never answering those two questions, I will always have my suspicions of your account as to what happened between you and your Uncle Leonard.

The Damages and the Kept Secrets

I offered to sit with you, Jeremiah, to share collateral damages of my life I never shared with anyone. I admit that I wanted more than to drag up old pains. I also hope you will feel the loving warmth you gave me years ago. You said I gave you strength for a lot of things. I am glad, but there are some things that I want to tell you face to face before we finish this book, not from behind a keyboard. I want to for once hear my voice say that my life was a wreck when we met, but you gave me so much hope. If I never win your love back, I wish we become friends. There were many reasons for our relationship to end. However, the way it ended was fixable had you not run and hid from me. I was confused about many things and found myself caught up in the spin cycle when I gave Lydia birth. If it were not for her, I would have run away, but I needed to keep her safe and take a crap I would never have taken if I hadn't had her. I was confused, lost, and felt all along, and I apologize for going behind your back to marry. ********, they were my get-out hell cards.

When I could not find you, and no one knew where you were or how to contact you, I learned that you were married to Sarah Dotson.

I was screwed and felt raped again, but this time of my chance to have true love and happiness with the only man I ever absolutely loved. When you came into my life, it was with high anticipations. But this is when we were kids hoping for a lifetime together. I felt that it was worth trying to chase you to rekindle a magical time in my life that was foolish on my part. In 1994 when you returned to Texas for good, I believe if we had gotten back together, it would have erased all the collateral damages. I would have had my soul mate that I could open and tell all the secrets I had kept bundled up inside. I never felt comfortable enough to fully trust me to tell you what I have just shared with you. I expected your reaction, which disappointed me because I hoped you would be that calm, quiet, and understanding person I once knew. Your actions, the look on your face, and Lydia's closeness and not with me said, no second chance. There was a time when the man with the shitty grin, bowlegs, and strong, loving arms always sent my heart racing, and to the moon is no more. And when he left me in 1978, it was forever.

Jeremiah: Annie, your second chance was so long ago. I cannot remember it. But I can remember the last episode and the loneliest drive of my life back to Missouri. Annie, old age, teaches us many things. I hope we both have learned our relationship was only a foundation to share our lives with someone else. Because we could not fully develop the kind of relationship that could withstand all the storms we faced, we must accept this fate because we know it was our fault. After all, what separated us were the secrets; we kept hidden. We never trusted each other enough to share secrets that could have saved us. Maybe knowing them would have brought us closer, but we will never know because we will never be able to return to that time in our history. We allowed them to become walls of separation instead of bridges to freedom. I pray that you will accept reality and try and move past the nightmare you state has haunted you most of your life.

Today, I would like to think of myself as Jeremiah wiser, a more deliberate decision-maker, when faced with challenging situations and needed a resolution. That is where we are and why I have stated that trying to rekindle or find fire in an old relationship was a non-starter for me from the beginning of this venture. I am in love with my wife, Ruth, very much. A voice that has whispered to me for many years to keep walking. And finally got my attention, and I found a permeant home for my heart. I am deliberate and decisive when making the right decisions for me. The impatient boy inside me who wanted to take on the world is now patient not to duplicate past mistakes. Falling in love with you was never a mistake, but trying to hold onto you too long, was indeed a big mistake. I did not do the right thing by not listening to the voice, telling me to keep walking. Therefore, with all the detours along life's way, I eventually found myself on the right road and with the right person.

When the rape/incest occurred, I failed to tell you my feelings. You had changed, and I felt I needed space before I could come back to you. Annie, I felt betrayed by you and your Uncle Leonard. I was the third wheel at that time and felt crowded out because you and Leonard had what I hoped someday you and I would have. There was no space for me in your life. I accept things as they are today and do not stew over them, knowing that it will change absolutely nothing. Not the worst time worrying about something I know is out of my control. I am confident Jeremiah and Annie's relationship was not long-term because it was missing a core element from the very beginning. That was trust. Neither of us trusted each other with the pain occurring in our lives, and we kept them hidden in dark closets. It was not just the things done to us that destroyed us. Still, the Collateral Damages, Kept Secrets we withheld from one another. And because of the lack of trust, we destroyed what perhaps could have been a good thing.

In my heart, I will always love you, adore you, and cherish all the happy moments that we had together. Those emotions and feelings are still unique because you made me feel special, Jeremiah. You gave me my start on how to love someone. You were the first girl I ever kissed. You were the first girl I held in my arms and told me I love you too. You were the first girl I made love to and was the only one I had hoped ever to make love to again. It was you, the first girl to tell me I love you. At the end of the beginning, you were the first girl to break my heart. Escaping the Malign Twins, my father, Mrs. Louser, and all the other negativity that came my way, you played a significant role in those victories. I am just learning we made a life together, and you and your family denied me a voice as to whether it live or die. The choice you made to abort a creation that we made together really hurts. You chose to keep the child conceived in rape/incest.

I would have reared the child myself since you did not want it. But I was not given a chance. You and your family played a God-denying life and refused me my right to have a say in a very crucial matter. Your selfish action makes it even more difficult to feel sorry for you because it eclipses all the other hurtful acts you committed against me. Thank you for helping me overcome the demons that forced me into a secret closet. And despite my overcoming, I still never admitted to you, Annie, that I gave you in 1969 was a defective Jeremiah. I feared that you would reject me, not because I thought I was not your type of guy or good enough for you but my dark skin. I spoke about forgiveness to you, Annie, for other people; I failed to tell you that I forgave you for all the pain and anguish you caused me.

Annie, in my opinion, I became a good man, father, and husband because of you. You were the key to unlocking the door to my heart by freeing my love to grow and flow. Thank you, but no thanks to the offer attempting to relive a dead dream. When I enlisted in the military, Jeremiah and Annie went on life support. Your third marriage pulled the plug, and we flatlined.

Dear Jeremiah,

When I learned that you had walked out and left me to find love and my way in a lonely and mean world. A world that had abused me and denied me opportunities to realize my dream. One such chance denied me the freedom to enjoy the kind of love you provided me when we were together. Jeremiah, I never had a vision more significant than one of someday becoming your wife and loving you for the rest of my life. Man, I cannot tell you enough that you were my life and always the only man I gave my honest love to for keeps. I hear your words and understand that Annie and Jeremiah's reunion is no chance. I will not pursue a rekindling of Jeremiah and Annie. However, I am not giving up on my dream because you believe you have realized your dream. Without the vision of you and me, yet old and unrealistic, it is what gets me through the day. It is what has kept me marginally sane and able to function all these many years.

Jay, I have been wrong because I have held on to the hope that we could still be lovers for forty-five years. If not, Mister and Mrs. Yes, I know that I married other men, and you feel that I did you wrong by not sharing with you before making those decisions. I was confused and pressured to do something. Jeremiah faced a rock and a hard place more than once because of my stepfather. What was even sadder is that my mother never once opened her mouth to defend me or protect me from his accusations and abusive language. You were always the center of his conversation, even though they had cut off our communication with each other. When I got pregnant with Lydia and came to see me because I asked you to come, I needed your comforting arms and a loving smile. Jeremiah, I expected you to take me away from that place and help me raise Lydia. We both knew that she was not your child, but I thought I was the love of your life, at least this is what all your letters used to say to me. I kept the nickname, Ebonic woman because you gave it to me. I have asked myself a million times. Why didn't I tell Jeremiah that I wanted him to take Lydia and me away from this situation? Until we started writing this book, I never knew you as someone who did not care about me. I know that you are married and dedicated to your marriage.

Still, I wonder how much of your disdain and hatred you perhaps developed over the years is because I was raped or married to other men. I am beginning to catch up on our conversations when you tell me how I hurt you by breaking your heart. Guess what I just allowed a new tenant to move in and torture me. Your voice tells me that you cannot let yourself become caught up in my drama by offering a sympathetic ear and a soft shoulder. Jeremiah and Annie's relationship death were not due to a tragic accident but homicide by both of their hands. And you blame me. There are four things that I want to say and make clear to you.

I loved you from the beginning to the present.

I will never stop loving you because the memories are as real today as in 1969 and were the happiest times of my life.

You buried Jeremiah Micah Ford and Annie Sims. Still, I wake up each day wanting to exhume and examine the body of love we created together.

Words can never say how it hurt me to tell you of a decision my mother and grandmother made for me. I am deeply sorry that I did not have the child we created together. You feel that I cared more about having the child conceived from rape or incest, which makes you think it hurt me the most.

I will never be able to make things right to your satisfaction. The more I think about it, the more I try to appease you because that is impossible. When I called you on the phone in November 1993 and heard your voice, I thought that I had located my once source of happiness. I cannot count the number of years that I asked about you to find out where you were, and nobody knew, or they were lying about not knowing your whereabouts. Eventually, I learned that you were married, and that was all; they did not know if you were still living in East Texas or your whereabouts.

I remember your surprise visit late one night when you were in Missouri, and too ashamed, I was even trying to explain what went down. I just knew that I hoped to see you again and tell you that it was not serious between that individual and me. The look on your face that night as we sat arguing in your car. And you are telling me that you never slept over because you had too much respect for Lydia when I got my place. I think that you loved her more and hated me greater. The look in your eyes and on your face said you were through with me because you asked me to leave your car. And it seemed as if you were in a hurry to get away from me. I had the feeling that you were telling me you were going away from me forever. You have never mentioned these words to me in any of our conversations, but I think we both have felt them and agreed that I had f...d up! And oh! By the way, I still have an Al Green record. Have you been Making out Ok that I asked you to buy me the day we met on the street downtown? Jeremiah, I am not making out ok, and you know why.

Ebonic Woman

Not A Love Letter This Time

Dear Annie,

I did not walk out on you; you replaced me with your ambitions and decisions to try and make it on your own. You can blame me along with everyone under the sun, but at the end of the day, I still hold you wholly responsible for all that separated us. You took away the hugs, kisses, and conversations we would share daily when you first left. Then you began to chip away at my emotions by being distant when we were together. It got to the point I was like someone trying to withdraw from drug dependency. I purposely did everything possible to avoid our friends by becoming a fixture in the library or doing chores for teachers. You were my comforter and blanket. And when you took your love away, you also took out the warmth of your arms, kissing of your lips, laughter, and that sweet voice that melted my heart; all were essential elements in my life. Anxiety began to set in as I feared that I would relapse and become shy and afraid by once again hiding in that secret closet in my mind. The woman I had planned to see many sunrises and sunsets existed no more. There would never be nights where we would hold each other tight or make love in such a passionate way that we begged each other for more. I would not be the man to wipe tears from your face when pain from our children's birth became too unbearable. I would not be able to say that this is the only woman that I have ever made love to or ever wanted to. I love my wife because I have not tried to duplicate us; instead, we have strived to create our mold by shaping our present for a long and happy future.

Today you are experiencing being pushed away just as I had to come to grips with the idea your love was no longer mine but belonged to others. As I have said often and will always tell you, I love you in our moment's past, and you will forever be in my heart because of what you were to me and how you came into my life at the right time. That love is not a rival with my love for my wife, Ruth, because she completes me. Unlike us, we only filled space and time when we each needed someone most to nourish us. We loved hard and unconditionally, but the sad commentary was that we never came clean with each other. My journey to Ruth involved falling in love with someone I thought would be the wife I dreamed of from a kid (you). I got on a road, not knowing where it would lead me, and all I know is that I started to feel free and hurting less each day that I was with a young lady named Dana.

Still unsatisfied and happy with life, my frustration leads me to stray and wander in the wilderness for thirteen years in a terrible marriage to Sarah Dotson. There was a time when I became a vagabond. I could not stay in love or have the desire to remain committed to one person. Jacqueline, Billie, Susanne, Donna, Evelyn, Rene, Mae, Andrea, and Carla; the list goes on. And none of them lasted more than two months. I had to move on because I thought none of them helped me duplicate our love. And finally, I realized that God was not trying to replicate our love but lead me to the love he had for me all the time. When Ruth came into my life, I didn't hear that voice telling me to keep walking. It was not until years after being married that I realized that you were just a part of the journey to Ruth, my love. I do not think you are a terrible person, just not the right person for me. God had the perfect mate for me as I believe that he also has someone for you if you stop focusing on how it was and start focusing on how it can become. Annie, I pray for you to find freedom from your torment and know that I forgave you a long time ago. When I saw Dana, who happened to be white, her love for me validated that my dark skin was not evil and that I was a decent person, and my skin color was not the problem. I hope you can still listen to Al Green's song because that was not the only question.

Annie: What Are the Damages? I remember you singing the **Friends of Distinctions song, Going in Circles,** to me over the telephone. I remember because I can still hear your voice singing it to me. What are the damages, others may ask? Two young people unfamiliar with the cruelty of humankind. If that moment were granted to me today, I would never want to leave the comfort and warmth of your presence. We were two young individuals that dared to venture outside of the world that had protected us and found true love in each other. Our love for one another was the only collateral that had freed us from homes of dysfunctional families and activities. When someone else interjected themself into our world, causing a detour, we forever lost our way back to each other, and we were never on the same path ever again. We could not overcome the many obstacles we faced once we were separated outside of our world without a map back into each other's hearts and physical presence. Every aspect of that song describes our demise and calamity. There is a real tragedy in our story as the two high school sweethearts who both kept secret hurts and pains for one another throughout our brief love affair. Angry loved ones threatened our lives because of their wrongdoings and unwillingness to accept the blame for the perpetrated transgressions they knew were happenings to me. Someone wanting to steal my innocence threatened my life despite my fight to keep what was forbidden and sacred; I lost every battle afterward. Inside my head are the voices and continuous movies of my wrongdoings. More than a million times, I have asked myself this one haunting question. Where would we be if I had not transferred schools farther away from you, thinking that I was running away from harm? Instead, I caused permanent damage.

What I know and feel is this, I will never become your best friend, lover, and wife. These are three failures in my life that somehow compound my hurting heart. Jeremiah, I feel worthless and not needed. Because you rejected me after being molested, abused, raped, I think that losing out on you and me is a more considerable pain to my heart than all of those put together. I know that I could have overcome all of them with you because of how much we loved each other. My regrets are few because I spent most of my life trying to survive and provide for my unplanned child. When I see old school and classmates married for forty-plus years, I instantly become jealous and feel that what we had together would have lasted through the test of times. I say that because you never showed any dislike or meanness toward Lydia, a child that you knew for sure was not yours, and you never made me feel guilty. The music I hear tells me that the curtain had fallen on the Annie and Jeremiah movie long ago. I noticed neither of us has said to each other that I am sorry. And I am because being young and energetic will not always bring you to the victory circle. I am not happy speaking to you with so many restrictions because I have a lifetime of memories or thoughts that I wish to share. With my head on my pillow, you have been imagined you breathing into my face on lonely nights. Your imaginary arms have held me because I never forgot how tight you used to secure me with those bear hugs. I keep ever familiar in my mind you were kissing my lips. Jeremiah, I remember our first kiss. That was a long passionate kiss, and I did not want to stop, and you showed no sign of wanting it to end either. Every day that I knew I would see you were a good day. Somehow, I feel that when we get to the end of Collateral Damages, Kept Secrets, it will be the end for us forever. I hope you feel some sadness that we conclude by saying goodbye instead of missing you and our past when we were together. You have shown me that you can move on and slam doors shut. Jeremiah, thanks for a lifetime of memories to help fill the lonely nights and days of gloom for one person that shall always keep a part of you in their heart. The dreams and hopes of a young girl that believed she would get rescued by the only true love she ever had.

Jeremiah, you felt trapped in your closet because of the ridicule you encountered regarding your dark skin. I never saw it as an issue either, or I probably saw the same individual that your White girlfriend saw because you made me your queen. But you did not need me to find your way out of the closet. All I ever experienced was inside a package that left a lasting effect on my life. Thank you for the brief moments of happiness, and if I had one wish, I would live every one of those moments with you again without hesitation. I would not keep any secrets, nor would anyone convince me to abort a part of you that had I not caved, we would still have something to connect us for a lifetime. I cannot wait to read what the writer has written. I know that it will be a picture I can see as I read. Thank you for being the best thing to come into my life. Good-Bye.

Jeremiah: You still believe that you are the only victim damaged by the fallout, but of what? Annie, I feel you are at fault for your plight today as anyone. Because you have spent most of your life watching your past instead of planning a future that did not include your history, all except Lydia, you should have moved on. You were not trying to press toward having a better and brighter future. Perhaps we could have made it together if only you had allowed me to help you face the things you were running from by burying those pains. But instead, you decided that hurting me was more of a priority than loving me. I left you physically, but you remained in my heart until I could no longer take the pain inflicted by you. You blame me for finally going on with my life after your three unannounced marriages. You are still holding your mother and everyone accountable for the visitors you provide rent-free space inside your head. And all those individuals are dead and gone. You have a love-hate relationship with your daughter because you cannot decide whether she was conceived by rape or a moment of incestuous passion. And Lydia is not the blame for either scenario. You are the landlord of your mind and soul, Annie, and it is your choice that you continue to give residents to your abusers by allowing them to stay on your brain.

When will you place the blame squarely on your shoulders? We never reunited again. After all, you refused to write me one lousy letter or just a note to let me know that we were still a couple in love because you did not like to write. But everything happens for a reason. Well, Miss Annie, you must accept the consequences of having it your way when you do it your way. Effective communication requires a sender, receiver with responders. You chose not to be either, and your silence became complicit by aiding me to take my show on the road if I wanted to find happiness. The communication or the lack of that destroyed us; I sent you received but never responded.

Because of some of my foolish actions and decisions after we parted ways, initially, my attitude was nobody gave me and Annie forgiveness or tried to enlighten us of its power. I learn to accept my failures and questionable indiscretions and my failures. Both God and man could have forgiven all, but by then, I had lost faith in man and doubted God wanted to ever hear from me again. Collateral Damages, Kept Secrets reveals the pain and disappointment of two individuals blinded by love and miscalculated humanity started us on a pathway to return. Annie, you decided never to seek or consider forgiveness for yourself or anyone that may have harmed you. Forgiveness would have freed you of the bitterness and hatred you have held in your heart for me and others for so many years.

CHAPTER THIRTY-SIX

CLOSING THE BOOK

By: Jeremiah Micah Ford

We have finally finished Collateral Damages, Kept Secrets without any physical touching or by succumbing to any emotional letdowns. I think we both can agree that we dreaded the demise of a courtship that appeared to have potential. We started and ended this experiment of remembering our first love. I think we both came in angry, bitter, and forgiveness was off the table. As I write the closing, I feel that Annie is still sore, not at me but more at the cold hand she was given. I, too, had some anger because I felt duped and left in the dark. Annie had the only key to my heart, and I had to find a new way to allow others to love me so I could begin to love again. My disappointments were the denial to be part of the decision to have a child born into this world for me. I leave with mixed feelings and suspicions about whether it was rape or accidental incest. And I no longer feel guilty. I didn't know how to handle the situation, albeit rape or incest. My presence when Lydia was born, and I believe, added more pain and shame. Although I could not see the expression on my face, I am sure Annie did, and if anyone could read my facial expressions, it was Annie.

As for me, I rode an emotional roller coaster at times through trying to get the truths and follow Annie's logic. And even though I have long moved on with my life, I still feel sorry for Annie because she was left to fend for herself long before I ever stepped into her life. After learning she was intentionally trying to get pregnant by me so that she could go home, I feel used by her and wonder if she loved me or the possibility of gaining her freedom from her family. I know that my love for her was genuine with no hidden agenda. I think I had to forgive Annie before we took on this joint project to share our stories hoping to explain our side, and we would both find it in our hearts forgiveness and satisfaction from the explanations we received.

I want to thank Annie for teaching me how to end a relationship. I walk out and never say goodbye, or it will not work out between us. Instead, I go on my way, and eventually, the other party gets the message. Annie, you taught me how to love and say hello, but exiting a relationship, I prefer to use your pattern. It is easy and less needed to be said.

We indeed had secrets, and I believe they damaged the collateral we shared: our love for each other because of those kept secrets. Annie never knew why I had my little nine-year-old cousin handed her the note that ignited our courtship. She is only learning now that I was afraid of her rejecting me because of my dark skin color and because of the teasing and reminders I hid in a closet behind a fence I had built for my protection. Annie took the note, read it, and confronted me with it tore down my protection fence. And responding with yes, stopped me from hiding my collateral to where I acknowledged its value. Annie's love allowed the good wrapped inside of the dark skin. I was so excited to write a letter and poem to her for the first time.

Unlike Annie, my collateral has served me well, and after her, I was never afraid to flaunt or step forth when opportunities have called. Annie's body was her collateral, but her mind was damaged. And neither was supposed to be abused and damaged by a raper. And because of one unfortunate event in her life, she has kept two secrets. First is the fact her uncle raped her. And secondly, she gave birth to her raper's baby, forcing her to relive each day since the rape by seeing a child's face forced upon her.

I can define my move as sympathetic and not empathetic because I could never have a baby; therefore, it would be impossible to empathize with her dilemma. For me, I learned why I chose to transfer colleges to be near Annie, even though what had happened to her was not my fault, and I wasn't going to be named the father of her daughter Lydia. And what was it that kept me always at the ready and her disposal? Because I was always readily available, Annie treated me more like something disposable than nonexpendable.

I never knew that Annie was living in a hostile environment because everything looked like a close-knit and loving family from the outside. I could feel the coldness whenever I would come around, but I never thought I was causing her and Lydia problems. My arms and heart loved the embrace and the affectionate way she took care and always made me feel good. I believe I will always long for the duplication of those feelings but have realized that only a special kind of person could have satisfied such a need because the time was right and necessary to see me through the roughest patch in my life.

I perhaps would have never gotten past my third-grade teacher, Mrs. Louser, who made me feel unworthy. I did not feel worthwhile when she explained that I was too black. Her opinion made me think I should not be among the other children because of my black skin because I was less intelligent. Mrs. Louser's hurtful words, I believe, will forever be etched in my mind. Part of the collateral damage I incurred early on as a child. But the cure repairing of those damages was the love and affection bestowed upon me by Annie Mae Sims. My secret was concealed so well kept hidden from her.

Whenever I felt down in my spirit or unloved, I reflected on the sunshine days I enjoyed with Annie. And use those moments as my battle-ax to overcome and motivate me when confronted or made to feel disrespected. As for me and my love for Annie, I never saw myself leaving her. And because I was unprepared for the sudden separation, which shocked me and caused me to still myself and refocus on the path forward that would best. It was not because of Annie, and I picked some wrong women and relationships. I don't blame Annie for setting me free. Because I am in a beautiful place in life today as far as marriage, all types of relationships, and achieving most of the goals I set for myself, like writing a book that when I started and thought of did not have her and my relationship in mind. I am thankful to God for my wife, children, grandchildren, and great-grandchildren. The career opportunities and success achieved.

My faith in God leads me to believe that He never makes mistakes but often shows tremendous patience and love for me. My prayer is for Annie to find someone to love her, and she loves them freely and unconditionally. And that is permanently freed of the voices of the unwanted visitors she describes inside her head is someday to love someone deserving of her love.

The End!

www.ingramcontent.com/pod-product-compliance
Lightning Source LLC
Chambersburg PA
CBHW030604180626
46816CB00005B/1673